PRAISE FOR DAVE H

"The Europe sequence is some of m century, and *Europe in Winter* is no exception. Mind-bending, smart, human, with espionage thrills wrapped up in a reality-altering Europe, all told with sparkling prose and wit that should, if there was literary justice, catch the attention of prize after prize. I love these books. I want more. Now."

Patrick Ness on *Europe in Winter*

"As rich and as relevant as its predecessor. It's funny, fantastical, readable and remarkable regardless of your prior experience of the series. Which just goes to show that, no matter how well you think you know something – or someone, or somewhere, or somewhen – there's almost always more to the story."

Tor.com* on *Europe at Midnight

"*Europe in Autumn* is one of the most sophisticated science fiction novels of the decade: a tour-de-force debut, pacey, startlingly prescient, and possessed of a lively wit. When approaching its follow-up, I felt both nervous and excited. Would Hutchinson be able to pull off the same magic a second time? The answer is undoubtedly yes. *Europe at Midnight* is pitch-perfect, bursting with the same charisma and intricate world-building as its predecessor."

LA Review of Books* on *Europe at Midnight

"In a way, what is most striking about *Europe at Midnight* is not the hard edge of its politics, or even the casual brilliance of its science fictional reworking of the political thriller, but Hutchinson's thrillingly assured control of his material. He writes wonderfully, his prose animated not just by a keen eye for character, but by a blackly witty sense of humor."

Locus Magazine* on *Europe at Midnight

"*Europe in Autumn* is the work of a consummate storyteller and combines great characters, a cracking central idea, and a plot that will keep you on the edge of your seat. Excellent."

Eric Brown on *Europe in Autumn*

"This awesome concoction of sci-fi and spies – picture John le Carre meets Christopher Priest – is an early favourite of the year for me."

Tor.com* on *Europe in Autumn

"The map of Europe has been redrawn, and its cartographers remain at work... the continent now exists as a patchwork of small nations and polities... for all that people want to carve out their own discrete realms, perhaps the greatest gift in Dave Hutchinson's future Europe is the ability to cross borders."

Strange Horizons* on *Europe in Autumn

"One of my best reads from the past year."

Huffington Post* on *Europe in Autumn

"One of the best novels I've read in a long time."

Adam Roberts, *The Guardian*, on *Europe in Autumn*

"With its understated stakes and imperturbable pace, its deliberate density and intellectual intensity... you have to work at it, but it's worth it, not least because what Hutchinson has to say about the world today is now more imperative that ever."

Niall Alexander, *Tor.com*, on *Europe in Winter*

"Hutchinson's entire Europe-series are wonderful: not quite science fiction, not quite crime, not quite current realism, but some of all."

***Benteh* on the Fractured Europe Sequence**

THE RETURN OF THE INCREDIBLE EXPLODING MAN

First published 2019 by Solaris
an imprint of Rebellion Publishing Ltd,
Riverside House, Osney Mead,
Oxford, OX2 0ES, UK

www.solarisbooks.com

ISBN: 978-1-78108-584-4

10 9 8 7 6 5 4 3 2 1

A CIP catalogue record for this book is available from the British Library.

Designed & typeset by Rebellion Publishing

Printed in Denmark

THE RETURN OF THE INCREDIBLE EXPLODING MAN

DAVE HUTCHINSON

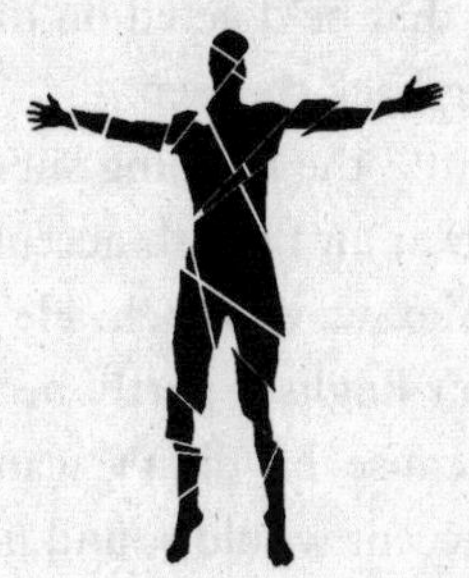

THE TOWN

It had been raining for days, the remnants of a hurricane which had chewed bits out of the Louisiana coast before tracking east across the Gulf and killing almost a hundred people in Florida. It had come ashore as a Category Four, but by the time it left Florida behind and wandered up the East Coast it was weakening steadily. It had made necessary the evacuation of a couple of coastal towns in the Carolinas, but by the time it reached Boston it was just a mass of rain and wind and misery. Standing in front of the bank of mailboxes in the lobby, Alex could look out through the double front doors of the building and see the rain still sheeting down. It looked as if the sewers were backing up again; passing vehicles were bearing shallow bow waves ahead of them.

It was a while since he'd been down here, but he couldn't quite remember how long. Certainly not yesterday, and probably not the day before that. After that it all got a bit vague, a mush of daytime television and social media he couldn't be bothered to engage with. He'd woken that morning with a distant sense that perhaps he should check the mailbox, if only as a reason to actually leave the apartment for a few minutes. What was quite remarkable was that he'd acted on the impulse instead of turning over and going back to sleep.

"What-ho, Mr Dolan!" the building superintendent called in a completely wild stab at an English accent, crossing the lobby with a bag of tools. Alex waved back. He'd given up trying to tell the super he wasn't English, partly because the man didn't listen, but mostly because he didn't want to hear what his version of a Scottish accent would sound like.

Alex unlocked the mailbox for Apartment 402 and peered blearily at the wad of letters and junk mail and leaflets and magazines crammed inside. Maybe it had been more than a couple of days since he'd been down here. What to do with it all? Take it, or let it pile up a while longer? It wasn't as if the mailman ever brought him anything that made the journey downstairs worthwhile.

Leaving the box open, he walked over to the doors and stood looking out, hands in the pockets of his sweatpants. The street was almost empty of people, just a few hardy souls battling along under umbrellas. The owner of the mini-mart opposite was standing in his doorway, looking glum. He saw Alex and waved. Alex waved back. The owner put a hand out into the rain, then shrugged hugely. Alex nodded and shrugged back. Which was about all you could usefully say about the weather using sign language. Alex waved goodbye and went back to the mailbox. *Ah, sod it.* He grabbed the whole wad of post, stuffed it under his arm, and went back upstairs.

In the kitchen, he dumped the post on the table, switched the kettle on, sat down, and sighed.

He looked out through the window into the building's airshaft. In the apartment directly opposite, a middle-aged bald man wearing only a pair of underpants was rearranging things in his fridge. From his body language, of which Alex could see far too much, it seemed to be a task which made him angry.

The kettle boiled. He made himself a cup of tea, took it back to the table and sat down again. He felt as if the act of getting the mail actually out of the mailbox and into the apartment had all but exhausted whatever resolve he had ever had for doing anything about it.

Bit by bit, he separated the junk from the legitimate mail on the table. Then he separated the letters from the obvious bills. Then he sat looking at the three piles. Three of the letters were identical. Same envelopes, same return address. Alex considered ignoring them—if he didn't actually *read* any of them, they technically didn't exist. Wasn't that how it worked? He dithered over them, then in what amounted, for him, to a headlong rush, he slit them open with the butter knife and took the plunge.

The letters were from his agent. The first wanted to discuss the advance she had loaned him and asked why he wasn't answering his phone or email. The second restated the first in rather more robust terms. The third thanked him for repaying the loan, asked him not to do it again, and suggested that at some point they might revisit the terms of their professional relationship.

Alex read this letter a couple of times, trying to remember when—and how—he had paid his agent back. But there was nothing. It seemed unlikely; he had barely managed to make the previous month's rent. Had he suddenly come into a large amount of money and subsequently suffered some kind of blackout? Was it a trap to make him call his agent and find out what the fuck was going on? The three letters covered a period of about a fortnight; the most recent was dated four days ago. Nothing out of the ordinary had happened during that time. Nothing had happened at all.

In a spirit of experimentation, he picked up one of the bills and opened it. It contained a receipt from the building's management company for the service charges on the apartment. It appeared he had suffered more than one blackout, because he couldn't remember paying this one either. The original bill was still, as far as he knew, sitting in a drawer, waiting for him to find enough money to do something about it.

He opened some more bills, and it was the same story with the electricity and water. A long-running and increasingly ill-tempered feud with the IRS had been settled. His credit cards had been zeroed. His accountant had—finally, it was noted—been paid.

Alex looked out of the window again. In the apartment across the airshaft, the bald man was standing motionless, a carton of milk in one hand and what looked like a package of bacon in the other, staring into his fridge with all the concentration of someone watching a complex subtitled movie.

The final envelope contained a letter and two printed airline tickets. It was a long time since Alex had seen a printed airline ticket. It was quite a while since he had seen an airline ticket of any kind. He read the letter. Then he read it again. He looked at the back in case there was a little note explaining the joke, but it was blank.

He got up and went into the bedroom, took his phone off its charger, and dialled the number in the letter. It rang twice, then a man's voice said, "Hi, Alex. Thanks for calling. You don't mind if I call you Alex, do you? It makes a difference to some people. I'm Stan, by the way. I guess you got my letter."

"Who is this, and why have you sent me tickets to San Francisco?" Alex asked.

"Yeah, well," said Stan, in a tone which suggested it wasn't the first time this had happened to him. "I'd give you my attorney's number but you wouldn't believe it was her, so what I'm going to do is tell you her name and you can look her up and call her yourself and she'll tell you this is on the level." And he said a name which Alex recognised because it belonged to someone who had spent quite a lot of the previous year in the news as the defence attorney for a Silicon Valley figure accused of spying on behalf of the Russians. "Call her now and call me back when you're done. I don't know what you've been dicking about with, but we should have had this conversation last week."

"Why?"

"Because the tickets are for tomorrow." And he hung up.

Alex stood there by the bed, phone in one hand, letter in the other. He looked at the phone, then at the letter, trying to work out what had just happened. Was this what a stroke felt like?

He googled the name of Stan's attorney. Then he googled the name of her firm. He thought for a moment, then dialled the number on the firm's website. When the switchboard answered, he expected to be put on hold or simply told to go away, but he was put through immediately.

"Mr Dolan," said the attorney. "We were expecting your call several days ago."

"I've been away." It didn't do to tell a Manhattan lawyer that you'd stopped checking your mail because you couldn't pay your bills.

"Right," she said in a voice which made him suspect she knew anyway. "You'll have spoken with Mr Clayton."

"I spoke with someone claiming to be Mr Clayton."

"That will have been Mr Clayton, then." Alex remembered that, in the face of what had seemed overwhelming evidence of his guilt, the Silicon Valley guy had been acquitted. "Okay. Well, you'll be aware of his proposal."

"I am." He wondered how much this call was costing Stan in billable hours.

"You're to meet Mr Clayton in San Francisco to discuss his proposal in person. For this Mr Clayton will pay you a per diem of two thousand dollars. This does not constitute a binding contract or a formal offer of employment. Do you understand?"

"Yes," he said. "No." He heard her sigh. "Yes."

She sighed again. "Okay. It's been good speaking with you, Mr Dolan, and I wish you joy of your trip. The Bay Area's lovely at this time of year." And she hung up.

Alex stood there with the phone in his hand. If this was someone's idea of a joke, he considered, it was a pretty good one. He looked at the letter again. It was written in a clear, looping, slightly adolescent hand, a chatty, informal letter from the fifth richest man in the world, offering him work. The envelope was hand-addressed, too, and it had a stamp rather than the mark of an office franking machine.

He went back into the kitchen and leafed through all the bills and outstanding debts that had suddenly blown away like leaves on an autumn breeze. There was, he realised, a part of him which had been praying for some sort of divine intervention. Now it had happened, he had no idea what to do next.

He took a breath, went back through the call list on his phone, and hit redial.

"So, you talked to my attorney," said Stan.

"She seems… feisty," Alex told him.

"Feisty is a good quality, in an attorney. I'll see you tomorrow, then?"

"Did you pay my bills?"

"Just as a gesture of goodwill."

Alex sighed. "This kind of thing doesn't happen to me every day," he said.

"Christmas doesn't happen every day," said Stan. "I don't hear anyone complaining about *that*."

"Isn't it illegal to do that? Go through someone's financial affairs like that?"

"It's just the same as doing a credit check on somebody," Stan said defensively.

"It's not remotely the same as doing a credit check. You can't just *datamine* someone's life like that without even a hint of implied consent."

There was silence on the other end of the line for a few moments, and then Stan said, "You know, this conversation's not going entirely the way I thought it would."

"You thought I'd be so grateful to you for hauling me out of the fire that I'd jump on a plane without even thinking twice about it."

"Sure," said Stan, as if it was absurd to think anything else.

"This is a lot to process. You must appreciate that."

"You can always give the money back, if that's what's bothering you." When Alex said nothing, he added, "No, I didn't think so." He sighed. "Look, Alex. Come out to the Coast for a couple of days and we'll discuss it face to face, no obligations on either side. You get a couple of nice plane rides and a night in a really great hotel. I know this terrific dim sum place in Oakland, we could go there. And you go home with four thousand bucks, no matter what you decide. How can that be bad?"

"I'll call you back," said Alex, and he hung up. He looked out of the window, but the bald man in the apartment opposite had gone. He'd left his refrigerator door wide open.

THERE WAS A man standing in Arrivals at San Francisco International Airport holding a sign with *DOLAN* written on it in orange Sharpie.

"Where's the rest of you?" he asked when Alex walked up and identified himself.

"This is all there is of me," said Alex.

The driver gave him a hard stare. "Are you the Dolan family?"

"I'm one of them," Alex allowed.

The driver narrowed his eyes. "The Dolan family of Pittsburgh? In town for a wedding?"

"The Dolan family of Edinburgh. In town to meet the world's fifth-richest man."

"You're a Brit? You have a weird accent."

"I'm a Scot."

"There's a difference?"

"Well," said Alex. "That is something of a bone of contention."

The driver was a very large man in a black suit that was ever so slightly too small for him. He grunted. "Rich folks don't impress me," he said.

"We have that in common, at least."

He sighed. "Every frigging time I do a pickup here, some asshole comes up and tries to hijack the ride by pretending they're the person I'm waiting for."

"Really?"

"And it's always rich folks. Poor folks don't do that shit."

"Right." This was obviously a subject on which the driver had been waiting for the opportunity to vent for some time.

"I've had guys just walk up to me and snap their fingers for me to take them to the car. Not a word from them. Just snap their fingers." He looked Alex in the eye. "And you can't punch them. You can't even use stern language on them. Just yes sir, Mr Rich Guy, no sir, Mr Rich Guy." He seemed perfectly calm, serene almost, but Alex didn't envy the Dolan family of Pittsburgh being stuck in a car with him.

"I'm not rich," Alex assured him. "I'm not even comfortably-off."

"Yeah," the driver said, looking him up and down. "I can see that."

Alex was rescued from having to respond to this by a voice behind him saying, "Mr Dolan? Alex Dolan?"

He looked round and saw a skinny black kid in jeans and a hoodie standing there. "Yes?"

She grinned. "I'm Lin, your driver. I'm late; I'm sorry."

They shook hands. "Hi."

She looked past him and nodded at the other driver. "Rick. How's it going."

Rick grunted and turned his gaze to the middle distance, scanning the crowds for signs of the Dolan Family. Lin looked at Alex, then at his overnight bag. "This all your luggage?"

"Should I have brought more?"

She grinned again. "Man travels light. I like that. So, shall we...?"

"Yes, of course." He turned to Rick and said, "Nice to meet you," but the driver didn't answer.

"Rick's cool," Lin said as she led the way across Arrivals towards an exit, "but he lives in his own head a lot."

"It seems a... disturbing place to live."

"Rick's cool," she said again. "You just have to get to know him." She took a card from a pocket of her hoodie and held it out. "Mr Clayton said you'd want this."

On the card, Clayton had written *Hi, Alex. This is Lin. She'll be late, because she always is. But she's a great driver and she'll get you here safely. See you soon. Stan.*

"I'm not, by the way," she said.

"Sorry?"

"Late. Not always, anyway."

"Right." Alex put the card in his pocket. "Is he always like this?"

"Mr Clayton? Best boss I ever worked for. You just have to get used to things, that's all."

"Things?"

"You'll see. Just don't let it faze you and you'll be fine."

"Okay." He was already fazed. He didn't think it could get any worse.

They walked for what seemed miles, along corridors and across concourses, and at one point even briefly went outside, before winding up in a parking garage packed with high-end vehicles. Rich people's parking. Alex thought he spotted, far down at the end of one row, what seemed to be a Bugatti Veyron, but that was impossible. You didn't own a Veyron and park it at an airport. Lin held up a zapper and pressed the button, and there was an answering blink of indicators on a silver-grey SUV a couple of rows away.

The SUV looked as if it had been driven here straight from the showroom. Even its tyres seemed to have been waxed. Inside, it was all leather upholstery and new car smell and a dashboard that looked as if it had been designed by a Hollywood CGI house. When Lin started it up a heads-up display appeared on the windscreen. Alex was surprised it was equipped with something as primitive as a steering wheel.

It took them about fifteen minutes to drive out of the airport and get onto the freeway, and a few minutes after that they drove into a wall of mist that rapidly thickened into fog and the world shrank to a ghostly procession of half-glimpsed vehicles and tail lights.

"I thought the Bay Area was lovely at this time of year," Alex said, looking out of the passenger-side window.

Lin chuckled. "Who told you that?"

"Someone I was talking to yesterday."

"The Bay Area is lovely at *all* times of the year," she said. "I love this town. Even in the fog."

"Hm."

"Is this your first time here?"

"No, I was here... a long time ago."

"Where did you stay?"

"I didn't. I was on my way to Santa Monica." She glanced at him and he shrugged. "Long story. Anyway, I was only passing through. I was only here about eight hours. I didn't even get a chance to ride on a tram."

"Cable car."

"Right. Well, I wasn't here long, anyway."

She grinned. "You seem to make a habit of flying visits."

"Yes," he said, looking out of the window again. "In and out, that's me."

The journey ended in yet another garage, this one under a towering slab of glass and steel that rose into the fog. Alex had no idea where he was. For all he knew, he was no longer even in San Francisco.

"Okay," Lin said, turning off the engine. "This is where we part ways for a while. The elevator's over there. You'll need this to operate it." She handed him a keycard. "You want the penthouse. That's button 'P'." She ignored his raised eyebrow. "I'll wait and take you to your hotel when you're done."

He looked out at the low-ceilinged Brutalist space of the garage. It was brightly lit, but there still seemed to be too many shadows in the far corners. "You're just going to sit here?"

She held up a Kindle. "I have something to read. Okay, so go. Don't keep him waiting."

"Right. Thanks for the ride."

She grinned again. "You're welcome. See you in a while."

At the lift, there was no call button, just a blank panel by the door. He touched the panel, and nothing happened. He put his hand flat on it, and nothing happened. He looked back across the garage and saw Lin sitting in the car, her face faintly lit by the screen of her Kindle. It would, he considered, be frankly embarrassing to have to go back and ask her how the lift worked. He looked at the panel again, and something occurred to him. He held the keycard against the panel, and the door slid smoothly aside. Score one for the Science Journalist.

Inside, there was another panel beside the floor buttons. Alex swiped the card against it, pressed button 'P', and the door closed and the lift took off fast enough to make his knees flex.

Forty-two floors up, he stepped out into bright sunshine. The penthouse level was above the fog, and looking out through the big windows of the lift foyer was like looking across a pale grey sea, from which the tops of a few other buildings rose. He thought he recognised the pyramidal cap of the TransAmerica building. In the distance, a range of hills lifted out of the mist like a far-off shoreline, and a few miles away he could see the suspension towers of the Golden Gate Bridge.

"It's quite a view, isn't it?" said a voice.

"Yes." Alex turned from the window. "I don't know how you

manage to get anything done."

"Oh, this place isn't mine," said Stan. "I just rented it for a couple of days."

In Alex's admittedly limited experience, the very famous—people you saw on the news or in films all the time—never seemed quite real in person. He'd done his share of showbiz stuff, back in his Fleet Street days, and it didn't matter how down-to-earth or 'normal' the subject seemed in private, there was always that sense of not-quite-normality.

Stanisław Clayton was different. He looked like someone you'd see shopping in the local supermarket, neatly upper-middle-class in chinos and an open-necked shirt and a plain grey jacket. He was going bald, and he wore John Lennon spectacles. There was no impression, Alex thought, that he was shaking hands with the fifth wealthiest person on the planet. You'd walk past Stan in the street and not notice him.

He led the way into the penthouse's main room, an enormous wood-floored space with floor-to-ceiling windows looking out on the sea of fog and its island high-rises. In the centre of the room was a big coffee table flanked by what appeared to be two pieces of chrome and black leather BDSM equipment. Stan lowered himself into one; Alex perched on the edge of the other.

"So," said Stan. "How was the flight?"

"It was good, thanks," Alex said, looking about him. The ceiling of the room was so high that it wouldn't have surprised him to see clouds gathered against it.

Stan saw him looking and grinned. "I'd have been happy to meet you in a coffee shop, but I had another meeting earlier and those are not guys you take to Starbucks." He nodded at a cafetière, cups, and assorted milk jugs and sugar bowls on the table. "You look like you could use a cup, yourself."

Alex blinked at him. "Yes. Thank you."

Stan hunched forward so he could reach the coffee things. "I think we got off on the wrong foot yesterday," he said, pouring.

"One of us did, anyway."

Stan glanced at him. "Well," he went on. "Let's start again." He handed Alex one of the cups. "I want to offer you a job. It'll be long-term. At least a year, possibly longer. You'll be well-paid for it and when you're done I don't see any reason why you shouldn't continue to work for us." He sat back with his own cup and smiled. "How about it?"

Alex dropped a couple of sugar cubes into his coffee. He said, "You said in your letter that you want me to write a book."

"That's right. And some newspaper and magazine articles."

"Why me? I've never written a book before."

Stan shrugged. "How hard can it be? I like your work. That piece about the biohacker guy in Portland was pretty good."

It had also been six years ago and it didn't dispel the feeling Alex had of being caught up in some profound and uncontrollable natural event, like a tornado or an avalanche.

Stan reached into an old-fashioned briefcase beside his chair—Alex was fairly sure now that it was a chair—and took out what looked like a printed brochure. "Take a look."

Alex opened the brochure, saw photographs of neat midwestern Americana. Clapboard houses, flagpoles, an Arby's. Cornfields. Soy fields. A huge blue sky dissected by contrails.

"It's called Sioux Crossing," said Stan. "Up by the Minnesota state line."

"It's pretty," Alex said, turning a page. A road running off into the vanishing point between fields. White silos in the distance off to one side.

Stan grunted. "It was dying on its feet," he said. "Half the farms went to the wall in the last decade, and the other half were barely surviving. We bought the town. Actually, we bought the county. And parts of the neighbouring ones."

He said it so casually that Alex glanced up, but there was no sense of boastfulness. If anything, sitting there on the other side of the coffee table, he seemed rather wistful, as if he'd been telling someone that his refrigerator had broken down and he'd had to go out and buy another one. We needed to buy northern Iowa, so we did.

"Bit like buying your own country," said Alex.

Stan tipped his head to one side and regarded him amiably. "You know," he said, "you have a pretty smart mouth, for someone at a job interview. I find that interesting. Not a lot of guys would talk back to a potential employer like that."

"Yes, well, it's been that kind of year." Alex strongly suspected that Stan knew exactly what kind of year he was having, but there was no harm in mentioning it.

"A disinterested observer might think you were almost trying *not* to get the job."

"How am I doing?"

Stan smiled. "I'll let you know," he said. "But it would make me feel bad if I didn't mention that it's a piss-poor negotiating strategy."

"Hm." He looked down and turned another page. These days, press and corporate materials came to you via a download link, full streaming video, all the bells and whistles. Some companies aimed at ironic retro and sent you memory sticks branded with kitsch logos and a knowing wink. It was rare—pretty much unknown, in Alex's experience—to receive anything on paper, but again there was no sense of boastfulness about the brochure. It was competently presented, well-written, printed on good, although not expensive, stock. Humble, unflashy. It could, of course, have been a one-off, printed just for him, which meant that it was not humble at all.

"What do you think?"

Another page. There were several photos of what appeared to be a small university campus, low brick buildings set in wooded parkland. There was a lake, wide white paths with people cycling along them. One of the buildings was three or four stories taller than the others. The following page was a single aerial shot of the same buildings, taken from a considerable altitude, set in a patchwork of fields arranged within a neat grid of roads. A huge circle had been superimposed on the photo. The campus, the town and several farms were all contained within the circle. Alex knew what it was, but to anyone else it would have been a bit of a mystery. What was this huge circle? The blast radius of a nuclear weapon? The spread of a pestilence?

"How did you talk them into it?" he asked. "Selling you all that land?"

"I told you." Stan shuffled forward until he was sitting on the edge of the armchair and he could reach out and put his hand against the cafetière on the coffee table. He seemed to take a moment to consider whether it was still warm enough, then he picked it up and topped up his cup. "The place was virtually bankrupt. Foreclosures everywhere, kids moving out of the area. Rural flight. It's the Twilight of the Gods for farmers up there."

It crossed Alex's mind to say something insubordinate, but he decided against it. He tried to remember who had done that line about the rich *not being like you and me*. Hemingway? Fitzgerald? Back in the nineteenth century the megarich—your Rockefellers and your Carnegies—used to endow public libraries or build whole towns for their workers. In the middle of the twentieth century they withdrew from view, Hughes-like, became shadowy, mythical. These days, they were all over social media. They gave TED talks, set up their own space programmes or railway companies. They fired convertibles into orbit. Stanisław Clayton had developed a taste for high-energy physics, and because he was the fifth wealthiest human being on Earth he was able to indulge his tastes and do Good Works along the way. Or, in his case, to buy an enormous tract of North America and bury a supercollider in it.

He didn't live anywhere. Or rather, he lived in a lot of places. He had an apartment in Berlin and a house in London and a small manor house in Normandy and a dozen or so properties scattered around North America, and he was in constant motion between them. As far as he was concerned, buying an entire county in northern Iowa wasn't much different to buying a brownstone in midtown Manhattan; it was just a matter of scale.

He said, "You don't have to give me an answer right now. Take some time. A week, let's say. Think about it."

"I don't do PR," Alex told him.

"Well, great. I already have more PR people than is probably good for me, and to be honest I'd prefer you to stay out of their way. You'd have complete autonomy, reporting only to me."

"So, not *complete* autonomy, then."

Stan shook his head wonderingly. "Good Christ, Dolan, are you *allergic* to money?"

"It's not that I don't want to do it," said Alex. "It's more that I don't understand what I'm supposed to do with this book. There are better science writers than me."

"I told you. I like the way you write." He shook his head. "I don't understand why you're so… *resistant* to the idea, Alex. How long is it since you had regular work?"

"You know how long."

Stan looked rueful. "Yeah, okay. Point taken. I handled that all wrong, and I apologise." He got up and walked to the window that formed one wall of the suite. "Have you noticed there's no sense of adventure any more?" he said to the view. "No sense of *wonder*?"

"I can't say I have."

He sighed. "When I was a kid I read all those popular science magazines, all those predictions of the future. We were going to have cities on the moon and habitats in orbit and we were going to irrigate the Sahara and farm the oceans and everything was going to be wonderful."

"Flying cars. Jet packs."

Stan turned and smiled and put his hands in his pockets. "You're too young to remember all that."

"I've seen the memes."

Stan looked sourly around the room. "The future has been a *disappointment*, Alex. We still haven't managed to get a manned mission beyond the orbit of the moon, let alone build cities there. And as for all that other stuff..." He snorted and waved a hand. "It's within our capabilities to understand and harness the fundamental forces of the universe, and instead of being bold about it we just *tick along*."

"I think there are scientists who would disagree with you," Alex mused. "The people at CERN, for instance."

"We are going to make the Large Hadron Collider look like a valve radio," Stan said solemnly. It was a good line, but he'd used it before, in press releases and speeches, and Alex was a little disappointed to hear him repeat it.

"Some of those old valve radios are pretty good."

"Bit of advice? Don't insult your prospective employer and his multibillion dollar vanity project. It's not a strong look."

"Duly noted." Alex looked down at the brochure and read through a bullet-pointed page of statistics. "Some of these numbers are pretty impressive."

"They are." Stan came back and sat down.

"But they're just aspirations right now, aren't they? You can't possibly know what sort of yield you'll get out of this thing until you fire it up."

Stan picked up his cup and saucer and took a sip of coffee. "You're interested."

Yes, well, who wouldn't be? He'd been too young for the LHC and there'd been nothing on that scale since, until now. But when all was said and done, he could still just read the results in *Scientific American*.

"You do it your way, warts and all," Stan told him. "But I want something that *inspires*, something that makes people *believe*. I want *sensawunda*."

"That's a word I haven't heard for a while."

"My point exactly." Stan nodded at the brochure. "We're setting out on a great adventure, a journey into the fundamental processes of the universe. I want people to be excited about it."

He wanted, Alex thought, people to be properly grateful, which wasn't happening at the moment. The project was drowning in bad press; its social media was a trainwreck. Last week there had been a rather cruel sketch on *Saturday Night Live*.

"Look," said Stan, "why don't you go out there? Take a few days, have a look around, see what you think before you decide." When Alex looked dubious, he went on, "My jet's out at SFO; you can be there by the evening."

"*Today*?"

"Sure, why not? Give me a few minutes and I'll make the arrangements." And with that he was on his feet again and wandering towards the kitchen, phone in hand. Alex sat dumbly with the brochure open in his lap, wondering why he hadn't had the wit to nail a sheet of plywood over his mailbox.

NIGHT WAS FALLING as the jet made its final approach to Sioux Crossing. Down below, the land was already in darkness, a great emptiness of farmland divided up by roads like a sheet of graph paper. Alex had managed to get some sleep, and he'd missed the Rockies.

Back on the ground, they taxied for ten minutes or so before coming to a stop in a complex of brightly lit hangars. Alex undid his seatbelt and stretched his legs out in front of him. In the past eighteen hours or so he had flown all the way across the country and halfway back again. He felt tired and achy and sweaty and his clothes were beginning to smell.

The door at the front of the cabin opened and the copilot stepped out of the flight deck. "All ready, Mr Dolan?" he asked. He looked neat and clean and well-rested and cheerful.

"Yes," said Alex, clambering to his feet and picking up his overnight bag. "All ready."

Outside, a grey SUV was parked on the concrete, a tall man wearing jeans and a Megadeth tee shirt standing beside it. There was no sign of anyone else, so Alex walked over to him.

He met him halfway, hand outstretched. "Mr Dolan? Danny Hofstadter. Welcome to Sioux Crossing."

They shook hands. "Thank you. I think." Close up, he smelled like someone who had, until an hour or so ago, been hosting a family barbecue.

"Can I take your bag for you?" Hofstadter asked as they began to walk towards the SUV.

"No, I'm good, thanks." The bag contained a single change of clothes, a shaving bag, a bottle of water, and a couple of trashy novels Alex had picked up at Logan when he'd left that morning. Hofstadter opened one of the rear passenger doors and Alex slung the bag inside, closed the door, and went to sit up front.

"This your first time in Iowa?" Hofstadter asked, putting the car into drive and pulling away from the hangars.

"Yes, I'm afraid so. Where are we going?"

Hofstadter glanced at him. He looked a couple of years older than Alex, which put him in his late forties, but he was in far better shape. His hair was buzzed down to a mousy fuzz, and his biceps bulged from the sleeves of his tee shirt. He looked like a farmer who moonlighted as a taxi service. "I'm going to take you to your hotel," he said. "I guess you're tired."

"It's been a long day," Alex agreed.

"Well, the rest of it's your own. What's left of it." He pulled the car to a stop at a gate in a high chain-link fence. A man in a uniform was standing beside a kiosk; Danny flashed a card at him, the guard reached into the kiosk and fiddled with something, and the gate started to roll aside. The guard sketched a salute as they drove through, which was a first for Alex.

They drove away from the airport along a road which seemed to Alex far too wide and smooth for a county road. He'd been on state highways that were in worse condition. It was also virtually empty, with just the occasional car or truck passing in the other direction. Apart from that, they drove through a great silence between cornfields and soy fields, the last faint light in the sky picking out distant farms and silos. They passed what looked like a brand-new ethanol plant, all lit up but otherwise deserted.

"Is it always this quiet?" Alex asked.

"Nah," said Danny. "Sometimes it gets really exciting. Fourth of July, Founders' Day, Thanksgiving. We have parades."

Alex sighed. "I'm sorry. I'm tired and that came out all wrong."

Danny chuckled. "I guess it is pretty quiet round here, if you're used to Boston." Like everyone who'd seen *Good Will Hunting* more than once, he tried to do the accent by pronouncing it *Bawstun*. "It's okay, though. Good country, good people."

"I heard the economy was on its knees."

"It is. Everywhere else."

After about forty minutes, buildings began to appear at the side of the road. Houses first, then public buildings and storefronts with a lot of space between them. Main Street was a double row of stores and bars, a firehouse, police station, a couple of diners. It was gone almost as soon as Alex realised it *was* Main Street, and they were heading out into the countryside again.

A couple of minutes after that, they were pulling into an almost-empty parking lot to one side of a big five-storey building with a sign outside that said *NEW ROSE HOTEL*.

"You're kidding me," Alex said half to himself, as the sign went by.

"The owner's a big Gibson fan," Danny said.

The foyer of the hotel was huge and empty and smelled brand new. Through a set of glass doors to one side Alex could see the tables of a dining room, and to one side a gift shop, which appeared to be closed. Behind the front desk, a young woman beamed at them as they embarked on the long journey towards her.

"Hi, Danny," she said when they finally reached the desk. "Hi, sir. How are you today?"

"I'm fine, thanks, Grace," said Danny. "This is Mr Dolan and he'll be staying with us for a couple of days."

"That's great," said Grace, smiling at Alex. "Welcome, Mr Dolan."

"Thank you," Alex said.

"We'll just check..." she said, consulting what Alex presumed was a computer monitor on a shelf below the desktop. "Yes, that's right. Three nights on Mr Clayton's account." She slid a pen and a registration card towards him. "If you'll just fill this in, Mr Dolan, I'll make up your room key."

Alex filled in the boxes on the card, ticked it in a couple of places, left blank the little space where it asked if he wanted to receive further information from the hotel, and when he slid it back across the desktop Grace was holding out a mobile phone.

"Excuse me?" he asked.

Her smile didn't waver. "Your key, Mr Dolan," she said.

Danny stepped in. "I haven't explained yet," he told Grace.

She looked at him and back to Alex, and he thought he saw her smile dim just a fraction. "Oh," she said.

"I've had a long day," Alex told them.

"The hotel uses electronic keys downloaded to your phone," said Danny. "Your own phone probably isn't compatible so we'll issue you this one for your stay."

"Okay." Alex took the phone. It sounded unnecessarily complicated, but Stan was paying for everything so it seemed ungrateful to complain.

"All the access to the Facility runs on the same system," Danny went on. "They'll program the relevant keys onto the phone when you go over there."

"Right." He turned the phone over in his hand.

"You can also use it to pay for stuff in the stores here. You'll find it's been loaded with a line of credit."

"Can it make calls?" Alex asked.

"Sure it can," Grace said proudly. "And we have a 7G network everywhere in the county."

"Just don't drop it in the toilet," Danny warned. "This batch of phones has a manufacturing fault. They're not *wildly* waterproof."

"Well," said Alex, looking at the phone again. "Thank the gods there's *something* it can't do." He saw them exchange glances and he sighed. "Sorry. I was still in Boston at seven o'clock this morning, I had lunch in San Francisco, and now I'm here. I think everything's starting to catch up on me."

"You don't travel much, do you," said Danny.

"Not a lot, no."

He didn't look convinced—what kind of Important Writer wasn't used to travelling?—but he let it go. "You go get some rest," he said. He put out a hand. "I hope I get to see you again before you go back to Boston."

"Sure." They shook hands. "Thanks for the ride."

He grinned. "That's what I'm here for." He nodded to Grace. "Grace. See you at the weekend?"

Grace bobbed her head, all smiles. "I'll be there."

"Okay, then." And with a nod to Alex and a last wave, he was gone.

"Danny's my brother-in-law," Grace explained.

Alex held up the phone and waggled it.

"Oh," she said. "Yes. Room 500. Top floor. Just hold the phone against the door and it'll unlock for you."

"Thank you," he said. He picked up his bag and began to trudge towards the bank of elevators on the far side of the lobby.

* * *

The fifth floor was a deeply carpeted silence. The elevator opened onto a small vestibule with a corridor to the left and the doors to the emergency stairs to the right. The corridor ended in a single door. No number, just a handle. Alex took the phone out and held it against the wood and heard a click somewhere inside the door. He pushed down on the handle and the door swung open.

"Oh," he said.

Room 500 seemed, at first glance, to occupy the entire top floor of the New Rose Hotel. He stepped out of a short hallway into a huge reception room, as if someone had mapped a high-end dentist's waiting room onto the inside of an aircraft hangar. The far wall—and it really was very far—was all window. He trekked across the room, his heels sinking into the deep-pile carpet, and leaned his forehead against the glass. The cold against his skin felt good, but when he straightened up he saw he'd left a greasy spot on the window and he had to polish it off with his handkerchief. Spread out in the distance, Sioux Crossing was slumbering in the moonlight, a neat vista of trees and houses. It was mostly level ground, but to the west the land rose and fell in a series of low hills that disappeared towards an uncertain horizon. He couldn't see the buildings of the Facility; either it was over on the other side of the hotel or it was just too far away. He tried to picture the maps and photos from Stan's brochure but he was too tired and the images wouldn't come. It was hard enough to imagine where *Iowa* was, let alone anything else. He just stood looking at the view, waiting for his brain to catch up. Somewhere out there, buried under the fields and the woods, was the most powerful particle collider on Earth. Or rather, it would be, if they ever managed to get it working; it had been, so far, a project beset by glitches and breakdowns and general snafus. Right now, it was merely a very expensive tunnelling project. And Stan expected him to change the public image of that somehow.

Eventually, he turned from the window and set out to explore the suite, which took a while. There were three bedrooms, all of them ensuite. There was a fully equipped kitchen, complete with a fridge that was taller than he was, stocked with beer and juice and water and bacon and eggs and a couple of steaks and a bag of granola. He spent some time pondering the world view of people who put granola in the fridge.

There was an old-style landline phone on a side table in the living room, along with a little laminated card with handy numbers. He dialled room service and ordered a club sandwich and fries. He thought room service sounded mildly reproachful that, given a perfectly good kitchen and all the food he could possibly need, a man couldn't be bothered to actually cook, but he might have been imagining it.

He hung up, and all of a sudden the day seemed to just sit down on him. He'd woken up in his own bed in Boston this morning, and now here he was in Iowa, in the world's largest hotel suite, and everything in-between seemed fractured and jumbled and out of sequence. Had he really been in San Francisco? Intellectually, he knew he had, because he was here now, but all he had in his memory was an hallucinatory impression of buildings in fog.

He took out his phone and speed-dialled a number.

"Hi," said Stan. "Alex. Are you there?"

"I am," Alex said, looking around the living room. "Wherever 'here' is."

Stan chuckled. "Are you being looked after all right?"

"Everyone seems very nice."

"You sound tired. Have you eaten?"

"I ordered something from room service."

"Well, good. You order whatever you want, it's all on my tab. Have dinner, then get some sleep. I want you to have a look round the town tomorrow. There's a guy up there, Mickey Olive, he looks after my interests. He'll be in touch."

"Mickey Olive."

"Great guy. You'll like him; he's a Brit."

That, in itself, was no guarantee. "I'm going to need some stuff."

"Stuff?"

"Clothes. Stuff. If I'm going to be here a few days. I've only got an overnight bag with me."

"Sure. Did you get the phone?"

"Yes, I got the phone."

"Good. There's a line of credit on it; you can use it to buy your stuff. Again, whatever you need."

"Okay. Thanks."

"Within reason. If you get the urge to buy a farm or something like that, you're on your own."

"There's no chance of that. I'm a city boy." There was a discreet knock on the door. "Dinner's here. Got to go."

The club sandwich was the size of a briefcase, and came with enough fries to feed a family of four.

BREAKFAST WAS SERVED in the Prairie Dining Room, a carpeted space large enough to host a medium-sized awards dinner. Each of the hundred or so tables was laid out with four place settings and a little vase containing a single flower. It was completely deserted.

Alex stood in the doorway for a couple of minutes, baffled. Then he hiked back to the front desk, where a young woman whose nametag read KATE was signing a wad of forms.

"Hi, Mr Dolan," she said as he approached. "Is everything okay?"

Alex was beginning to feel a faint nostalgia for the time when no one knew who he was. "Have I missed breakfast?" he asked.

"No," she said brightly. "Just go in and sit down anywhere. Someone will be out to take your order."

Okay. He went back into the dining room. There was a small stack of fresh newspapers by the door, and he took one as he went past, then dithered for a few moments before seating himself at a table right in the middle of the room.

A minute or so later, a waiter came out with a menu. "Bacon, scrambled eggs, hash browns, sausage," said Alex, reading down the list. "Toast. In small portions, please."

While he waited for his breakfast to arrive, Alex looked at the newspaper. The *Rosewater County Banner*, according to its masthead. *Est. 1932*. That was a pretty good age, considering the catastrophe which was overtaking print journalism. The front page headline was about a new building opening on the Clayton Campus, and the announcement of another seventy job vacancies. The rest of the paper was a compendium of small-town news. Someone's sow had won first prize at the County Fair. In the photo, the animal appeared to be the size of a Volkswagen.

He glanced up and saw someone walking across the dining room towards him. The newcomer was wearing a long dark-grey overcoat over a black sweatshirt and jeans, and there was a white silk scarf around his neck.

He reached the table and held out a hand. "Mr Dolan? I'm Michael Olive." He had a plummy, deep-brown voice and a Home Counties accent. "Everyone calls me Mickey."

"Alex." They shook hands.

"May I join you?"

"Stan told me to expect you." As Mickey sat opposite him, his breakfast arrived. It wasn't quite the colossal portions he had been fearing, but it was still going to be a while before he needed to eat again. "Why is everything so *big* here?"

Mickey raised an eyebrow. He was tall and broad-shouldered, with a broken nose and untidy brown hair. "You're not in the normal world any more, I'm afraid," he said. "It takes a little while to get used to it."

Alex picked up his knife and fork and looked at his plate. "Do you want some of this? I'll never eat it all."

Mickey shook his head. "I already ate. I was going to pop over last night, but I thought it would be best to let you settle in."

"Yesterday was pretty weird."

"Yes. Well, the dangerous thing is when you stop noticing just how weird it is. Is everything all right? Is there anything you need?"

"I need to do some shopping, if I'm going to be here a few days."

"Stan emailed me about it." Mickey picked up the vase from the middle of the table, sniffed the flower, wrinkled his nose, and put it back. "I'm afraid I'm going to be out of town most of today, otherwise I'd show you around, but I can get someone to give you the grand tour."

Alex shook his head. "I can manage."

"Good." Mickey put his hand in his coat pocket and rummaged for a moment, then came up with a bunch of keys threaded on a length of string. "This is for you."

There was a cardboard tag on the string too. *24 EAST WALDEN LANE* was written on it in block capitals. "What do I need these for?"

"They're the keys to your house."

"I have a house?"

"You will, if you decide to accept Stan's offer. I thought you might like to take a look, while you're here, but you don't have to."

Alex looked at the keys again, then put them down beside his plate. "Will I get to see the facility while I'm here?"

Mickey nodded. "That's all in hand. How does the day after tomorrow sound?"

Alex glanced at him, then went back to his breakfast. "It sounds okay, but I don't want to be here too long."

Mickey regarded him sadly. "I know this is all new to you, but perhaps it's best to look at it as a bit of a holiday, with someone else paying for everything. Stan's very keen to have you on board. Just relax and enjoy yourself."

"In *Iowa*?"

"Well," Mickey mused. "Quite." He twitched up the sleeve of his overcoat and looked at his watch. "I have to go. Are you sure there's nothing you need?"

"I'll manage."

"Right." Mickey stood. "I'll see you soon, then. If you do need anything, my number's on the phone they gave you."

"Okay. Thanks. Nice to meet you." They shook hands again and Mickey left, and all of a sudden Alex felt very alone in the middle of the huge dining room.

THE CENTRE OF Sioux Crossing—if it could be called the centre—was a mile or so west of the hotel. Kate on the front desk offered to organise a cab for him, but he wanted to walk.

It was a nice day, but there was a chill in the air that reminded him he had dressed for the West Coast. The sky was blue and cloudless and almost derangingly huge. He kept to the verge, his shoes slipping on grass still damp with dew, and the cars rolled past him. Most of them seemed new, and many of them appeared to be carrying young families.

As he'd noted the previous evening, Main Street was modest to the point of being shy. A couple of dozen brick buildings, none of them more than three storeys tall. He looked at the fire station and the sheriff's office and the post office. He made a note of the Telegraph Diner and a Starbucks and a department store called Stockmann. There was something not-quite-right about the scene, something too neat and clean.

He went into Stockmann, which turned out to go quite a way back from the street and seemed to contain pretty much everything a human being might consider useful for modern life. He dumped jeans and underwear and tee shirts and fleeces and a couple of Rosewater High sweatshirts into a trolley, found a warm jacket, and at the last moment added a pair of stout workboots.

At the checkout, an eye-hurtingly-neat young man with a badge which read *JIM* scanned his purchases through. The total was more than Alex had spent on clothes in the previous couple of years. He held out the phone he'd been given at the hotel, and Jim pointed a little black box about the size of a pack of cigarettes at it. There was a moment's suspense, during which Alex became convinced that this was the point at which a film crew would leap out of hiding and inform him that he was the victim of a particularly involved practical joke, but then the till beeped and, yes, he now actually owned all these things.

"I can parcel these up and have them delivered to the hotel if you'd prefer, Mr Dolan," Jim said brightly.

Alex supposed the phone had told him who he was and where he was staying, but it was still getting a bit eerie. "Yes," he said, putting the phone away again. "That would be great. Thank you."

Outside again, he wandered unhurriedly. Main Street was busy, but the demographic seemed wrong. Most of the people here were not what he thought of as farming types. He spotted a few large men in jeans and checked shirts and baseball caps—and a couple of old faded MAGA hats worn, he presumed, unironically—but the majority were young and multicultural, the kind of people you'd see on a university campus or at the headquarters of a tech startup. A lot of them had kids with them.

He stopped outside the Great North Bookshop and looked about him, wondering what was troubling him about Sioux Crossing. It wasn't that everything was neat and clean, or that almost everyone he could see appeared to have been transplanted from elsewhere. It was something else, something that niggled at the edge of his attention.

A sign over the front of a building across the street proclaimed it to be the headquarters of the *Rosewater County Banner*. Alex thought about it for a few moments, then crossed over and opened the front door.

Inside was a smallish room with about half a dozen desks, piles of newspapers, file folders. A large potted palm was dying in a corner.

The only person in the room was an African-American woman in her mid-sixties, her grey hair in cornrows. She looked up as the door opened. "What."

All of a sudden, Alex was unsure what had possessed him to come in here. "I'm new in town," he said.

"Yes." She got up and walked over to him. "I know who you are. What do you want?"

After the general Stepfordness of the town, it was kind of refreshing to meet someone who was straightforwardly grumpy. "I don't really know," he confessed.

The woman regarded him sourly over the top of her spectacles. "Come to see how the smalltown press works?" When Alex didn't answer, she said, "What," again.

"I just realised what's wrong with this place," he told her. "It looks brand new."

She sighed. "I'm Dru Winslow," she said. "Editor of the *Banner*. Let me buy you a cup of coffee, Mr Dolan."

NOW HE SAW it, it was obvious. At most, Sioux Crossing looked about five years old. There were barely any signs of wear and tear. It was like a peculiarly detailed movie set. The interior of the Telegraph Diner was the same. The vinyl of its seats was unpatched and almost unworn, its counter polished and unchipped. Rhoda, the waitress who brought them coffee and slices of apple pie on plates that looked as if they had still been in the shop the previous day, was wearing a uniform so crisp and clean that it might have been delivered to her that morning. The pie was very good, though. And it came in normal human-sized portions.

"Long story short," Dru told him, "they rebuilt the town."

"Why?"

"Ah. That's the long story." She took a sip of coffee. "When Clayton's people first started buying land round here, ten years or so ago, the place was on its knees. Farms were going bust, families were moving out. Half the storefronts were boarded up. It was pretty bad."

"So I heard."

"It was a lot worse than you heard. We had suicides. More than one."

Alex stared.

She shrugged. "Anyway, Clayton wanted to build goodwill, win hearts and minds. So he started to endow public buildings. First thing he did was buy us a new firehouse. Just demolished the old one and built a brand new one on the site. New engines and ladders, new equipment, the whole thing."

"Must have made him popular."

"Most of us couldn't see the point of it. Why build a new firehouse for a town that was going to be deserted in a couple of years?" She shrugged again. "Still, it was his money. Anyway, next it was a new post office. Then it was a new library. By then they'd started to build the Facility and suddenly there was a lot of work, money started to come into the county for the first time in... oh, Christ, I don't know how long. People started to talk about it as if it was a miracle."

"It sounds like you don't agree."

Dru nodded. "Clayton couldn't stop building; it was like he'd got a taste for it or something, and in a couple of years we had a brand new Main Street and coffeeshops and fast wi-fi and we were all properly grateful. Haven't had a suicide in, oh, almost a decade, I guess."

"I'd guess there are a lot of rural towns who'd give their right arms for an opportunity like that."

She gave him that look over the rims of her spectacles again, as if she was trying to decide whether he was serious or just playing devil's advocate. "I grew up here, and I'm old and cranky now and I don't like the idea of being *bought*."

"It strikes me as being more of a bribe."

"I was going to retire," she said. "The *Banner*'s circulation was down in the low three figures, ad revenue had tanked—you know the story, it's happening everywhere. I was going to sell up and take a cruise."

"But Stan came along with his magic fairydust."

"We got a brand new building, new presses, new computer equipment. I got a nice fat loan to keep the paper going, and after a few years the scientists started to move in and circulation began to go up and now we're ticking over very nicely, thank you, and I still owe Clayton that nice fat loan."

"Why did you take the money? Why didn't you do what you planned and take the cruise?"

She pulled a face. "I'd have gone out of my mind in the first couple of days. I've been in the business more than forty years. You know how it is."

"Yes, I do." He looked round the diner. Here and there, fliers were stuck to the walls with the words VOTE HOFSTADTER and Danny's face on them. He nodded at one. "He drove me from the airport last night."

Dru half turned in her seat and looked. "Yup, he's running for re-election in the spring. Not that anyone's running against him yet, but I guess he wants to start early."

"Re-election?"

"Yes, he's the Mayor." She smiled broadly at the look on his face. "Oh yes. And shall I blow your mind a little more? He owns the hotel where you're staying."

"Good lord."

"The SCS has been *very* good to the Hofstadters. Did you ever hear of the Osage?"

He shook his head.

"Native American nation," she said. "Back in the 1920s huge oil deposits were discovered under their land in Oklahoma and all of a sudden the Osage were the wealthiest people in the country."

"And that's you," he said. "Everyone in the county."

"Well, the story didn't have a very happy ending for the Osage, but yeah, that's us. We're not the wealthiest people in the country, but we're sure as hell the wealthiest people in Iowa."

He thought about it. "That's... quite something," he said.

She drank some more coffee and regarded him steadily. "So, what's your story?"

"Me? Very similar to the one you just told me, actually. I lost my job three years ago, been trying to freelance ever since. No money. One day out of the blue Stan comes along and does some *rebuilding*."

"How do you feel about that?"

"I don't know yet. Why does everyone seem to know who I am?"

"Oh, we were told you were coming."

"Really?"

"Yup. Big-shot journalist from out East, blowing into town and showing us how to do things."

Alex found that he didn't know how to feel about this, either. He said, "When did you get the word?"

Dru thought about it. "A week, maybe? Be easy to check; I've still got the memo at the office."

Alex shook his head. "That's okay." A week ago was more or less when Stan had posted his letter. Long before Alex had seen it. "That's a bit annoying, actually."

"Isn't it just?" Dru chuckled and forked some pie into her mouth. "Your basic offer-you-can't-refuse."

He looked around the diner. There were a couple of farmer-types on stools at the counter, but everyone else here seemed to be the younger, nerdy types he'd seen on the street. "Is everyone here a scientist?" he asked.

Dru looked about her. "Scientists, admin people, techs, support staff. Clayton was keen to bring young families into the county."

And that was good, wasn't it? Stan's methods might have been unorthodox, but it sounded as if he really had single-handedly regenerated the entire county.

As if reading his mind, Dru said, "Even an asshole can do something good every once in a while, right? Well, I remain unconvinced, Mr Dolan."

"Alex."

"So. Alex. I presume you haven't given Clayton a yes or a no yet."

"Not yet, no. He wanted me to see the town and the Facility first, get a feel of the place, I suppose."

Dru laid down her fork and dabbed at her lips with a napkin. "Look," she said. "You seem a decent enough man. It sounds as if you're already beholden to him; get out while you still can. Don't let him own you."

"It's not that simple," he said.

She looked at him a moment later, then folded her napkin and put it on her plate. "No," she said. "It never is. I should interview you."

"Beg pardon?"

"Big-shot journalist comes to our humble town, that's news. I should run something about you."

"Everyone already knows all about me, by the sound of it."

"Don't underestimate small-town gossip. You're going to be the object of a lot of curiosity for a while; might be better to get it all over with in one go."

Alex laughed. "You shouldn't try that line on another journalist, Ms Winslow."

"Dru."

"Tell you what, if I do take the job I'll think about it, okay?"

"Fair enough."

"There is one thing you could help me with, though. Where's East Walden Lane?"

"Three or four miles that way." She pointed back in the direction of the hotel. "Why?"

"Something I have to go and look at."

"Ah." Dru smiled knowingly. "I think I can guess."

"You can? Why are you smiling?"

"You'll see. Well." She stood up. "I have to get back to the office, but it's been good meeting you, Alex. I hope I see you again." They shook hands. "Or rather, I don't."

"Yes," he said.

"Flee," she said seriously. "Save yourself."

He spent half an hour wandering around the Great North Bookshop, then went back to the hotel via Carl's MultiMart, where he bought a couple of bags of groceries. At the checkout, Carl—at least his nametag said he was *a* Carl—offered to have the groceries delivered, but by now, notwithstanding his conversation with Dru Winslow, Alex was starting to feel more than a little weirded out by the town and he was succumbing to the urge to run for cover.

Back at the New Rose, the lobby was still deserted, apart from Grace, who was back on the front desk. Through the half-open doors of the Prairie Dining Room he could hear the distant sound of an industrial vacuum cleaner. The gift shop was still shut. It occurred to Alex that apart from Grace and Kate and the waiter who had brought his sandwich the previous night—who was, he was half convinced, the same waiter who had taken his breakfast order that morning—he had not seen another living soul at the hotel.

Upstairs, his purchases from Stockmann had been delivered and were sitting in the suite's hallway. He gathered up the bags and took everything into the kitchen, where he spent half an hour putting things in the fridge and cutting labels and price tags off pieces of clothing.

When that was done, he made himself a coffee, then dragged one of the armchairs across the living room and sat in front of the windows, looking out over the panorama of Rosewater County. It was quite a view—better than the one in San Francisco. At least there was no fog.

The problem, he thought, was that he had believed himself to be bombproof, that he was so good, so indispensable, that the catastrophe sweeping the newspaper industry would pass him by. So, unlike wiser heads, he hadn't made any escape provisions. Looking back, he wasn't quite sure why he hadn't. Maybe he'd been afraid that acknowledging the possibility would have made it come true. Maybe it was just a simple, and somewhat out of character, act of hubris. Whatever. He'd been wrong; he wasn't indispensable, and when the first wave of layoffs went through the *Globe*'s newsroom he'd been left holding a severance notice and a redundancy cheque, not quite understanding what had just happened.

"You'll be fine," his editor told him, not quite able to look him in the eye. "You're a good writer; you'll find something else."

But of course he hadn't. He wasn't prepared, and those who were snapped up the dwindling number of available staff jobs elsewhere. He scrabbled for whatever freelance gigs he could find. In the past three years, he hadn't even come close to getting a full-time job.

And now… this. Sitting here with a mug of very good coffee cradled in his hands, looking out across the late-summer panorama of a new world. Out there, among the trees and the fields and the neat houses, was a brand new life. All he had to do to secure it was sell his soul to a man who, for all his amiable goodwill, basically got whatever he wanted by buying it, whether it was journalists or towns. It occurred to him that an outsider would find it hard to understand why he hadn't chewed Stan's hand off the moment he made the offer, but there were lots of things an outsider would have found hard to understand.

He took out his phone and scrolled down its contact list until he came to Stan's number. He sat looking at it for quite some time. Then he put the phone away again.

Outside, the sun was beginning to make for the western horizon. Somewhere out there, a couple of timezones away, it was still only late afternoon in San Francisco. He wondered if the fog had cleared yet.

There was a knock on the door. Alex put his mug on the floor beside the chair and made his way towards the hallway. About halfway there, the knock came again, and this time there seemed something wrong about it. There was a weird *scrabbling* quality to it that made him miss a step and then come to a stop a few feet from the door.

There was a soft *thump* on the other side of the door, then that weird knocking again. It sounded, he thought, inexpressibly *weary*. He took another step towards the door, then another, trying to tread as softly as possible. He bent slightly and, holding his breath, put his eye to the little viewer.

Outside was a fish-eye view of the lift vestibule. It appeared to be quite deserted. Alex reached for the handle of the door, intending to have a quick look outside, when something dark moved across his field of view and he started back.

Another knock.

He stood where he was, heart pounding. He was alone on this floor. He was, he was beginning to suspect, almost alone in the hotel. The door and its lock had seemed solid, but there was no way to be sure. He backed slowly away from the door until he was able to turn his back on it and go into the kitchen.

In one of the drawers was a roll of stout cloth tied with a tape. He undid the tape and unrolled the cloth on the worktop and regarded what seemed to be a full set of Sabatier kitchen knives. Ignoring them, he took out the sharpening steel, which was a lot heavier than it looked, had a satisfying heft and a sharp point, and posed little danger of him cutting off one of his own fingers.

Back at the door, he looked through the viewer again, but the vestibule still appeared to be empty. He took a shaky breath and called, "Hello?"

No answer.

"Who's there?"

No answer.

He put his ear against the door, but all he could hear was a distant low humming which was probably something to do with the hotel's aircon. Straightening up, he cocked the sharpening steel up beside his ear and reached for the handle with his other hand. But he stopped before he touched it. For a fraction of a second—just a fraction—he thought he saw blue sparks on the metal. He blinked, and they were gone.

Okay.

He went back into the living room, picked up the house phone and dialled zero.

"Hi, Mr Dolan," Grace said brightly. "How may I help you?"

"Has someone come up to my room in the past five minutes or so?"

"No." All of a sudden Grace didn't sound quite so perky. "Why?"

"Someone was knocking on the door." His voice, he thought, sounded remarkably steady. "I thought it might be one of the housekeeping staff."

"No, your suite was serviced while you were out earlier. Did you see who it was?"

He thought of the dark shape that had moved across the door viewer. "No. Not clearly. But there *was* someone there."

"I didn't mean to contradict you, Mr Dolan." Grace was all business now. "Are you okay?"

"Yes. A bit puzzled. Maybe someone got the wrong door."

"Yes," she said, the tone of her voice telling him everything he needed to know about what she thought of *that*. "Please just sit tight where you are, and I'll send someone up."

"You don't have to do that. I just wondered who it was."

"Please, Mr Dolan. We have procedures for this."

For what? "Okay." He hung up and went back to the window. The sun was closer to the horizon now, shadows starting to gather between the trees and across the fields.

About ten minutes later there was another knock on the door, this time firm and confident. He went to the door and said, "Hello?"

"Mr Dolan?" said a man's voice. "Officer Muñoz, Sioux Crossing Police Department."

Alex put his eye to the viewer, got a fisheyed look at a short young man in a crisp blue uniform. "Hello."

Muñoz held up to the viewer a badge which might as well have come out of a Christmas cracker for all that Alex knew. He said, "Are you alone in the apartment?"

"Yes."

"Could you open the door, please, and then stand aside?"

"Okay." Alex opened the door and stood to one side, and Muñoz, who looked and moved more like a dancer than a law enforcement official, stepped inside and closed the door behind him.

"You reported some suspicious activity," he said.

"Someone knocked on the door," Alex said. "I don't know who it was. It might have been perfectly innocent."

"Okay." Around his waist, Muñoz was wearing a belt festooned with arcane equipment, as well as an oddly foreign-looking sidearm. "May I take a look around the apartment?"

"Sure. But there's no one here. They were outside."

Muñoz gave him a level look. "Please let me do my job, Mr Dolan."

"Okay." Alex waved into the suite. "Help yourself."

"Are there any weapons in the apartment?"

"What? No."

"Okay. Please stay here." And he went into the suite and for the next five minutes or so Alex heard him moving almost soundlessly around.

"Well," he said when he finally came back, "the apartment seems clear."

"It *is* clear, Officer Muñoz."

"Yes." Muñoz unbuttoned one of the breast pockets of his shirt and took out a little black notebook and a pen. "Could you tell me what happened, Mr Dolan?"

"I was expecting they might just send up hotel security," Alex told him. "Or even just a waiter. This seems a bit like overkill."

Muñoz gave him that look again. "It's my job to decide what is and isn't overkill, sir. So. In your own words?"

Starting to feel a little self-conscious, Alex told the story. He left out the bit about the little blue sparks, though. He was beginning to think he'd imagined them. Muñoz wrote everything down without comment, only interrupting a couple of times to clarify something which Alex didn't think needed clarifying.

When they'd finished, Muñoz quickly paged through his notes, then snapped the elastic band back round the notebook and buttoned it into his pocket again.

"Thank you for your cooperation, Mr Dolan," he said. He took a folded piece of paper from his other breast pocket and held it out. "Could you fill this in, please?"

Alex unfolded it, saw a list of bullet points and little checkboxes. "What is it?"

"Customer satisfaction survey."

Alex looked at him. "I'm sorry?"

"Customer satisfaction survey." There was no indication that

Muñoz was anything but serious. "You don't have to fill it in right now. You can do it later and leave it at the front desk; they'll make sure it gets back to us."

"Okay." Alex scanned down the page again. "So, what happens now?"

"I'll check the perimeter of the hotel and we'll get a specialist to run a review of their security arrangements."

"Seriously, Officer, that seems way over the top."

"Maybe to you, sir," Muñoz said soberly, "but from time to time we have some very high-status guests at the New Rose, guests whose security people take their jobs *very* seriously. We'll have to report this incident to all of them."

Alex tipped his head to one side. "High-status like whom?"

"I'm not allowed to say, sir."

"Okay." Bemused, Alex folded the piece of paper and put it in the back pocket of his jeans.

"Did they give you the phone?"

"Yes, Officer Muñoz, they gave me the phone," Alex sighed. "That's how I get into the room."

The sarcasm bounced right off Muñoz. "The number for Headquarters is in the contact list. If you see or hear anything unusual, give us a call and either ask for me or Chief Rosewater."

"Chief Rosewater."

"Doesn't matter how insignificant it seems. It could be important."

"Nobody told me about this when I checked in."

Muñoz pursed his lips. "That will have been an oversight, Mr Dolan." He reached for the doorhandle. "Don't forget to fill in the survey."

When Muñoz had gone, Alex closed and locked the door and put on the chain. He went into the kitchen. A few moments later, he came out again and dragged one of the living room armchairs across the suite to the door. By tilting it back a little he was able to wedge it under the handle. Sod fire regulations.

He cooked himself a beef stir-fry and sat on a stool at the kitchen counter eating it. Later, he took one of the beers from the fridge and sat in front of the window again, staring out across the darkened countryside through his reflection. Presently, for something to do, he filled in Muñoz's customer satisfaction survey.

He woke the next morning feeling well rested but with a nagging conviction that at some point during the night he had dreamed there was someone in the suite with him.

SHOWERED AND SHAVED and wearing some of his new clothes, he went straight past the Prairie Dining Room and out the front doors of the hotel. Forty minutes later, he was sitting in one of the booths at the Telegraph Diner regarding his breakfast.

He'd barely started to eat when Mickey Olive came in, nodded hello, and slipped into the booth opposite him.

"Heard you had a little excitement yesterday evening, old son," Mickey said.

Chewing a mouthful of bacon and eggs and hash browns, Alex blinked at him. He nodded.

"Do us a favour and let us know if anything else happens, will you?"

Alex swallowed. "Someone knocked on my door, Mickey. That's all. Everyone's behaving as if it was the third act of *Die Hard*."

"It bothered you enough to call the police," Mickey pointed out. "Hi, Rhoda," he added, beaming at the waitress who had materialised silently beside them. "I believe I'll have bacon and pancakes this morning. And coffee, of course." He looked at Alex. "You good?"

Alex glanced down at his breakfast. "I'm good." He had been literally tightening his belt, and he usually just had a slice of toast or—if it was a good month—a bagel for breakfast. He planned to put on a few pounds while he was there and it was on Stan's dime.

When Rhoda had gone back to the counter, Mickey said, "Something about it bothered you enough to call the cops."

"I called the front desk," Alex said. "*They* called the police."

"And quite right too. But why would you call them if it was just someone knocking on the door?"

There were little blue sparks on the door handle. "I was twitchy, that's all. Still a bit tired." He put some more food in his mouth, chewed, swallowed. "The police officer said you sometimes have high-status visitors at the hotel."

"He did?"

"He did."

They embarked on a brief staring match, which Mickey finally broke. "Yes, we do get VIPs staying there from time to time. Security's important."

"VIPs?"

"Oh," Mickey waved it away. "People coming to visit the Facility. Scientists, senators, congressmen. The president."

"Really?"

"Really. I believe you're in the Presidential Suite, in fact." He saw the look on Alex's face and added, "He's only been here a couple of times. The suite's been sitting empty since last October; someone might as well have use of it."

Alex thought about it. "Well," he said.

"It's got all kinds of hidden extras I'm sure no one's told you about," Mickey went on. "I'll have to get the hotel to show you the briefing book; it's rather fun."

"Can I launch an airstrike from there?"

Mickey deadpanned him. "Anyway, as I said, security is important. If people are just wandering in and out and annoying the guests without the staff noticing, that's an issue. We have to report stuff like that to the Secret Service."

"Good lord."

"What I'm *really* here for," Mickey said, taking a couple of folded sheets of paper from the inside pocket of his jacket, "is to tidy up some rather tedious legal stuff regarding your visit to the Facility." He handed the sheets over and watched Alex unfold them. "Bullet points, you won't be allowed to write or speak about anything connected with the Facility until you sign a formal contract with us. Basically, if you want to see The Beast you'll have to sign this, and if you subsequently decide not to come on board and go away and write something about it anyway we'll pursue you and your extended family through the courts for the rest of your lives, kill your pets, kill your *friends'* pets, demolish your home and plough salt into the ground where it stood so nothing will ever grow there again." He smiled happily. "What do you say?"

"I think it's a remarkable work of compression," Alex said, holding up the two closely printed pages. "In the hands of a lesser attorney this thing would run to almost a hundred pages."

Mickey inclined his head. "Concision is a wonderful thing, Alex. There should be more of it. Would you like to borrow a pen?"

"It's okay, I have one." Alex read the agreement one last time to make sure he wasn't signing himself, his mother, his sister and his cousins into a lifetime of indentured servitude. Then he flattened the document on the table beside his plate and signed where indicated.

"Don't get grease on it, there's a good chap," Mickey advised. "We'll only have to do it again."

"Does grease make it null and void?" Alex asked, folding the sheets up again and handing them back.

"Nah," he said, slipping them back into his jacket. "Just makes it look unprofessional." Rhoda returned with a plate bearing a two-inch stack of pancakes and several rashers of crispy bacon and Mickey sat looking at it solemnly. "I can feel my arteries closing up already," he said.

"What are you doing here, Mickey?"

He looked up. "Breakfast."

"No, *here*. Claytonland. I never saw a man who looked further from home."

"Oh." He unwrapped his knife and fork, settled the napkin in his lap. "That. Well, I was a barrister back home." He drizzled maple syrup onto the pancakes. "I was doing all right, had a nice house, interesting work. And then..." He paused and looked off into a distance far beyond the end wall of the diner, the little syrup jug still in his hand. His silence lasted so long that Alex started to fear he'd suffered a stroke or something, but then his eyes focused again and he went on, "I had a bit of a *mid-life crisis*, I suppose. Stan Clayton got in touch one day, just out of the blue, and suddenly everything was so much... *more*." He looked at Alex and shrugged. "I don't suppose that makes much sense," he said apologetically.

It not only made sense, it sounded familiar. Alex said, "He's done the same thing with me."

"If you're thinking this whole thing is just a rich man's toy, don't," Mickey said solemnly. Alex didn't try to deny it. "This is serious science, genuine fundamentals of the cosmos stuff. When they get The Beast working it could change everything."

"*If*, Mickey. *If*."

"Well, indeed." He busied himself with his breakfast for a little while, then said, "It's a nice town, isn't it."

"Yes," Alex said. "Almost everyone has been telling me how nice it is."

Mickey glanced at him, fork loaded with pancake and bacon. "'Almost'? Oh. Yes, I heard you'd been chatting with our friendly local newspaper editor. How is Dru? I haven't seen her for a couple of weeks."

"Have you been keeping tabs on me?"

"Of course not, old son. Someone just mentioned they'd seen you in town, that's all."

That could have been anyone. "Dru told me how you rebuilt the place."

"Ah, now that was before my time, I'm afraid." Mickey sat back and took a sip of coffee. "I've seen the 'before' photos, though. It wasn't very pretty."

"If I tell you something, will it eventually find its way back to Stan?"

Mickey went back to working on his breakfast. "Not if you don't want it to, no."

"Seriously?"

"He's my employer, not my owner."

Alex leaned his elbows on the table and said more quietly, "I really don't like what you've done here."

Mickey looked at him, glanced around the diner. "What have I done?"

"Not you personally. Stan."

"Oh." He went back to his food. "How so?"

"You've bought this county and everyone in it, and they're *happy* about it."

"It's an arrangement of mutual benefit," Mickey agreed around a mouthful of pancake and bacon. "Don't quite see your problem."

"Mickey, I'm going to have to *write* about that."

He started to say something, thought better of it and put another forkful of breakfast in his mouth instead.

"Have you *any* idea what that will look like to, you know, *normal people*?"

He sat back, chewing, then took another swallow of coffee. "We don't have copy approval?"

"I don't know. I've been promised complete independence but I haven't seen a contract yet."

Mickey thought about it. "*I've* seen it," he said. "Can't remember a clause about copy approval, though, now you mention it. Which seems a schoolboy error." He grinned. "Have to rectify that." When Alex didn't answer, he added, "This is a nice town, Alex. Everyone loves us."

"They don't have any choice."

"Oh come on now." Micky looked mildly disappointed. "Don't be like that."

Alex sat back and crossed his arms. "So, what happens now?"

Mickey gave him that disappointed look for a few moments more, then decided to park that part of the conversation and said, "A car will come and pick you up from the hotel tomorrow morning. It might be good not to be late; Professor Delahaye doesn't like to be kept waiting. He'll give you a tour of the Facility." He thought about it. "Well, he'll probably hand you over to one of his assistants, but that's the Professor. I think they'll probably lay on a lunch for you."

"And then I can go home?"

That disappointed look again. "You can go *now*; you're not being held against your will. Give me a few hours to have the jet ready and you can be home by suppertime." He drank some coffee, returned his mug to the table. "Of course, if you do that you'll never get to see The Beast." He dabbed his lips with his napkin and dropped it beside his plate. "But you should go to the Facility. The food's terrific; they have a Michelin-starred chef."

Of course they did. Nothing but the best for Stan's Cosmic Warriors. "I think I'm the wrong person for this job."

"Stan speaks very highly of you. I'm afraid I haven't read your work yet, but I'll get round to it."

"That's not the point, Mickey. I'm not going to be able to do the job Stan wants me to do."

Mickey sighed. "You know, it's not my job to talk you into taking up the offer; I'm just here to handle admin. But between you and me, there are worse places to be."

* * *

On the way back to the hotel, he stopped off at Stockmann and bought a couple of notebooks and a pack of cheap ballpoint pens, then he spent most of the day sitting in the armchair at the window trying to put his impressions of Sioux Crossing into order. He told himself he wasn't working, that he was just noting down the pros and cons of taking the job, but by lunchtime he'd half filled one of the notebooks and he was no closer to working out what to do.

For lunch, he made himself a bacon sandwich, and when he'd finished that he stood at the window with his hands in his pockets. After a while, he took out the bunch of keys Mickey had given him and weighed them in his palm.

At the front desk, Grace provided him with paper maps of the town and the county. When she discovered where he was planning to go, she wanted to organise a cab. "It's a bit off the beaten track," she told him. "Hard to find, if you don't know your way around."

"I'll be fine," he said, looking at the maps. "It doesn't look so hard."

But, of course, it was. Following the maps and Dru Winslow's directions, he walked away from the town. The day was cool and overcast and there was no sense of that impossibly huge sky hanging over him. Not far from the hotel, the houses and buildings thinned out and the road gently undulated away into a vanishing point. He could hear tractors in the distance in the fields on either side, and from somewhere the breeze brought the smell of manure.

After a couple of miles, he came to a crossroads. He went straight across, and half a mile further on, consulting the maps, he turned off the main road and down a dusty side road. A few hundred yards or so further on, the road narrowed down to a rutted track and then petered out in a field.

Alex stood at the end of the track, maps in hand, looking about him. He held the maps up and turned to orient them with the main road. Then he looked up again. According to the maps, he should be standing outside the house Clayton's people had organised for him. Looking about him, he could see no signs of habitation at all.

Back at the main road, he looked in both directions. According to the maps, East Walden Lane was definitely on this side of the intersection. He trudged away from town for another twenty minutes or so, but he didn't pass any more turn offs.

"Well, okay," he muttered to himself, and turned back towards town. A minute or so after crossing the intersection, he came upon a turn off. It was almost hidden by bushes, but he was still somewhat baffled that he'd managed to walk right past without seeing it. According to the map, it wasn't there at all.

Cursing the makers of hotel maps, he stomped off down the side road. It wound gently between fields and little stands of trees for about three quarters of a mile, and then just came to a stop in a wall of weeds. Alex checked his watch. It was going to start getting dark in another hour or so.

Fine. He started back towards the main road, but after a hundred yards he came upon a track leading off the side road. Once again, he had walked right past it. He dithered at the junction for a minute. He wasn't particularly worried about getting stuck out here after dark; he could always phone the hotel and no doubt a search party would be sent out to rescue him. But it would be intensely embarrassing. On the other hand, he was here, he'd walked a long way, his feet hurt, and he still hadn't found East Walden Lane.

Ah, sod it. He started to walk down the track.

Almost immediately, it widened out again and became a paved road. A couple of minutes later he spotted a house sitting among the trees, and then another, and then another, and suddenly he came to a place where the road made a loop around a neatly mowed oval of grass, like a village green large enough to host a cricket match. Along one curve of the green a dozen or so houses were arranged, each perched at the back of shallowly sloping lawns. There were cars and trucks parked beside the houses, and a smallish powerboat sat on a trailer on one driveway.

Okay. Feeling self-conscious, Alex walked along the line of houses. There were not twenty-four houses here, but one of the mailboxes did indeed have the number *24* on it. Alex stood looking at the house the box belonged to. It was a neat, white-painted two storey clapboard with a shingled roof and sash windows. Its lawn was freshly mown and the bushes dotted around it seemed well-tended. The house next door was not nearly as well kept; it looked dingy and disreputable and its lawn was overgrown and full of weeds.

Well. There was still no indication that this was actually East Walden Lane; it might be best to be careful. He walked up onto the porch of Number Twenty-Four and rang the doorbell. He heard the sound echo in the space beyond the door and knew immediately that the house was empty, but he tried again anyway. Then he knocked. Still no response. He leaned forward and looked through the tinted and rippled glass panes of the door. He got an impression of a long hallway, but no sense of any movement.

So, moment of truth. He took the bunch of keys from his pocket and looked from them to the two locks on the door. He tried one key but it wouldn't go into either of the locks. Tried another and this time it slid in and turned easily, which suggested that he was at least in the right place.

Heartened by this, he tried the other keys, and a few moments later the door was open and he was looking down the wood-floored and panelled hallway. On the left, a flight of stairs rose to a dogleg and on up to the first floor. On the right, three closed doors. Straight ahead in the failing light, he could see what seemed to be the appliances of a kitchen.

"Hello?" he called. "Anyone here?"

No answer, no sound of anyone moving about. He took a breath and stepped into the hallway. "Hello?" He closed the door behind him. The air in the house was cool and still and smelled ever so slightly musty. "Hello?"

Fine. He found a switch on the wall by the door and clicked it. Five bulbs in a little brass chandelier halfway along the hallway ceiling came on. He walked towards the kitchen, trying the closed doors as he passed. The first opened onto a dining room with a big table and six chairs; the middle one turned out to be a cupboard containing a Hoover and shelves neatly stacked with cleaning products. The third was a big living room. Three-piece suite, a lounger, huge flatscreen television on the wall. There seemed to be no personal possessions here. Furniture, but no paintings or prints on the walls, no ornaments, no vases with flowers, no coats hanging on the rack in the hall. Whoever had lived here was gone.

In the kitchen there was a range and a big fridge and an island with a tiled top and four stools. Under the window there was a Belfast sink large enough to bathe a Shetland pony. Alex tried the taps. Then he looked out of the window into the backyard and tipped his head to one side.

There was a little old man standing in the backyard looking at him.

The little old man was wearing a pair of pyjama bottoms, a grubby-looking sweatshirt and a tatty old towelling dressing gown that hung open, the ends of its belt trailing on the ground. On his feet was a pair of Converse All Stars. He looked at Alex for a while, then raised one hand and waved. Alex waved back, and the little old man moved out of view around the side of the house. A minute or so later, the doorbell rang. Alex stood where he was, thinking. Then he went to the door.

The little old man was standing on the porch, a ragged unlit stub of a cigar plugged into one corner of his mouth.

"Hello," said Alex.

"Are you burgling the place?" He was short and wiry and his voice was phlegmy.

"No, I'm just taking a look round."

"Mm hm" He leaned to one side and looked past Alex down the hall. "What do you think?"

"It's very nice."

"Hm." The little old man looked him up and down. "Ralph Ortiz," he said. "I'm your neighbour."

"Alex Dolan. I don't actually live here." Leaving the *yet* hanging.

"You're the writer, yeah?"

"I guess."

Ralph nodded. "I'm a writer too. Used to be, anyway. They said you were coming."

"'They'?"

"Danny Hofstadter and them." He put out a hand. "Welcome."

"I haven't decided yet," Alex said, but he shook Ralph's hand anyway. They stood there a little awkwardly until he added, "Would you like to come in, Mr Ortiz?"

"Ralph," he said, stepping past into the house. "And yeah, that's very kind of you, Mr Dolan."

"Alex," said Alex, closing the door and following him down the hall.

Ralph was looking in through every open door as he passed by. "So the Shanahans beat feet then."

"Shanahans?"

"The people who used to live here." He'd found his way to the kitchen and was looking in the fridge. "Can't say I'll miss them; their kids were little bastards. They shot my dog. Ah, good." He reached into the fridge, and backed away holding two bottles of Budweiser.

"I'm sorry," Alex said. "About your dog."

He snorted. "It was a BB gun. They only winged him. Couldn't prove anything, of course." He held one of the beers out. "You have an opener?"

Alex stood there holding the bottle, looking helplessly at the drawers and cupboards. "I have no idea."

"Never mind." Ralph dug a Swiss army knife from a pocket of his dressing gown, levered the cap off his bottle, did Alex's for him and handed it back. "So," he said, pulling a stool away from the island and perching on it, "what do you think of Stanisław Clayton's little kingdom?"

"I've only been here a couple of days. I'm still processing. Or not."

Ralph took a long drink of beer and belched. "Don't let them railroad you."

"I don't mean to pry, but what were you doing in the garden?"

"Saw the lights come on. Thought I'd better scope things out before I called the Law."

"Right." Alex took a sip of beer. "This is quite a hard place to find, isn't it."

"Ah," Ralph said with a satisfied smile. "That's because it doesn't exist."

"Does it not?"

Ralph shook his head. "This is actually the independent township of East Walden. Or it would have been, if the developers hadn't gone bust back in the eighties. They lasted long enough to build this street and then they just dried up and blew away. There's been a case in the courts about our status ever since. Are we an independent entity? Are we part of Sioux Crossing? No one's been in much of a hurry to sort it out." He drank some more beer. "We're a bit of a thorn in Clayton's side; because of the legal case we can't be sold, so this is the one part of the county he doesn't actually own."

"He owns this house, though, I presume."

Ralph nodded. "He can't buy the legal entity, but there's

nothing to stop him buying the properties privately."

Alex wondered if he had been deliberately parachuted into the situation, for reasons which would not become apparent until it was too late. He decided it was just too complicated to think about right now.

"Anyway," Ralph went on, "because a whole bunch of people have been arguing about it since the dinosaurs roamed the Earth, we appear on some maps and not on others. And I kind of like it like that."

"Why would he want to buy it, anyway? It's miles from the Facility."

Ralph took another mouthful of beer. "Man like that, he sees something he can't have, it just makes him want it all the more."

Alex looked out into the backyard. It was almost completely dark outside now. "This place is utterly fucked up, isn't it."

"And they haven't even turned the damn thing on yet." Ralph raised his bottle in a toast, and the doorbell rang. They looked at each other. "Expecting guests?"

"No," said Alex. "I'm really not. Excuse me a moment."

He went back down the hall and opened the front door, and found himself staring at the chest of a quite enormous man wearing a police uniform. A badge with the word ROSEWATER was pinned to one of his breast pockets, at roughly the same level as Alex's eyes. He tipped his head back, saw a shaven scalp, intelligent eyes and a kindly face. "Yes?"

"Mr Dolan?" said the enormous man.

"Yes."

He smiled. "I was driving by, saw the lights on, thought I'd better check." This was patently a lie; nobody just 'drove by' on East Walden Lane. He put out a hand large enough to park a Volkswagen on. "Bud Rosewater, Chief of Police."

"Nice to meet you." Alex surrendered his hand to the Chief's vast grip, was mildly surprised when it was returned unharmed. "Would you like to come in?"

"That's very kind of you," said Rosewater. "Just for a moment."

Alex led the way back down the hall, feeling a colossal displacement of air behind him. He didn't see whether Chief Rosewater had to duck his head to get through the kitchen doorway, but when he turned he was standing there taking up more or less all the available space at that end of the room.

"Ah, you have guests," he said, nodding hello to Ralph. "Mr Ortiz."

"Bud," Ralph said. He drank some more beer.

"So," Chief Rosewater said, "how are you settling in?"

"I'm not," Alex told him. "I haven't decided whether I'm going to yet."

"Hey, that would be a shame," the Chief said, shifting the utility belt that hung around his waist.

"Would it?"

"It would." He looked round the kitchen. "This is a nice place."

"I was telling Alex about Vern and Pam," Ralph piped up. "Where did they go off to? Duluth? Sioux City?"

The Chief gave it some thought. "Twin Cities, I heard," he mused. "Didn't Pam have family in St Paul?"

"Any place that's seen a spike in dog shootings, that's where they are."

Rosewater gave Ralph a good-natured and avuncular smile. "We never established that the boys were responsible for that, Ralph. And you're giving Mr Dolan the wrong idea about the neighbourhood."

Ralph shook his head. "You're a sad excuse for a law enforcement officer, Bud Rosewater. Did you catch that guy yet?"

Rosewater gave him a Look. Alex had only just met him so he wasn't familiar with all his facial expressions, but it was definitely a Look, and it did its job because Ralph looked at Alex and asked, "Do you have a dog?"

"Me?" Alex's life appeared to have entered a period of rapidly escalating surrealism. "No."

Ralph waved it away. "You'll be fine then, probably."

Alex looked at them, feeling completely lost. It seemed that some fundamental anchor had come loose in his life around the time he boarded the flight to San Francisco, and it had let these people in. He said, "Gentlemen, it's been great to meet you, but I've had a long couple of days and I'm not processing very well right now. I think maybe I'll get back to the hotel."

"You're not staying here?" Ralph asked.

"No, Ralph, I'm not."

"I'll give you a ride back to the New Rose," said Rosewater. "I'm going that way."

"I can walk," Alex said, but he didn't put any force into it because he wasn't at all certain he'd be able to find the main road in the dark.

"Don't be ridiculous," said Rosewater. "Easy for a stranger to get lost."

"Okay. If you promise to put the lights and the siren on."

Rosewater guffawed, and Alex thought he felt the entire kitchen relax. He wondered what he'd just witnessed, and whether or not he'd imagined it. "No," said the Chief. "I'm afraid I can't do that. I can't remember the last time I fired up the lightbar."

"Maybe next time," Alex said. He looked at Ralph, who showed every sign of having taken up residence. "I'm going now," he said.

"Yeah," said Ralph, levering himself unwillingly to his feet. "I guess." He shook Alex's hand again. "We have to get together again when you're all moved in."

"I still haven't decided," Alex reminded him.

"Yeah, well," he said, going over to the fridge and opening it again. "You will." He took a couple more bottles of beer, closed the door, and nodded to Rosewater. "Bud."

"Mr Ortiz," said the Chief, who was clearly used to turning a blind eye to minor instances of theft.

They watched him shamble down the hall towards the front door. When he'd gone, Alex said, "This has been quite a peculiar couple of days."

"Hey," Rosewater said, landing a hand on Alex's shoulder softly enough not to dislocate it, "if nothing else you've been to new places and met new people. Shall we?"

Alex turned off the kitchen lights and followed him down the hallway to the door. A truck in Sioux Crossing PD livery was parked on the drive. Alex presumed it was difficult to find a normal police cruiser that fitted Chief Rosewater. He turned off the hall light, locked up the house, and climbed into the truck.

The twisty, confusing combination of lanes and side roads which had kept him wandering around for what seemed hours were actually only a couple of minutes' drive, and then they were back on the main road.

After a couple of minutes or so, Alex said, "I may be new here, but even I know we're going in the wrong direction."

"That's right," Rosewater said amiably without looking at him.

"Are you kidnapping me, Chief?"

He grunted. "My friends call me Bud."

"Ralph calls you Bud."

"Well, Ralph and I have a complicated relationship."

"You might as well call me Alex," Alex told him, staring out into the tunnel of headlight. "Because I think you and I are going to have a complicated relationship too."

"There's something I want to show you," the Chief said. "It won't take long. I'll have you back at the hotel in time for Happy Hour."

"There's a Happy Hour? How did I miss that?"

They drove for a couple of miles or so, then Bud took a right turn onto a bumpy dirt road between fields that seemed to run away into infinity under the light of the half-moon. A couple of minutes later he stopped the truck and opened his door. "Come on."

Alex followed, trying not to stumble on the uneven ground. They were parked in the middle of a great expanse of gently rolling farmland, row after long row of thigh-high plants. He could smell the vegetation and the damp soil. It suddenly occurred to him that Bud was armed and that there was no sign of human habitation.

"Okay," he said.

Bud hitched up his belt and looked around him. "This used to be my family's farm," he said. "We farmed here for almost a hundred and fifty years. Now it belongs to some sort of hedge fund in Belgium and they lease it out to some damn agribusiness or other."

Alex wondered why he was telling a complete stranger about this. He didn't seem angry; maybe a little wistful.

"We used to own a *lot* of land," he went on. "They named the county after my great-great-grandfather. Now? All gone." He pointed out into the field. "This is soybean," he said. "Once upon a time we'd sell every other row to China, but those days are long gone. The Chinese don't want our soy any more. Farming families just dried up and blew away."

"People keep telling me this story," Alex said.

Bud nodded. "Well, the whole county was dying. And then the SCS came along, and now maybe two-thirds of the county work for the Facility and the other third have *something* to do with it."

Alex sighed. "Chief. *Bud*. I get it, I really do."

"I'm not sure you do," said Bud. "What you write is going to be important, to a lot of people. Some of them maybe not so obvious."

"Are you *threatening* me?"

That made Bud smile, in an if-I-was-threatening-you-you-wouldn't-have-to-ask sort of way. "I just want you to know that the stakes here are really high. Not just for Clayton and the scientists and what-all. For ordinary people too. You'll finish up here and go back East, but we can't do that."

"I think everyone's overestimating how good I am," Alex said. "And I haven't even decided to do it yet."

The Chief sighed and walked back to the truck. "If you don't, Clayton will get someone else," he said. "He's paying you a lot to do this, yeah?"

"Yes." There seemed no point in denying it.

Bud opened the driver's side door. "Might as well be you, then, right?"

Back in the truck and heading for the hotel, he said, "We don't care what the rest of the country thinks about us. I find some of those *SNL* sketches funny, myself. What we're worried about is what *Clayton* thinks about us. The government can pull out, Defense can pull out, and we'd survive. If Clayton decides he's had enough of the whole thing, this county might as well pack up and move to Minneapolis."

If Dru Winslow was telling the truth, they could certainly afford to do that. Alex sat looking out the passenger side window, thinking about it. "Okay, point taken," he said. "But maybe in a couple of months you'll be having this conversation with someone else."

Bud nodded. "Okay." Bud pulled to a stop at the end of the track, looked both ways, then turned the truck back onto the road. "You might want to think twice about taking notice of Ralph's opinions."

"Why?"

"He's had a bit of a chequered past, I guess. His judgement's not quite right. A lot of folks round here tend to give him a wide berth."

"He seems harmless enough. What did he do?"

Bud thought about it, then he said, "He was a big-shot writer, back in the day. Haven't read his books, myself, but that's what people say. He was teaching at some fancy college out East and he got caught having an affair with one of his students. Big scandal. It was all over the papers, I hear. Came out here to hide, is what people say. Doesn't get out much."

"You don't strike me as someone who pays much attention to gossip, Chief."

Bud shrugged.

They drove a while longer in silence. Alex couldn't get over how *quiet* it was here. He wondered what the population—the native population—of Rosewater County was these days, after foreclosures and rural flight.

He said, "What was Ralph talking about? The guy you haven't caught yet?"

Bud scowled. "I told you not to pay any attention to what he says."

"Come on, Bud. I saw your face when he mentioned it."

Bud frowned. "Some folks have been reporting a prowler. He seems harmless at the moment, but sometimes these things escalate. I'd like to take him into custody before somebody gets hurt, and he's proving... elusive."

Alex thought about that, thought about the knock on his door and the way everyone had over reacted to it. Was that really just a security thing? Or was something else going on? He said, "Is there much crime here?"

"Most of what we get is domestic," said Bud. "Big guy gets resentful about something, takes it out on his wife and family, that kind of thing. The usual stuff with high-schoolers—underage drinking, grass." He shrugged. "We've got a lid on it."

Alex had known what the answer would be almost as soon as he asked. Sioux Crossing was virtually crime-free; none of the locals wanted to poison the well. No wonder they were worried about Stan closing down the project. Quite why they thought he could do anything to help was a mystery.

As he got out of the truck at the hotel, something occurred to him. He took the sheet of paper Muñoz had given him and held it out. "This is for you."

Bud unfolded it and shook his head when he saw what it was. "Muñoz and his fucking customer satisfaction survey," he muttered.

"I thought it was your idea."

"No," Bud said with a sigh, folding the survey again and slipping it into his breast pocket. "Between you and me, half the time I don't even read them."

Alex raised an eyebrow.

"Muñoz is a great cop," said Bud, "but there are times when I'd swear he'd be happier working in Human Resources. Have a good evening, Alex. I'll see you soon."

"I don't doubt," said Alex.

He watched Bud drive away, then he turned and went into the hotel, waving to Grace as he went past.

Back in the suite, he got a beer from the fridge and stood at the window. Clearly the whole of Rosewater County had been driven batshit crazy by the sudden eruption of Stan and his project into their lives, and if he still had the sense he'd been born with he'd get out of here tomorrow morning and never come back. On the other hand, there was something intriguing about the situation, and he was still enough of a journalist to respond to that. He sighed and slumped into the armchair.

His phone rang. He looked at it, saw an unfamiliar number, thumbed the answer icon. "Hello?"

"Oh, hullo," said a diffident English accent. "Alex Dolan?"

"Yes?"

"My name's Kitson. I wonder if I could have a moment of your time?"

"I've had a long day, Mr Kitson."

"Yes, I appreciate that, but it's a rather tricky matter and we'd appreciate your help in sorting it out."

Alex sighed. "Yes, okay. How can I help?"

"Could you meet me in the Telegraph Diner in about half an hour?"

"Can't it wait till tomorrow?"

"Afraid not."

Alex closed his eyes. He was too tired to cook, and he didn't think he could face one of the hotel's family-size meals. At least he could have a bite to eat while he was at the Telegraph. "Yes, okay. I'll see you there."

HE'D BARELY LEFT the hotel's car park when a silver-grey Accord pulled up alongside him and slowed to keep pace with him. The driver wound down the passenger window and called, "Mr Dolan? Sam Kitson. We spoke on the phone."

Alex stopped. So did the Accord. He bent over slightly so he could see into the car. The driver was a young man wearing jeans and a chunky sweater against the cool evening air. "We did?"

"Yes, just a few minutes ago. I'm just on my way to the diner. Can I give you a lift?"

Alex was tired and mildly fuddled by the events of the previous few days. "Thanks." He got into the car and Kitson drove off again.

"Can I ask a huge favour?" Kitson asked.

"I don't see why not; everyone else does."

Kitson reached into the caddy in his door and came up with what looked like a small cloth bag. He held it out. "Would you mind putting your phones in here?"

"What?"

"I'll explain in a moment."

The bag felt surprisingly stiff. When Alex opened it he saw that it was lined with what looked like copper mesh. He put his phones inside and zipped it up. "Okay," he said. "Why did I just do that?"

Instead of replying, Kitson took a laminated card from his pocket and passed it over, then he switched the overhead light on so Alex could read it. The card identified the bearer as

Samuel J Kitson, a British consular official.

"I thought you worked for Mickey Olive."

Kitson shook his head. "I'm attached to the British Consulate in Minneapolis."

Alex looked at him. "No you're not."

"Ah, but I am, and most of the work I do is *stultifyingly* dull. But every now and again I get sent out on a little excursion."

Alex looked at the card again. "Any idiot could make one of these up in twenty minutes with a laptop and a laminator," he said.

"I'm not sure there's any way to convince you in a hurry," Kitson said. "I'm not going to show you my Licence To Kill or my Winston Churchill tattoo. You'll just have to take my word for it for now. You can call the Consulate later. Ask for Colin and tell them it's about a visa and they'll put you through to me." He looked apologetic, but not much. "Best I can do. Sorry."

Which sounded a lot like the little bit of business Stan had pulled with his attorney. Alex looked out of the windscreen. Main Street and the Telegraph sailed by. "We're not stopping," he said.

"I just wanted a quiet little chat," Kitson told him. "How long would it take you to walk from the hotel to the diner? Fifteen minutes? Twenty? Twenty-five after dark when you're making sure you don't trip over something?"

"About twenty-five."

"Good. I'll drop you off there when we're finished. Now then, we understand you've been offered a position here."

"I don't think I should be talking to you," Alex said.

"We're just having a friendly chat," Kitson told him. "Two Brits together in a foreign land."

"You've kidnapped me."

Kitson snorted. "Don't be silly. I'm giving you a lift into town. We're just taking the scenic route. You can tell me to stop at any time and you can get out and walk back and you'll never hear from me again. But I would strongly advise that you listen to what I have to say."

Alex sighed.

"So. You've been offered a position here, yes?"

"I haven't even decided whether to take it yet."

"Oh?" Kitson looked surprised. "Whyever not?"

Alex felt his spirits sag. "I'm tired of having this conversation. I just haven't decided yet, okay?"

"Well, we can't have *that*."

"You can't force me to do it if I don't want to."

Kitson smiled. "This is really going to be something of a voyage of discovery for you, Mr Dolan. I understand they want you do do some kind of public relations thing?"

"Stan Clayton wants me to write a book and a series of articles about the Collider."

Kitson nodded. "And in support of this work you will of course need to have access to the Collider itself and the scientists working on it."

"Yes."

"Good. Mr Dolan, have you ever considered working for your country?"

"For Scotland?"

Kitson sighed. "I'd rather you weren't tiresome, Mr Dolan. There isn't time."

"You want me to spy for you."

"We'd like you to carry out your work for Mr Clayton but let us know if you come across anything... unusual."

"Unusual how?"

"We don't know."

"That's... helpful." Alex looked out of the windscreen again. "Pretty much everything anyone could ever want to know about the SCS is in public domain," he said.

"Well, not *everything*. The US Defense Department has quite a large stake in the project, and that part of it is classified."

"I've signed an NDA."

Kitson chuckled, as if to show what he thought about quaint concepts such as NDAs.

Alex thought about it. "You might as well get it over with. What happens if I say no?"

Kitson nodded approvingly, as if pleased that Alex had decided to play the game. "Well, there's the question of your green card, isn't there."

Alex looked across at him. "Is that all you've got? Really?"

"You mustn't underestimate how unpleasant deportation procedures can be," Kitson told him. "Also, it's not a good look when prospective employers run a records check on you."

Alex looked down at the bag in his lap.

"Not that there's a lot of work anyway, back home. Not for someone in your line, anyway," Kitson went on. "And then, where would you go? You haven't paid National Insurance for eleven years so claiming benefits would be tricky. You'd wind up living with your mum, and I doubt her pension would stretch very far trying to support both of you." He paused, to let that sink in. "And that would be a shame, particularly when it's all so easily avoided."

"What's to stop me just going to the Americans and telling them you've approached me and threatened to get me deported? I haven't signed the Official Secrets Act or anything."

"Ah, now," Kitson said. "I'm afraid you have."

"No I haven't."

"You really have."

Alex thought about it. "You can't do that."

"No," Kitson said sadly. "No, I daresay we can't. You'd have a hard time trying to prove anything, though." He glanced over at Alex and his expression softened. "I'm sorry about the thick-ear stuff, I really am. We wouldn't normally play so rough, but we only heard about you yesterday and we've had to wing it, rather."

"Suppose I don't find anything?" said Alex. "Suppose I genuinely come up empty-handed. What happens then?"

Kitson smiled. "You won't. There's something there."

Alex thought some more. "How do I get in touch? Dead drops? Secret postboxes?"

"Look in the glove compartment."

It took a few moments for him to work out how to operate the catch, but he finally got the glove compartment open. Inside, among wads of hire company documents and dusters, was a mobile phone. He took it out and looked at it.

"There's a number in the contact list under 'Colin'," said Kitson. "It's encrypted and frequency-agile but try to use it where nobody's likely to overhear you. It might be best if you didn't use it indoors, at least not in Sioux Crossing."

"You think they have the whole place wired?"

"A project this size? With Defense Department involvement? I'd be surprised if there wasn't *some* kind of surveillance. The phone they gave you is probably bugged. Certainly it's got a GPS tracker."

Alex held up the bag. "And I thought this place was weird enough already."

Kitson glanced at the clock on the dashboard. He pulled the car to a stop at a crossroads out in the middle of nowhere, looked both ways, then did a U-turn in the middle of the intersection and started driving back towards town. "So," he said. "Are we in agreement?"

Alex sucked his teeth. "I want it on record that I'm doing this under coercion."

Kitson beamed. "Bless you, Mr Dolan, you're such an innocent. If I give you my word that such a note will be made, will that do?"

Kitson's word was, of course, essentially worthless. For all Alex knew, this was some bizarre scenario cooked up by Stan to test his loyalty. If so, it was a test he felt quite relaxed about failing. "I'll call the Consulate."

"Please do; the number's on the website. I'd wait till tomorrow evening, though; I've got a bit of a drive ahead of me now." Kitson pulled the car to a stop just outside town. "I'll drop you here. There's a blind spot in the traffic cameras. Talk to you soon." He didn't offer to shake hands.

Alex unzipped the bag, took out his phones, and put them in his pocket. He dropped the bag in the footwell and got out of the car. Kitson drove off without another word.

It was busy in the Telegraph. Alex spotted Dru Winslow, and Danny Hofstadter wearing a business suits and sitting at the counter chatting to a couple of farmer-types, and after a few moments he recognised Officer Muñoz in civvies, sitting with a pretty young woman with long brown hair. He sat down in the only unoccupied booth, and had just ordered steak and potatoes and a green salad when something like an eclipse occurred and Bud Rosewater sat down opposite him.

"Hi," he said.

"Hey," Bud said amiably. He nodded hello to Muñoz. "You okay?"

"I will be once I've had something to eat. I missed lunch."

Bud nodded. And then they sat looking at each other. Finally, Alex said, "Was there something you wanted?"

Bud put his hand in his trouser pocket, brought it out dangling a bunch of keys. Alex squinted at the tag.

"I guess these are yours," said Bud. "I found them in the truck after I dropped you off."

Alex took the bunch. They were, indeed, the keys to Number Twenty-Four. He patted his pockets. "I must have dropped them," he said. "That's very kind of you."

Bud grinned. "No problem."

"You could have just dropped them at the hotel, though," Alex said. "Or I could have picked them up from the police station. You didn't have to come chasing me around town."

Bud got to his feet. "It's all part of the service. Have a good meal."

Alex thought of the mesh-lined bag, of how his phones must have seemed to disappear from the network when he zipped them up inside. "I'm sure I will."

His steak, when it arrived, was very good, but suddenly he didn't have much of an appetite.

THE CAR THEY sent the next morning was another of those brand new silver SUVs. Its driver was named Doug and he wore a suit and tie, and he introduced himself and got Alex settled in the back of the car and then didn't say another word for the whole journey.

Which was good in one way—Alex didn't feel much like talking. On the other hand, he could have used the distraction. While he watched first Main Street and then the countryside going by beyond the smoked windows, he thought about Stan coming in and buying up and then rebuilding the town. He thought about all the people who owed their livelihoods to Stan and who would suffer if the Collider project was shut down. He tried not to think of Kitson's phone—the 007 Phone—in his pocket. He tried not to think of Kitson at all. Grace had said that there was 7G all over the county, which presumably meant that its broadband and mobile contact with the outside world ran through cell towers and routers owned by Stan. The people of Rosewater County probably used their phones and their fast download speeds and didn't have a second thought about them, but from a certain point of view—Alex's this morning, for instance—it did look a bit like a deal with the Devil. He wondered just how much data wound up in Bud Rosewater's hands, to help in his never-ending fight to keep the town crime-free.

And that was before you factored the Defense Department in. That probably meant the NSA were involved, and the NSA just *loved* to listen. Quite how *closely* they were listening was anyone's guess. Kitson hadn't been too concerned about phoning him last night, but that didn't necessarily mean anything. He'd just have to assume that unless he used the 007 Phone an algorithm somewhere would be listening in and looking for keywords. He wondered what would happen if he called his dentist back in Boston and started talking about Al-Qaeda.

For quite some time now, the road had run parallel to a high chain-link fence, through which Alex could see what appeared to be neatly tended parkland, great sweeps of grass dotted with stands of trees. Occasionally, he spotted low white buildings in the distance.

The car slowed and made a right turn onto a wide, smooth road between two high fences. The road ran dead straight for about a mile before ending in a gate manned by uniformed security guards. One of them came over to the car. The driver lowered his window and showed an ID, which the guard checked off on a tablet. Then the guard came to the rear of the car and knocked on the window. Alex spent a few moments trying to find the button that lowered it.

"Hi," he said when he finally got the window down. "Alex Dolan. I'm supposed to be meeting Professor Delahaye."

The guard didn't look impressed. Alex noted that his belt was festooned with tasers, cans of mace, and a sheaf of cable ties. One of those weird foreign-looking pistols was in a holster strapped to his thigh. He typed something on the tablet, looked at the result, looked at Alex, looked at the result again, then stepped away from the car and waved at one of his colleagues in a kiosk beside the gate. A few moments later the gate slid to one side and the car drove through. This time nobody saluted.

The main road continued straight ahead, but the driver turned off shortly after passing through the gate, onto another road which wound gently through the parkland. Looking out, Alex saw people cycling along wide white cycle paths between the low buildings. He saw a huge ornamental lake with a fountain jetting a horsetail of spray into the air. The place looked like a large and sparsely inhabited university campus.

Eventually the road brought them to one building that was larger than the others, a five-storey brick cube faced with lines of tinted windows, its roof cluttered with many different kinds of aerial. There wasn't a soul about.

Doug got out of the driver's seat to open Alex's door, but Alex already had it open. "No welcoming committee, then," he said as he stepped out. Doug looked at him as if he was unfamiliar with human speech. "Never mind. Thanks for the ride, Doug."

Doug closed the door and went back to the driver's seat.

Inside, the foyer of the building looked like the waiting room of an upscale graphic design house. Soft furnishings, low tables with carefully arranged magazines, plant displays. Behind a desk, a young man smiled as Alex approached.

"Hi, sir," he said.

"Hi, I'm here to see Professor Delahaye."

"Certainly, sir." The young man was wearing a badge on a lanyard around his neck. The badge had a full-face colour photograph and the name CHARLES in big letters. "Could I have your name, please?"

"Alex Dolan."

Charles consulted a monitor on the desk, scrolling down with his finger. "I'm afraid I don't seem to have you here, sir."

"Mr Olive made the appointment."

Charles looked at the monitor again. "I have a Dorman here at ten a.m. Alan Dorman." He looked up hopefully.

"Dolan," Alex said patiently. "Alex Dolan."

Charles frowned a little. "Do you have your phone with you, sir?"

Alex handed over the hotel phone and Charles put it down on a little silver disc set into the top of his desk. He typed briefly, looked at the screen. "Well, yes," he said. "That's you, Mr Dolan. I'm sorry about that; I don't know how it happened."

"No worries. Is Professor Delahaye about?"

"I'll just page him." Charles typed again and a little box on the desk beside the monitor made a soft whirring sound and ejected a laminated badge. "In the meantime, could you please wear this at all times while you're on the campus?" He clipped the badge to a lanyard and held it out.

"Sure." The badge was warm from the printer. On it were his passport photo and the name ALAN DORMAN, overprinted with VISITOR in big red letters. He sighed and slipped the lanyard over his head.

Charles was typing again. "I just paged Professor Delahaye," he said. "If you'd like to wait?"

Alex wondered what else Charles was expecting him to do. "Yes, that would be great."

"Can I get you a coffee? Juice? Water?"

"No, thank you, Charles." Alex wandered over and sat on one of the padded benches near the window. All the magazines on the coffee table in front of it were latest editions, and none of them looked as if they had ever been opened. He picked up a copy of *Scientific American* and paged through it, trying not to burn down to the ground with jealousy at all the journalists who had articles in it. He'd been trying to pitch pieces to *SA* for the past year, without success.

He read the magazine from cover to cover, and there was still no sign of anyone coming to collect him. He looked at his watch, saw Charles watching him. Charles shrugged helplessly. Alex sighed and picked up a copy of *Newsweek*. People came and went through the foyer, but apart from the occasional curious glance nobody paid him any attention.

When he'd read the magazine, he put it back on the table, got up, and ambled over to the desk. "Look," he told Charles. "Maybe there's been some kind of mistake. Maybe I'm not supposed to be here today."

"No," Charles said, indicating his monitor. "You're right here. Alan Dorman, ten a.m."

"Dolan," said Alex. "And it's..." he checked his watch again, "...twenty to twelve."

Charles thought about it. "I've paged Professor Delahaye," he said apologetically.

"Well, perhaps you could page him again?"

Doubt crossed Charles's face. "That's probably not a good idea," he said. "The Professor doesn't like to be bothered."

That much was obvious. "I can't sit here all day, Charles. This is ridiculous."

Indecision replaced doubt. "I could maybe page someone else..." he mused. "But the Professor doesn't like me doing that. He likes to be in the loop."

"You've already told him I'm here," Alex said. "I don't know how much more in the loop he could be, unless I go and sit on his lap."

This was obviously an alarming image. Charles typed again. "Okay, I paged Dr McCoy."

Alex narrowed his eyes.

"And she's on her way," Charles said, reading from the screen. "She'll be here... ah." He looked past Alex.

Alex turned and saw a tall woman with short curly brown hair walking across the lobby towards the desk. She was wearing jeans and sneakers and a long grey cardigan over a faded tee shirt with the face of Frank Zappa on it.

"Hi," she said when she reached them. "Wendy McCoy. You must be Mr Dorman."

"Dolan," Alex said, shaking her hand.

"Oh." She looked at Alex's badge. "But it says..."

"Yes," he said. "Yes, I know."

"I paged Professor Delahaye," Charles put in.

She pursed her lips. "Yeah, well Professor Delahaye's an asshole." Charles looked as if he was about to keel over. She beamed at Alex. "So," she said. "You're here for the tour, right?"

"I'm supposed to be, yes."

"Okay, so let's do that." She beamed at Charles. "I'll take it from here, Charles." The look of relief on Charles's face was the kind of thing that wound up becoming an internet meme.

As she led the way back towards the front doors, Alex said, "Thanks for doing this, Dr McCoy."

"Wendy," she said. "And if you have any *Star Trek* gags it might be best to get them out of the way now."

Alex shook his head. "Never crossed my mind."

"Hm. Are you a cyclist?"

"I haven't been on a bike since I was sixteen."

"We'll take a moke, then."

There was a long, low structure beside the main building. Parked inside were thirty or so small vehicles which looked like the products of the forced marriage of a quad bike and a golf cart, all of them lined up and plugged into charging points in the wall. Wendy went over to the nearest one and unplugged its cable. They climbed in, she touched her phone to a pad on the dashboard, pressed the accelerator, and the moke moved off with a high-pitched whine.

"The motors are completely silent," she said as they left the garage. "They had to put in a noise generator so people would hear them coming."

"Couldn't they have come up with a less annoying sound?"

"The whole point is for people to notice it," she said, turning the moke onto one of the cycle paths. "They did try having them play 'Ode to Joy' but that was *really* annoying."

He looked at her. "You're kidding."

She shook her head. "I've seen footage of the tests; it's pretty terrible. I hear you haven't decided whether to take the job or not yet."

Except I don't have a choice any more. "Yeah. Kind of."

Wendy shrugged. She glanced over and saw him looking at her. "What."

"I think you're the first person I've met since I got here who hasn't either tried to talk me into taking the job or warn me off."

"You're over twenty-one," she said. "You can make up your mind without my help. How much do you know about the Sioux Crossing Supercollider?"

"Just the broad stuff."

"Okay. Well, there's a lot of technical detail which I guess can wait for another time, if there *is* another time. I was on the way over to Susan when Charles paged me, so maybe we'll head over there and I'll show you some of the Campus on the way. How does that sound?"

"Sounds good. Who's Susan?"

She grinned. "You'll see. Don't be afraid to ask questions as we go, but I should warn you I don't have every little nitpicking detail at my fingertips and there may be things I'll have to get back to you with."

"Fair enough." He looked out over the neat parkland of the Campus. "How long have you been here?"

"Since the start," she said. "I was one of the original team who surveyed the site. I was still a grad student back then, of course; I was just carrying gear around for course credits."

"That must be quite a thing, watching a project like this come together over… how long has it been? Ten years?"

"Twelve. Nearly thirteen. Yeah, it's been a wild ride and no mistake." He couldn't tell if she was being sarcastic or not.

"What do you think about the setup? Clayton buying the county and everything?"

She glanced at him again. "These are strangely nontechnical questions."

"I'm still trying to get a feel of the place, fit it all together in my head." She didn't look convinced. "Trust me; I'm a writer."

She shrugged and pulled out to pass a couple who were cycling unhurriedly two abreast. "None of my business. I just do the science I'm told to do; I leave the rest of it to Admin. I'm on the

Liaison Committee that deals with relations between us and the town. I could probably scare up a couple of the other committee members for you to talk to if you give me an hour or so."

He shook his head. "Maybe some other time." He doubted he'd hear anything from the liaison people except the company line that the project had been good for the county and the locals were all grateful. Everyone smile and nod. "How many people are on the project?"

She thought about it. "Can't remember, exactly. About nine thousand, give or take."

"That's a lot of people."

"It's not as many as the LHC, even though it's a bigger project." As if anticipating his next question, she added, "About three quarters of them live on-campus; the rest have homes around town, mostly people with families. We're planning a new housing development south of town, for people who want to move off-campus, but that's a way in the future."

"Do you live in town?"

She chuckled. "We don't know each other that well yet, Mr Dolan. Oh, for fuck's sake." This last because she'd spotted an obstruction on the cycleway ahead of them.

When they got closer, Alex saw that it was a 1968 Ford Mustang GT Fastback, the make of car Steve McQueen drove in *Bullitt*, except this one was sprayed bright tomato red. It was parked diagonally across the cycleway at the end of a long, curving double line of churned up grass that ran away out of sight in the distance.

Wendy stopped the moke a few feet from the car and got out, taking her phone from one of the pockets of her cardigan. She speed-dialled a number and held the phone to her ear. "Hi," she said when the call was answered. "He's done it again." She listened. "Who do you think?" Another pause. "I'm standing right next to it. Tag my location and get someone to come out and pick it up." She bent down and peered into the car. "Keys are still in the ignition." Straightening up, she looked around. "No, I don't see him anywhere. He's probably sleeping it off under a tree like last time." The two cyclists they had passed went by, pulling off onto the grass to go around the obstruction. Neither of them bothered to look at either the car or the moke.

Wendy came back and climbed into the driver's seat. Alex said, "What's that all about?"

"That, Mr Dolan," she said, pressing down on the accelerator and driving around the marooned car, "is just one of the crosses we have to bear."

THE CAMPUS OF the Sioux Crossing Supercollider was about three miles across. Most of the buildings were clustered over to one side, where the buried ring of the collider itself ran under the facility, but the residences were scattered all over the site, each one named after a famous scientist. Wendy pointed a couple of them out as they went by, each one an identical brick cube. The campus was neat and clean and well kept, but none of it was going to win any architectural awards. Driving by, they saw more mokes and cyclists, but not very many. Alex wondered where the rest of the nine thousand people were hiding.

Presently, they came to another building not far from the perimeter fence, basically a big cinderblock cube with windows covered in wire mesh. Wendy stopped the moke and led the way to the door. Most of the ground floor of the building was a single open cement-floored space, with a pair of huge sliding doors at the far end. Wendy took a couple of hard hats from a rack on the wall and handed one to Alex. "Better put this on," she said. "Don't want you bumping your head."

Beside the rack was a set of lift doors. Wendy put her phone against the sensor on the wall beside the doors and they slid open. Inside, she pressed a button and Alex felt the lift floor sink beneath his feet.

It felt as if they descended quite a distance, but there was no way to tell because there was no indicator beside the panel of buttons. Eventually the lift bumped softly to a halt and the doors opened onto what could have been an office corridor anywhere in the world. Hard-wearing carpet underfoot, rows of office doors on either side, walls painted beige. Through windows beside the doors, Alex could see into the offices as they passed. People were sitting in cubicles, intent on monitor screens. So that was where everyone was.

At the end of the corridor was a short flight of steps leading down to another corridor, this one floored with vinyl and walled with white-painted cinderblock. This led to a large vestibule with boxes and bits of electronic equipment stacked against the walls. There was a solid-looking metal door with an alphanumeric keypad and an emergency pull-handle in a glass-fronted box. Wendy tapped in a code and the door swung open. It was about four inches thick and edged with rubber gaskets. Beyond, Alex could see a big room and another metal door. He had a sudden image of moving through the interior of a submarine.

Inside, Wendy pushed the door shut and typed on another keypad, and for a moment nothing seemed to happen, then Alex felt his ears pop. A little green light on the keypad turned red.

At the other door, there was a green light on the keypad. Wendy typed again and the door swung open and she indicated he should step through.

"Oh," he said.

The door opened onto a cavern the size of a cathedral, almost filled by the most complex-looking device Alex had ever seen.

"Oh," he said again.

"Alex Dolan, meet SUSAN," said Wendy, closing the airlock door behind them. "SUSAN, meet Alex Dolan."

They were standing on a metal catwalk about halfway up the wall of the cavern, and still the great metal device towered over them. Parts of it had been opened up and people wearing hard hats were clambering all over it. Alex went to the railing of the catwalk and looked over. The floor of the cavern was full of equipment and scaffolding.

"We've got four detectors," Wendy said, stepping up beside him. "SUSAN, HELEN, ROSE, and WENDY. Not me," she added. "The detectors are all named after Delahaye's nieces."

"That's quite something," he said, staring at the device. There had been a photograph of one of the detectors in Stan's brochure, but it hadn't done it justice.

Wendy smiled at him. "I do believe you have the sensawunda, Mr Dolan."

"Who wouldn't?" Alex said, unwilling to look away from the scene.

"Okay, so I have to go down there and have a word with a couple of people. You're not cleared to go any closer yet so you'll have to stay here. Can I trust you not to drop stuff over the railing or go around pushing big red buttons?"

He laughed. "I'll be a good boy. Promise."

She grinned again. "I'll bet. See you in a few minutes." And she walked along the catwalk to a set of steps leading down to the floor of the cavern.

Alex stayed where he was, looking at the detector, a camera aimed at the most fiercely hidden secrets of the universe. Despite himself, despite everything that had happened to him over the past few days, he felt the beginnings of a thrill of excitement.

ON HIS FINAL morning in Sioux Crossing, Alex walked into town to buy a rucksack to carry his new clothes in, and afterward he walked on to East Walden Lane. Now he knew the way, it seemed ridiculous that he had ever got lost in the first place.

He walked past Number Twenty-Four and up the front path of the house next door. He tried the bell but nothing seemed to happen, so he knocked, and a minute or so later Ralph opened the door. He seemed to be wearing the same things he'd been wearing the last time Alex saw him.

"I've got a favour to ask," Alex told him.

"You'd better come in, then," Ralph said. "You can't ask a favour standing on the porch."

Inside, the house was dark and stuffy and it smelled of greasy food and cigars. Books and magazines were stacked knee-high along one wall of the hallway. A plump and aged golden retriever waddled out of the living room and stood in the hall looking at him with milky eyes.

"That's Homer," said Ralph.

"Hi, Homer," said Alex.

Homer let go a loud and eyewatering fart, then turned and toddled in the direction of the kitchen, wagging his tail slowly as if he was pleased with himself.

Ralph led the way to a chaotically untidy living room and collapsed into a lounger. "Heard you went over to Black Hole Central yesterday," he said, taking the stub of a cigar from the table beside the lounger and lighting it.

"How do you hear stuff? You never go out."

Ralph puffed on the cigar. "Bud told you that, huh?"

"He told me a lot of stuff."

Ralph snorted. "I'll bet he did. What was the favour?"

Alex took the keys to Number Twenty-Four from his pocket and held them out. "Could you look after these for me till I get back?"

Ralph looked sadly at the keys. "You decided, then."

It hadn't been much of a decision really, what with Stan's money and Kitson's threats. Saying no had never, in the end, been an option, however much he kidded himself. "I have sold my soul," he agreed.

Ralph took the keys. "How long will you be gone?"

"A couple of weeks. I need to put my stuff in storage, give

notice on my apartment. I'd be happier if someone kept an eye on next door while I'm gone."

"Okay." Ralph put the keys in a pocket of his dressing gown. "Your funeral."

"I'm over twenty-one," Alex told him, walking over to the wall and looking at the dozen or so framed photographs hanging there. "As someone pointed out recently." In the first of the photographs a young man with a great deal of dark curly hair and a Zapata moustache was standing grinning beside a much older, cadaverous gentleman in a suit and a fedora. The cadaverous gentleman was not smiling. "Hey, is this...?"

Ralph looked up. "Burroughs was an asshole," he said. "You don't have to be an intellectual giant to stick junk in your arm. I'm sorry he's gone, though. He made life interesting."

In the next photo the young man was wearing a dinner suit and bowtie and he was standing beside an intensely-scowling, white-haired Norman Mailer.

"Mailer was an asshole too," Ralph said, behind him. "I'm not sorry *he's* gone. He challenged me to a fistfight at that dinner, even though he was, like, four times my age or something."

Alex went along the line of photos, watching Ralph age with each image. Here he was with Gabriel Garcia Marquez. Here he was with David Foster Wallace. Here he was shaking hands with Bill Clinton in the Oval Office.

"You're him," Alex said, a sudden light going on in his head.

"I'm *a* him," Ralph grunted. "I couldn't admit to being *the* him."

Alex turned from the wall. "I read you at university. *Aztec Snow*."

Ralph waved it away. "That was a long time ago."

"I just didn't connect the name with..." Alex looked around him.

"Yeah," said Ralph. "Yeah, I know." He got up from the lounger and ambled towards the door. "You want a beer?"

Alex checked his watch. "There's a car coming to take me to

the airport at four and I still have to pack, but yes, I'd like that."

Ralph's kitchen was a disaster area. The stove was camouflaged with grease, the sink was full of dirty plates and pots and pans, and every flat surface was stacked with old pizza boxes and Chinese food containers. Ralph took a couple of beers from the rust-spotted fridge, levered the caps off, and handed one to Alex.

"To your great project," he said wryly, lifting his bottle in salute.

"Cheers," said Alex, taking a sip. He moved some copies of the *Banner* from a chair to the floor and sat down. "Look, tell me to sod off if this is too personal, but what happened?"

Ralph leaned back against the fridge and looked at him. "What did Bud tell you?"

"He said there was some kind of scandal. One of your students."

Ralph nodded. "Yeah. Well, what he probably didn't tell you was she was a *mature* student. She was thirty-two when we met." He took a drink of beer. "But rules is rules. No fraternisation. The university had to let me go."

He said all this so matter-of-factly that he might have been talking about one of the characters in his books. Alex said, "How did you wind up here?"

Ralph shrugged. "We just wanted to get away from all the publicity. Marion was a local girl. Her parents owned a farm somewhere out west of town, and when they died she sold it, so she had some money and we bought this place and got married and lived happily ever after. I was going to settle down and start writing again, but somehow I never quite did." He smiled sourly. "She got a job teaching at Rosewater High. One evening she was driving home after work and a drunk in a truck T-boned her car at an intersection. He walked away from it. She was in a coma for eight days and then she just seemed to give up."

"I'm sorry."

Ralph shook his head. "I guess Bud didn't tell you that bit."

"How do you... look after yourself?" Although it was obvious Ralph was barely doing that.

"What? Oh, there was still a big chunk of Marion's money left when she died. And I still get royalties. A couple of years ago someone decided to make a movie of *Aztec Snow*. The movie's still not been made but I get option money every eighteen months or so. I get by." He looked at Alex. "And you can take that look off your face. I'm not going to be one of your projects. You're not going to tidy this place up and redecorate it and get me to shave and put some clothes on. I like things the way they are and I really don't need your pity."

"It's not pity," Alex told him. "It's..." He thought about it. "Okay, maybe it is pity. I'm sorry."

"I think you're an asshole for taking the job."

"I think I probably agree with you." He wanted to explain about Kitson, but he had the hotel phone in his pocket and there was no way to know whether it was transmitting his conversations, even though he'd turned it off. Powering it down didn't seem to disable its GPS tracker, certainly, because nobody had come around to see where he was. And anyway, he had the 007 Phone in another pocket—he didn't dare let it out of his sight—and that would almost certainly relay every word, even if he took its battery out. He sighed. "I should be getting back to the hotel."

Ralph nodded and got up from the lounger. "So I'll see you in a couple of weeks."

"About that. Just keep an eye on the house."

Ralph frowned slightly. "You expecting visitors?"

Alex smiled and said, "Out here? Nah." But he was nodding as he said it.

Ralph gave him a hard stare. "Okay," he said. "Hey, you play chess?"

"It's been a while."

"Maybe we could have a game, when you get back."

"Yes," Alex said, shaking his hand and sensing opportunity. "Yes, I'd like that."

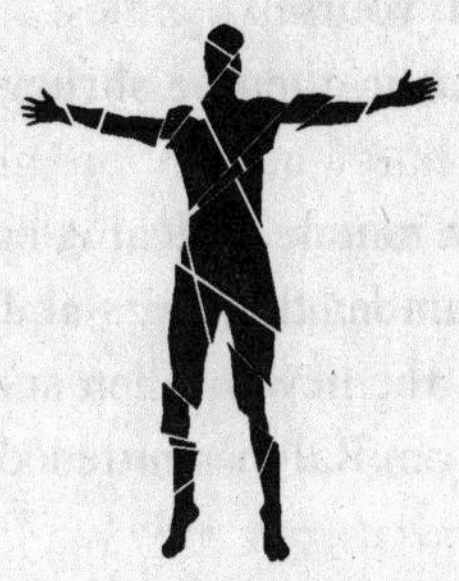

THE SNOW

Winter came late to Rosewater County that year. First there were a few days of frost that silvered the trees and fields and turned the land to stone. Then, improbably, there was a thaw and it was mild enough for Alex to sit out on the back porch with his laptop quite late into the evening, working on the book and listening to various unknown representatives of the local wildlife crashing about in the woodland his yard backed onto.

And then three separate blizzards swept across northern Iowa, and when they were gone there was about five feet of snow on the ground. Municipal snowploughs didn't clear the roads around East Walden Lane, probably out of spite, so the inhabitants were stuck there.

One morning Alex looked out of the living room window and saw Ralph, wearing a snowsuit that made him look like a permatanned Michelin Man, labouring at the snow on his front path with a broad-bladed shovel.

Alex opened the front door and stood on the porch. "What the hell are you doing?" he called.

Ralph looked at him, then held up the shovel and indicated

the snow.

"You're going to kill yourself."

Ralph thought about it, then he shrugged and indicated the snow again.

Alex sighed. "Wait a minute." He dug boots and a warm coat out of the cupboard under the stairs and went outside again, highstepping through the newly fallen snow on his own path, and took the shovel from Ralph's mittened hands. "You bloody old idiot."

Ralph was wearing a tattered old woolly hat and a tartan scarf wound around the bottom half of his face, so all Alex could see were his eyes. He said, "I'm not your project."

"I don't fucking care. I'm not going to wind up on my hands and knees in this bloody snow trying to give you CPR."

"I'd be snowblind long before you needed to do that," Ralph mused, squinting about him. The sun had come out, for a while at least, and the light reflecting off the snow was almost unbearable.

"Is it always like this?"

Ralph shook his head. "Nah. Sometimes it's worse. We had twenty-foot drifts the year Marion and I moved in here."

"Jesus." Alex bent his knees and tossed a shovelful of snow to one side of the path.

"Guy at the end of the street ran out of food. Ended up eating his dog." Alex stopped shovelling and looked at him, and Ralph grunted happily. "Jeez you're gullible."

"I must be; I'm shovelling snow for you when I could be sitting at home under a pile of blankets." The rackety furnace in the basement appeared to have given up all pretence of trying to heat the house and would only dispense enough hot water, at any given time, for a very quick shower. Alex had woken up a couple of mornings ago and found frost flowers on the inside of the bedroom windows. There was a heating engineer in town, apparently, but short of helicoptering him in the furnace was going to have to wait until there'd been a thaw.

"You should call your friends at Black Hole Central and get them to come out and fix that thing," Ralph mused.

"Yeah, right." It had taken him a little longer than he'd anticipated to get things in Boston straightened out, and it had been almost a month before he moved into East Walden Lane. During which time, according to Ralph, no less than four different groups of cleaners and decorators had visited Number Twenty-Four. The place did not seem notably cleaner or more decorated than when he'd first seen it, so he presumed they'd been there to wire the house. He found he didn't mind the idea of surveillance so much—he was hardly doing anything to be embarrassed about and if someone wanted to spend hours listening to him snoring, that was their business—but the thought that he was somehow deemed untrustworthy nagged at him. Ralph said he knew a hotshot civil rights lawyer in Philadelphia who would blow through whoever had bugged Alex's house like a ball of napalm through a flowerbed, but Alex couldn't see the point. He had a feeling that if he ever read his contract of employment properly there would be some small print somewhere which had him giving his consent.

Ironically, considering he was now under twenty-four-hour surveillance, his employers seemed to have lost interest in him. As soon as he'd signed the contract, he had magically ceased to be the Special Boy. Stan's phone number cut to voicemail whenever Alex tried to call him; interactions between them were mediated by Mickey Olive, who no longer magically popped up whenever Alex was eating. No drivers at his beck and call, no one inquiring if everything was all right or offering to help him with stuff. After some effort, he'd managed to buy an aged Accord to get himself to and from the Facility, but it was sitting in the garage beside the house, entombed behind a snowdrift that reached halfway up the door.

He said, "I wish you'd stop calling it that."

"What?"

"'Black Hole Central'."

"Why?"

"There's more chance of Elvis touring again than the Collider creating a black hole, Ralph. How many times do I have to tell you?"

Ralph grunted. "So *you* say." He watched Alex working for a while. "Have you never shovelled snow before?"

"You know, I could brain you with this thing and bury your body in the woods and nobody would find you till the spring."

Ralph squinted past him, then shaded his eyes with his hand. "Are you expecting a delivery?"

Alex stopped and leaned on the handle of the shovel. Looking in the same direction as Ralph, he saw a tall, bulky figure wearing snowshoes coming down the lane. The figure was wearing a parka with its hood pulled up, and it seemed to be towing a small canoe and using a pair of ski poles to help itself along.

"No," he said. "I didn't order anything."

"Me neither. Maybe one of the neighbours."

"Could be." But it was almost a week since either of them had seen anyone who didn't actually live on East Walden Lane, so they both stood watching the figure slogging its way towards them. Ralph found the remains of a cigar in a pocket of his snowsuit, and he pulled down his scarf, put it in his mouth, and lit it. The smoke hung in the still, cold air. The figure seemed to notice them for the first time, and it waved. Alex and Ralph waved back.

As the visitor drew closer, Alex saw that they really were towing a small canoe. The canoe was full of insulated picnic coolers and bags and it appeared to be generating its very own faint cloud of steam. The figure plodded right up to them, planted its ski poles in the snow, pulled back the hood of its parka, took off its ski mask and its goggles, and it was Wendy McCoy.

"Hi," she said.

"Hello," said Alex.

"We hadn't heard from you for a while," she said, running a hand through her hair. "We got worried."

"'We'?"

"Well, me and Rob Chen. We thought someone ought to come out and see if you were still alive." She added, "I drew the short straw."

"You could have phoned."

"System's down," she said. "We've had engineers checking the cell towers for the past four days."

That was interesting. "Well," he said. "It's good to see a friendly face." Beside him, Ralph blew a quiet raspberry.

She unclipped the harness that attached her to the canoe. "I brought you some supplies, just in case," she said. "It's good to see you're alive because otherwise I'd have had to haul it back to the car."

"Never had a woman trek through the snow to bring *me* supplies," said Ralph.

Wendy raised an eyebrow.

"Wendy McCoy, Ralph Ortiz," said Alex. "It's okay; he's kidding."

"No I'm not," Ralph said. "I never had a woman bring me supplies. My hand to God."

Alex sighed.

"What have you brought us, in your little boat?" Ralph asked.

Wendy narrowed her eyes at him. "I know you," she said. "You're Marion Hofstadter's husband."

Alex turned and looked at him, hearing the surname. "As in Danny Hofstadter?"

Ralph waved it away with a mutter.

"I'm sorry for your loss, Mr Ortiz," Wendy said. "Your wife was one of the great American poets."

Ralph was clearly completely disarmed. He muttered some more and then fell to puffing on his cigar. Wendy smiled and said, "We'd better get this stuff inside before it starts to freeze."

They towed the canoe up to Alex's front porch, then formed a human chain to unload it and stack the boxes and bags in the hallway. Tucked between the containers were catalytic hot packs, the kind of thing hikers used, to help keep the supplies from freezing. When the boat was empty, they formed another human chain to move the supplies into the kitchen and unpack them.

There was tinned food and bags of prewashed salad and shrink-wrapped steaks and burgers and boxes of cereal and bags of oranges, and freshly baked bread from DeKeyser's Deli, miraculously still warm in its insulated bag. "Got to hand it to scientists," Wendy said. "We know how to keep stuff warm. Or cold."

"This is great," Alex said, surveying the piles of produce on the kitchen island and the worktops. "I thought I was going to have to eat Ralph's dog."

Ralph refused to rise to the bait. "How bad is it out there?" he asked.

Wendy was shrugging out of her parka. Underneath, she was wearing a down vest over a couple of sweaters. "The major roads are clear, mostly," she said, draping the parka over a stool. "There was a pile-up on I-35 south of here during the blizzard on Tuesday night, and that's still blocked. Schools are closed, of course." She unzipped the vest and dropped it on top of the parka. "Jesus, it's cold in here," she said.

"Furnace," said Alex. "It's warmer in Ralph's house, but you'd be in therapy for the rest of your life if you saw his kitchen."

Wendy looked at them. "You probably think you're funny," she told them. "But you're really not. Do you have any tools?"

"I have no idea," said Alex.

She sighed. "Basement, right?"

"Second door under the stairs."

"I'll be back in a minute," she said. "Try not to laugh yourselves to death while I'm gone."

"Who is she?" Ralph asked when she'd gone.

"Works at Black Hole Central," said Alex. "Give me a hand to put this stuff away."

A few minutes later, while they were arguing about what meat to put in the fridge and what to put in the freezer, the lights went out. Then they came back on again. Then they went off, and they stayed off for about ten minutes. Then they came back on and the vents around the base of the walls began to exhale warm air.

"I don't know who installed that thing," Wendy said when she came back into the kitchen, "but they need to be prosecuted for crimes against engineering." She looked at the thermostat on the wall beside the door, gave the dial a fractional twist.

"Whatever you did, thank you," said Alex.

She shook her head. "Get a qualified engineer to look at it as soon as you can. Better still, call someone in from Des Moines and have a new one installed. Put it on Clayton's tab."

"Well, the least I can do is cook you lunch," he said.

"Yes, it is," said Ralph.

She took her phone from the back pocket of her jeans and checked the time. "Okay," she said. "But I want to be out of here before dark; I still have to get back to the car."

Alex looked at Ralph, who clearly had no intention of going anywhere. "All right," he said. "You too."

"I'll find some plates," said Ralph. "You got any beer?"

He cooked them steaks and fried potatoes and made a green salad with the mortal remains of a head of Romaine lettuce he found in the fridge. They ate in the dining room, which was probably the first time the room had been used for anything at all since the unlamented Shanahans had moved out, and Ralph mercilessly interrogated Wendy about where she was from (Duluth, via Caltech and MIT) her marital status (divorced and currently single) and whether she would be willing to give the electrics in his house the once-over.

"I'm really not qualified to do that," she told him. "You need to get a proper electrician to have a look."

"What *are* you qualified to do then?" he asked.

She thought about it. "I could make you an atom bomb," she said. "If you could scare up the components."

Ralph beamed at her. Then he looked sad. "There's nobody left to use it on. All my enemies are dead."

She laughed. "I'd call that a win." She looked at Alex. "How about you? Anyone you want to nuke?"

Alex imagined a fuming crater in the ground where the *Boston Globe* had been, but he shook his head. "I'll pass."

"Ah, you're no fun," Ralph said.

"Chief Rosewater was asking about you," Wendy said.

Alex cut a slice off his steak. "Was he?"

"I bumped into him in town while I was loading the car. He said he hadn't seen you for a while."

Alex wondered if this meant his company phone, issued to replace the one from the hotel, was off the network and no longer broadcasting his conversations. He also wondered whether it meant he could expect a visit from Bud in the near future.

"It's nice to know people are thinking about me." Thing was, he liked Bud. He liked Stan. He hadn't met anyone he didn't like in the town since he'd arrived. Hell, he even liked Ralph. But the surveillance thing did nag. He understood why it was happening. Stan had secrets to protect and Bud didn't want anyone rocking the boat and jeopardising the future of the county. But it still nagged. And that was before he even got to the other thing.

Wendy must have heard something in his voice, because she frowned fractionally, then changed the subject and started to talk to Ralph about his late wife, who apparently had won a Pulitzer Prize, which Ralph hadn't bothered to tell him about.

Back in Boston, he'd taken the 007 Phone out onto the Common and used it to phone the number of the British Consulate in

Minneapolis and ask for Colin. Kitson had come onto the line, sounding a bit miffed that Alex had taken so long to call. He'd used it twice more since he moved to East Walden Lane, both times to report that he had nothing to report. He thought it might be best not to use it too much, just in case. He hadn't actually done anything yet, but the thought of facing Stan's attorney in court with an industrial espionage charge hanging over him had been responsible for at least one sleepless night.

A flicker of motion caught the corner of his eye. He looked over Wendy's shoulder, out of the window, and saw dry snow blowing up into the air in lazy whirls. The trees on the other side of the green were beginning to stir sluggishly, snow drifting down off their branches. Alex tipped his head to one side.

A shockwave went through the trees, blowing all the accumulated snow off them in a single huge exhalation. Then he couldn't see anything at all outside, just a howling whiteness. He heard the house actually creak fractionally in the wind.

"Jesus Christ," said Wendy, who had turned to see what he was looking at.

They all sat there mutely watching the storm for some minutes. Then Ralph said to Wendy, "I hope your car's insured, because I think you just drove it for the last time."

As NIGHT FELL and the screaming white blankness beyond the windows gave way to a screaming black blankness, Ralph became more and more restless, saying he wanted to go home.

"It's Homer," he said. "He's got food and water and I put a litter box in the downstairs bathroom in case he decides he wants a dump in the middle of the night, but he'll fret over there on his own."

"Mr Ortiz, you *can't*," Wendy told him.

"I can go straight from your side door to my side door," he said. "It's, what, a hundred feet? You'd walk that in a minute without even thinking about it."

"You mad old sod," said Alex. "The wind'll pick you up and when the thaw comes some farmer in Wisconsin's going to find you in one of his fields."

"I don't like to think of him over there on his own," Ralph said. "He'll fret."

For supper Alex cooked cheese and ham omelettes, and they sat in the living room with their plates on their laps, listening to the wind trying to pry the house off its foundations and send it bowling across the state line into Minnesota.

They tried the television, but all the channels were dead. Alex had, though, found an old transistor radio on a shelf in the basement. He had no idea how much life the batteries still had in them, but he managed, amid static and white noise and automated country rock stations, to find a station in Des Moines, and while they ate they listened to reports of what sounded like the end of the world in northern Iowa. Half the state was paralysed. Hail the size of grapefruit had swept across Sioux City, destroying vehicles and damaging buildings and causing at least a dozen fatalities. Every airport north of Fort Dodge was closed. People were phoning in from places like Algona and Spencer and Emmetsburg and West Bend, places that might as well have been on the other side of the galaxy tonight, with stories of power blackouts and hurricane-force winds and blinding, impossible snow. Some of them sounded calm and fatalistic about it all—faintly amused even—and content to wait it out, but quite a lot of people sounded terrified. Loved ones hadn't come home, windows had been smashed by flying debris. Around half past ten, there was a statement from the Governor to the effect that citizens should remain in their homes and try to keep warm. This was clearly a once-in-a-century weather event and emergency services were working as hard as they could, but everyone should be patient and under no circumstances go out. The Governor sounded tired, and

Alex suspected from his voice that the emergency services had mostly had to give up until the weather eased.

There was an airing cupboard stuffed with bedding on the landing upstairs, and Alex used some of it to make up the beds in the two spare rooms. He was just finishing the second one when he felt the air pressure in the house change suddenly and he heard Wendy shouting.

He ran downstairs and found her in the kitchen, leaning against the side door. The floor, and one of the side walls, was covered with melting snow, and stuff had been blown off the worktops. "Oh, he didn't," he said.

"He said he was going to the bathroom," she said in a horrified voice.

"Stupid, stupid, stupid..." *Oh, for* fuck's *sake*. He ran into the hallway and opened the door to the basement.

"What are you doing?" he heard her call behind him.

The Shanahans, whoever the hell they had been, must have enjoyed climbing or potholing or something, because there was a big canvas bag of climbing gear tucked away in a corner of the basement. Pitons, crampons, other bits of metal equipment he couldn't recognise. There were also three neatly coiled climbing ropes. He grabbed two and carried them back upstairs.

"You're not serious," Wendy said when she saw them.

"I can't just leave him out there," he said, putting on his boots.

"You're as crazy as he is," she told him. "Just a minute." She went into the living room and came back a moment later with her vest, ski mask and goggles. "Here."

Masked and dressed in his warmest coat, Alex tied a wide loop in the end of one of the ropes and dropped it over the island in the middle of the kitchen and tied the other end around his waist. "Try and keep some tension in this," he said, handing the rope to her. "If you feel me tug twice on it, pull as hard as you can."

"Stupid man," she said.

He turned and flicked the switch beside the door that turned on the intruder light on the side of the house. Then he pulled the goggles over his eyes, flipped up the hood of the parka, opened the door, and stepped out.

The wind blew him off his feet the moment he got outside, tumbling him through a blinding gale and sprawling him on his face in foot-deep snow. He thought he could hear Wendy shouting from the open kitchen door.

He managed to lever himself onto his hands and knees and then get unsteadily to his feet, leaning against the wind. The light on the side of the house was almost useless; it just lit up the howling storm around him. He could barely see his hand in front of his face. He steadied himself and set the light at his back and started to plod slowly across the space between the properties, arms outstretched in front of him, leaning forward against the tension in the rope.

It was impossible. His left side was already plastered inches deep with snow where the wind blew it against him. His face felt raw even under the mask, and he had to keep stopping every couple of agonised steps to clean snow off the goggles. He'd barely gone a couple of yards before his feet started to feel cold, and after a few more steps he couldn't feel them at all. He called Ralph's name, but there was so much noise in the air that he could barely hear himself.

Abruptly, the tension went out of the rope and he lost balance and the wind blew him over again. He scrambled to his knees and put out his hands to push himself up, and he felt them land on what felt like a body.

"Ralph? Ralph!"

Obviously it was Ralph. Who the hell else was out here? Alex felt along the body until he found an arm, and he tugged on it. Ralph didn't seem inclined to move under his own steam, so Alex struggled him into a sitting position, then managed to get his hands under the old man's armpits and lift him up enough to drape an arm around his neck and hold him upright.

There was no way to tell where he was; he was standing in the middle of a howling illuminated madness. One-handed, he got hold of the rope and pulled at it, intending to follow it back to the kitchen, but it stayed limp and eventually—way too soon—he was holding the end of it. He rubbed snow off his goggles and held the rope close to his face. At a distance of an inch or so, he could just see that the end looked charred.

The light was booming and directionless; there was no way to tell where the house was. He was already exhausted from the cold and from continually fighting the wind. He was going to die here, a few feet from his own home.

Ralph shifted against him and he thought he heard the old man say something in a loud voice, but it was lost in the noise of the wind. They were *both* going to die here.

There was nothing else for it. Alex shouldered Ralph's weight, picked a direction, and staggered on.

He fell several times, and each time it was harder to get up and to get Ralph up too. He thought, with growing horror, that he might be walking in circles. Every step was more difficult than the last.

He stumbled again, and this time his face smacked into a hard surface with enough force to make him see sparks. Something warm and wet ran down inside the ski mask and he realised his nose was bleeding. He reached up and felt the wall of the house and he almost screamed with relief.

Pressing himself against the wall, he pulled Ralph to his feet and managed to get his arms round the old man's waist. Okay, if this was the house, which way was the door? Half supporting, half dragging Ralph, he staggered along the wall.

His hand, outstretched against the house, encountered a change in surface, something that felt like tight-stretched metal mesh. Screen door. He didn't have a screen door; this was Ralph's house.

Fine. Shelter was shelter. With burning lungs, he pulled back the screen door and groped for the handle of the wooden door beyond. He found it, tried to turn it, but it wouldn't move. It was locked.

"You fucker!" he yelled in Ralph's ear. "You *stupid* old fart!" Ralph did not respond.

Holding the old man up with one hand, Alex groped down his body with the other, trying to find the pockets of his snowsuit. At the second try, he encountered something. Putting his hand in the pocket he felt, dimly through his glove, what his brain could only decipher as being a bunch of keys.

He rested his forehead against the door, trying to think. His mouth was full of the taste of his own blood and he kept having odd moments of what felt like weightlessness. If he dropped the keys, they were dead. Even if he could find the way back to his own house, he didn't have the energy to get there. He tugged the ski mask up enough to expose his mouth, feeling the windblown snow flaying the exposed skin of his face. With his teeth, he tugged off his glove and let it fall to the ground, then he put his hand in Ralph's pocket again, rooted around for a moment, found the keys, made sure he had a good grip, and took them out.

There were six keys in the bunch. There was nothing else for it. He released Ralph and let him slide down the wall until he was slumped against the house. Then, working by touch, he found the keyhole in the centre of the doorknob and tried the first key. It didn't fit.

"Don't be frozen," he muttered to himself. "Don't be frozen." He tried the second key, and that didn't fit either.

By the fourth key, his fingers were so cold he could barely tell whether he was holding anything or not. He pulled off his other glove and used his other hand to guide it to the keyhole. This one went in, but it refused to turn. He wiggled it, but nothing.

The fifth key fitted the lock and it turned smoothly. He

screamed in triumph and turned the knob and decided that if Ralph had bolted the door from the inside he would use the last vestiges of his strength to throttle the old man.

But the wind blew the door open with such force that it tore the knob from his hand. Alex reached down, grabbed Ralph by the hood of his suit, and dragged him step by step over the threshold and into the kitchen, and then his legs gave way and he toppled and smacked his face on the floor.

He rolled over on his back, gasping and pulling off the ski mask, which was crusty with snow and frozen blood. And then he got a proper look at the kitchen and thought for a moment that it was on fire.

Electric blue sparkles covered every surface. The walls, the floor, the fridge, even the ceiling. They were crawling in thick, wavering lines, like fingerprints, so bright they were hard to look at. Alex felt every hair on his body stand on end.

"Oh, fuck off," he said, and passed out.

Sometime later, he woke up in bed covered with blankets. He ached all over, his hands and face felt raw, and he couldn't breathe through his nose. He lifted his head a little and realised he wasn't in bed but on a couch in a darkened room. There was also someone with him on the couch, hugging him from behind.

"You were right," said Wendy sleepily in his ear. "I saw his kitchen. It's the worst thing in the world."

He went back to sleep.

The next time he opened his eyes, a faint semblance of daylight was fighting its way around the edges of the curtains. He rolled over slowly, but there was nobody else on the couch with him. He pushed down the pile of blankets and duvets covering him and saw that someone had managed to get him out of his outer clothing and into a pair of sweatpants and a pullover.

Gradually, he sat up. He felt as if someone had come into the room during the night and spent a happy hour or so hitting him with a length of scaffolding. He touched his face. His nose felt swollen and misshapen and his forehead appeared to be one large bruise.

He swung his feet off the couch and tried to stand up, but he had another moment of weightlessness and he had to wait until it passed. The second time, he made a better job of it and when he was on his feet he limped slowly to the window and pulled back the curtain. The world was still a featureless driving screen of white. The wind didn't sound as if it had dropped at all.

In the kitchen, Wendy had cleared a small space for herself and she was frying bacon. "Hey," she said when he came in. "You should lie down."

"Hm." He dropped onto one of the kitchen chairs. "Ralph?"

"On the couch in the living room." She turned the bacon over in the frying pan. "Fast asleep. I don't think he's in any danger right now, which is a miracle, but he needs a doctor. Do you want some of this?"

He could, just barely, smell the bacon, and it made his stomach growl. He got up and poked carefully around the kitchen until he found a loaf of white bread hiding under a stack of fast food containers. In the fridge... he closed the door after a single glance inside and wondered whether he would ever be able to forget what he'd just seen. "Margarine?" He said. "Butter? Anything?"

Wendy indicated a tub of margarine on the worktop at her side. Alex found a plate which didn't seem to be harbouring too many lethal bacterial cultures and spread margarine on a couple of slices of bread. "What happened?"

"I don't know," she said. "I was paying the rope out to you and all of a sudden the end of it just ran through my fingers and out the door. So I roped myself up and came looking for you."

He looked at her.

"You were already here so I made sure you weren't both going to kick on me and put you to bed."

"Hm." He gave her the plate and watched her putting bacon on the bread. She topped it with the other slice and cut it in half and gave him the plate back.

"There's coffee," she said. "I think it's coffee."

There was a half-full jug sitting on a corner of the stove, keeping warm. He poured some into a mug and dropped a couple of sugar cubes into it, then he took everything back to the table and sat down. "Well," he said.

"What happened to your face?"

He touched his nose again. "Bumped it a couple of times."

Wendy took some bread, made herself a bacon sandwich, and sat down opposite him.

"Thank you," he said. "For coming to find us."

"Well, don't get too excited about it because we're not out of the woods yet. There's almost no food in the house; it looks as if Ralph lives mostly on takeouts. And I don't like the sound of his breathing. I managed to find some aspirin and get those into him, but he's running a fever. I'm worried about pneumonia."

He bit into his sandwich. In spite of the extreme unhygiene of the kitchen, it tasted delicious. He took a swig of coffee, looked at the mug.

"Told you," she said.

He swallowed. "So," he said. "What do we have?"

She shrugged. "Food for today, maybe tomorrow as well. After that we're eating the dog's food; Ralph's got a stack of tins taller than I am. We're safe and warm and dry. There's still running water. There's no cell coverage and Ralph's wi-fi is down but I can't tell whether that's because of the storm or because his router was probably first used to relay news of the Fall of Khartoum."

That made him smile, despite everything. Wendy nodded at the window, which was a rectangle of raging whiteness. "People at the Facility are going to be wondering where I am, but nobody's going anywhere until this thing blows itself out."

"Any news on that?"

She shook her head. "No television coverage, and if he's got a radio I can't find it."

He took another bite of sandwich, washed it down with another mouthful of coffee. "One of us is going to have to go back to my place and get supplies," he said.

"Not today."

"No." He winced. "Christ, no."

"The whole front of the house is under a snowdrift," she said. "Right up to the bedroom windows. But the wind funnelling between the properties stopped it getting too deep out there." She waved at the door, which was wedged shut with a length of rope hanging from the gap.

He remembered that from last night; it was only a foot or so deep. "Did you close my door?"

"I pulled it shut on the rope," she said. "It was pretty firmly wedged; you'll be fine so long as it didn't blow open."

"So at least it's doable. We go out, we follow the rope, get some stuff, follow the rope back." They looked at each other. "But not today."

They sat for a while in silence, eating and listening to the wind howling around the house. Wendy said, "The dog's upstairs on Ralph's bed, fast asleep. I don't think it's even noticed anything's going on yet." She wrinkled her nose. "That dog smells."

He looked around the kitchen. "Did you see anything last night? When you found us?"

"Like what?"

He shrugged. "Anything… unusual."

"I saw two assholes who didn't have a quantum of common sense between them lying on the floor. There's this, though." She got up and went over to the corner by the door and picked up a soggy length of rope.

It was the rope he had tied around his waist last night. He ran it through his hands until he reached the end, and, just as he remembered, it was charred. He squinted at it and turned it this way and that.

"That looks deliberate," said Wendy.

He frowned. The rope had been in the basement for a while. Maybe at one point it had been stored too close to the furnace and wound up scorched. Maybe the Shanahan children, alleged dog shooters, had decided to off their parents in a climbing/caving accident. There could be any number of reasonable explanations, although he couldn't think of any right now. "I don't know," he said.

The living room seemed hot and feverish. Ralph lay on the couch, under a pile of duvets and blankets and coats. His breathing did seem laboured, although considering what he'd gone through the previous night that was hardly a surprise.

Alex sat down on the side of the couch and Ralph stirred under the blankets and slowly opened his eyes and looked at him. "He's a threat," he said distinctly.

"I beg your pardon?"

"He does fret," Ralph said again. "Homer. How is he?"

Alex frowned at him. "He's fine. Farting like a champ."

Ralph settled back in his nest. "That's good. What happened to your face?"

"Took a bit of a tumble. It's nothing."

"Thank you for last night."

"It's Wendy you should really be thanking. If it wasn't for her we'd probably both have died on the kitchen floor."

Ralph closed his eyes and shook his head. "Tell me later," he murmured.

"Do you have a radio?"

Eyes still closed, Ralph thought about it. "Yeah," he said

finally. "One of those wind-up things. In the closet in my bedroom. Unless I threw it away. I can't remember."

"Okay." Alex tucked the blankets around him. "You rest now. Everything's going to be fine."

THEY SAT IN the kitchen listening to the radio. The whole of northern Iowa and southern Minnesota and a big chunk of Wisconsin was, officially, a disaster area. The National Guard had been called out to help FEMA in what relief efforts they were able to mount at the moment. Confirmed fatalities—and the newsreader emphasised these were only the confirmed ones—ran into the high three figures, the majority due to traffic accidents. No flights had been able to take off from or land—or even approach—anywhere in a huge swathe of the Midwest since the storm began. Scanning along the dial they found a station which styled itself *The Home of Free Speech*—never a good sign. In the space of half an hour, the presenter blamed the storm on the Democrats, the Russians, the Zionists, socialised medicine, the anti-gun lobby, chemtrails, geoengineering, Mexican immigrants, Islam, black helicopters, and the European Union.

"That guy needs to cut down on his caffeine," Wendy said, tuning the radio to a country rock station.

Alex, who had long ago come to the conclusion that the United States was way too twitchy for its own good, said, "Kind of impressive, though. In its way."

She said back and looked at him. "So," she said. "How did you wind up here?"

"Here?"

"In the US. You're a long way from home."

He remembered asking Mickey Olive the same question, what seemed like a thousand years ago. "Oh. Long story."

"We've got plenty of time," she said. "Unless you've found a stash of board games around here."

"There's a chess set," he suggested.

"I don't play."

He raised an eyebrow.

"It's not obligatory for scientists, you know," she said. "Don't get cute with me. I think it's a stupid game."

"Why?"

She crossed her arms and glared at him. "I asked first."

"Okay." There was no arguing with that. He took a few moments to arrange it all in his head. It felt, if he was going to be honest with himself, as if it was the first time he'd done it. "Well, I was still working in London back then. *The Guardian*. I was doing okay, and one day I got an invitation to go out to Livermore Labs. They were announcing a joint Anglo-American nanotechnology project, hands across the sea, that sort of thing. Stepping forward together into a golden future." He scratched his head. "Anyway, they were prepared to pay my fare, my editor thought we could turn out a good piece about both sides of the project, and I'd only be gone a couple of days, so I went."

Wendy narrowed her eyes. "Was this JTAC?" She pronounced it 'Jay-tack'.

"You heard of it?"

"I saw some of the Congressional hearings."

He smiled sadly. "Yes," he said. "They were fun, weren't they? Anyway, I went, and I got the tour and the lectures and about a hundred flash drives full of presentations and it all looked very wonderful but it was all a bit dull. There were about thirty journalists from almost everywhere except China and Russia, being herded from room to room and getting PowerPoint Rage.

"There was this chap there, none of us could ever work out quite what he was doing. He didn't seem to be attached to any particular project, he was just wandering about poking into things. Chap named Larry Day." He saw her raise an eyebrow. "You've heard of him too."

She nodded slowly. "Oh yeah, I've heard of him," she said

with a heavy irony that she didn't seem inclined to explain.

"Well, I hadn't, not back then. But we got chatting and he said it looked as if I needed a break and we wound up spending an evening going round the bars in Livermore."

She nodded as if she was completely familiar with the situation.

He looked around the kitchen. "And at some point, in some bar or other, I couldn't tell you where, I wound up chatting to this girl. Chatting for quite a long time. Larry wandered off at some point, I didn't see him go, and this girl and I—her name was Kim—went to an all-night diner and had coffee and pancakes and bacon and we talked a *lot*."

Wendy reached out and turned the radio down a little.

"And we kept on talking, after I came back. And one thing led to another and eventually I was flying to California to meet her parents and a few months after that we were getting married."

"That's sweet."

"Yeah." Except it hadn't been quite that easy. Kim's parents had lived in Santa Monica back then, but she'd told him to fly to San Francisco and make his way south from there by land, and she'd given him a very tight schedule within which to do it. It had seemed a harmless bit of fun back then, a bit of an adventure, but looking back it was just one of a series of tests she'd put him through during their marriage. "So I managed to get a job with the *Boston Globe*, we got a flat in Boston, Kim got a job teaching at a local high school. And that, constant reader, is why I'm in the United States."

"What happened?"

"Beg pardon?"

"You're not married any more, yes?"

"Yes, I am not married any more," he agreed.

"So what happened?"

"She joined the Marines."

Wendy barked a single astonished laugh and almost simultaneously stifled it with both hands, her eyes wide with shock. "Sorry," she said, taking her hands away from her mouth. "That was horrible of me."

Alex shrugged. "Her father was in the Corps, and her grandfather." He thought about it. "And I seem to remember something about her great-grandfather, too. She wanted a proper career. What she thought of as a proper career, anyway. We'd sort of stopped talking to each other so much by then. I didn't want to be an Army bride, things were going pretty well for me at the *Globe*. We just agreed to part amicably."

"That's..." She shook her head.

"We stayed in contact, for a while. She did a couple of tours in Afghanistan. Then we just lost touch. Last I heard, she was a colonel and she was teaching counterinsurgency techniques at a staff college somewhere down South." He looked at her. "Sorry you asked now, aren't you."

"Oh, Christ, no," she said. "I wouldn't have missed hearing *that* story for anything."

He smiled. "Everything else is pretty simple, really. I bumbled along for a couple of years, then I lost my job at the *Globe*. Then I bumbled along for another couple of years. Then Stan Clayton rode in on a multicoloured thundercloud and scooped me up and here I am, sitting in the middle of the New Ice Age."

"Speaking of which," she said, getting up, "I'd better check on Ralph. You could make yourself useful by doing a proper inventory of our food, then we can work out how long we've got before we have to start panicking."

"Oh, that's easy," he told her. "I've already started."

The following afternoon, the wind dropped enough for Alex to decide it was worth risking the trip to his house. Visibility was still poor, but at least he could see the building now, and the intruder light still burning beside the door, as he plodded along holding onto the rope with one hand.

He filled a rucksack with tins of soup and vegetables and some of the fresh produce Wendy had brought the day the storm began, bagged up some burgers and steaks and added them. On top, he stuffed some fresh clothes. There was a chunky green knapsack with a white cross on the front of it in the basement, yet another part of the Shanahan Legacy, and he grabbed that. He didn't know what kind of medical supplies it contained, or whether any or all of them would have expired, but it couldn't hurt to have it.

Back upstairs, he went into the living room and stood looking about him, thinking. Then he said out loud, "Hi. I know you've bugged the house. I don't know whether you've lost contact for the moment, but we have someone here who needs a doctor, so if you could send help sooner rather than later I'd really appreciate it. Thank you." He stood there a few moments longer, feeling slightly ridiculous. Then he headed for the kitchen.

He was about to open the side door when a thought struck him, and he went through the kitchen cupboards again, adding coffee and sugar and teabags. Then he went up and ransacked the bathroom cabinet and stuffed everything into his coat pockets along with a bottle of shower gel.

"Oh bless you," Wendy said when she saw the shower gel and the toothpaste and spare toothbrush. The subject of how Ralph managed to maintain his personal hygiene had become something of a conversation between them. There was a single rock-hard sliver of soap in the shower upstairs, and a tin of dentifrice so ancient it might have come from the kitbag of a Civil War infantryman, and that was about it. Wendy, who had got them both out of their outer clothes when she rescued them from the kitchen floor the night the storm began, was of the opinion that Ralph had reached an age where he simply absorbed any dirt. "How is it out there?"

"It's still snowing hard." Alex sat on one of the kitchen chairs and unlaced his boots. "Not nearly as windy, though."

Although there had still been a couple of moments when gusts had almost knocked him off his feet.

"We got a television signal while you were gone," she said, starting to unpack the rucksack and arranging its contents on the table. "Scared me half to death; I hadn't realised it was on."

"What was it?"

She shook her head. "Some old science fiction movie. People screaming. It was hard to tell, there was so much interference. It only lasted a few minutes before it went down again, anyway."

"But it's got to be a promising sign, right? If infrastructure's starting to come back."

She pouted at a couple of tins of soup. "Could be." She put the tins on the table. "But let's not have a big celebratory dinner just yet, eh?"

Two days later, Alex woke in his bed in one of the spare rooms and realised he couldn't hear the wind outside. He got up and went to the window and pulled back the curtain and was almost blinded by bright sunlight.

Downstairs, the side door was open and Wendy was standing outside, knee-deep in fresh snow. "I was just coming to get you," she said.

He put on his coat and went out to join her. "When did it stop?"

"I don't know. The wind was still blowing when I went to sleep. I woke up about fifteen minutes ago, and..." She gestured at the world before them.

Together, they crunched through the crusty snow to the front of the house and looked out at East Walden Lane. The whole world was a landscape of brilliant glittering white, the fronts of the houses hidden behind drifts that in places were roof-high. The green was a smooth dome of snow taller than a bus, and beyond it the trees were just vague shapes, almost buried. The sky was immense and clear and eye-crunchingly blue, a single lonely contrail creeping slowly across it.

Alex looked down the curve of houses. "Maybe we should check—" He stopped and cocked his head to one side. "Do you hear that?"

Wendy looked off to the left. "Yeah."

A couple of moments later, the helicopter popped up over the trees and howled across the sky at an altitude of about five hundred feet. "Shouldn't we set off a flare or something?" Alex said, shading his eyes with his hand as he watched it fly past.

"Do we have any flares?"

He couldn't, in all honesty, discount the possibility that the Shanahans hadn't left some in the basement. "I don't know."

"Let's just do it the old-fashioned way," said Wendy, and she waded through the snow down the slope of the lawn and out onto where the road was, waving her hands above her head. Alex joined her, and together they jumped up and down and waved while the helicopter came round for another pass, and another, while the pilot checked out the landing area. It came in to hover over the centre of the green, and snow erupted in a blinding cloud. The helicopter flew slowly back and forth for a while, blowing snow out of the way, until the pilot decided it was safe enough to land.

Before the rotors had stopped turning, a door in the side opened and a huge figure in a bright orange snowsuit clambered down and started wading through the snow towards them.

It was, of course, Bud. He pulled back the hood of his suit and grinned at them. "Alex," he said, "Wendy. Good to see you."

"We thought you'd forgotten about us," Wendy told him.

"Well, no, we didn't," he said, still grinning. "Do you have any casualties?"

"We're fine," she said. "Mr Ortiz needs to get to a hospital as soon as possible." She looked along the curve of the lane. "I don't know about anyone else. We haven't seen anybody since it started."

Other people were starting to emerge from the helicopter, several of them police officers, including Officer Muñoz. Bud turned to them and said, "Okay, you guys check the other houses. See if anyone needs urgent help."

"When did it stop?" Alex asked.

"Storm passed over about three hours ago," said Bud. "The trailing edge is about a hundred miles east of here. West, it's clear all the way to the Rockies."

Another figure climbed down from the helicopter, which appeared to be larger on the inside than the outside, judging by the number of people it was carrying. As it approached, Alex saw it was Mickey Olive. He was wearing a ski jacket and a sort of Tibetan knitted hat, and his jeans were tucked into a pair of brown furry boots that looked as if they'd been made by cutting the feet off a Wookiee.

"Hello, Alex," he said when he reached them. "What happened to your face?"

"I walked into a door," Alex told him.

Mickey winced. "Ow. You should get that looked at."

"There's a bunch of National Guardsmen clearing their way down the road with supplies," Bud said. "Should be here in two, maybe three hours."

"They should be careful," Wendy said. "My car's parked up on Blackfish Road. It's probably completely buried; they won't see it until they run into it."

"They know what they're doing, Wendy," Bud said. "But I'll let them know."

"How bad's it been?" Alex asked.

"Ah, pretty bad." Alex belatedly realised that behind his grin Bud looked exhausted. "Town's been without power since the day before yesterday. We lost some folks down by Cooper's Hollow. County Sheriff's checking on outlying communities but I expect we'll find we've lost others too."

"I'm sorry."

Bud nodded. "We'll roll with it. We always do." He blinked at Alex. "Is there anything you need?"

"So long as you get Ralph out of here, we'll be fine until the National Guard arrives."

"Okay." Bud looked along the lane, where his officers were slogging from house to house trying to find unburied doors to knock on. "Well, I guess I'd better help take care of this." And he set off down the curve of houses.

"You gave us a bit of a scare," said Mickey. He was looking at both of them, but he was talking to Wendy.

"We were perfectly safe," Alex said.

"Eventually," Wendy added.

"There were a couple of moments," Alex admitted.

Mickey looked from one to the other, then back again. He said, "Excellent. Well, no doubt I'll hear all about it. Dr McCoy, would you do me the honour of coming back to the Facility with us?"

Alex and Wendy looked at each other. "What, now?" she said.

"Well, as soon as Chief Rosewater's satisfied himself with the situation here," he said, watching Bud clambering up a snowdrift to knock on a first-floor window a few doors down. The drifts must be frozen solid almost all the way through, for it to bear his weight like that.

Wendy looked nonplussed. "Sure. I guess. What about Ralph?"

"We'll drop Mr Ortiz and any other casualties off at County General on the way. Professor Delahaye *is* quite keen to have a chat with you."

"Has something happened?"

"I don't know. And even if I did, I doubt I'd understand it; I'm not a scientist, just passing on a message."

Alex got a sense of Subtext, of something significant. He said to Wendy, "You might as well; what were you planning to do? Wait till the thaw?"

"No, of course not," she said. "It just feels like I'm abandoning you, flying off like this."

"You can always come back and visit in the spring."

"Yeah." She thought about it. "Yeah." They turned at the sound of boots crunching in the snow behind them. A paramedic and a police officer had Ralph on a stretcher, wrapped up in what must have been his own bodyweight of blankets. He seemed to be asleep. They carried him carefully down the slope of the lawn and out towards the helicopter. "I hope he's going to be okay."

Some of the neighbours had come out of their besieged homes by now and were standing, all wrapped up, and gawking at the helicopter sitting in the middle of their village green. Some of them were chatting to Bud's officers.

It took another hour or so for the police to complete their sweep of East Walden Lane. Alex and Wendy and Mickey went back to Ralph's house, where Mickey stood looking around the kitchen and said, "And you've been *here* since the night the storm began?"

When it came time to leave, Alex went outside to watch everyone clamber back into the helicopter. A couple of the neighbours—older folks—went with them, and a few doors along the lane Alex saw that four of Bud's officers had stayed behind and looked like they were securing one of the properties, and he felt his heart sink.

As the rotors wound up, lifting a new blizzard from the ground, he saw Wendy's face in one of the windows. She was mouthing something and pointing at Ralph's house. Alex waved to her, but that just made her gesture more emphatically and mouth whatever it was she was saying even more exaggeratedly. He raised his hands and mimed a big shrug and she glared at him. Then the helicopter lifted itself up out of the snow, rose straight up for about three hundred feet, tipped its nose down, and howled away into the distance.

Alex watched until the helicopter was nothing more than a speck in the great blue vault of the sky, then he turned and trudged back up the lawn. As he came round the side of the house, he saw Homer sitting in Ralph's doorway, sniffing suspiciously at the snow just outside. Alex scowled.

"Well, shit," he said.

THE COLLIDER

THE SIOUX CROSSING Supercollider was a hollow ring twenty-three miles in circumference, a tunnel buried two hundred feet below the farms and towns and settlements of Rosewater County and a couple of the neighbouring counties. Twin beams of particles, running in opposite directions through a pair of beam pipes along the centre of the tunnel, were accelerated by superconducting magnets up to within a tiny fraction of the speed of light, at which point they were crashed into each other at enormous energies, the collision throwing off increasingly exotic particles, deep building blocks of the universe.

In theory, anyway. In practice, the SCS had suffered years of delays and technical problems. In test runs it had barely achieved half its target energies. It was regularly referred to by commentators—who clearly felt very clever for coming up with it—as 'Stan Clayton's Shitshow'.

Which was unfair, Alex thought. A lot of very smart people were working very, very hard to make the SCS work. They were building the most complex piece of machinery ever created, not putting together a kit-car.

He wondered if he was going native. He'd planned to keep a distance, try to be objective, but that had proved difficult. Everyone on the Campus was enormously enthusiastic and committed, and that tended to be infectious. It was disturbing; he'd thought himself more cynical than that. He was even starting to feel comfortable in the town, now that people had stopped staring at him.

One morning, parking his car outside the main Facility building, he saw Lin, Stan's driver, sitting at one of the picnic tables outside with a go-cup of coffee, thumb-typing on her phone.

She looked up as he approached, and grinned. "Hey, Alex. How's it going?"

He sat down opposite her. "What brings you here?"

"The boss wanted to see what all you crazy people are spending his money on."

Alex doubted anyone was keeping Stan in the dark about *that*. He said, "Nobody said you were coming." Although to be fair, that was hardly a surprise. He hadn't had any direct contact with Stan since before Christmas. He had more meaningful conversations with the dog.

Lin put her phone away and took a sip of coffee. "Some bigwigs wanted a tour, very hush-hush. Mr Clayton decided to host them himself." She was wearing a black suit, white shirt, and a narrow dark green tie, and a pair of wraparound sunglasses was perched on top of her head. "You're looking well. The countryside obviously agrees with you."

"It has its compensations."

"I heard about the storm you had. That must have been a hell of a thing."

Alex looked out across the brilliant green lawns and little woodlands of the Campus. It was hard to believe that just a couple of months ago it had been under tens of feet of snow. Like winter, spring had come hard to northern Iowa. The freeze had been followed by an abrupt thaw, widespread flooding, people winched into rescue helicopters from the roofs of their homes. Some of the newspaper op-eds believed they could detect a definite post-apocalyptic flavour to the times. "Yes," he said. "Yes, it was a bit." He stood and picked up his bag. "I'd better go to work. Are you staying at the New Rose?"

She shook her head. "We're flying back tonight. Mr Clayton's off to Paris tomorrow morning."

"I thought things got quieter when you became a billionaire."

Lin laughed. "That money doesn't just make itself."

"That's not what I heard."

Inside, one of the seemingly endless line of eager young interns was at the front desk, BRIAN on his nametag. "I'm late," Alex told him, putting his ID into the slot in the desk to sign in. "Have I missed them?"

Brian consulted his monitor. "They have a meeting scheduled on the third floor, Mr Dolan," he said. "That should be ending soon."

"Thank you, Brian." Alex hung his ID around his neck on its lanyard and headed for the stairs.

People were just emerging from the third-floor lecture theatre when he got there. He spotted Stan, Mickey Olive, and Professor Delahaye and his senior staff among a group of very expensively suited strangers and a scattering of security men, identifiable because their suits were not terribly expensive, their expressions grim, and they were not speaking to anyone.

"Hi," Alex said in a loud voice, walking down the corridor towards the group. "Sorry I'm late." He saw the security men tense up, but Mickey spoke quietly to one of them and they stood down, although at least a third of them at any one time proceeded to stare at him.

"Alex," said Stan, smiling and shaking his hand. "It's been too long."

"Yes," Alex said. "It really has."

A cloud crossed Stan's face, was gone almost as soon as it appeared. "Alex, do you know Brigadier General Bell?" He indicated the man standing beside him.

"I'm afraid not." Alex put out his hand.

"Brigadier General J Arthur Bell, Alex Dolan," said Stan. "Alex is writing a history of the project."

Bell was in his early seventies, wearing an exquisite suit, but his body language was so obviously military he might as well have been wearing full dress uniform. He looked as if he'd been left outside for a very long time in some of the world's worst places and allowed to petrify, and his handshake had all the human warmth of a small bag of gravel. He didn't bother quite looking at Alex, and when one of his aides whispered in his ear he turned away without saying anything.

In the meantime, Stan had also managed to get himself into a conversation with Professor Delahaye. Mickey came up soundlessly to Alex's side, gently grasped his elbow, and steered him away from the group. "There must have been some kind of mistake, old son," he said conversationally. "You weren't invited to this one."

"I could have sworn I got an email about it," Alex told him. "Sorry I'm late. Car wouldn't start."

"You didn't miss anything. Terribly dull." They reached the doors at the end of the corridor, pushed through into the stairwell beyond. "I'm glad I've seen you, actually. I wanted to have a quiet word about your expenses."

"Oh yes?" Alex allowed himself to be gently urged down the stairs.

"It's a little delicate, but really those expenses are to cover your day-to-day outlays in the course of doing your job, not paying vets' bills."

Alex, guessing it might have been a while since Homer had had a checkup, had taken the dog to see the vet in town. It had left him with the news that Homer had a heart murmur and the early stages of cataracts, and a bill for a little over a thousand dollars. He'd submitted the bill in his expenses more out of mischief than anything else.

"That sounds like an admin error," he said. "My bad. I'll pay you back."

"Oh, there's no need for that," Mickey said, growing more amiable with every step he put between Alex and General Bell's people. "Mistakes happen. What's the word on Mr Ortiz?"

"The hospital say he could be coming home next week." They were back on the ground floor by now, heading across the foyer towards the doors.

"Really? That's excellent news. He gave us all quite a scare."

Alex doubted whether Ralph had crossed Mickey's mind since he flew away from East Walden Lane the morning after the storm. He said, "His hospital bill's going to be astronomical."

"He'll have insurance."

"I'm not so sure about that. Couldn't we do something for him? As a gesture of goodwill?"

The doors opened for them and they stepped outside, where Mickey came to a halt, thinking. "Well, I'm sure we can look into that." He thought some more. "Yes, excellent idea. I'll put it to Stan."

"Does it have to go past Stan?"

"Everything," Mickey said heavily, "has to go past Stan. Anyway, I should be getting back." He clapped Alex on the arm. "Good to see you again, Alex. Truly. Have a good day." And he was gone.

Alex sighed and started to walk around to the moke garage when he heard a motor behind him. He stopped and looked round and saw the bright-red Mustang he had seen apparently abandoned on the Campus on his first visit. The car was pulling into the car park, but it didn't bother parking. The driver just stopped arbitrarily, turned off the engine, and got out. Despite something of a bite still in the air, he was wearing cargo pants and a Hawaiian shirt of spectacular ugliness. He was a big, broad-shouldered man with a spectacular mane of prematurely white hair, and he was carrying a plastic shopping bag stuffed with papers in one hand and what seemed to be a six-pack of Miller Lite in the other. He didn't bother locking the car, just headed for the main building and went inside. Alex watched him go, tipping his head to one side.

LATER, AFTER DINNER, he took Homer for his walk. The dog didn't seem to require exercise—he seemed to get all he needed by dreaming about chasing rabbits, judging by the way his legs motored when he was asleep—but the vet had said he was overweight and Alex found it a relaxing routine.

Their usual route went across the green and through the trees on the other side and along the edge of one of the fields beyond. Alex took off Homer's leash when they got to the field, but the dog seemed content to amble along beside him. Alex had a quick look around in case someone else had had the same idea, then he took out the 007 Phone and dialled Kitson.

It had taken a couple of days, after the storm, for the phone network to come back up, and when he'd phoned to check in Kitson had been in a mood to muse about US deportation procedures, even after being informed that Alex had been in the middle of the worst blizzard to hit the Midwest since records began. Since then, he'd been careful to report every few days, staggering his calls just in case someone noticed a pattern. He never had anything to report, but that didn't matter to Kitson. Obedience was the important thing.

"Were you introduced to anyone else?" he asked when Alex finished telling him about the meeting earlier that day.

"Just the Brigadier General. I was walked out of there fairly quickly."

"Hm. Well, Brigadier Generals tend to be more decorative than anything else, usually. The important ones will have been the ones you weren't introduced to."

"I didn't get a good look at them."

"Hm."

"And to be fair, this is outside my brief. I'm supposed to be telling you if there's something weird about the hardware. I only mentioned it because I've got nothing else to tell you."

Kitson gave this some thought. He said. "You should keep in mind that the parameters of your 'brief', as you rather charmingly call it, are not yours to set."

Alex looked at Homer. The dog was sitting a few feet away, looking out over the field. He could, he supposed, just quit. Write a letter to Stan and get on a plane. He could be back in Edinburgh in two days. He said, "There's something else. Larry Day's here."

"Who?"

IF ONE HAD taken any interest at all in science over the past fifteen years or so it was impossible not to have heard of Larry, because he seemed to be omnipresent. Trouble was, the majority of people were not remotely interested in science in general, and particularly not the esoterica that attracted Larry's hungry attention.

Rolling Stone had called him 'Steven Hawking's Evil Twin'. A big *Atlantic* profile of him had been titled 'Professor Gonzo', something he played up to. One of the most brilliant physicists of his generation, a giant at the age of 27. Of course, by that time he had been thrown out of MIT for an incident involving a home-made railgun, a frozen chicken, and his supervisor's vintage Trans Am, but that was just part of his mystique, and pretty much every other university on earth had offered him a place. His doctoral thesis was titled *Why All Leptons Look Like Joey Ramone But Smell Like Lady Gaga*, and it was generally agreed that it would have been embarrassing if it *had* won him the Nobel Prize. His postdoc research had been a mixture of the mundane and the wildly exotic; he cherry-picked his way through some of the wilder outlands of quantum mechanics and nanotechnology, came up with a brand new theory of stellar evolution, published a paper which not only challenged the Big Bang but made it seem rather dull and simple-minded. Larry Day. Brilliant physicist. Brilliant drunk. Brilliant serial womaniser. The smartest man most people had never heard of.

It was no great surprise that he was here; the SCS promised energies higher than those attained by any other collider in history, insights into impossibly tiny and fundamental corners of Creation, but the thought of Professor Delahaye working with him, willingly or otherwise, was out of the question, and anyway, when all was said and done he could just read the results in the science journals like everyone else. And why, if Larry *was* here, working on some weird fold of physics only half a dozen people in the world had even heard of, had nobody bothered to mention it?

"He comes and goes," said Wendy. "Sometimes we don't see him for months, and then suddenly he's there, poking at things, being rude to people. I mostly try to stay out of his way."

They were sitting in the commissary in the Facility's main building. The food was as good as Mickey had promised. Alex said, "*Somebody* must know what he's doing."

She sighed and poured herself a glass of water from the carafe in the middle of the table. "I don't think *he* knows. I think projects like this are like attractors for him; he just orbits from one to the next looking for stuff that gets his juices flowing and eventually he grinds out a paper and everyone thinks he's God."

"You don't think he's God."

"I think he's an asshole. He's got that Hunter S Thompson gonzo schtick going on, but he's really just a big spoilt kid."

He poked his fork into his spaghetti carbonara. "I thought maybe he was working on the defence stuff."

She raised an eyebrow. "Defence stuff?"

"I bumped into some sort of general here the other day."

She waved it away. "There's no defence stuff. We're doing pure research here."

"But Defense *has* put a lot of money into the project."

Wendy gave him a long, level look. "Are you interviewing me, Alex?"

He chuckled. "Force of habit. Sorry."

"Defense *always* puts money into projects like this," she said. "Just so they have rights in case something bangy spins off. They can't afford to build their own collider." She took a sip of water. "And anyway, can you imagine the military letting Larry Day anywhere near classified stuff?"

This was a fair point. Kitson seemed to believe some kind of military research was going on at the SCS, but maybe he, like the Defense Department, was just covering all bases, placing an asset just in case something useful popped up. Maybe all these people were just chasing each others' tails. He sighed and looked across the commissary. Over at a corner table, Professor Delahaye was in earnest conversation with Mickey Olive and Danny Hofstadter. Alex played a little game, trying to imagine all the possible Venn diagrams which would result in those three sharing a table. Rosewater County was like that. Everything was connected. Even the stuff that wasn't connected was connected, because Stan Clayton owned it all.

Their meeting over, the three men stood and shook hands. Danny and Mickey headed for the exit, but Delahaye, spotting Wendy and Alex sitting at their table, came over.

"Mr Dolan," he said. "Dr McCoy." Paul Delahaye was basically an event horizon of mindbending neatness enclosing a singularity of intellectual snobbery. Today he was wearing a three-piece tweed suit, a cream cotton shirt, and a plain grey tie. A silver chain curved between the watch pockets of his waistcoat over the smooth swell of his little pot-belly. His nails were immaculately manicured, and there was not a single visible hair anywhere on him that was out of place. "How are we today?"

"We were just talking about Larry Day," said Wendy.

"Yes." Delahaye was one of those Englishmen who pronounced it 'ears'. "Is he here today?"

"Haven't seen him."

"Good." It was some considerable time since Delahaye had done any kind of science; these days he was an administrator from the ground up, and Larry's on-off presence threatened the smooth running of his life. "Mr Dolan, I was promised a sight of the first draft of your book."

"You were?"

"I was. And I was wondering when I might have a chance to read it."

Unlike the NDA Alex had signed when he first arrived in Sioux Crossing, his contract of employment was not a masterpiece of concision. It ran to over a thousand closely spaced pages and he'd only managed to skim it before its legalese stunned his brain. He didn't remember anything about Delahaye having advance reading rights, though.

He said, "I'm still quite a long way from having a first draft finished, I'm afraid, Professor."

Delahaye made a little *hmph*ing sound. "You've been working on this book for more than six months. I do hope you're not one of those writers who contracts for a deadline and then has to beg for an extension."

Down the years, Alex had met any number of people he hadn't liked, but he had never met anyone he'd wanted to punch quite as much as he wanted to punch Delahaye. He said, "It's not rocket science, Professor. You of all people should appreciate that."

"What was all that about?" Wendy asked, stepping in before they grabbed cutlery off the table and started stabbing each other.

Delahaye held eye contact with Alex for a couple of moments longer before breaking off and looking at her. "All what?"

"All that." She nodded towards the corner table.

"Oh. Just a liaison meeting."

"No it wasn't. Liaison meetings are on Tuesdays."

Delahaye tugged down on the front of his waistcoat. "We're all busy men," he said. "We have to meet when we can."

"Why weren't the rest of the Committee informed?" Wendy claimed to be baffled that she was a member of the committee which liaised between the town and the SCS. It was, according to her, a committee of staggering dullness.

Delahaye opened his mouth. Closed it again. "I'm sure minutes will be circulated," he said finally. "Please excuse me." And he walked away.

"That guy is such a malignant dicksplash," Wendy said, watching him go. "When's Ralph coming home?"

"There's a car picking him up from County General at six." They'd been taking turns to visit the old man at the hospital every couple of days, as soon as it was possible to travel around the county again.

"They kept him a long time," she said.

"Yes," he said. "They did." Ralph's doctor had been unwilling to discuss his condition in anything but the most general terms with someone who wasn't a close family member. Alex had thought he detected subtext, but he hadn't pushed it and Ralph, though tired, seemed as cranky as ever.

"I'd like to be there," she said. "When he gets back. If that's okay."

He smiled. "I think he'd like that."

She nodded. "Okay." She checked her watch. "I have stuff to do," she told him, standing up. "Thanks for lunch." She picked up her bag and started to go, but she thought of something and turned back. "Just out of interest, how much of the book *have* you written?"

"I have a lot of notes."

She chuckled. "Thought so. See you later, Dolan."

* * *

As it turned out, it was Danny Hofstadter who brought Ralph home from the hospital. Of course, they were related by marriage. Everything in Rosewater County was connected.

They went out to meet the car as Danny helped Ralph out. The old man had lost weight, although the doctors had assured Alex that was mostly due to physio and eating a healthy diet for the first time in about twenty years.

"Place looks different," he said, standing beside the car and looking around him.

"That's because it was under a glacier the last time you saw it," said Alex.

Wendy gave him a gentle hug. "Welcome back, you stupid old man," she said.

"Hey, kid," he said, hugging her back. "Haven't you gone home yet?"

"I have a nice comfortable apartment with a PX and a three-star restaurant on the doorstep," she told him. "If you think I'm moving out here to the frontier to live in a sod hut, you're crazier than I thought."

He chuckled. "Good for you."

Danny handed Alex a small zip-up tote bag. "He comes with optional extras," he said.

"What, like power steering and air conditioning?" said Alex, unzipping the bag. Inside were dozens of pill bottles and little white cardboard boxes.

"Vitamins," Ralph said.

Alex took one of the bottles out and squinted at the label. "Oh aye?"

"Dietary supplements," Ralph went on. "Dieticians aren't real doctors."

"They really are, you know," Wendy told him seriously.

"I've got to go," Danny said, hauling a larger tote out of the car and putting it down on the pavement. "Town Hall stuff. I'll come by later and see he's okay."

"Thanks, Danny," Alex said, shaking his hand.

"Hey, I couldn't let my favourite uncle just walk home, could I?"

"You'll only ever be a small-town politician, Danny Hofstadter," Ralph told him, as if revisiting a conversation they'd been having on the way from the hospital.

Danny sighed. "I'd say he's feeling better," he told Alex. "See you later."

Danny drove off, and the three of them started to walk up the path towards Ralph's front porch, but he stopped and looked along the lane, to where a police cruiser was still, even after all this time, parked outside Number Thirty. "Amy finally had enough of Simon, huh?" he said.

"Let's not think about that," Wendy told him. "Come on. It's still not very warm."

"Warmer than the last time I was here," Ralph snorted. "You'd better not have cleaned up," he told them as Wendy opened the front door. "I'll never find anything."

As they stepped into the hall, Homer came waddling out of the living room and stared at them.

"Hey," Ralph said, bending down to let the dog sniff his hand. "He lost weight. Have you been feeding him?"

Not only had Alex been feeding Homer, he'd built a litter box in his living room for the dog, which he thought was above and beyond the call of duty. It was going to take weeks to air the house out. "He's overweight, Ralph," he said. "It's not good for him." He decided to wait before discussing the results of the vet's checkup.

Homer finished sniffing Ralph's fingers, and his eyes went wide. The dog took a single step back, sat down, lifted his head, and howled.

The three of them stared. Apart from the continual flatulence and a tendency to slobber at mealtimes, it was the first sound

Alex had ever heard Homer make. He just sat in front of them, yowling.

"He's probably confused now you're back," Wendy said doubtfully.

"Stupid dog," Ralph grumped.

Abruptly, Homer stopped howling, got up, and went back into the living room. They heard the sound of a single massive fart.

"See?" Ralph told them. "See what happens when you don't feed him right?"

LATER, WHEN RALPH had settled down for a nap, Alex and Wendy stood outside the house. "He's still not well," she said.

"It's hardly surprising," said Alex. "*I'm* still not well." He didn't mention the bag of pills.

"Well, you're just a typical ninety-pound weakling." She looked down towards Number Thirty. "Why are the police still here?"

"Bud says it's still a crime scene."

"After all this time?"

"Something about forensics."

The truth was, no one was entirely sure what had happened. The Abrahamsons had been, on the face of it, a perfectly ordinary, quiet, middle-aged and middle-class couple. On the day Bud had flown in to rescue them, his officers had found Simon Abrahamson lying on the floor of his kitchen with massive blunt trauma injuries to the back of his head. Amy was nowhere to be found until the snow began to thaw, when her body was discovered almost two miles away, still clutching a bloody claw-hammer in her fist. Judging by the amount of frozen snow under her body, she had been there since the day after the storm began.

"Surely there's no doubt that she did it?" Wendy said.

"Bud's just trying to be thorough. Everyone's upset about it; he wants to make sure he has all the boxes ticked." People in town were still gossiping about what might have gone on at Number Thirty, but as far as Alex was concerned, his memory of trying to cross between his property and Ralph's was still painfully strong and they all missed the important point, which was that Amy, who stood about five foot three in her socks and weighed almost nothing at all, had managed to get two miles from the house before she dropped.

"Did you know them?"

Alex shrugged. "I saw them about. Said hello once or twice."

"They were on the Liaison Committee for a while. I thought they were sweet. Always holding hands."

"Hm." He put his hands in his pockets, lost for words.

"Larry's back," she said. "I saw him this morning having an argument with Delahaye." She thought about it. "Well, Delahaye was doing the arguing; Larry was just standing there looking at him."

Alex had lately been formulating an idea to interview Larry, either for the book or for an article for the *New York Times* which Stan was keen on him doing. Stan was disappointed that Alex hadn't managed to place more pieces in the popular press; he was currently trying to buy his way into the *LA Times, The Atlantic,* and the *Chicago Tribune* with a view to gently persuading them to run Alex's articles. Mickey Olive seemed to acknowledge Alex's horrified opposition to this, but if the message was reaching Stan he was choosing to ignore it.

"Do you know how long he's going to be around?" No one seemed to know where Larry was when he wasn't at the SCS; it seemed best to catch him while he was here.

Wendy shrugged. "For all I know, he's already gone again."

Alex sighed.

THERE WAS A mall a couple of miles outside town. The sign at the entrance proclaimed it to be The Hundred Acre Mall, but Alex suspected that referred to the size of its car park, which seemed easily large enough to accommodate a rocket launch facility. The mall itself was a modest group of buildings clustered in the middle of the great wilderness of asphalt. Alex had visited a mall outside Washington into which the Hundred Acre would have fitted maybe a dozen times. But it had a bowling alley and a three-screen multiplex and a couple of restaurants and some chain stores.

It was also, he discovered, where the locals went. He'd started to notice that, apart from the people who actually worked in the stores and cafés and so on, pretty much everyone he saw around town worked at the Facility. There were locals about, of course, but he suspected that there were some days when he could have stood on Main Street and thrown a rock and been more likely to hit a particle physicist than someone who drove a tractor for a living.

"Yeah, it's been commented on," Wendy said. "Nobody knows why that happens. We get on pretty well with the townsfolk, there's certainly no friction between us, but we do seem to drift apart."

They were sitting in the mall's bowling alley, which called itself, with admirable directness, The Twenty Lanes. Except this evening it was only nineteen, one of them being out of action. It was packed with locals, most of whom seemed to take the business of bowling very seriously, with the exception of a group of teenagers down the far end, who were being politely rowdy.

There were a number of bowling teams at the Facility, and Alex and Wendy were watching a match between two of them, The Strange and The Charm. Alex, who did not understand bowling, had no idea what was going on and who was winning, if indeed anyone was winning at all, but everyone seemed happy and relaxed.

"We've been trying to get a mixed league going," Wendy went on. "Teams from the town playing teams from the Facility. We go to church events, give regular tours. We're doing our best."

"Pretty much everyone here works for the Facility, though, one way or another," Alex said.

"Yeah, pretty much."

"Maybe they're all just trying to get away from it for a while."

She watched while one of the Strange team members—green silk shirts—sent a ball down the lane and demolished the pins. The red-shirted Charm team booed goodnaturedly. "I did wonder about that," she said. "We're always going to be outsiders, but I don't like the idea that we're crowding them out."

"I don't think I've met anyone who's ungrateful about you being here."

Wendy sighed. "No. That makes it worse, somehow." She sipped some Coke. "Is East Walden still a crime scene, by the way?"

He shook his head. The last remaining law enforcement presence on the lane, a sheriff's deputy, had departed a couple of days ago.

"Did they work out what happened?"

He nodded. "Simon had an affair," he said. "About twelve years ago. Amy found out about it somehow, the storm was going on, they were cooped up in the house, and she snapped."

Wendy thought about it. "I never heard of anybody killing someone because of an affair they had twelve years previously."

"Ralph says it was Amy's sister."

She shook her head. "How does Ralph hear this stuff? He never goes anywhere."

"He's been pestering the deputies Sheriff Brandt posted at the house. You know what he's like. Eventually one of them caved and told him about it to get him to go away."

"Well," she said. "I liked them."

"Yes, you said." One of the Charm team took their turn, but only managed to clip a couple of pins. Both teams booed.

She looked at him. "You're bored."

"Not at all."

"Yeah, right."

"I was just thinking about Larry Day."

"Oh, don't," she groaned. "It's been a perfectly nice evening so far." After his flying visit a couple of weeks ago, Larry had departed again for parts unknown.

"He must have some pull with Stan, to be able to get access. There's no way Delahaye would let him into the Facility if it was up to him."

"I guess."

"So he must be doing *something* that interests Stan."

"I haven't met Clayton very often," she told him, "but I got the impression that he likes people like Larry. People who are, you know, a little bit off the beaten path."

"Like me, you mean?"

She chuckled. "Yes, Alex. Just like you."

He decided to take it as a compliment. "I should try and corner him for an interview," he said.

"Yeah, well," she said, politely applauding one of the Strange crew. "Good luck with that."

NOT LONG AFTER the official onset of spring—everyone in Rosewater County had already been wandering about in shirtsleeves for a couple of weeks—Alex finally got round to exploring the basement of his house. The book was stuck again, a series of disconnected chapters and notes, but he'd finally managed to place an article at the *NYT*, so he felt vaguely virtuous and inclined to indulge a little displacement activity.

Apart from a brief look-see when he first moved in, his initial struggles with the furnace, and his raid on the Shanahans' mountaineering supplies on the night of the storm, he had barely gone down into the basement, and it remained a vaguely mysterious cement-floored space lined with shelves and stacks of boxes. He had an idea that it extended beyond the boundaries of the house, out under the backyard, but it was hard to tell.

He took a mug of coffee and a torch down the wooden stairs and stood at the bottom. The ceiling was a good three feet above his head, but sound down here felt dull and suppressed. It was warm and dry, didn't smell mouldy, and was well lit by two twin rows of LED lights set into the ceiling.

In front of him was the furnace, a completely unknowable metal box the size of a small car that sprouted metal pipes near the top to carry heat and hot water around the house. It might have been a modern sculpture or something left behind by a UFO for all the sense it made to him. On a plate affixed to the front, just above the little window through which one could spy on the flames within, was the word BANGER. Whether this was the furnace's make or a warning about its nature, he couldn't say. On Wendy's advice he'd got an engineer to come over and have a look at it. The engineer, like engineers the world over, had sucked his teeth and shaken his head and given a couple of rueful chuckles and presented him with a bill which, before encountering Stan, would have bankrupted him.

Anyway, now the weather was warming up the furnace seemed to be working okay, which was par for the course. Like the kitchen range, it ran on gas, which was periodically and entirely without any intervention on his part delivered by a small tanker truck, the driver of which ran out frost-encrusted hoses and filled up the tank beside the house.

To his left was the near wall of the basement, lined floor-to-ceiling with well-made wooden shelves. On the shelves were toolboxes and various power tools, their cables neatly coiled. There were jars full of nails and screws and other, less obvious, small metal objects. Little cardboard boxes of brackets, the purpose of which remained unknown. Light fittings, some of them brand new, others obviously quite old. Alex opened a couple of the toolboxes and poked around inside. Just your usual collection of hand tools. The Shanahans seemed to have amassed a selection of every kind of screwdriver ever manufactured.

Behind the furnace was a stack of plastic storage boxes with more tools and coils of electrical and coaxial cable, all neatly arranged and hand-labelled according to load and purpose. Under those was another box full of wall switches and sockets and junction boxes.

To the right of the furnace, the basement stretched away for a surprising distance. Both walls were shelved, and a line of freestanding shelves ran down the middle, creating a pair of aisles. He went down the left-hand one, looking at the boxes stacked on the shelves against the wall. More tools, kids' toys, odds and ends of camera equipment, an ancient photographic enlarger, a box of miscellaneous computer parts, old motherboards and components. He reached the end of the aisle, turned back along the shelves in the middle of the room. These were mostly stacked with old suitcases and steamer trunks. A couple were unlocked, and poking through these he found neatly folded clothes, underwear, shoes, coats. He took a mouthful of lukewarm coffee and looked along the shelves of suitcases. If they all contained the same thing, he thought, that was an awful lot of clothes.

The final row of shelves was jars. Dozens and dozens of jars, of all sizes containing preserved fruit and jams, all of them labelled and dated in the same cramped, nearly illegible hand. Some of them were almost a decade old, which seemed, to Alex at least, a very long time to keep jam.

At the far end, tucked between the end of the shelving and the far corner of the basement, was a narrow metal cupboard he hadn't noticed before. It was almost as tall as he was, and it was, he saw, ballistic-bolted to the floor. He tried the handle, but it was locked.

One of the keys Mickey Olive had given him fitted the door. He unlocked it, opened the door, and found himself looking at a rack containing a pump-action shotgun, a hunting rifle, and an AR-15 semi-automatic rifle.

He tipped his head to one side. Kim had grown up around guns, and to her it had not been out of the ordinary to keep a handgun, a somewhat aged Glock, in the apartment, but Alex had never quite managed to get used to it. It lived on the top shelf of one of the closets, in a locked case, and every now and again Kim had taken it out, stripped it down, cleaned it, and reassembled it. As she had said, there was no point keeping the thing if, when they needed it, it didn't work. He'd tried to get into it; they'd gone to a range on the outskirts of Boston and he'd paid for a couple of hours' instruction, but the first time he fired at a target the pistol's recoil almost broke his wrist and he'd known guns and him weren't going to get along. When she'd moved out, Kim had taken the gun with her, but sometimes, usually late at night, he'd still sensed its presence, as if the apartment was haunted.

A shelf at the top of the gun safe had boxes of shotgun shells and rifle rounds, and a couple of magazines for the AR-15. At the bottom were three cases like the one which had once sat in the closet in his apartment. He picked up the top one and it was heavy enough to contain a weapon, but there was no way to check because it was locked and none of the keys on the bunch fitted it. There were, however, half a dozen boxes of 9mm ammunition in the bottom of the safe, like the ammunition Kim's Glock had used.

He stood there for quite a long time, looking into the safe. The fact that an American family kept weapons was essentially meaningless. He'd heard of perfectly normal, law abiding people whose personal armouries were larger than this. What did seem puzzling was that the Shanahans had left them behind.

"THE WHO?" MICKEY asked.

"The Shanahans," said Alex. "The people who used to live in my house."

Mickey thought about it, then shook his head. "Don't know the name, old son. Sorry."

They were having breakfast in the Telegraph. The place seemed busier than usual, for a weekday. A lot of scientists and tech types, some of whom he recognised but most of whom he didn't, were sitting in the booths and bellied up to the counter. In fact, now he looked properly, he didn't see anyone who presented as a local. It was as if Stan's people had finally driven them all out.

"I keep getting mail for them," he said. "There's quite a stack now." This was true, but it was all junk mail.

"I'd have thought they'd have got their post redirected."

"Maybe it slipped their minds."

Mickey thought about it. "It was quite sad, really," he said. "She had a problem with prescription painkillers, if I remember rightly. We had to let them go."

"Well, their post is piling up."

Mickey shrugged and cut a slice from his ham and cheese omelette. "Their forwarding address will be on record somewhere. Let me have the stuff and I'll see it's sent on."

"I can do that myself," Alex said casually, sitting back and taking a mouthful of coffee.

Mickey glanced at him, then went back to his omelette. "Up to you, old son. I'll email you the address."

"Thanks."

"Everything else going all right?"

"Larry Day," said Alex.

Mickey winced, momentarily.

"Is he actually working here?"

Mickey chewed some omelette, swallowed. "I only do admin, Alex, as you well know. You'd have more luck asking about Professor Day at the Facility."

"No one there seems to want to talk about him."

Mickey chuckled. "That sounds about right. Have you met him?"

"Once. A long time ago."

"He can be quite the nuisance, our Professor Day."

"Why do they keep letting him in, then? Just revoke his access."

A brief look of pain crossed Mickey's face. "Professor Day is..." he searched for the right word. "Resourceful. Friends in high places."

"Brigadier General Bell?"

Mickey gave him a long, level look before saying, "Quite." He wadded up a piece of bread and butter and swiped it around his plate. "I'm not a writer, of course, but if I were asked for my opinion, I'd say that Professor Day could quite easily become a distraction."

"Oh?"

"He's not an official member of the team; he's not going to give you any insight into the project." Mickey popped the wad of bread in his mouth.

"It sounds as if you're warning me to stay away from him."

Mickey washed his mouthful of food down with a swallow of coffee. "In my experience," he said, "that's more or less the default reaction to Professor Day."

"No," said Margaret Owen. "Absolutely not. Are you crazy or something?"

"Come on, Maggie," said Alex. "Just five minutes."

"Delahaye's told us not to talk to you," she said.

"I know." This, of course, was Delahaye's revenge for not being allowed to read an early draft of the book. It would be reasonably straightforward to pass a message to Stan via Mickey Olive and get Delahaye's ban lifted, but Alex was interested to see how long the Administrator's fit of pique was going to last.

"Isn't it worth it, just to wind him up?"

"No." Margaret, a tall, elegant Korean-American with a severe look and an astoundingly dirty laugh, was standing on a stepladder beside HELEN, adjusting something behind a panel on the detector's side. "He's told us anyone who talks to you will be thrown off the project."

"He doesn't really mean that."

"You want to bet the five years' work I've got invested in this thing on that?" Margaret came back down the ladder, put the tool she'd been using in a little plastic case, and closed the lid. About a dozen other scientists and techs were working on the detector, studiedly ignoring the conversation. "He's a prissy little anal-retentive dickwad, but he *runs* things here, Alex." She picked up the box and she suddenly looked up, behind him. "Nothing personal, but will you go away and annoy someone else, please?"

He half-turned to see what she was looking at. Up on the catwalk that ran around the room, Larry Day was leaning on the rail. He appeared to be wearing US Army desert camouflage fatigues. "I think I'll do just that, Maggie," Alex said. "See you later."

Larry was gone when he got up the stairs to the catwalk, but he caught up in the airlock. "Hi," he said.

Larry squinted at him. "I know you," he said.

"We met at Livermore, about ten years ago."

Larry thought about it. "Dolan," he said, as if excavating a particularly delicate fossil, although it wasn't quite the prodigious feat of memory that it seemed. "I heard you were here." He didn't offer to shake hands. "You want an interview, yeah?"

"Sure. If you have time sometime."

Larry thought some more. "Okay," he said. "Let's get a drink."

* * *

Getting a drink proved slightly more complicated than it sounded. It transpired that Larry had experienced a series of unfortunate reversals which had resulted in him being thrown out of every bar in Rosewater County and a large number in neighbouring Blackfish County. Escaping his personal exclusion zone required a two-hour drive over the state line into Minnesota. They took Alex's car because Larry admitted to having snacked on a six-pack of Bud that morning. He climbed into the passenger seat of the Accord without bothering with the seatbelt, gestured in a vaguely northward direction, said, "That way," and fell asleep.

Leaving Rosewater County for the first time in more than eight months was something of a shock. Alex hadn't realised the extent to which he'd grown used to the all-pervading newness and prosperity around Sioux Crossing. It had become so familiar that he'd stopped noticing it, but now, driving north, he could see his surroundings becoming progressively shabbier and run down, as if they were travelling out of a zone of fallout.

The townships they drove through were increasingly worn out and depressed, storefronts either empty or boarded up completely, buildings old and decrepit. Foreclosure signs were everywhere, on the overgrown front lawns of houses and at the end of roads leading to farms. Everything seemed wilder and dirtier and more broken.

He was just pondering whether to turn round and take the snoring form of Larry back to the SCS when Larry opened his eyes and said, "Here."

"What?"

"Here," Larry told him, gesturing at what seemed to be a large public lavatory set back from the road. "Ah, hell," he said. "You missed it."

Alex drove a mile or so further down the road, made a turn in a farm road, and came back, pulling into the parking lot behind the building. It was a mouldering windowless single-storey cinderblock construction. What paint there was on it was flaking off, and larger pieces of the frontage had come adrift and lay on the ground. A dozen or so shabby pickups were parked in the lot, along with a line of four cheaply customised motorcycles. A sign outside proclaimed the building to be the BLACK COUGAR ROADHOUSE. Alex's heart sank.

"Maybe we should drive a bit further," he suggested. "There might be somewhere better a couple of miles down the road."

"Nah," said Larry, getting out of the car. "This'll be great, Alex." And he wandered a little unsteadily towards the front of the roadhouse.

Inside, the Black Cougar was dim and stank of beer and tobacco smoke and bleach and greasy food. It was basically just one big L-shaped room. There was a bar down one side of the long arm of the L, with booths down the other side and tables arranged in the free space between. Most of the short arm of the L was occupied by a low stage entirely encased in a cage of chicken wire. Alex had no idea what the purpose of this was, but it was one of the most disturbing things he'd ever seen in a bar. A group of biker-types was clustered around a tatty-looking pool table in one corner, and there were a dozen or so large and rather unpleasant-looking men at the bar. The place was such a dive that it seemed it didn't even have a jukebox. Alex had a very strong urge to flee, but Larry was already sitting in one of the booths and talking to a waitress.

"Well," Alex said, sitting opposite him. "This is nice."

"Pure Americana," Larry said, smiling and looking about him. The waitress had gone to the bar and was talking to the barman, a skinny shaven-headed man with a black tee shirt and tattoos. "So, what do you want to know?"

"If you think I'm doing an interview here, you're crazier than people say you are."

Larry pouted theatrically and said, "Aw. And I thought you really wanted to talk to me." The waitress returned with a pitcher of beer and two glasses and set them down on the table between Larry and Alex. Larry filled the glasses, picked one up, and drained half of it in one swallow.

Alex clasped his hands in front of him on the tabletop, then thought better of it. The tabletop was sticky. He sat back and rubbed his hands on his jeans. "What are you doing at the SCS?"

Larry raised his eyebrows. "So we *are* doing the interview now?"

"I'm just trying to make conversation." Alex picked up his glass and took a drink. The beer tasted as if it had roughly the same alcohol content as a glass of Perrier, but there was a faint and completely baffling afterburn of what tasted like paprika.

"I read that thing you did for the *New York Times*," Larry said.

"Oh?" Alex waited for him to continue, but all he did was sit there. "Thank you," he said eventually.

"And you're writing a book too."

"Yes."

Larry finished his beer, topped up his glass from the jug. "I guess Clayton's paying you a lot of money to do that."

"He's paying above market rates, certainly."

"How's that going?"

"It's going." Alex took another sip of his beer and scowled. "And I thought I was supposed to be interviewing you."

Larry grinned a buccaneer's grin. "Just making conversation. Shall we see what the food's like in this place?"

Alex shuddered. "Shall we not?"

"Ah." Larry looked sad. "You've got no sense of adventure."

"What I do have is a highly developed sense of self-preservation. What *are* you doing at the SCS? You're not on any of the research projects."

Larry shook his head. "I'm just a tourist, taking in the pretty sights." He drained his glass again, refilled it.

"Are there any?" Alex asked. "Pretty sights?"

Larry grinned that grin again. "Sure. The SCS is the largest privately funded science project in the world. Don't you think that qualifies it for a look-see? Isn't that why *you're* here?"

Well, no. "Stan wants me to create *sensawunda*."

Larry gave him a level look. "*Stan* wants gravity."

"Beg pardon?"

"Gravity. He wants to know how it works." He sat back. "Actually, he's self-aware enough to realise he probably won't be able to understand it, but he's got people who can boil off a cartoon version for him. He can hold up a piece of paper and say 'Behold: The Graviton'. Cue music, crowd goes wild."

"Is that a bad thing? Particularly?"

Larry shrugged. "Good, bad, it doesn't matter. If they come up with some solid proof about the nature of gravity, he gets the bragging rights. They find themselves a massless spin-2 boson and they get to rewrite quantum field theory."

"So it's quite a big deal, then."

Larry squinted at him. "What kind of science journalist did you say you were?"

"The wrong kind, obviously."

Larry picked up his glass, half emptied it in one swallow, put it back on the table. "Most people believe it's experimentally impossible to detect individual gravitons. Gravitational waves? Sure, we got those. But the individual particle, nope. They interact very weakly with normal matter. You'd need to put a detector the size of a gas giant in orbit around a neutron star, and even then you'd only pick up a graviton once in a blue moon, and even *then* you couldn't be certain it *was* a graviton."

"So the SCS is a waste of time? Is that what you're saying?"

"Well, I've seen some papers which suggest it *would* be possible to detect gravitons in a collider. I'm not convinced, myself." He sniffed. "But it's Clayton's money."

Alex thought about it. "I've been here almost eight months," he said, "and this is the first time I've heard anyone mention gravitons." Now he thought about it, nobody had ever mentioned a specific task for the SCS; they were just going to smash up particles at energies no one had reached before and see what came out. It was research for research's sake, and that was one of the things that made it a hard sell.

"Well, that's PR for you, isn't it." Larry refilled his glass again, then held the empty pitcher above his head to indicate he wanted more. "They're going to get all kinds of interesting results, once they get the thing working properly, but if word got out that they were tilting at windmills..." The waitress took the empty pitcher from his hand, replaced it with a full one, and went away again.

"How do you know all this stuff?"

"They got in touch, six, seven years ago and asked me to lead the research. I wasn't interested in being a figurehead."

Alex suddenly had a horrific thought. "Is that why the military are involved?" Because the merest hint of being able to manipulate gravity would have been enough to interest the defence industries.

"Ah, well," Larry said. "What motivates our friends in uniform, I can't say."

Alex rubbed his eyes. This was a scandal of enormous proportions. Or was it? Could it be a scandal if everyone went into it with their eyes wide open, knowing what they were trying to do was impossible? "Stan's not a stupid man," he said.

"No sir, he is not. What he is, is obsessed. I told you. He wants gravity, and he's found a bunch of people who've told him, whether they believe it or not, that he could have it if he builds his toy just... *so* and presses the big red button." He drained his glass in one go, refilled it. "Actually, what I think *really* happened is that he found a bunch of people who told him it was impossible, but that it shouldn't stop him from trying. A lot of people have been feathering their own nests from Clayton's piggy bank."

"Jesus. So what *are* you doing here?"

"Like I said, they're going to get some cool results whatever happens." Larry drained his glass again. "And all kinds of interesting stuff happens when a failure mode kicks in." He got up. "Back in a second."

While he was gone, Alex stared into space, trying to think. There was probably a book in Stan's quixotic pursuit of the force of gravity, but it wasn't the book that Stan wanted him to write.

There was a sudden commotion at the other end of the bar, the sound of breaking glass and raised voices. Alex turned his head and saw Larry and one of the pool-playing bikers standing toe-to-toe, yelling at each other, and he felt his heart sink. As he watched, Larry, still shouting, took a step back, grabbed one of the cues from the pool table, and broke it over the biker's head.

THEY SPENT THE afternoon and early evening in cells at the local police headquarters. Alex sat on the grubby mattress with his back against the concrete wall, knees drawn up to his chest. Periodically, he could hear one or other of the bikers, along the row of cells, shouting threats and obscenities at Larry, but the only response from Larry was snoring.

At some point, there was the sound of heavy footsteps in the corridor outside, a key in the lock, and the door swung open and Bud Rosewater was standing there. They looked at each other for a while.

"Alex," said Bud.

"Bud," said Alex.

Bud gave a little jerk of the head. "Let's go."

The local police chief, a man named Lundgren, was waiting by the front desk, looking stern. Alex thought Chief Lundgren spent quite a lot of time looking stern. He looked on while the desk sergeant produced Alex's personal effects in an A4-

sized envelope. Alex opened the flap and looked inside without taking anything out, because he didn't want Bud to see the 007 Phone. He signed for his belongings.

"What about Professor Day?" he asked.

"We'll let him sleep it off, then we'll probably let him loose with some harsh words," said Lundgren. "We found crystal meth on the other guys, so we'll want to discuss that with them in more detail." He watched Alex signing a couple of other forms. "You might want to consider not coming back to this county again, Mr Dolan."

"I've been considering it ever since I got here," Alex said. "No offence."

"None taken."

Alex rolled up the mouth of the envelope and turned to Bud. "Are we done?"

"I'm parked out front." He nodded to Lundgren. "Chuck."

Lundgren nodded back. "Bud."

In the truck and heading south towards Rosewater County, Alex sat with the envelope in his lap, staring out at the passing countryside. He felt tired, somehow jetlagged.

"You okay?" Bud asked after a while.

"Me? Oh, I'm grand, thanks. Never better."

"What happened?"

"I don't know. We were having a quiet drink, Larry got up to go to the loo, the next thing I knew we were being arrested." One of the unpleasant-looking men in the Black Cougar had turned out to be an off-duty police officer, who had restored order, of a sort, by breaking a couple of heads before calling for backup.

"That place has a bad reputation," Bud told him.

"It wasn't my idea."

Bud grunted. "I guess not." Without taking his eyes off the road, he unbuttoned one of his breast pockets and took out a folded slip of paper and held it out.

"Another customer satisfaction survey?" Alex asked, taking it and unfolding it. A Minnesota address was printed on it.

"Mickey said you were asking about Vern and Pam," said Bud. "The Shanahans."

"Oh. Oh. Thank you." He unrolled the mouth of the envelope, dropped the note inside, rolled it up again. It occurred to him to ask why Bud had the address, but he kept his mouth shut.

They drove on for a while in silence. A sign went by welcoming them to Iowa. After a few more miles, Bud said, "Technically, Chuck didn't let you go. He released you into my custody."

Alex thought about it. "So what happens now?"

Bud shrugged. "I could take you back to town and put you in a cell until I decide what to do with you."

"Okay."

"Or you could make a spectacular escape and I'd never see you again."

Alex said nothing.

"Hey!" Bud shouted all of a sudden, making Alex jump. "Where'd he go? How'd he get out of the truck?"

"Very funny."

Bud chuckled. "Word to the wise, Alex? Stay out of that guy's way."

There was no need to ask who 'that guy' was. Alex looked out of the passenger window. "Thanks for coming," he said.

Bud nodded. "Don't mention it."

A COUPLE OF weeks passed. Larry was not seen at the SCS; there was anecdotal evidence that he was making a nuisance of himself at MIT, but no one knew for sure. Alex tried to get his head back into the book, which comprised about fifty thousand words' worth of disconnected bits. He'd been promised an in-depth interview with Stan about his motivations for launching the project in the first place, but somehow that kept never quite materialising, so in the end he'd had to make do with press releases and media profiles. He was sort of tempted to write Stan out of the book altogether, leave him as a mysterious, unnamed presence in the background. He quite liked that idea, in fact.

Most evenings, he went over to Ralph's for a game of chess. He thought his game was improving, although he had not once come close to winning, or even forcing a draw.

"You're getting better," Ralph said one night, after thoroughly destroying him in a dozen or so moves.

"No I'm not."

"Yes, you are," Ralph insisted. "You're... no, you're right. You're a lousy chess player. It's embarrassing."

"Cheers." Alex gave the board one last look, then he started to reset the pieces. "Do you ever miss writing?"

Ralph raised an eyebrow. "Miss it?" He settled back in his chair and lit a cigar. "I guess not, no."

"What happened?"

Ralph shrugged. "I just woke up one day and I couldn't do it any more. Ran out of words." He regarded Alex through a cloud of cigar smoke. "You don't believe in writers' block?"

"It's not an excuse most of my editors would have accepted."

Ralph grunted. "You're in a different part of the business, of course. I kind of admire journalists, having to churn out copy day after day, come rain or shine or hangover. It's quite a discipline."

"It doesn't feel that way." He held out his fists. Ralph leaned forward and tapped one; Alex opened it to reveal a black pawn. He turned the board around.

"You want me to read what you've got so far?"

Alex shook his head. "There's nothing *to* read. Just a lot of bits." He looked at the board for a couple of moments, then played pawn to king four.

"What's your deadline?"

"There isn't one."

Ralph narrowed his eyes at him.

"I haven't asked anyone, but I've been through my contract and there's no delivery date."

Ralph thought about it. "This is why amateurs shouldn't be allowed to mess around in the business," he said finally. "You think they're actually serious about this?"

Alex shrugged. "I'm here. And the money seems to be real. I do wonder sometimes, though."

"Seems a peculiar thing to do, ask a man to write a book and then just forget about it."

"That never happened to you?"

Ralph laughed. "Hell no. I had editors on my back the whole time, especially when I was hot. Do us this thing, Ralph, do us that thing, Ralph. We think you're really great. And then all of a sudden they stopped."

"I'm sorry."

"Don't be." Ralph pushed one of his pawns forward. "I'm not."

Alex looked at him. Despite almost constant grumbling about dieticians, the old man was sticking to his diet and he hadn't put on the weight he'd lost while he was in hospital. Instead, he seemed to be slowly mummifying. He said, "I'm a spy."

Ralph glanced up from the board. "Say what?"

He couldn't believe he'd actually said it, out loud. For a moment, he doubted that he *had* said it. He habitually left his phones at home when he visited Ralph, and he was as sure as he could be that Stan's people hadn't wired this house. But still.

He said, "I'm a spy." And he told Ralph about Kitson's approach, the *fait accompli* he'd been presented with.

When he'd finished, Ralph spent a while regarding the end of his cigar. Finally, he said, "Well, *this* is exciting."

"It's really not."

"Here I was, thinking you were just another halfwitted journalist, and now it turns out you've been James Bond all along."

"Ralph. I'm serious."

Ralph looked at him and pursed his lips and said, "Well. I'd say you were in a *situation*, son."

"No shit." Alex looked at the chessboard but suddenly none of the pieces made any sense. "I don't know what to do."

"Have you told anyone else?"

Alex shook his head. He'd almost told Bud, on the drive back from the Black Cougar the other week, but had thought better of it. It had never even crossed his mind to tell Wendy.

Ralph stared into space. "The government tried to get me to spy for them once," he mused.

"What?"

"Back in the late 90s. I was touring *Aztec Snow* and my publishers got me a gig in Moscow. The usual stuff, interviews, bookshop signings, a lecture at the university. Five days of vodka and pickles and black bread. Anyway, this pencilneck turned up a couple of weeks before I was due to leave. Said he was from State and they'd be *ever* so grateful if I'd keep my eyes and ears open while I was in Russia and if I saw or heard anything *interesting* I could let them know when I got back."

"Wow. What did you do?"

"Said yes, sure. I was hoping they'd send me to spy school, teach me how to do invisible writing and use a one-time pad and set up dead-drops, but they didn't. So I just forgot about it. Went to Moscow, had a great time. When I got back the pencilneck turned up again and I told him I didn't have anything to report, and I never saw him again."

"Good lord." Here they were, a pair of amateur spies.

"Anyway," Ralph went on, "the *point* of telling you all that is that you haven't been sent in here to steal blueprints or some new weapon of mass destruction. It sounds to me as if all they want you to do is keep your eyes and ears open. If there's nothing here for you to see or hear, that's not your fault."

"Kitson's very keen," said Alex. "He's sure something's going on." He thought about it. "Also, nobody threatened to have you deported."

"They can't deport you for not telling them about stuff that isn't there. Why would they do that? Spite? It's a lot of effort and all it does is increase the chance of you going running to Wikileaks."

"Nobody goes running to Wikileaks any more, Ralph. Those days are over."

Ralph waved a hand. "Whatever."

"I remain unconvinced."

"That's your business, Alex, and nothing I say's going to make you feel any better. But if you want my advice? Fuck 'em." He leaned forward and moved one of his knights. "You don't even know he's really an intelligence officer."

"He's on the end of the right phone number."

"You sure about that?"

Alex brought his bishop back across the board. "Pretty sure."

"Pretty sure isn't sure. For all you know, this is some sort of industrial espionage thing. Some jealous scientist wanting to find out the inside scoop from Black Hole Central."

"Scientists don't do that, Ralph."

Ralph stared at him. "Oh, please." He looked at the board again. "Thing is, you don't *know.* All you know is what this guy told you. Ever hear the phrase 'false flag'?" He moved his knight again. "Mate."

Alex looked at the board. "You asshole."

THE ADDRESS BUD had given him for the Shanahans was not in Minneapolis or in St Paul, but further to the west of the Twin Cities, in a town called St Christopher. It was an almost four-hour drive from Sioux Crossing, and the Accord was more than equal to an eight-hour round trip, but instead he drove over to Mason City and parked at the long-stay car park at the airport, then went inside to the Hertz desk and hired a Lexus, with cash. He did all this almost without thinking, an indication of the generalised air of paranoia which had begun to settle on his life. He had no evidence that there was a tracker on his car, but equally he had no evidence that there was not, and if anyone did, in future, ponder why the car had spent all day in the car park at Mason City airport, well, he'd have to cross that bridge. He'd left his phones at home, so before leaving the airport he bought a preloaded burner in case of emergencies, and set off north.

He was in St Christopher just after lunchtime, following the Lexus's GPS to find the Shanahans' address. As a town, it didn't seem all that much larger than Sioux Crossing, and if it didn't have that brand-new patina, it seemed prosperous enough.

The address turned out to be a small apartment complex on the edge of town, set in its own grounds and looking out across farmland that seemed to go on forever into the west. A sign with the words *WINDY RIVERS APARTMENTS* went by as he drove through the gates.

He parked in a little parking lot to one side of the complex and walked back round to the front. The Shanahans were in one of the ground-floor apartments. He walked up to the door, took a moment to gather his thoughts, then rang the bell.

There was no answer, and it belatedly occurred to him that he might have driven all this way only to find nobody here. He rang the bell again, and this time he heard the door being unlocked. It opened, and a young boy was standing there, blond and big-boned and about eleven years old.

"Hi," said the boy.

"Hi," said Alex. "Are your parents home?"

"Who is it, Timothy?" called a man's voice from inside the apartment.

"Mr Shanahan?" Alex called. "My name's Dolan. I'm from Sioux Crossing."

"You sure don't *sound* as if you're from Sioux Crossing," the voice called. It sounded weak and reedy and far-away.

"I'm living there at the moment," Alex said. "In your old house."

There was no reply to this. After a while, Alex heard someone moving around deeper inside the apartment, and a few moments later a figure appeared in a doorway, supporting itself on a Zimmer frame. "That house is cursed," said the figure.

VERN SHANAHAN WAS only a couple of years older than Alex, but he looked about a thousand years old, nothing but yellowish skin stretched tightly over bone. His clothes were about two sizes too large for him. His feet, stuffed into worn slippers, were swollen, and Alex could see the loop of a Hickman line taped to his chest.

"Liver cancer," he said before Alex said anything.

"I'm sorry," Alex said. He'd brought some of the Shanahans' junk mail with him, as camouflage, but it stayed stuffed in his coat pocket. The apartment was too hot, and it smelled of antiseptic and sick.

"It's been eight months," said Vern. "They gave me six, so."

They were sitting in the apartment's living room. Beyond the windows, Alex could see neat formal gardens. Vern had one of those old person's chairs, built up to make it easier to sit and stand. On a little table beside it were various bottles and boxes of pills, a jug of water and a glass. On the floor under the table were a little stack of disposable cardboard sick-bowls and a lidded metal bucket.

Now he was here, Alex had no idea how to proceed. "Is your wife about?"

"She went into town to pick up my meds. Not that they're going to do any good."

Another blond boy came into the room with a mug of coffee,

handed it to Alex, and left again. These would be Ralph's nemeses, the Shanahan Boys, dog shooters. They seemed harmless enough, but there was an atmosphere here, a sense of waiting, of a death which had not happened yet.

He said, "What did you mean about the house being cursed?"

Vern snorted. "How long have you been there?"

"About nine months now." Alex tried the coffee. It was monumentally strong.

"You work at the collider?"

"Kind of. I'm a journalist; I'm writing something about the project."

Vern shook his head. "We were there three years and we weren't happy a single day. Haven't you noticed there's something *wrong* about it?"

"How do you mean, 'wrong'?"

"Something uncomfortable. Like the house didn't want us there." He looked at Alex. "I know how that sounds. The neighbours were all assholes, especially that poisonous old bastard next door. Always coming round and banging on the door to complain about something. I hadn't mowed my front lawn, my car was blocking his driveway, the boys were making too much noise."

"Right."

"I mean, they're *boys*," said Vern. "Boys make noise. And he doesn't even have a car."

Alex heard the front door open and close, and a moment later a small woman with a pinched face and weary eyes came into the room and stared at him.

"This is Mr Dolan, Pam," Vern said. "He's living in East Walden Lane."

Pam stared at Alex a few moments longer, then she held out a big white paper bag. "Here's your medication, Vernon," she said. Then she turned and left the room.

"It's hard on Pam," Vern said, setting the bag down beside

his chair. "Well, it's hard on all of us, but her in particular." He settled back against the cushions. "Of course, it's hardest on me, because I'm the one who's going to die."

Alex was beginning to regret coming here. It was impossible to decode the situation. He said, "Why were you in Sioux Crossing?"

"We worked at the SCS." Vern saw the look on Alex's face. "Oh, we're not scientists. We got a tour of the collider when we arrived, but that was the last we saw of it. We worked in admin."

"And you left when you got ill?" Alex felt uncomfortable about that. The Shanahans didn't seem to have been well-treated by the SCS. The apartment was less than half the size of Number Twenty-Four.

"No, I got sick after," said Vern. "A month or so after we moved up here."

"Why are you here, Mr Dolan?" Pam asked from the doorway.

I brought your junk mail. "I've found quite a lot of your stuff at the house," Alex said carefully. "In the basement, particularly. I wanted to see if I could return it to you."

"We don't have room here for all that stuff," Pam said stonily. "Keep it, throw it away. We don't care."

Alex looked from one to the other. "Well," he said. "If you're sure..."

"We're sure," Pam said. "We just want to forget that place ever existed. And now I want you to leave. You're tiring Vern."

Vern didn't look any more or less tired than he had when Alex arrived, but he'd been in enough interview situations to know when it was time to go. He stood up. "I'm sorry to have disturbed you," he said.

"Good to meet you, Mr Dolan," Vern said, offering a hand that felt like a bundle of sticks.

Alex thought Pam would simply close the door on him, but she surprised him by walking him to the car. "I don't want anyone else from the SCS coming here," she told him. "Tell them that."

"They don't even know I'm here," he said.

She glanced at him. "You should get out of there while you still can, Mr Dolan. That place made Vern sick."

"The SCS?"

"The house."

They reached the car. Alex blipped the door unlocked, paused with his hand on the handle. "You left in a big hurry," he said. "You left half your stuff behind."

Pam sighed and looked about her. "Okay," she said. "Okay. Things were happening there, things we didn't understand. We kept hearing noises. Knocking sounds in the walls. The place was suddenly full of static; you couldn't touch *anything* without getting a shock."

Alex thought of blue sparks.

"I was in the kitchen one morning and I looked out of the window and there was someone standing in the backyard. I turned and called to Vern, and when I turned back they'd gone."

"Chief Rosewater said something about a prowler."

She shook her head. "I only looked away for a moment, Mr Dolan. One second they were standing there, the next they were gone. When we went outside the grass was charred where they'd been standing."

Alex waited with his hand on the handle.

"One night, a couple of days later, we were in bed and I heard someone walking around downstairs. I thought it was one of the boys—they went through a spell of sleepwalking—so I got up and went downstairs and there was static *everywhere*. And there was this..." She stopped. "There was someone standing in the kitchen. He turned and looked at me and I screamed and screamed and screamed." She stopped again, fists clenched. "By the time Vern and the boys came running downstairs to see what the noise was, he was gone. Just vanished, right there in front of me in a cloud of static." She looked away. "We put the boys in the car and we left right there and then, drove to my parents in St Paul."

Alex didn't know what to say.

"I know what you're thinking," she said. "But I didn't imagine it. I know what I saw."

"Did you tell anyone else?"

"Vern called Chief Rosewater when we got to my parents'. He said he'd check the house. A few days later this Brit from the SCS turned up. Tall guy, sounded like Hugh Grant with a bad cold. He said the police hadn't found any sign of a break-in and maybe I'd had a bad dream or a reaction to my hayfever meds or something. I just refused to go back and eventually he said he'd get our personal stuff sent on and organise severance for us. He was sorry we felt that way, we were valued employees, and could we sign these NDAs and he'd get our severances processed right away, etcetera and blah blah blah. And that was the last time anyone from the SCS bothered to get in touch with us until today."

"I don't really work for the SCS," he told her. "I'm writing a book."

She looked at him. "I don't care," she said.

"Don't tell anyone I was here," he said, opening the door. "Please."

"Just go, Mr Dolan," she told him. "Leave us alone."

He'd planned to stop somewhere for something to eat, and then drive straight back to Mason City, but as he worked back towards the interstate he saw signs for Minneapolis and something occurred to him and he drove into the city instead. Pausing briefly to use the burner phone to google the British Consulate, an hour or so later he found himself standing outside a smallish, modern-looking building surrounded by a high brick wall which looked like an addition which had come along with the Global War on Terror.

There was a pair of iron gates at the front, and mounted in the wall beside them was an entryphone panel with a big fat steel button, a little camera, and a speaker grille. He stood where he thought the camera could see him, and pressed the button.

"Yes?" said a voice from the grille.

"Oh, hello," he said, trying to appear as British and harmless as possible. "I wonder if it would be possible to speak to Colin? It's about my visa."

There was a silence, then the voice said, "Just a moment, please."

It was, actually, rather more than a moment. He stood there for five minutes before the grille said, "Come in, please," and the gates buzzed. He pushed them open against their springs and stepped into the consulate compound.

Kitson was waiting in the foyer of the building, a look of fury on his face. "Mr Ross," he said, approaching across the parquet with his hand out.

It was the first time Alex had heard the name 'Ross', but he rolled with it. "Hi," he said. "Just checking on my visa." They shook hands. He got the sense that Kitson was struggling not to crush his fingers.

"Certainly," Kitson said. "I was just going to get myself a sandwich. Perhaps you could walk with me?"

"Of course."

Kitson waited until they were through the gates and out of sight of the consulate before he said, "What the *actual fucking hell* do you think you're playing at?"

Alex shrugged. "I was in town; I thought I'd look in."

"This way." Kitson pointed down the street. "You do *not* just 'look in'. You are never, *ever* seen with me. Do you understand? Why is your phone still in Sioux Crossing?"

"I didn't want anyone to know where I was."

Kitson shook his head angrily. "Yes," he said, pounding along the pavement. "Yes. Very fucking funny. Well done." He stomped to a halt outside a deli and thrust his hands in his pockets. "Do you have any news?"

Everyone's looking for the secret of gravity and they're afraid that if word gets out people will laugh at them. "Nope."

Kitson nodded. "Okay. Look, don't do this again, Alex, right? I can't be seen with you, otherwise there will be awkward questions, and neither of us wants that."

"Do we not?"

"No. We don't. Now, if you'll excuse me, please fuck off back to Iowa and keep reporting on your usual schedule." And he pushed open the door of the deli and went inside.

"Righto," Alex said to himself with a little smile. He went to find the car.

"PAM SHANAHAN."

"What about her?" asked Ralph, looking down at the chessboard.

"Someone told me she had a problem. Prescription drugs."

Ralph grunted. "I heard a rumour she was using painkillers a bit too *enthusiastically*. Don't know how true that was. I do know she's batshit crazy." He reached out and moved one of his knights. "She's crazy, Vern's an asshole, their kids are dog killers." He took his beer from the table beside his chair and took a swallow. "Whole damn family's dysfunctional."

Alex thought of the blond boys at Windy Rivers Apartments. "They didn't kill Homer."

Ralph snorted. "Only because they couldn't shoot straight."

"Vern has liver cancer," Alex said.

Ralph looked at him. "How do you know that?" When Alex didn't answer, he narrowed his eyes. "Ah hell," he said. "Why did you do that?"

"I found a gun safe in the basement. There are enough weapons inside to start a small civil war."

Ralph raised an eyebrow. "Didn't know Vern had guns. The kids, yeah, but not him. He didn't seem the type."

"It sounded as if Pam was having hallucinations while she was here."

"That doesn't surprise me. Are you going to move, or are you just going to stare at the board until we both die of old age?"

Alex took one of Ralph's pawns with his rook. "Why doesn't it surprise you?" he asked. "Pam seeing things?"

"Not particularly tightly wound, Pam," he said, taking Alex's rook with his knight. "Always banging on my door to complain about some damn thing. Check."

Alex looked at the board. "Bollocks." He moved his king.

"I'm sorry to hear that about Vern," said Ralph. "I never liked the man, but liver cancer?" He shook his head. "That's a fuck of a way to go."

"Have *you* ever seen things round here?"

"Me? Like what?"

"I don't know. Unusual stuff."

"Like those guys going in to decorate your house?"

"Pam said the place was full of static."

Ralph thought about it. "Can't remember anything like that. I told you; Pam's nuts. She probably took a few of her little pills and imagined it."

"You really are an unpleasant old man, you know."

"You didn't have to live next door to them." Ralph moved his queen. "Check."

Alex scowled and moved his king again.

"What are you going to do about Vern's guns?"

"Haven't decided yet."

"You should take them to Bud," Ralph told him, studying the pieces. "Or get him to come out and collect them, if you don't want to mess with them. I know how you Brits feel about guns."

It wasn't that. The presence of the guns seemed to him to be evidence that Stan's operation was not infallible. The safe was tucked away in a corner of the basement, hidden from view from the bottom of the stairs. He hadn't seen it until he was almost on top of it. If someone had checked out the house before he moved in, he got a sense that they'd only given the basement a cursory look. He didn't *want* shotguns and rifles, particularly, but the fact that they'd been missed was kind of comforting, proof that there were still surprising little hidden corners in his life.

"We'll see," he said. "Maybe."

"Before I forget, there was a guy looking for you the other day, when you were away." After the events of the previous autumn, Ralph had appointed himself the guardian of Alex's house.

"Guy?"

"Big guy, white hair, dressed like a clown. Drove a red car."

Alex winced.

"Sounds familiar?"

He nodded. "Yeah. Did you speak to him?"

Ralph shook his head. "He banged on your front door for a while, then he looked in the windows, then he went away again."

A lot of the younger scientists at the SCS thought Larry was pretty cool; some of them appeared to regard him as a kind of trickster god. Alex thought that was one of the reasons he hung around the project; that kind of adulation could be addictive. Most of the older staff just thought he was a nuisance, but even they were slightly in awe of him.

"Did you see them go?"

"Who?" Ralph looked at him. "Oh, we're talking about them again. No, I didn't see them go. I have better things to do than watch my asshole neighbours. Particularly those asshole neighbours."

"They left in a hell of a hurry. The SCS delivered their stuff afterward. The stuff they could fit in their new apartment, anyway."

"I don't know about that. I'm just glad they're somewhere else."

"I dropped in on Kitson, while I was in Minneapolis."

"Oh yeah?" Ralph took another drink of beer. "How'd that go?"

"Well, he's certainly *at* the consulate."

Ralph went back to examining the board. "I'm hearing a 'but', there."

"I don't know." Alex pondered whether or not to move his queen back down the board. "Something odd going on. He was *really* pissed off that I'd turned up."

"As you'd expect." Ralph waved at the board. "Come on, move already, for Christ's sake."

Alex sighed and moved his queen. "It wasn't that. It was more like he was embarrassed or something."

"You expected him to offer you tea and cucumber sandwiches? You have a *lot* to learn about how spies work."

Alex had been going over and over Kitson's reaction since he got back. True, Kitson had been annoyed, and it had been worth the trip for that alone, but it had been something *more* than annoyance, more than professionalism. At the moment, he was working on a theory that Kitson was actually engaged in some kind of private enterprise, something not officially sanctioned, something he'd cooked up in his own time to impress his masters. If that was true, what did it mean? Could Alex just ignore him? If he did that, could Kitson still cause problems?

"It's all very complicated," he admitted.

"Well, that's life for you," Ralph said. "You're boogieing along without a care in the world, then some guy comes along and does *this*." And one of his rooks came out of seemingly nowhere and took Alex's queen. "Mate."

Alex looked at the board. "Fucksake," he said.

"Hey, you *are* getting better," Ralph told him. "You lasted a whole fifteen minutes that time."

"I don't know about that," [illegible]

[illegible]

[illegible]

[illegible]

[illegible] the board. [illegible]

"I don't know," Alex [illegible] whether or not [illegible]

[illegible]

[illegible]

[illegible]

[illegible]

[illegible]

[illegible]

Alex [illegible] the board. [illegible]

[illegible]

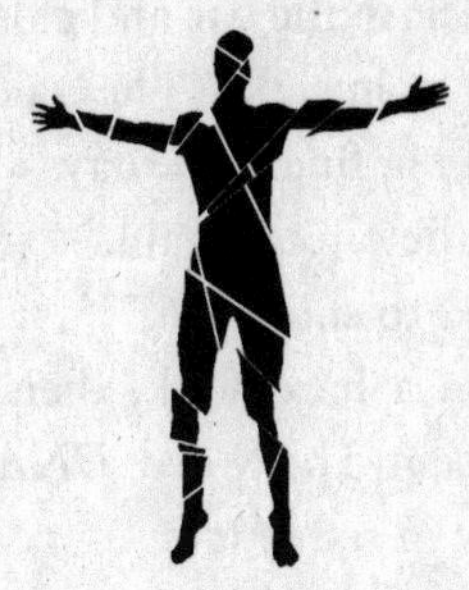

THE RACCOON

He visited the SCS two or three times a week, usually to mooch around and pick up gossip and have lunch with Wendy or one of the other scientists and techs he'd managed to strike up a friendship with. He couldn't have said, hand on heart, that he had established an easy relationship with the contractors who guarded the Facility, but he was at least a familiar face. Usually all that was required was a quick scan of his phone and he was waved through the gates. Usually.

"Your authorisation has been withdrawn, sir," said the guard, who, like all the guards, wore no name tag.

"I'm sorry?"

The guard consulted his pad and scanned Alex's phone again. "Your authorisation has been withdrawn."

Alex thought about it. "Nah, that doesn't make any sense." He started to open the door. "Let me have a—"

"Please remain in the vehicle, sir," said the guard.

Alex put one foot on the ground. "Don't be—"

The guard took a step back. "Please remain in the vehicle, sir." His hand hovered over his belt, either near the pepper spray or the taser, it was hard to be sure. At least he wasn't reaching for his pistol. Alex got back in the car and closed the door.

"There's got to be a mistake," he said through the open window. "It was working fine yesterday."

The guard scanned the phone again.

"And there's no need to shoot me."

The guard gave him a hard look, then held up the pad so he could see the screen. The word *UNAUTHORIZED* was displayed prominently in red letters.

Alex sighed. "Call Professor Delahaye. He'll sort this out. It'll just be a glitch somewhere."

"It says your authorisation was withdrawn at Professor Delahaye's request, sir," the guard told him.

Alex squinted at the screen, saw a tiny four-digit serial number under the much larger *UNAUTHORIZED*. "You utter bastard," he muttered under his breath.

"I have to ask you to leave, sir," said the guard. "Please vacate the area."

It occurred to Alex to make a Thing about this, but life was too short to be spent annoying armed humourless men, so he started the car up, reversed back onto the road, and drove into town.

It turned out that the phone not only no longer worked to let him into the Facility, it no longer even worked as a phone. Its contact book and call logs were blank, and he couldn't raise a dialling tone. He sat in the Telegraph with a cup of coffee and a doughnut and poked at the phone. He tried turning it off and back on again. He took the battery out and replaced it. Nothing.

"You look like a man with a problem," said Dru Winslow, sliding into the seat opposite.

"Quite possibly," he said.

"Anything I can help with?"

"Probably not." He put the phone down beside his plate. "But thanks for offering. How've you been?"

"Me? Fine." She ordered a coffee and a chicken salad.

"Actually, I'm glad I've seen you. I've been meaning to pop in."

She raised an eyebrow.

"Did you ever know the Shanahans? The people who used to live in my house?"

Dru shook her head. "I don't get over to East Walden much. No reason to go there. Unless you live there. Something wrong?"

"Don't know." He looked around the diner. The lunch crowd had been and gone and the place was nearly empty. "When I first came here last year, Ralph Ortiz and Chief Rosewater said something about a prowler."

She snorted. "You mean the angel."

"I'm sorry?"

Dru settled herself in her seat and clasped her hands on the tabletop in front of her. "For a few weeks towards the end of last summer, we had a bunch of sightings of an unidentified guy hanging round town. Didn't seem to be doing any harm, just wandering across people's property, standing in their backyards, not really doing much of anything. We all figured it was some drifter, lost his job and his home and his family somewhere and he was just looking for a place to rest for a spell."

The people of Sioux Crossing sounded very understanding. "I sort of lost track of the story," he said. "Did they ever catch him?"

She shook her head. "Nah. Nobody even managed to get a good look at him apart from Walt Brooker." She saw the look on his face. "No, you can't speak with him. Walt passed just after Christmas."

"I'm sorry."

Dru shrugged. "I didn't know him that well. He wasn't local. His dad was some kind of small-time preacher, had himself one of those cable television channels back in the nineties." She looked off into the distance. "In Macon, if I remember rightly. Anyway, there was some kind of scandal and his dad went to jail and Walt and his mom made a run for it and wound up here. She was..." She looked into the distance again. "Jessica must have been, wow, she must have been in her nineties when they arrived. Walt was sixty-something. Bought a place south of town, didn't mix much. Wanted to keep their heads down, I guess. Jessica died a couple of years later and then it was just Walter on his own. Didn't even have a dog."

"And he died after he saw the prowler."

She looked at him for a moment. "It wasn't that that killed him; he died months later. Walt weighed more than three hundred pounds; he had a massive heart attack. Died on the toilet."

"Oh."

Rhoda delivered Dru's salad and coffee and went back to the counter. Dru unwrapped her knife and fork from their napkin. "So where was I? Oh, yeah. Right. Anyway, Walt was the only person who ever got a good look at the prowler. Everyone else saw them from a distance, but Walt said they were in his house."

Alex thought about a massively obese senior citizen suddenly finding a stranger in their home and wondered if it hadn't, in fact, had something to do with Walt Booker's death after all, but he kept his mouth shut and let Dru tell the story.

"I went out there and interviewed Walt for the *Banner* a couple of days after it happened," she said. "I could describe what shape the house was in, but I won't, although I will mention that Walt's personal hygiene was on the poor side. He said he'd been to his kitchen for something and when he went back into the living room there was someone just standing there in the middle of the floor."

"That must have been quite a shock."

"You would think that, wouldn't you?" She put a spoonful of sugar in her coffee and stirred slowly. "But Walt was happy." She thought about it. "No, actually, he looked *radiant*. He was just a big harmless kid, really, maybe not all that smart. I guess his folks never really let him grow up. But he was... beatific." She raised her eyebrows and tried her coffee. "I couldn't figure it out, so I asked him. 'Most people would have been scared witless if they found an intruder in their living room,' I said. And he just *beamed* at me and said, 'That weren't no intruder, Miss Drusilla. It was an *angel*.'" She nodded and sipped some more coffee.

Alex thought about it. "Okay," he said.

"I thought about that a lot, after he passed," she said. "Walt told his neighbour that his dad once felt the Voice of the Lord move through him. But Walt went to his reward believing he'd actually met an angel in his living room."

Alex picked up his doughnut and tore off a piece. "Did he happen to mention," he said casually, "static?"

Dru tipped her head to one side and gave him a look of such calmly intense interest that it was quite scary.

"Pam Shanahan says she saw an intruder in her kitchen. My kitchen." He popped the bit of doughnut into his mouth, chewed, and swallowed. "She didn't think it was an angel, but she did say there was static."

Dru sat back. "Well... shit," she said.

"That was the reason they left in such a hurry," he said. "Conventional wisdom is that she was off her face on painkillers or something at the time."

Dru shook her head. "Walt never touched a harmful substance in his life. Unless you count Twinkies." She sat forward again. "He said everything in his living room was 'sparky'. I thought he meant the Holy Spirit or something. I didn't think he meant *literally* sparky."

"I've had a couple of sparky moments myself, since I got here." He looked at the phone. Either it was dead or it wasn't, and if it wasn't it was probably relaying every word of this conversation, and he was fast approaching the point where he didn't care any more.

"Where's Pam now?"

"Her husband's dying, Dru." He realised they were speaking very quietly by now. "She wouldn't thank you for going up there."

"You think this is something to do with the SCS."

"I don't see how it can be. Colliders don't do that. It's not a black hole machine. And besides, it was out of action most of last year; they couldn't get the magnets working properly."

"But you think *something's* going on."

"I think maybe someone's not been telling me all the bits of the story," he said. He picked up the phone. "Unfortunately, I seem to have been fired."

"IT'S DELAHAYE," SAID Wendy. "He's *really* pissed with you."

"That's hardly news," said Alex. They were sitting at the island in his kitchen, eating omelettes. He'd never bothered to memorise any of the numbers on the phone—who did, any more? They were all on the phone to start with—so he'd had to use Ralph's phone to call her. She'd made the old man put her number on his speed-dial list in case there was an emergency when Alex wasn't about.

"He's read your book."

"No he hasn't. *Nobody*'s read it yet."

"I've read it too," she said, popping a forkfull of omelette in her mouth. "We all have."

He stared at her.

"It turned up in our inboxes this morning," she told him. "Not a book; more a quarter of a book and about a quarter of a million words of notes."

He felt a cold sensation in his chest. "Could I see, please?"

"Sure." She reached down into her bag, took out her pad, poked at its screen for a few seconds, then handed it over, and he found himself reading his own notes, the ones that were supposed to be safe and secure on his laptop.

"Bollocks," he said.

"I tried to call you when it happened," she said, "but your phone wasn't working. I didn't realise Delahaye had done that, the vindictive little shit. Why aren't *I* in there?"

"This isn't funny."

"You've got notes about Delahaye and Clayton and Larry and Bud and about two thirds of the staff, but nothing about me." She pouted theatrically. "That kind of thing can hurt a girl, you know?"

"It's not funny," he said again.

She wrinkled her nose. "Is a bit."

He opened his mouth to say something, but there was a knock at the door. "Excuse me a second."

Mickey Olive was standing out on the porch, a wry look on his face. "Oh god," said Alex. "Not you too."

"Afraid so, old son," said Mickey. "Could you pack an overnight bag and come with me? Stan wants a word."

Alex looked past Mickey's shoulder. Another of the seemingly limitless fleet of brand new silver-grey SUVs was sitting at the bottom of his drive. Glancing to his right, he saw Ralph's curtains twitch in a way which had not been caused by a stray breeze. "Fine," he said. "Give me a minute."

"I'll wait in the car," Mickey said amiably.

Back in the kitchen, Wendy raised an eyebrow.

"I've been summoned to the Mother Ship," Alex said.

Wendy's eyes widened. "Jesus," she said. "You think *Clayton* was in on the mass-mailing?"

"Oh, I'd put money on it." Not that he was going to have money for much longer. He gave her the keys to the house. "Can you lock up after I've gone?"

"Sure."

"And look in on Ralph while you're here," he said, heading for the stairs. "Leave the keys with him. I should be back tomorrow, but if I'm not I'll try to let you know."

"Right." She thought a moment, then called down the hallway, "Hey, do you want me to come with you?"

"No," he called back. "I've been bawled out by editors before. I'll be fine."

HE'D EXPECTED SAN Francisco, but what he got was Chicago, a fast two-hour flight in the corporate jet, barely time for sandwiches and coffee. Mickey made small talk for a while, then lost interest and sat staring out of the window as the Midwest passed by far below.

Lin was waiting for them at O'Hare, drove them downtown to the Four Seasons. Alex had an impression of an impossibly tall monolith of creamy grey stone, then he was being ushered inside gently but efficiently by Mickey.

The penthouse was an extraordinary space, complete with a grand staircase that looked as if it belonged in a theatre rather than someone's flat. The view out over the city and the lake was the kind of thing a person could become physically addicted to.

"So," said Stan. "I read your book."

"You weren't supposed to see it yet," Alex said. "It's not finished. Someone hacked my laptop."

Stan pouted. Today he was dressed to kill. Suit worth almost as much as Alex's old flat, crisp white shirt, Harvard tie, diamond tiepin, Oxfords buffed to a high shine. The costume of a man who was visiting old money or a firm of attorneys which had once represented Theodore Roosevelt. He said, "I think it's pretty good, actually."

"You do?"

"For something that isn't finished yet, yes. I am a little disappointed with that, but you work at your own pace, I guess." He sat back in his chair and crossed his legs. "But you nailed the *sensawunda*, and that makes me happy."

"I haven't made Delahaye happy. He withdrew all my access."

Stan guffawed. "I don't blame him. Why did you have to actually *write down* those things about him?"

"They're only notes. Just to nudge my memory."

Stan subsided. "Yeah. Yeah, I had him on the phone this morning, about fifteen minutes after your stuff hit the intranet—and it was only the project intranet, which was fortunate, otherwise pirate sites in Uzbekistan would be selling ebook copies of your *notes* right now. Paul wants you off the project. Says he'll walk if I don't fire you."

Alex found himself grinding his teeth.

"So," Stan said. "If I fire you I'll lose what's shaping up to be *exactly* what I want. And if I don't, I'll lose Paul, who in spite of—or possibly even *because of*—being an Olympic-level asshole, is actually very very good at his job and will be hard to replace. What would you do?"

"I quit," said Alex.

Stan's face fell. "Aw, don't be like that. What about the book?"

"You've got my notes. Get someone else to finish it."

Stan looked at him for a long time without speaking. "Here's what I'm going to do. I'm going to fire you, which will satisfy Paul, and then I'm going to retain you on a freelance basis, same terms as before, so you can finish the book. Where you choose to do that is entirely up to you. You could stay in the house, you could go back to Boston. Hell, you could even go home to Scotland. I won't restore your access to the Facility, but what I *can* do is issue you a phone with a sockpuppet ID, on condition that you use it very *very* sparingly."

"That'll never work. Someone will tell Delahaye."

"Well, I'll leave you to work out the nuts and bolts. As far as Paul's concerned, you're just sitting in your house finishing the book. How about it?"

It occurred to Alex to demand that the listening devices be removed from the house, but it was pointless. He'd only ever have Stan's word that they were all gone. He said, "Delahaye's never going to go for this."

"Yes, but you have to keep three things in mind about Paul. One, he wants you off-site. Two, he wants you punished for the things you said about him. And three, he's never going to get another job like this anywhere else. It's not ideal, but you get to finish the book and Paul gets to think he's fucked you over." He smiled. "Come on, Alex. The restaurant in this place is *outstanding*. Let's wrap this up and we can go and eat."

Alex thought about it. "Well," he said.

"So," Stan said crisply. "The next thing is, I'd like to find out who hacked your laptop and leaked the book."

"I'll take care of that."

"This *is* a tech company, Alex," Stan reminded him. "I have people who are very good at that sort of thing."

Alex shook his head. "Nobody touches that laptop but me. I'll sort it out."

"Okay. But if you need support, you'll let me know."

"If I do."

"If you do." Stan sat forward. "So, do we have a deal?"

"There may be other stuff I'll need, further on down the road."

"Anything you want. Within reason."

"Not good enough, if you're deciding what's within reason or not."

Stan looked at him. "Okay, Alex. Just don't ask me to sign the company over to you."

"All right."

Stan grinned and put his hand out. "You're fired," he said. "Welcome to the family."

And as if by magic, Mickey appeared from one of the many other rooms in the apartment, bearing another thousand-page contract.

* * *

The obvious suspect for hacking his laptop was Delahaye. He was desperate to see what Alex had written about him, which gave him motive, and Alex used his laptop a lot at the SCS, sitting in the commissary transcribing notes or fighting a losing battle against spam emails, which gave him opportunity. He had a bunch of sycophants at the Facility, and it wouldn't have taken much to get one of his flying monkeys to do the deed for him.

But.

"There's someone new at the Facility," Alex said. "I've seen him a couple of times, from a distance, so he's not just visiting for the day." There were always new faces at the SCS, people dropping in for a few days to help out on some project or another.

"Did you get a good enough look to describe him?" Kitson asked.

Alex looked around his backyard, located an old log near the edge of the woods, and went over to sit down. "Indian or Pakistani, mid fifties, greying hair, little goatee beard," he said. "About your height but a couple of stone heavier. *Very* nattily dressed. Grey pinstripe suit."

There was a silence at the other end of the line, as Kitson jotted all this down. "What was he doing?"

"The first time I saw him, he was in a corridor chatting to Delahaye. They spotted me and Delahaye hustled him away. The second time he was down in the tunnel with a bunch of the particle scientists and one of the people I saw with General Bell that time."

Another silence. "Okay. Could you get a wee *snapshot* of our mystery man, do you think?"

"I didn't agree to take happy snaps for you, Kitson."

"You agreed to do as you're told," Kitson told him crisply, but Alex could hear a thin edge of excitement in his voice.

"If I get the chance," Alex said unwillingly.

"Good. See if you can pick up any gossip about this chap, some bona fides perhaps. And call me if you see him again." He hung up.

Alex looked around the backyard again, and this time saw something half hidden in some bushes. He got up and walked over to it.

There was actually an Indian high-energy physicist called N.N. 'Tony' Narayan, who had briefly become notorious a couple of years ago for hawking around something he called a *Meson Gun*, which he claimed could knock down supersonic aircraft at a distance of several hundred miles. Chubby chap with a beard and a taste for good suits. His claims had been mostly debunked, except on the wilder edges of military-industrial conspiracy theory, and he'd dropped out of sight, some said to work on particle beam weapons for the Russians. He was not, as far as Alex knew, at the SCS, or indeed anywhere near Iowa.

The object in the bushes was covered with a green plastic tarpaulin, which was probably why he hadn't noticed it before. He gathered a double handful and pulled the tarpaulin up and off, and found himself looking at a medium-sized gas barbecue.

He had no evidence that Kitson was responsible for hacking his laptop and releasing his notes—although Wendy had asked one of her nerdier colleagues to have a look at it on the quiet—but it was just the kind of thing he thought Kitson would do, out of nothing more complicated than spite, for turning up at the consulate in Minneapolis. That it had almost got Alex thrown out of the SCS altogether probably never crossed his mind.

Anyway, let him obsess over Tony Narayan for a while. It would give Alex some time to work out some other bullshit to feed him. And if it did turn out that Delahaye had been responsible, well, it wasn't time wasted. He'd had enough of Kitson.

The barbecue looked almost brand new, considering it had been out here in the worst winter the area had ever seen. In fact, it looked as if it had never been used. It looked as if it had been delivered, then just wheeled into the bushes, covered up, and abandoned. There was no gas bottle attached. He fiddled with the knobs for a while, thinking, then he went back into the house.

* * *

As far as Stan was concerned, Alex's status was unchanged—he was, after all, still working on the book—but for Alex everything felt different. There was the period Before Email Fiasco, and there was the period After Email Fiasco, and he was definitely living in post-EF times. He spent most of his time at home, picking away at the book. Most evenings, he went over to Ralph's and cooked dinner—it was a way of making sure the old man ate at least one healthy meal—and in return received sound thrashings at chess. He'd managed to get his survival time up to twenty minutes, but he thought that was more because he was taking more time thinking about his moves than because his game was improving.

A new phone had been delivered by Mickey Olive, who seemed to think the whole business was amusing in some distant esoteric and lawyerly fashion, but Alex hadn't been back to the SCS since his flying visit to Chicago. BEF, he'd had quite a long wish list of interviews still to complete. Now, AEF, it was going to be trickier. Wendy had managed to get round his supposed exile from the Facility by getting some of the subjects to come out to the house and do the interviews there. Two of them had managed to get lost trying to find East Walden Lane, and he suspected several more had done the same but were embarrassed to admit it.

Once a week, he drove into town for groceries and lunch with Dru Winslow, who was working her way through back copies of the *Banner* looking for stories of paranormal activity or static electricity. It was a long job—only the past five years or so of the archive were in digital form; the rest was in thick, bound volumes in a back room, shelf after shelf of them.

One afternoon, he got back from Sioux Crossing, parked in front of the house, opened the back of the car to get his shopping out, and only then noticed something hanging on one of the supports of the porch. He stood looking at it, head tipped to one side, trying to work out what it was. It looked, he thought, like a teddy bear.

He left the car open and walked up the drive, but he it was only when he was a few feet from the object that he realised it wasn't a teddy bear at all.

"WELL," SAID BUD. "I've not seen *that* before."

"No?"

Bud shook his head. "Nope. This is a new one to me."

They were standing by the porch, looking at the raccoon which had been nailed to the post which supported the porch roof. There was a long metal spike protruding from the raccoon's right eye; it had been driven through the back of its skull and into the wood of the support.

"That there is an old-style railroad spike," Bud said.

"Do you think that's significant?" asked Alex.

Bud shrugged. "And it wasn't here when you went out?"

"I'd have noticed."

"Anyone see anything?"

"Ralph was having a nap; the house could have blown up and he wouldn't have heard it. I haven't had a chance to talk to the other neighbours."

"Mm hm." East Walden's peculiar legal status meant it sat outside, in normal circumstances, the jurisdiction of the Sioux Crossing Police Department, but Bud was the first person Alex had been able to think of to call and he seemed unwilling to hand this off to the County Sheriff. "Well, do *you* have any idea who could have done this? Anyone got a beef with you over something?"

There were a couple of names Alex could mention, but he said, "Not that I can think of, no."

Bud looked up and down the shallow curve of East Walden

Lane and nodded to himself. "It's quite a thing to do in broad daylight, when you think about it," he said. "This isn't exactly Broadway, but someone could have come out of their house and seen what was going on. You'd have to be really confident to do something like that, or really angry."

"Neither of those possibilities is filling me with joy, if I'm honest with you."

"I'll have somebody come out and recover it. Maybe we can get some forensics off it."

"You can dust a raccoon for fingerprints?"

"We can certainly dust the spike. Also, you don't see spikes like that very often nowadays, not outside of museums anyway."

"You seem to know a suspicious amount about railroad spikes, if you don't mind me saying."

"My mom's grandfather worked on the Union Pacific for a while," he said. "He left her a whole bunch of junk, including some spikes. I've still got them somewhere."

"I'd say that makes you the prime suspect, then."

Bud looked at him. "You sure you don't have an idea who might have done this?"

Alex shook his head.

"You've not had anything else? Crank emails? People phoning you and then not saying anything? Hate mail?"

"I haven't had *any* mail."

"You'll let me know, if anything else happens."

"You'll be the first person to know, trust me." Alex looked at the raccoon, a horrible thought occurring to him. "You don't think it was alive when that happened, do you?"

Bud grunted. "Nah. You tried to do that to a live raccoon, you'd end up losing your face."

"Did anything like this happen to the Shanahans?"

Bud raised an eyebrow. "The Shanahans? Why do you ask?"

"Maybe whoever did it doesn't know they've moved."

"I think anyone who would take the trouble to nail a raccoon to someone's porch would make sure the right people were still living there." Bud turned and started to walk back down the path to his truck. Alex followed. "Good thought, but Vern and Pam never reported anything. I think the only time I ever spoke to them was when Ralph said their kids shot his dog."

"Did they? Shoot Homer?"

Bud shrugged. "They didn't seem the type. Quiet kids. Vern said they didn't even have a gun. There was a mark on the dog's back leg, but I couldn't tell what made it. You could barely even see it, to be honest."

"You think Ralph made it up?"

"Now *that* sounds more in character." They reached the truck and Bud opened the driver's door. "No way to prove it, though. And then they moved out anyway."

"In quite a hurry."

Bud looked at him. "Who told you that?"

"One of the neighbours." Alex waved vaguely down the street. "One of the Abrahamsons, I think."

Bud shook his head. "They'd been gone a couple of weeks before I even heard they'd left. Pam was ill, I heard. They wanted to be closer to her folks." He climbed into the truck. "This is a small town, Alex," he said. "Small town gossip is the worst kind of gossip; maybe best to take it with a pinch of salt."

"I'm a journalist. We love gossip."

Bud glanced past him, up the slope of the lawn, to the raccoon nailed to the porch. "I'll have someone come out for that in an hour or so," he said.

"Okay. Thanks."

"And let me know if anything else happens."

"Will do."

Alex watched Bud drive off, then he walked back up to the house. Inside, he went down to the basement and unlocked the gun cabinet. He stood looking at the guns for a while, then he locked the cabinet again and went back upstairs.

* * *

Towards the end of spring, the book stalled again, at just over fifty-seven thousand words, and he sat staring at the screen for days on end. He'd solved the problem of hacking by buying a new laptop from Amazon—the courier had got so lost trying to find East Walden Lane that he'd retreated to the New Rose and phoned Alex to beg him to come and collect it from him—and doing some research online. Then he'd gone into town and bought a bunch of tools from Stu's Radio Shack, where Stu seemed serenely unconcerned about the possibilities of trade-name violation. Back home and following a YouTube tutorial on his phone, Alex had opened up the new laptop, removed the machine's wireless card, wrapped it in tinfoil, and dumped it in the trash. The thing with the tinfoil was more symbolic than anything else, more a manifestation of his state of mind at the moment.

The laptop was now isolated from wi-fi and remote hacking. To keep it secure, he bought a safe from Stockmann. The safe was the size of an old-style television and weighed more than the sun; it took three of Stockmann's delivery men to get it down the stairs into the basement, where it would probably have to remain for the rest of human history because no lifting machinery known to Man would ever get it out again. If he put the new laptop in it diagonally, it just fitted. He copied his files onto a couple of memory sticks and let Wendy's nerdy friend pronounce them clean of any infection, then transferred them over. He kept the memory sticks in the safe, just in case.

All of which was jolly fun, and he learned more than he probably would ever need to know about the inner workings of the average laptop, but it didn't help the book along. He wandered around the house indulging in displacement behaviour, which had helped in times past but didn't help this time. He dusted and tidied, took apart the litter box he'd built for Homer and stacked the pieces in the basement, just in case. He went back to Stockmann, the eyes of whose staff now lit up the moment he walked through the front doors—and bought paint and brushes and some other bits and pieces, and one week he sanded and painted the front porch, somewhere in the back of his mind erasing the ghostly presence of the dead raccoon. Ralph came out, now and again, with helpful decorating tips and the occasional bottle of beer.

And again, all this was jolly fun, but he couldn't say he was making any progress with the book, unless you counted one evening where he spent two hours adding and removing a single comma. A couple of times, he stopped himself on the edge of getting in the Accord and driving over to the Facility and seeing if his sockpuppet ID actually worked.

The garden offered less scope for displacement activity. Firstly, he had spent an appreciable percentage of his life avoiding gardening, and he wasn't quite desperate enough yet to break that habit, and secondly there was very little to do. Someone came to tend the backyard and mow the lawns, but they always turned up when he was out and he could never detect any trace of their presence. He suspected he was subject to the visitations of elves or ents or something. He wandered around the garden anyway, looking for things that looked like weeds and pulling them up, and one day he approached the barbecue and took its cover off again and he stood looking at it, thinking.

"Do your people even barbecue?" Ralph asked.

"'Your people'?"

"Scottish people."

"I'll have you know that at the first sign of spring sunshine the smell of burning meat hangs heavy over the back gardens of Kirkaldy," Alex told him. "Sound systems are moved outside. Pallid, pasty legs are exposed to light for the first time since the previous summer. Much beer is drunk. Do my people barbecue? Pft."

"Remarkable," said Ralph. "Is there footage of this?"

"Oh God, yes. Just google it."

"I can't remember anyone *ever* having a barbecue out here," Ralph said thoughtfully. "I didn't even know Vern and Pam had that thing."

"I'll have to invite the neighbours. Can you bear not to insult anyone for an afternoon?"

"I'm not going to make any promises I can't keep. Check."

Alex moved his king, exposing his bishop. "Well, can you bear not to *speak* to anyone for an afternoon?"

"There's always body language." Ralph brought one of his knights round in preparation for a pincer movement.

Alex moved his rook. "Maybe we can sit you in a box and feed you through a slot in the side. Check."

Ralph sat back and looked at the board, a slow smile coming over his face. "You bastard," he said. "I never saw that coming."

"No?"

Ralph shook his head. "Not for a moment. Well done." He moved his queen one square. "Mate."

Alex sighed. "Definitely put you in a box," he said.

He started in the morning by putting two dozen chicken drumsticks, six at a time, into a plastic freezer bag, pouring marinade on top of them, and jiggling them about until they were coated, then putting them in the oven. By the time he'd done that, two deliverymen from Stockmann had arrived with a pair of big folding tables and two sets of garden furniture, which the store had rented to him on the understanding that he would buy anything that got broken.

He spent an hour or so arranging the furniture and putting up a couple of big umbrellas and making sure they were properly weighted down. Then he dragged the barbecue out of the bushes and took the racks into the kitchen for a wash.

Opening the fridge, he was confronted with a solid wall of meat. Trays of steaks, sausages, lamb chops, ribs, burgers. It occurred to him that he might have overdone things a bit. There was a box the size of a chest freezer in the hall, full of burger buns and hot dog rolls and loaves. Several catering-size bottles of ketchup and mustard, and, flying the flag, a single bottle of HP Sauce, bought from the Cost Plus in Mason City. There was a bucket, a literal plastic bucket, of barbecue sauce on the back porch.

"You've only ever seen American barbecues in the movies, haven't you," Wendy said.

Struggling to connect a gas bottle to the barbecue, Alex said, "I could really use a hand here."

She laughed. "I'm going to go visit with Ralph for a while. See you later."

He'd managed to get the barbecue lit by the time the first guests arrived, Rob Chen from the SCS, along with his wife and their two little girls. Conscious of East Walden Lane's stealth status, Alex had printed out maps and GPS coordinates for the non-locals, but he suspected a percentage of the guests would still be wandering hopelessly around the countryside come nightfall. He fixed Rob and his wife up with beers, and the girls with juice, and put some food on the grill.

People began to drift in over the next hour or so. Almost everyone brought food and drink with them. The neighbours brought home made pies and then stood in a group by the house, drinking beer and wine and watching the scientists and techs. Dru Winslow turned up with a bucket of home made potato salad. Officer Muñoz and his girlfriend, who turned out to be Wendy's nerdy computer friend from the SCS, brought catering-size tubs of ice cream. Smoke and the sound of conversation and the smell of cooking meat hung over the garden. There were about a dozen kids running about and crashing through the woods and dropping bits of food all over the grass. At one point, a dimming of the sun announced the arrival of Bud

Rosewater and his family with a truck full of beer.

"Lot of folks turned up," Bud commented, coming to stand beside Alex at the barbecue.

Alex looked around the garden. At a guess, there were forty or so people here. "They're not mixing much," he said.

Bud took a drink of beer. "A lot of the townsfolk are related to each other, one way or another, so this is basically a family gathering," he said, raising his bottle in salute to Muñoz, who was chatting to the people from two houses down the Lane. "They've got gossip to catch up on. Give them time. Can I give you a hand?"

Alex was sweaty and stank of smoke, and barbecue sauce coated his arms up to the elbows and was splashed on his jeans and tee shirt. He rubbed his smoke-stinging eyes. "I think the worst's over, for now. Everyone seems to have something to eat. Did you get anywhere with the raccoon?"

Bud looked at him. "I wasn't planning on talking shop today."

"Sorry."

Bud thought about it. "Nah, you're right, I should have been in touch. No, we haven't got anywhere with the raccoon yet. No prints on the spike, no real leads on where it might have come from, none of your neighbours saw or heard anything."

"I know; I asked them myself."

"I figure whoever it was came in through there," he said, nodding at the woods at the end of the garden. "Then round the side of the house to the front. That way they could have snuck in unobserved. From the other side, they could have come in over the fields and through the trees, but then they'd have to cross the green in full view of every house on the street."

Alex looked at the trees. "Blackfish Road's on the other side, isn't it?"

Bud nodded. "About a mile."

"So whoever it was knew the way through the woods to here."

"Now, Alex," Bud said in a disappointed voice. "Don't jump

to conclusions. Sure, it could be somebody local. Equally, it could be someone from out of town who did a lot of reconnaissance."

So it could be someone he might have stood next to at the counter in the Telegraph, or it was someone who had stalked him for some time, scoping out where he lived. He couldn't decide which was worse.

"So, not a prank."

"We've not entirely ruled that out, but with a prank you'd expect it to have been done at night, when the chances of being seen were lowest. This was something different."

Kitson had crossed Alex's mind, but it was a long drive from Minneapolis to nail a dead raccoon to someone's house, and it didn't seem his style. And anyway, assuming he'd released Alex's notes, he'd made his point. If it turned out he wasn't responsible for that, well, it was still a long way to come to nail up a dead raccoon.

He said, "Well, anyway," and he felt something tugging at his jeans, somewhere down around his knee. He looked down and saw a little girl standing next to him, one of the Chens' daughters, he thought. He smiled at her and said, "And what can we get you? Hot dog? Some juice, maybe?"

The little girl—she couldn't have been much more than five or six—put her thumb in her mouth and tugged his jeans again. Then she half turned and very solemnly pointed at the house.

Alex looked, and for a moment he couldn't see what she was pointing at. Then he noticed a wisp of what looked like smoke curling from the edge of one of the little horizontal windows that ran along the base of the house and let a little daylight into the basement. As he watched, the wisp became denser and he thought he saw something orange-yellow flickering behind the dirty glass of the window.

"Oh, what?" he said quietly.

Bud looked and saw it too. "Is there anyone in the house?" he said.

"I don't know." Alex started to move. The front door was shut, but he'd left the kitchen door open so people could put gifts of food on the worktops or use the toilet.

"Alex," said Bud, who had somehow telepathically summoned Muñoz to his side, "maybe let us handle it, okay?" But Alex was already at the kitchen door.

Inside, he could smell smoke, not barbecue smoke but something more acrid. Outside, he could hear Bud calling in a calm voice of authority, "Folks, could I have your attention? Folks? It looks like we might have a little situation here, so I'm going to ask you all to gather out on the far side of the green. No need to panic, but could you please move now?"

Alex went down the hallway and reached for the handle of the door to the basement, and as his fingers brushed the metal he felt rather than heard an electric *snap* and snatched his hand back. He reached out again and tapped the handle, but nothing happened, and he took hold of it and turned it.

Before he could open the door, someone stepped up beside him and put their hand on it. "Sir," Muñoz said calmly, "please don't do that."

They exchanged a look, then Alex let go of the handle and put his hand flat on the door. It was hot. "Fuck," he said.

"Please leave the building, sir," Muñoz said.

Alex took his hand off the door and headed down the hall towards the stairs. "Check there's nobody down here," he said. "I'll do upstairs."

There was nobody in the upstairs bathroom, or in his bedroom, or the bedroom he used as a study. The smell of smoke was stronger now, and there was a smell of electricity in the air too, almost as if a thunderstorm was gathering in the house. Downstairs, he could hear Muñoz shouting, but he couldn't make out the words.

He opened the door to the third bedroom and stopped dead in the doorway.

The room was full of sparks. They covered the walls and the floor and the furniture and danced in the air, and they outlined the figure standing in the middle of the room.

Alex said, "Hey," and the word barely made it past his lips.

The figure was hard to see, somehow, not blurred so much as hard to *understand*. It seemed to be male, and wearing dark clothing. It turned and Alex could see that it had no face. Or rather, it had *all* faces, a montage of human and animal faces that cycled almost too fast to resolve.

The last thought that went through Alex's mind before his knees gave way was, *So that's what Walt Booker meant*. Then Muñoz, who was considerably stronger than he looked, had him in a fireman's carry and was heading down the stairs and out the front door.

When his head cleared, he found himself sitting on the grass on the far side of the green, among the crowd of barbecue guests. On the other side, Bud and Muñoz were organising people to move their cars off the street so the emergency services could have access, and some vehicles had already been driven onto the grass. Smoke was pouring out of the open front door of the house.

"Fuck," Alex said again.

Wendy knelt down beside him. "Hey," she said. "You okay?"

"Yes," he said, confused. "I saw—" and then there was a *thud* that he felt through the ground and the house seemed to slump, almost disappointedly. He heard glass breaking and walls cracking.

"That'll be the furnace," he heard Ralph say, behind him.

EVERYONE WOUND UP, temporarily, at the New Rose Hotel. Bud and his men took statements and then rides were organised to take people home. Which left the residents of East Walden Lane sitting in the Prairie Dining Room drinking coffee and talking in low voices and occasionally casting angry looks in Alex's direction.

"You should have told me there were firearms and ammunition on the property," Bud said.

"I've had a lot on my mind," Alex told him. "The Shanahans left them behind."

"I don't care whose they were; you should have told me."

Rosewater County's emergency services, firetrucks and paramedics and police and Sheriff's Department, had all arrived more or less simultaneously within about ten minutes of being alerted, and had then been forced to hang back while they listened to the ammunition in the gun safe cooking off and flames licked out of the ground floor windows.

"Okay," Alex said, feeling beaten. "I'm sorry."

Bud looked at him, judged that he had been bawled out enough, and his expression softened. "How are you feeling?"

He nodded. "I'm fine. What state's the house in?" Bud and Muñoz had stayed behind when everyone else was ferried into town.

"Well, the fire's out. There's a crew still out there, damping down. The propane tank didn't go up, for a miracle."

"That's something, anyway." He watched Homer wandering around the dining room, sniffing at all the new things and pestering people for ear scritches. Ralph had refused to leave his house without him.

"Nobody's going to be living there for a while, though."

"Was anyone hurt?"

"One of your neighbours turned his ankle, out on the green, but apart from that everyone's accounted for and safe and sound."

"That's good," Alex said tiredly. "That's the main thing." Across the dining room, he saw Danny Hofstadter, newly reelected Mayor, chatting with a few of the neighbours. What Alex really wanted to do was talk to Dru about what he'd seen upstairs in the house, but after gathering a few quotes she'd headed for the *Banner* offices to write up the story.

"That was quite a brave thing to do, going into the house like that," Bud said.

"I wasn't thinking," Alex said. "Could you say thank you to Officer Muñoz for getting me out of there?"

"I'll do that. But, Alex? The line between brave and stupid is sometimes really *really* thin."

"He gets it, Bud," said Wendy, who was sitting on the other side of Alex.

Danny came over, shook hands with Bud, and looked down at Alex. "Hey," he said, "how are you doing?"

"I'm okay, thanks, Danny," Alex said. "Nobody was hurt, that's the main thing."

Danny looked at them, then back at Alex. "Look, I want you to stay here, okay? On the house. Until things shake out and you know what's going to happen."

Alex looked blankly at him. "Thank you, Danny."

Danny grinned. "We can't put you in the Presidential Suite again because we've got someone coming through in a couple of days, but we'll make sure you're comfortable."

"Okay." Alex nodded.

"Okay," said Danny. "I have to take care of something, but I'll speak with you soon."

"Right."

As Danny walked away, Bud said, "Folks round here are pretty good, generally. We'll look after you." Alex burst into tears.

THE CORNER ROOM they put him in, on the third floor, was smaller than the Presidential Suite, but only in the sense that it was possible to trek from one side of it to the other without stocking up on a couple of days' food and water. It was still at least twice the size of his old apartment. It was on the other side of the hotel, and from its big windows he could just see, in the far distance, the top floor of the main building of the SCS poking up above the trees.

The first evening, when everything got too much for him, he left everyone downstairs in the dining room and went up to the room and had a long hot shower. A remarkable amount of grime pooled around his feet and went down the plughole.

His clothes were filthy. He wrapped himself in one of the hotel's fluffy blue towelling robes and lay on the bed, exhausted. He was just drifting off to sleep when there was a knock on the door. When he answered it there was nobody there, but on the floor outside were two plastic carrier bags full of clothes, a couple of pairs of jeans, underwear, tee shirts, sweatshirts, and a couple of hoodies, and he almost broke down again.

Mickey Olive turned up a few minutes later, all efficient and concerned. "Sorry I wasn't here earlier, old son," he said. "I only just heard what happened." The fact that he hadn't been invited to the barbecue was not mentioned. "Is there anything you need?"

"I think I could do with going to sleep, Mickey," Alex told him. "I've had a day."

"Of course. Do you have your phone?"

Alex shook his head. "In the house." One of the hotel staff had let him into the room with a passkey.

"Right." Mickey took a phone from his pocket and handed it over. "I brought this one, just in case. I'll pop round tomorrow, see how you are, but in the meantime if you do need anything, give me a call. All right?"

"Sure. Thanks, Mickey."

"Do you know how it started?"

Alex shook his head. "I had some trouble with the furnace when I first moved in, but I got that fixed. I don't know."

"Right. Well, get some rest and I'll see you tomorrow. And don't worry about anything."

After he'd gone, Alex lay down on the bed again and closed his eyes, and the phone rang. He considered just turning it off, but he checked the caller ID and pressed 'answer'.

"Alex," said Stan. "How are you?"

"I'm fine, Stan," he said. "Really. Nobody was hurt, we don't know how it started, and everyone's being really nice to me."

There was a brief silence. "Good. I just wanted to tell you not to worry about anything. We'll get this fixed."

Considering what the house had looked like the last time he'd seen it, Alex thought this was quite a commitment, but he just said, "Okay, Stan."

"You're at the New Rose, yes?"

"Yes."

"Good. They'll take care of you. The restaurant's terrific. Rest and recover. Don't worry about the book."

Alex groaned.

"What?"

"Nothing." He'd forgotten the laptop, and all the backups of his work, in the safe in the basement, along with the 007 Phone. He closed his eyes and grimaced. "Listen, Stan, I'm really tired. Can we talk tomorrow?"

"Yeah, sure. I just wanted to make sure you were okay and being looked after. Talk to you tomorrow. Take care, Alex." And he hung up.

Alex turned the phone off and dropped it on the bed beside him. After a couple of moments, he got up and opened the door to hang the Do Not Disturb sign on the handle. Outside were another two bags of clothes.

THE NEXT MORNING, unwilling to face the world, he ordered a room service breakfast. He'd just finished when there was a knock at the door, and he found Bud outside blocking pretty much the whole corridor.

"Alex," he said.

"Bud," said Alex.

"How're you doing?"

"I've more or less reached the limit of the number of times I can hear people asking me how I am, to be honest."

Bud grunted. "I was going to head over to East Walden. Want to come along?"

Alex had been dreading going back, but he supposed it was better to get it over with. "Yes, okay."

He stopped at the front desk on the way out, to get Grace to put the room's key on his phone, then they drove through town. When they got to East Walden Lane, the first thing he saw was the green, its grass all chewed up by the tyres of the vehicles which had been parked on it the previous day.

The house was still standing, but it had settled in on itself, as if it had tried unsuccessfully to hide in its own basement. All the windows were broken, the ground floor was charred. The front lawn was a mess, soaked with water from firefighters' hoses and then trodden into mud. The smell of burning was still very strong. A County Sheriff's car was parked outside, East Walden being outside the jurisdiction of the Sioux Crossing PD. Bud went over to have a chat with the deputy in the cruiser and Alex stood by the truck, hands in the pockets of his donated hoodie, staring up at the place where he had once lived. He was surprised by how much it hurt.

"At least the roof's okay," called a voice.

He looked over, saw Ralph standing on his porch. "Yes," he said. "We only need to demolish everything underneath it." He walked up the path to Ralph's house. "When did they let you come back?"

"Ten, eleven last night." Ralph took the cigar out of his mouth. "I would be lying if I said you were wildly popular around here right now."

Well, it wasn't as if he was ever going to live on East Walden

Lane again. He looked around, at his house, at the green. "Christ, what a mess."

"It was the furnace, right?"

"Nobody knows for sure, yet. I only had the damn thing fixed a few months ago."

"Knew a guy in Philadelphia, his furnace exploded one night," Ralph said thoughtfully. "They found it a block away on the roof of a school." He puffed on his cigar. "They never found him at all."

"Thank you for using that charming little anecdote to make me feel better."

"What's going to happen now?"

Alex sighed. "I don't know. I'm at the New Rose for the foreseeable future, however long that is."

Ralph looked at him. "You're not thinking of leaving, are you?"

"It's crossed my mind."

"Jesus, Alex. This was an *accident*. Could have happened to anyone."

Bud came up the path. "Deputy Lofgren says it'll be a couple of days before anyone can go in there and assess the structure," he said. "Ralph."

"Bud," said Ralph.

So the damn thing could *still* fall down. "My laptop's in a safe in the basement," Alex said.

Bud raised an eyebrow. "Well, I wouldn't get your hopes up that it still works."

There was also the 007 Phone. If he stopped checking in with Kitson, what would happen? Would the junior spy just decide to cut his losses and have him deported? He could still call the consulate from a public phone, but he was going to have to drive out of the county to do that. He said, "Can I pick up my car while I'm here?"

They all looked at the garage beside the house. It looked

lightly scorched, but otherwise undamaged. "If you can get it started, I guess that's okay," Bud said. "Make sure you let the Sheriff's Department know, though. They're treating the place as a crime scene."

"What?"

"Because of the raccoon."

Alex thought about it. "Ah, *bollocks*." That had never occurred to him.

"You think this was *deliberate*?" Ralph said with interest.

Bud looked at him. "Now you know I'm not going to discuss that with you, Ralph. And I'll thank you not to go off spreading the word to anyone who'll listen."

Ralph looked affronted. "I have no time for gossip."

"Yeah, right." Bud said to Alex, "I have to get back to town. Can I give you a lift?"

"Can you drop me at Stu's? I need to see if I can get a new laptop."

"Sure."

Alex turned to Ralph. "I'll be over later."

"I'll be here," Ralph said sullenly. "It's not like I'm allowed to go anywhere and *talk* to anyone."

Back in the truck, Alex said, "What the fuck's going on, Bud?"

"Sheriff Brandt's concerned that the raccoon thing and the fire could be connected," Bud told him. "Also, you had your computer hacked, right? Lost a lot of stuff?"

Not lost, *as such*. Lost *would have been better.* "That was something else," he said.

Bud sighed. "Why don't you *tell* me stuff, Alex?"

"That was different. And you seem to be hearing about these things fine without my help."

"You do realise how this all looks from the outside, don't you? It looks like someone has a grudge. I can't do anything to help if you won't level with me." Bud turned the truck onto the main road. "Is there anything else you haven't told me?"

I saw something in the house yesterday that you wouldn't believe. "No, there's nothing else."

"What makes you so sure the thing with your computer isn't connected?"

"It's just not."

"That sounds as if you have an idea who did it."

"No." Alex shook his head tiredly. "No, I really don't."

"Okay, *you* say so." Bud pulled out to pass a tractor, pulled back in again. "I'm not saying everything *is* connected," he went on. "But it does look a little suspicious, wouldn't you say?"

"The mind always looks for patterns, even when they're not there," Alex said. "That's how we get conspiracy theories."

"It's part of my job to look for patterns. That's how we catch bad guys."

Alex looked out of the window for a little while. "So," he said. "What now?"

"We'll wait for the fire department investigators to do their job before we make any decisions. Till then, I guess I'd ask you to be careful. You're safe enough at the New Rose, but try not to wander about too much on your own. And if you see or hear anything out of the ordinary, *tell me.*"

Bud had no idea that the boundaries of *out of the ordinary* had been redrawn in Rosewater County. Alex looked out of the window again. "I'm really tired," he said.

HE WENT TO Stu's Radio Shack and bought a cheap, basic notebook computer and some accessories, but it was more for camouflage than anything else. Then he walked down the street to the *Banner* offices.

"I was meaning to come round and see you," Dru told him. "I could use a quote for the story."

"How about 'I'm utterly fucked-off'?"

"It's short and to the point," she admitted. "Maybe a little strong for our readership, though. You look terrible."

He sat down opposite her and told her about what had happened in the upstairs bedroom of the house the previous day. The sparks. The figure with all the faces.

"That's what Walt Booker meant," he said. "There's a description of angels in the Bible, something about them having many faces."

"Four faces," she said. "One human, three animal. It's in Ezekiel. And it's cherubim." She looked at him. "You think this thing set fire to your house?"

"Bud Rosewater thinks I'm being chased by a serial killer." He told her about the hacked files and the raccoon, and she sat back behind her desk and folded her hands in her lap, her expression unreadable.

When he'd finished, she said, "Well, you have had a time of it. Any suspects?"

"I don't know any more."

She looked at him a moment longer, then she opened a folder on her desk and took out a sheet of paper. "A few editors ago, the *Banner* ran a series about local history," she said. "The editor at the time was a man called Palgrave—a Brit, as it happens; I have no idea how he wound up here, he was long gone by the time I was born. Anyway, Palgrave tracked down the oldest residents of Rosewater County and he interviewed all the ones that would talk to him.

"One of the residents was a farmer called Christensen, and he told this story about *his* father, round about the turn of the last century. He said his father saw a cherub out in one of their fields." She looked at the sheet of paper, then passed it over.

It was a photocopy of a newspaper article. *Biblical Manifestation In Rosewater County*, read the headline, which was not exactly snappy. Alex scanned it quickly and said, "Sparks."

Dru nodded. "'A mist of blue light'. Mr Christensen had quite a turn of phrase, didn't he?"

Alex looked at the article again. "This was in 1907."

"It was."

He did the sums. "A hundred years before they even started work on the SCS."

She nodded again. "Which blows my theory out of the water. Looks like this has *always* been happening here. Although you'll notice that 1907 is *exactly* a hundred years before they started work on the SCS."

Alex shook his head to clear it. "Sorry. Too much stuff."

"I told you to get out of here while you could," she said.

"Yes, you did. I remember that." He took one last look at the photocopy. "Can I keep this?"

"Sure. I still have a few volumes of back issues to go through. There might be more."

"You know, I wonder how many times stuff like this has happened round here and nobody's said anything because they thought they were seeing things or they were afraid people would think they were crazy."

"Short of running an ad that says 'Have you, or a member of your family, ever seen an angel or a cloud of blue sparks', I doubt we'll ever know." She saw the look on his face. "And no, I *won't* do that."

"It might be worth asking a few people. Informally."

"It might. And I may do that." She closed the folder. "But I guess the question we should be asking ourselves is, what are we going to do with this?"

He looked at her, mind blank. He tried to imagine going to Bud with it. "I don't know."

"But you're going to stick around? Angels and serial killers notwithstanding?"

"I've got nowhere else to go. I've got to finish the book, whatever happens, or Stan's people will sue me until the end of time."

"Forgive me for saying this," she told him, "but I think the book is the least of your problems."

Back at the New Rose, he set up the notebook. Then he went through the nitpicking process of extracting its wi-fi card. Then he sat looking at it.

He phoned Wendy. "Do you still have the files that leaked?"

"Delahaye ordered us to delete them," she said. "But I copied them onto a stick. Why?"

"Could you bring them over? Otherwise I'm going to have to start this fucking book again from scratch."

"You lost your laptop?"

Well, no, I know exactly where it is. "Kind of, but it's inaccessible at the moment and it's probably ruined anyway."

"Things are a bit busy here today," she said. "VIP visit."

He recalled Danny saying someone was going to be using the Presidential Suite. "Okay. Later? I'll buy you dinner."

"Sounds good to me. I'll see you around seven."

He hung up and looked around the suite. Then he got up and went downstairs.

Apart from Grace, the lobby was deserted. He took the lift back up to the second floor, where there was a bar. It was the first time he'd visited it—he had a suspicion that it was the first time *anyone* had visited it. It still smelled of new carpeting, and the furniture looked as if it had only just been delivered. The barman had probably been standing behind the bar since the hotel was built, waiting with diminishing hope for a customer to come along.

He ordered a beer and went over to a table by the window. The bar overlooked the main road in front of the hotel, and the occasional car and truck went by. Alex took a sip of beer, leaned back in his chair, and closed his eyes.

If he was honest with himself, the urge to just get in the car and drive away from Sioux Crossing was very strong. He felt as if the wheels had fallen off his life the moment he set foot in the town. Screw Stan, screw the SCS, screw Kitson, screw angels and dead raccoons, and screw the book. He could go home and try to forget they'd ever existed.

Except he wouldn't. As always, it was easier to stay here, not do anything. Just carry on doing what he was doing and not make a fuss. And anyway, it occurred to him that his passport was in the house. It might be okay—it was in a drawer in his bedroom—but there was no knowing when he'd be able to retrieve it.

He opened his eyes and saw a big black SUV driving down the road outside. It pulled to a stop a few hundred yards past the hotel, and turned so it was parked across the road, almost entirely blocking both lanes. Alex took another drink of beer as five more identical SUVs came down the road. Four of them turned off into the hotel forecourt, while the fifth stopped just short and turned to block the road.

Alex leaned over close to the window so he could see the four vehicles parked outside in a line outside. A large number of men wearing suits and sunglasses emerged from the front and rear SUVs and took up station around the vehicles. After a few moments, the doors of the second car opened and it disgorged another large number of men, who surrounded an older, white-haired man and hustled him in through the front doors of the hotel.

Alex got up and wandered across the bar to the door, but before he reached it one of the men in sunglasses stepped into the doorway and took up station there. Alex walked right up to him, but he didn't budge.

"Hi," he said.

The man didn't reply. Alex could see his reflection in the mirrored lenses of his sunglasses.

"My name's Alex," he said.

"Please return to your seat, sir," the man said.

"I really wanted to go up to my room," Alex told him.

"Thank you for your cooperation, sir."

Alex was in the mood for a row, but he could see the wire of an earpiece curling out of the Secret Service man's ear and away down inside the collar of his jacket and the fight slowly drained out of him. He nodded and went back to the table. Outside, the cars were slowly pulling away and driving to the car park behind the hotel. He wondered why the vice president had to stay at the New Rose, why they hadn't just helicoptered him in and out of the SCS, what he was doing here in the first place.

A few moments later, the Secret Service man called from the doorway, "You can go now, sir," and with a little smirk he walked away.

THE TELEGRAPH WAS busy that evening, so they walked a little further down Main Street to a restaurant called Gino's, which was almost deserted. Alex ordered veal, Wendy carbonara, and then they sat looking at each other.

"Before I forget," she said, taking a memory stick from her pocket and putting it on the table.

"Thanks," he said. "For a moment I thought I was going to have to start again from memory."

She sat back. "You're looking better that the last time I saw you, anyway."

"That's because the last time you saw me I was watching my house burn down." He wondered how bad he'd looked yesterday, if today was an improvement. "Bud thinks it's all connected, the hacking thing, the raccoon, the fire."

Wendy thought about it. "I guess you could look at it that way," she allowed. "Seems unlikely, though, doesn't it? To my knowledge the only person you've pissed off since you got here is Delahaye, and he's not the arsonist type."

Alex, who was still oscillating between blaming Kitson and blaming Delahaye, wasn't so sure. The leak of his documents could have been intended to get him fired. When that hadn't happened, there was the raccoon, then the fire. He still had Delahaye in the frame one way or another. He said, "Well, according to Bud the County Sheriff is on top of it. And nobody's going to try anything here; the place is full of Secret Service men."

"You've seen Gray Goose, then?"

"Who?"

"Gray Goose. That's his Secret Service code name, apparently."

"Oh. Yeah, he turned up earlier. What's he doing at the SCS?"

She shrugged, and smiled at the waiter who brought their food. "The place represents a substantial government investment, I guess. He had some meetings with Delahaye and some of the higher-ups. I was not party to their discussions."

That had been troubling Alex ever since he got here. The project was sold to the public as the first privately funded supercollider; while it was a given that other entities would want to invest in it, that wasn't widely publicised. He hadn't known how to present that in the book, quite, and Mickey Olive had seemed unwilling to give him much of a steer.

"I need a phone," he said.

"Didn't they give you one here?"

"A private one."

She looked at him.

"I can't buy a phone here with my line of credit, because someone will spot it," he went on. "And all my bank cards went up with the house. It'll be days before I get access to my bank account again." Also, there was that uncomfortable feeling that Stan was watching his accounts.

"Okay," she said. "You could use mine. Wouldn't that be simpler?"

Simpler, but no more secure, and he didn't want to drag her into it. He was still going to have to leave the county to contact

Kitson, and he was going to have to think up a good excuse for that, or wait until he wasn't such an object of attention and then sneak out for a couple of hours. "Can you lend me a hundred dollars or so?"

"Sure. That's not a problem. But what's this all about?"

"I can't tell you," he said. "You're better off not knowing."

"This is kind of a shitty thing to do," she said, pointing her fork at him. "I thought we were friends."

He winced. "Don't," he said. "I'm miserable enough as it is."

She looked at him a few moments longer, then put down her fork, took out her wallet, and handed over four twenty dollar notes and a ten. "That's all I have on me right now."

He took the money and put it in his pocket. "It'll be enough," he said. "Thank you."

Wendy picked up her fork again and poked it into her spaghetti. "But you'll tell me what's going on at some point," she said. It wasn't a question.

"Yes," he said, knowing it was a promise he was going to have to break.

"Okay," she said, knowing it too. She took a breath, didn't quite sigh. "So, what happens now? Will they rehouse you?"

"I don't know. I'm not sure I want them to. I liked East Walden."

"You can't want to stay at the New Rose?"

He shrugged. "Could be worse."

"But you're going to stick around? Even though someone's out to get you?"

"I'm not convinced someone's out to get me." He cut a piece off his veal and put it in his mouth.

She deadpanned him. "You are *so* convinced."

"I don't want to think about it," he told her. "Otherwise I won't be able to get anything else done, and I need to finish the book. I'll let Bud and Sheriff Brandt worry about it for now. It's their theory, after all."

They ate in silence for a while. Alex said conversationally,

"When you fire up The Beast, do you get... edge effects?"

"Edge effects how?"

"Static discharge, stuff like that."

She tipped her head to one side.

"People in town say they've noticed a lot a static electricity about lately."

She looked at him a moment longer, then went back to her meal. "I hadn't heard that. No, The Beast wouldn't have anything to do with that. More likely to be the weather and a larger concentration of artificial fibre carpets than normal."

He nodded.

"You know," she said, "around this point a paranoid person would be pretty much convinced there were a *lot* of things you weren't telling her."

He almost told her about the angels, but he didn't. Best to wait until he had some idea what was going on. He said, "It was just a thought."

"There were protests when we first started building the collider," she told him. "Religious nutjobs, people who thought it was going to give everyone in the county cancer. I hope you're not thinking about putting all that stuff in the book."

He'd heard about that, and he had in fact made a contact at County General, who had reassured him that cancer cases hadn't spiked since the SCS went live. They had actually gone down a fraction. "Background," he said. "I wasn't planning on mentioning it."

"You're different."

"Pardon?"

"Something's different about you today."

"I watched my house burn down yesterday," he said. "That'll change a person."

She shook her head. "It's not that. Not just that, anyway. You seem more focused." She studied his face. "Not sure what on, though."

* * *

Back at the New Rose, there was no outward sign that the vice president was in residence. Grace was as perky as ever, the Prairie Dining Room was still empty, the gift shop was still closed. No men in sunglasses. Maybe they'd all left while he was in town, although he didn't think so.

He got a beer from the fridge—this room didn't have a kitchen, but its minibar was better stocked than the fridge he'd had in Boston—and stood at the window looking out over the darkened town. The presence of the vice president was something he ought to tell Kitson about, he thought. He was tempted not to, but he was starting to wonder about the junior spy. Would he really have leaked the documents, knowing there was a chance that Alex would be fired and mess up his intelligence gathering operation? Just because Alex had turned up unexpectedly and with clearly malicious intent on his doorstep? Had that one incident driven Kitson to heights of spite which had led him to have Alex's house torched? Did that really, if he was honest with himself, scan?

Similarly, for Delahaye, the pieces didn't quite fit. He could imagine the administrator having his laptop hacked to see what he'd written, and then being so pissed off that he'd release the product to embarrass him. But arson? And what the actual fuck was the raccoon all about? It seemed too uncomplicatedly *grotesque* for either Delahaye or Kitson, unless he'd seriously misread them both.

The problem was, he couldn't tell anyone about Kitson. *Oh, by the way, Bud, there's this MI6 officer who forced me to spy for him and he could be responsible.*

Someone knocked on the door. He went and opened it, and found Bud standing outside.

"I was just thinking about you," he said. Then he saw the look on Bud's face. "What."

"I need you to come with me, Alex," Bud told him.

* * *

The morgue at County General was down in the basement of the building, down a long, chilly corridor with ducts running along the walls.

Inside, everything was neat and clean and tidy, with that all-pervading Sioux Crossing feeling of newness. A technician was waiting for them, and he went to a wall which seemed to be composed entirely of little square doors. He opened one and pulled out a long stainless steel tray on which lay a pale blue body bag. The technician unzipped bag a fraction. Alex looked down.

"Do you know this person?" Bud asked, beside him.

For a moment that seemed to last forever, Alex's mind went blank. Apart from a cut on the forehead, Kitson's face was unmarked, drained of colour. He heard himself say, "Never seen him before."

Bud gave him a stare that was powerful enough to make the air between them ripple. "You sure you don't know him?"

Alex shook his head. "No, I don't."

Bud nodded to the technician, who zipped up the bag and slid the tray back into its compartment. Bud turned on his heel and headed for the doors. After a moment, Alex followed. "What's going on? Why did you bring me here?"

"He was carrying a British passport," Bud said, pushing open the doors. "He was a Brit, you're a Brit. I figured you might know each other."

All of a sudden, Alex felt a wave of dizziness pass through him. He stopped and leaned on the wall.

Bud walked a couple of steps further along the corridor, stopped and turned. "You okay?"

"I don't get called out to look at dead people very often. Give me a second."

"Someone ran him off the road, south of town, last night," Bud told him. "His airbag failed and he took the steering wheel in the chest. Killed him instantly, the EMTs said."

"Maybe he worked at the Facility," Alex said, trying to force his brain to work again.

"Don't bullshit me, Alex," Bud said, his face stony. "There's three reasons I know you know who that guy is. First, the look on your face when you saw him. Second, the fact you didn't ask me who he was. And third, he was driving your car when he died."

The headquarters of the Sioux Crossing PD resembled a small, comfortable office building. It was not at all the way Alex imagined a police station would be; even the front desk looked like the foyer of a little motel. Bud's office was on the third floor. There was a desk and a couple of comfortable guest chairs, some framed photos and diplomas on the walls, filing cabinets, a photo of the president on the wall behind the desk. No American flag, Alex noticed. Was that normal, or was it only in films that police chiefs' offices had American flags?

"Okay," Bud said heavily from his chair on the other side of the desk. "Let's try that again."

Alex looked at him for a few moments. "His name's Kitson," he said. "Sam Kitson. He works at the British Consulate in Minneapolis." He watched Bud grimace. "He was—he claimed to be—an officer with SIS. MI6."

Bud put a hand to his head and groaned gently. "And you know this how?"

"He contacted me shortly after I arrived in town and tried to get me to spy at the SCS on his behalf."

"'Tried'?"

"He threatened to have me deported if I didn't cooperate. I didn't see that I had any choice."

Bud stared at him. "So you're admitting to carrying out espionage on American soil."

Alex nodded.

Bud shook his head. "Well, fuck, Alex," he said with a mixture of exasperation and wonder.

"I didn't do it willingly."

"I doubt whether that will carry much weight in court. What was he doing here?"

"I don't know. I didn't even know he was in the county."

"He wasn't coming to meet with you?"

"Not that I know of. Our last contact was the day before the barbecue and there was no reason why he'd have needed to come here."

"And you can't tell me why he was in your car."

"As far as I knew, it was still in the garage at East Walden. We were talking about that this morning, remember?" Christ, it had been a long day.

"I remember. You didn't go collect it?"

"I haven't had the time. Or the brain power."

Bud settled back in his chair and clasped his hands across his stomach. "So this guy was your, what, your *case officer*."

"I suppose. I got the impression he was doing it on his own initiative, putting a source into the SCS because the Department of Defense is involved in the project. Maybe he thought he could impress his superiors."

"I should book you right now and try to figure this out afterward," Bud told him. "Can you think of any reason why he would steal your car?"

"I have no idea." Alex rubbed his face. "I still have the keys." He put a hand in his pocket, took them out, and held them up. "Look."

Bud made a gimme gesture, and Alex tossed the keys on the desk. Bud looked at them. "This is a hell of a thing," he muttered.

"I thought he might have something to do with the fire," Alex said, because why not. "And the raccoon. And the hacking thing."

Bud raised an eyebrow.

"I had a bit of a crisis of confidence," Alex confessed. "I didn't have any proof that he was who he said he was. So I went to Minneapolis and visited the consulate to see if he really did work there."

"And did he?"

Alex nodded. "He was annoyed. Apparently you're not supposed to turn up where your case officer works."

"He'd have to be *astronomically* annoyed to burn your house down because of it."

Alex shrugged.

"When did you go up to Minneapolis?"

"A few weeks ago." Alex considered stopping right there, but he said, "I didn't originally go to see Kitson, that was just because I was in town. I went to see the Shanahans."

Bud scratched his head. "You did, huh."

"Because of the guns."

"Which you never told me about."

"We've been through that already."

Bud sighed. "Well, we're going to have to go through it again on an *official* basis now." He looked at Alex. "This is a genuine mess," he said.

They looked at each other for quite a long time. Alex said, "So. What happens now?"

"I have to alert the British authorities," Bud said. "The nearest of which just happen to be at the consulate in Minneapolis. I guess they'll blow smoke up my ass, but they'll want to know what this guy was doing down here. You're sure he was acting on his own?"

"No. Not by any stretch. It was just a feeling."

Bud pouted. "If you're wrong, they'll want to contact you, make sure everything continues to run smoothly." He brought his fists down on the desktop very gently, but Alex still fancied he felt the floor shake. "You see what happens when you *don't tell me things*?"

"Sure, I was just going to run up to you and confess to being a spy."

"I should be—and in fact I am—*really* pissed off with you."

"I'm sorry."

"You're sorry. And is there any reason I shouldn't book you on suspicion of this guy's murder?"

That hadn't occurred to Alex. "Well... lots of reasons," he said.

"Because if he *was* blackmailing you, and he *was* harassing you, and he *did* set your house on fire, I'd say you had motive."

Alex sagged back in his chair. "I wish I'd never heard of this fucking place."

"This fucking place which is my home," Bud pointed out. "*Did* you kill him?"

"No, of course I didn't. What with? He was driving *my* car."

"You could have got another car easy," Bud mused.

"Oh, please. I was at the hotel all last night. And before that I was standing with you, watching my house burn, and I can't believe you asked me that."

"Hey, you just admitted to being a spy."

Something belatedly caught up with Alex. "You're sure this wasn't an accident."

Bud lifted his hand and tipped it from side to side. "Jury's out until we examine his car. *Your* car. But it looks deliberate to me."

"So maybe somebody thought *I* was driving."

"*I* sure thought so, when I first saw the car."

"Why didn't you come and find me straight away?"

"The place where it happened is County Sheriff's jurisdiction. Guy Brandt didn't call me about it until this afternoon, when they found out whose car it was."

Alex looked at his watch. "It's almost eleven in the evening."

"You may have noticed," Bud said, "living, as you now do, at the New Rose, that we have had other things to worry about today."

Dammit. Trumped by Gray Goose. "So what are we going to do?"

Bud thought about it for a while. "I'm going to keep you here tonight," he said finally. "While I untangle this clusterfuck some. I'll contact the consulate momentarily; if this guy Kitson really was a resident intelligence officer they'll want to send someone down ASAP. If they don't ask after you, well, that might be significant, it might not, and we'll visit that when the time comes." He saw the look on Alex's face. "Think of it as protective custody; if someone *is* wandering around Rosewater County trying to kill you, you're better off here anyway."

"All right."

"But the espionage thing?" Bud shook his head. "I can't let that go, Alex. You literally admitted it."

"Don't tell Mickey Olive," Alex said. "Not just yet."

"Alex," Bud said, "the *best* possible outcome here is that you wind up thrown out of the country. These are not good times to be caught spying on the US. If there ever *was* a good time."

"Just hold off telling them," said Alex. "Until we have a clearer idea what's going on."

"That could be a while. Eventually they're going to wonder where you went."

"Let them wonder."

Bud thought about it. "Okay. For the moment we'll say you're in protective custody, following recent events, and we'll take it from there."

"Okay."

Bud stood slowly, like a continent shifting. "What did the Shanahans tell you?"

"They said my house was cursed."

"Well," Bud said, indicating that Alex should lead him out of the door, "I can't disagree with them, right now."

THE POLICE DEPARTMENT cells looked as if they had never been occupied. The mattress was thick and brand new, and there was a flat-screen television in a glassed-in alcove on one wall. It played American football during daylight hours, a couple of hours of Fox News in the evenings, then it switched itself off and the lights dimmed for sleep. The cell smelled clean and it was warm. He'd slept in worse hotels.

The morning after his protective arrest, Bud came in and told him that someone had turned up from the consulate at a little after four a.m. "Name of Goddard," he said.

Alex shook his head.

"Older gentleman," Bud went on. "Tall, thin, grey-haired. Had an air of attorney about him. One of those troubleshooting ones."

"Never met him," Alex said.

"He did an ID of Kitson, signed a bunch of forms, took the remains away in a van. Said the Brits would take care of an autopsy and share the results with us, but I'm not holding my breath."

"Can they do that? Just go off with the body in the middle of an investigation?"

Bud shrugged. "Mr Goddard had letters signed by some extremely important people, strongly recommending that I offer him full cooperation. I could have dug in my heels, but I doubt it would have changed anything in the end."

"Wow. They organised that in a hurry."

"Yeah, I thought that. Anyway, he didn't mention you."

"I'm hurt," Alex said, not feeling in the least bit hurt.

"It's not conclusive."

"It's something. I've been thinking about Ralph."

Bud nodded. "Me too, but Brandt's got deputies stationed outside your house; they'll keep an eye on him too."

"Kitson stole my car from my garage right under everyone's noses," Alex pointed out.

"When did you last see it?"

Alex thought about it. "Fair point," he said. "I used it to do the shopping a couple of days before the barbecue, put it in the garage, forgot about it. He could have taken it the night before."

"So if he was in the county at that time, he could still have caused the fire."

Alex shook his head. "He didn't seem the type."

"You'd be surprised at the kinds of people who turn out to be 'the type', Alex."

Alex scowled. "Okay. So, Kitson's gone and we're still none the wiser. What now?"

"It wasn't an accident. Preliminary findings indicate he was sideswiped by another vehicle and driven into a ditch. Forensics got some red paint off the side panels of your car; we sent that off for analysis, but it'll be a few days before we get any results."

"Traffic cameras?"

"Not that far out of town. We're reviewing the footage we do have from that night to see if we can spot anything. So far it's all just emergency vehicles hightailing it to your place."

"None of this helps very much, does it."

"Nope." Bud turned and thumped his fist on the door. An officer outside opened it. "The Brits will have an investigation into Kitson's death. Unless he was doing the whole thing in his head, there will be documentation, and when they find that they'll come looking for you."

Would there be anything to identify him? Alex had no idea. Maybe he had a codename, and Kitson had been the only person who could connect him to it. *My information comes from Source Halfwit*. That wouldn't be too hard to figure out. "I've got enough to worry about, without adding MI6 to the list."

"You got that right, at least," Bud said, leaving the cell and letting the officer close the door behind him. Alex heard the key turn in the lock.

* * *

HIS NEXT VISITOR, the following day, was a bit of a surprise. She looked around the cell and said, "Well, *this* is nice."

"The food's terrific," he told her.

Wendy snorted.

"No, really. They bring it over from the Telegraph. Full menu, all you can eat."

She shook her head. "What have you done, Alex?"

"I'm in protective custody. Bud has evidence that someone's trying to kill me." *I'm also a British spy, but let's not get into that right now*. "What are you doing here?"

"Nobody had seen you for a couple of days. I asked Bud where you were."

Alex was more than a little annoyed with Bud for telling her where he was, although he supposed the Chief had kept his word and not told Mickey Olive, because Mickey hadn't turned up yet.

"Who's trying to kill you?" she asked. "What for?"

"We don't know yet. That would make things too easy."

Wendy came over and sat down beside him on the mattress. She said, "Isn't this a bit... *extreme*?"

"Bud doesn't like to take risks."

This clearly didn't impress her. She said, "Mm hm."

"How's the outside world? Is there still an outside world?"

She sighed. "Don't try to change the subject, Alex. This isn't protective custody. It's something else."

"It's protective custody," he insisted. "And something else."

"What else?"

"Can't say."

She half turned and thumped him on the shoulder a lot more soundly than he thought strictly necessary. "Dickhead. What did you do?"

He sighed. "I got into something over my head. Bud's helping me sort it out."

"Dude. You're in a *cell*."

"Bud says I can leave any time I want." Although Bud had

added that he would arrest him if he tried it, "And put you in *real* jail."

"Ralph's going frantic," she said. "He's really worried about you."

It occurred to him that Ralph was probably the only person in Rosewater County who would actually understand what was going on. Dru Winslow too, maybe. He was going to have to sit those two down next to each other and get them talking, if he ever got the chance. "Tell him I'm okay. I'll be over to see him soon."

"Well, *that* was said with conviction," she told him.

"Seriously," he said. "I promise."

The look she gave him told him everything he needed to know about what she thought about *that*. They sat quietly together for a while, then she said, "Oh, we found out who hacked your laptop."

"*What*?"

She nodded. "Maia left me a note this morning. There's a calling card."

He turned so he was facing her. "What was it?"

"There's some malware on your laptop. It's meant to look like something else, but it opens the machine up to remote access. Maia says it's really complicated, much more complicated than it needs to be, thousands of lines of code. And among all those lines of code there's a single line of plain text, like a trademark almost. *Peacocks can't live at this altitude*."

Alex blinked.

"So we googled that, and it turns out to be a quote from Hunter S Thompson."

He blinked again. Red paint traces on his car.

"And who do we know who has a thing about Thompson?" Wendy went on, while light years of possibility unfolded themselves in Alex's head. "And it's *just* the sort of childish prank he'd pull."

"I only went for a drink with him," he said, half to himself. "Have you seen him lately?"

"Yeah, he's out at the Facility, pissing people off."

"Now? Right now?"

She looked at her watch. "I guess. He was there when I left."

Alex looked around the cell, trying to get his brain to work. "I need to talk to Bud." He got up and went to the door and started to hammer on it with the flat of his hand. "Hey!" he shouted. "Hey!"

"Alex?" said Wendy from the bed. "What are you doing?"

"Hey!" Alex shouted again. Abruptly, the flap in the door snapped open and a police uniform moved into view. "I need to speak to Chief Rosewater," Alex said through the flap. "Right now."

The officer outside bent down slightly to see into the cell. "Sir," he said. "Step away from the door please, sir."

Alex took a couple of steps back. "I have to speak with the Chief," he said. "It's very important."

"The Chief's not here, sir," said the officer, a man named Jackson.

"I need to get a message to him then. Right now."

"I'm sure we can get word to him, sir," said Jackson. "In due time."

"That's no good."

"To be fair, sir, you're in no position to tell me what's good or not."

"Oh, for fuck's sake," Wendy said. She got up off the bed and came over to stand next to Alex. "Can I go now, please?" Alex heard a faint jingling sound, looked down, and saw Wendy's hand, down out of Jackson's sightline. Her car keys were dangling from her fingers. They exchanged glances, and she shrugged.

"Sir, would you step back further?" Jackson said. "If you do not, I will be forced to mace you."

Wendy looked at him. "What the fuck did you *do*?"

"I made the mistake of talking to strangers," Alex told her, unobtrusively taking the keys from her and taking another step back.

Jackson's key turned in the door, and it opened, and Wendy moved forward all of a sudden, crowding Jackson to one side while berating him about something in a loud voice. Alex slipped through the door behind her, turned right, and ran down the corridor away from them. He heard shouting, but didn't look round.

There was another door at the end of the corridor, this one with a crush bar on it. He hit the bar and the door opened and an alarm went off everywhere in the building. More shouting, behind him, and people running.

He was in another corridor, this one lined with office doors. It made a right-angle turn about halfway along, then came to a dead end. "Bollocks," he said. He tried one of the doors, and it opened onto a small office with a desk and a couple of chairs. He slammed the door shut and dragged the desk against it, just as something large and annoyed hit the other side.

The office had a window. He pulled the blinds open and found himself looking out on a little patch of grass at the side of the building. The window was locked. He picked up one of the chairs and swung it and it just bounced off the glass. *Of course they're going to have toughened glass; it's a police station.* He swung the chair again, and again. On the third try, the glass starred. *Not tough enough, though.* Another swing cracked the glass, and with the next the window suddenly shattered into thousands of tiny round-edged particles. Alex climbed out, dropped to the ground, and took off at a full run from the police headquarters.

Wendy's car was parked down the street. By a miracle, he'd actually wound up running towards it. He skidded to a stop beside it, unlocked the door, jumped inside. The engine started first time, which was also a miracle. He put the car in Drive and sped off down Main Street, jumping the red light outside the Telegraph. He spotted Dru Winslow standing on the pavement.

Well, that was absurd. He looked in the rearview mirror and didn't see any police vehicles in pursuit, which was also absurd. He was also going in the wrong direction. If he wanted to get out to the Facility he was either going to have to make a five-mile detour or turn round and go back through town *and where were the police?*

He'd got about a mile out of town when his phone rang. He took it out and thumbed the answer icon.

"Now what do you think you're doing, Alex?" asked Bud.

"Your security is *terrible*," Alex told him. "What sort of police station do you call that?"

"Just come back right now and we'll forget this ever happened."

"It wouldn't be happening at all if you'd been there. I know who did it."

"Did what?"

"Everything. My laptop, the fire, Kitson. Everything."

"Fine, well, you come back to headquarters and we can talk about that."

"Not a chance."

There was silence, at the other end of the line. Then Bud said, "Okay, then. Who is it?"

"If you wait five or ten minutes, I'll tell you."

"That's not going to work, I'm afraid, Alex. I know exactly where you are because I'm tracking your phone. I've got officers and Sheriff's deputies heading to your position right now. There's nowhere for you to go."

Alex took the phone from his ear, looked at it. He couldn't throw it out of the car; he needed its sockpuppet ID to get into the Facility. He said, "It's Larry Day."

Another silence. Alex took a left, then a right onto a bumpy farm road. Bud said, "Fine. Now stop the car, wait for my officers, and let us deal with it. Okay?"

"Not okay." He was having to fight the wheel one-handed. He put the phone on speaker and dropped it on the passenger seat. "Not at all okay. He set fire to my fucking house."

"Maybe he did, maybe he didn't. This is not the final act of a Hollywood movie, Alex. You're not the hero going to bring down the villain single-handed while the Law bumbles about in the background. We're actually smarter than you."

"You're not smarter than him, though." A fence was coming up, strands of wire strung between wooden posts. Alex put his foot down and the car went straight through and slewed out into the field beyond. The suspension bottomed and he almost bit his tongue in two before he regained control. "I'm really sorry, Bud, but I'm a bit busy right now." He reached over and switched off the phone.

Fine. So here he was, bouncing across the fields of Iowa in what was, to all intents and purposes, a stolen car, without anything even resembling a plan. Actually getting out of the cell hadn't crossed his mind until Wendy held out her keys, but he didn't think blaming her was going to work. The police knew where he was, and in a couple of minutes they would be able to make a shrewd guess at where he was going, but by then it would be too late. All his access codes were false, and he didn't think anyone would be able to cancel them in time to stop him getting into the Facility. Quite what he was going to do when he was inside, he didn't know yet.

He went through a couple more fences, across a couple more fields, then out onto another farm road. The road came out onto the main road half a mile from the Facility, and a minute or so later he was pulling up at the front gate.

The guard looked at the car, which was covered in dust and bits of chewed up vegetation, then at Alex, who was sweaty and red-faced and breathing hard, but the ID on the phone checked out and he stepped aside and waved the visitor through.

Alex parked outside the main building and pushed through the front doors. Charles was on the front desk. He smiled at first, when he saw Alex enter the foyer, but the smile faltered a little as Alex reached the desk and held his phone out to be identified.

"Have you seen Professor Day?" Alex asked.

Charles was frowning at the monitor on the desk. "I'm sorry, Mr Dolan, but this says you're somebody else."

"I know," Alex said. "I'm going to get that fixed while I'm here. Where's Professor Day?"

"But I can't let you through," Charles said, still reading. "It says here that your access has been revoked."

"Where is he?" Alex yelled.

Charles actually took a step back from the desk. He raised a finger and pointed at the ceiling. "Control room," he said.

"Thank you," Alex said, and he started to run up the stairs.

The control room was on the top floor, at the end of a long corridor. Its door had a security lock, but the sockpuppet ID let him through. The room beyond was large and full of people, either sitting typing at consoles and staring at monitors, or watching screens suspended from the ceiling. Nobody noticed him, but he spotted Delahaye on the other side of the room, deep in conversation with Brigadier General Bell, and perhaps a dozen other techs and scientists he recognised.

Rob Chen came over and shook hands. "Hey, man," he said. "Come to see the main event?"

"What's going on?" Alex asked, scanning the room.

"We're going to run the thing at full power for the first time. Delahaye's being a prick."

"What's new? Listen, is Larry here?"

"Yeah. I saw him earlier." Rob looked around the room. "Over there."

Alex looked, saw Larry Day's leonine features over the heads of a group of people in a corner of the control room. He was wearing Bermuda shorts and a desert camouflage jacket and he was holding a tin of beer. His hair looked as if he had been dragged back and forth through a hedge a couple of times, and his eyes were hidden by mirrorshades with lenses the size of silver dollars.

"Okay," said Alex. "Rob, do me a favour and go and get Security, please."

"What?"

"Just do it, please. And hurry."

Rob looked at him, then at Larry, then back to Alex. "What's going on?"

"It's a long story. Please, Rob."

Rob came to a decision. "Okay." And he turned for the door.

Alex pushed his way through the press of people. In the background, he heard a couple of voices raised in a countdown, and more voices joined them as he moved towards Larry. By the time he reached him, most of the room was happily counting down.

Larry turned his mirrored gaze towards him and beamed. "Alex," he said.

He had absolutely no idea what to do next. In the background, he heard the countdown continuing, then Delahaye's voice raised over the noise shouting, "What the *fuck* is he doing here?"

Alex lunged forward, grabbed Larry by the front of the camouflage jacket, and drove him two steps back against the wall.

"...Three...two..." everyone counted.

"You fucking *bastard*!" Alex yelled into Larry's face.

"...One...zero!" and the world filled with a sudden flash of something that was not blinding white light.

THE MANIFOLD

THERE WAS A place that was not a place. It was too small and too large all at once, and it was either dark or it was lit by something that wasn't light at all but came in from the edge of vision like a hypnagogic nightmare. There was an 'up' and a 'down'. Or maybe it was a 'down' and an 'up'. He screamed and he screamed and the noises he made were not sounds. He was... He was...

He drifted, or perhaps he didn't. Perhaps he remained still and everything else moved around him. Perhaps there was no everything else. Perhaps there was no him.

He went away, came back. Went away, came back. There was a howling... sound? Vibration? Light? He went away, came back. Time passed. Or perhaps time stood still and he passed. He was larger than the universe and small enough to hide within the electron shell of an atom.

Objects which were not objects at all boiled at the edges of his perception. He moved towards them, or perhaps he stayed still and they moved towards him. They were shapes that were not shapes, too small to see and too large to comprehend, shapes that curled away tightly into infinity. He couldn't understand what he was seeing, couldn't be sure he was seeing it at all. He wanted to lie down and die, and he did in fact try that a couple of times, but he found that he couldn't even lie down, in the sense that he had once understood it. He held up his hands and looked at them. They were... They were...

He went away, came back.

He made a choice. If he was perceiving an environment, even though he couldn't understand what he was perceiving, he must exist, in some form or other. The very fact that he was able to make the choice to believe that meant he must exist. That was a start. He existed. He was real. A wave of panic the size of the bow-shock from an exploding galaxy passed through him.

He went away, came back.

At some point, maybe instantly, maybe it took a hundred billion years, he encountered a... structure. It looked like... there was no way for him to understand what it looked like, but he *touched* it and he *curled around* it, and the next thing he knew he was lying on his back looking up at a starry sky and someone nearby was screaming, "Don't move, you fucker! You stay right where you are!"

It was an effort to remember how to breathe; his chest hurt and his eyes hurt and he was freezing cold. By somehow *not thinking about it*, he managed to trick his body into remembering how to turn his head. A man in a military uniform was standing a short distance away, pointing an automatic rifle at him. There was no moon, no light at all—the soldier was wearing a bulky pair of image-amplifying goggles over his eyes—but he could see the soldier perfectly well.

"Who are you?" he asked, and almost choked himself because he was still trying to speak as he might have when he was *there*. He coughed and retched and felt a wave of tremors pass through his body. At some point, he realised he was stark naked. "Who are you?" he said again.

"Who are *you*?" shouted the soldier.

"Dolan," he said, and this time he managed to say it without strangling. "Alex Dolan. There's been some kind of accident."

There was a squawking noise and the soldier lifted a walkie-talkie to his lips. "Fenwick here, sir," he shouted into the radio. "I've got a civilian here. He says there's been an accident."

"Is he awake?" a voice said.

"I don't know, sir," answered another. "I can't tell."

"What do you mean, you can't tell?"

"Sir, none of these readings make any sense."

There was something wrong with his eyes. They were open, but the right was blind in the centre of his vision and was only perceiving blurred colours at the periphery. The left felt as if it was looking upward and to one side, but otherwise it wasn't working at all. He tried to blink, but it was as if his body had forgotten how.

He was aware, though, of the room. It was not large and there was something not *right* about the walls. He could feel the mass of various pieces of equipment, and four people in the room with him. He only knew they were people because they were moving around and making noise; otherwise they were indistinguishable from the inanimate objects. He was afraid that he was paralysed, somehow. When he tried to wiggle his fingers and toes he felt them move, but they seemed to move somewhere *else*, not where he was. Some kind of brain injury? He remembered that momentary flash of blinding not-light which had seemed to last for ever, and he wondered if this was what a stroke was like.

He could not say to himself, with any great certainty, that he was breathing.

He lay there—he had a sense he was lying down—for some considerable time, listening to the other people in the room moving about and talking. Sometimes he could understand what they were saying, sometimes not. Sometimes it didn't sound like speech. Or even like sound.

Strangely—and he noted it in a distant, almost uninterested way—he felt no sense of panic. He remembered panicking back *there*, a crashing wave of anxiety the size of a galaxy, but it seemed to have altered him, bent him into another shape somehow. He was paralysed and almost completely blind, and he was taking it in his stride, which was a surprise.

He slept—at least it felt like sleep—and dreamed he was back *there*, in that dimensionless space with too many dimensions, and when he woke again there was screaming in the room and people running about and things falling over and he wondered what that was so he *concentrated* and found himself back in his own body, more or less, and able to see, more or less.

He was lying on a hospital bed, one of those beds with rails on each side to stop people falling out. The head end of the bed was elevated slightly, so he could see around what seemed to be a perfectly ordinary hospital room. Perfectly ordinary apart from the way the walls didn't seem to connect with each other, and the figure in doctor's scrubs which lay on the floor near the door, whimpering. Everyone else seemed to have gone.

With an effort of will, he said, "What's going on?" and the whimpering figure screamed and covered its ears and curled up in a ball.

Fuck this. He tried to sit up and discovered that one of his wrists was handcuffed to the bed rail. Except there was an optical illusion and if he looked at it in a certain way the bracelet didn't seem to go around his wrist at all. He made a fist and rotated it and the handcuff seemed to *miss* his wrist altogether and fell on the bed.

He clambered down from the bed and stood unsteadily beside it, feeling the cold floor under his bare feet. "Hello?" he said to the figure on the floor—was it male, or female? He didn't seem able to tell. "Are you okay?" There was no answer. He took a wobbly step away from the bed, then another, then another, and then all of a sudden he was right up against the door without remembering the intervening space. He tried the handle, but it was locked.

Okay. Well. He went back to the person on the floor and squatted down beside them. "Hello?" he said. "Do you need help? Can I call someone?" The only response was a hysterical high-pitched sob.

He stood up again and looked around the room. There were signs of panic here. Bits of medical equipment, monitors, instruments, strewn around the floor, stuff knocked over. What the fuck was he doing here? Where *was* here? Why had they handcuffed him, however sloppily, to the bed? Who *were* they?

He moved along one wall until he reached one of those troublesome corners. Here, there seemed to be a space wide enough for him to slip through, so he did, and found himself standing in the corridor outside the room. It ran off left and right, lined with doors, some of them open. He leaned round one and saw another hospital room, like the one he had just left. But this place didn't feel remotely like a hospital. It had the dead dullness of an office building, and that was before you got to the way none of the walls connected with each other. Some kind of film set? How did that make any sense?

He picked a direction and set off down the corridor, but he'd barely taken half a dozen steps when he heard the sound of booted feet running behind him, and when he turned he saw six or seven men in military uniform blocking the corridor. They were all pointing assault rifles at him. He put his hands in the air.

"Sir!" barked one of the... not soldiers, the uniforms were wrong. Airmen? "Stand *down*!"

"What?"

"Stand *down*!"

"My name's Alex Dolan," he said, a little startled by how

calm he felt, considering. "I think I've been in an accident. Who are you and what am I doing here?"

"This is your final warning, sir!" the airman yelled. The airman did not seem calm at all. "Stand down and *stop doing that*!"

"Doing what?" He looked down at his body and it seemed that there were two parts of his brain, one of which understood what it saw and the other of which did not. "Oh. That."

"Open fire!" the airman shouted.

He *let* go, and felt himself fall in all directions, and somewhere in an impossible distance he thought he heard gunfire and screaming.

TIME PASSED. OR did not. Like all the other dimensions here, it seemed either impossibly complex or absent altogether, or a combination of both. He imagined himself sitting very still, but that didn't work very well, so he allowed himself to drift, or everything to drift around him.

He thought he must have been severely injured in the explosion—surely it had been an explosion. He was in a medically induced coma and he was hallucinating all of this. It was the only explanation that made any sense.

Once he had that straight in his head, it gave him a perspective to hang on to. There was nothing to fear here; it was all a construction of his subconscious, a *Pincher Martin* simulation, and keeping that in mind he could set out and explore.

Having said that, there wasn't much here to see, or at least to understand. The space, which could still not make up its mind to be infinitely large or infinitely small, was empty until he looked at it in a certain way, at which point it became crowded with an impression of objects which he could not understand. He trekked across the space for a length of time which had no meaning.

Remembering how he had returned the first time, he paid more attention to some of the structures around him. He picked one, turned it over in his mind, slipped *inside*, and found himself standing in the middle of a field.

He was naked again, which was annoying, so he imagined clothes for himself. It was late afternoon or early evening, the light beginning to fail. He could see, in the distance, a line of trees, but no buildings, no sign of habitation. He had no idea where he was.

The air was full of blue sparks.

He turned slowly, looking around him, and was startled to see someone standing behind him, a couple of yards away, a middle-aged man in old-fashioned work clothes.

"Hello," he said as unthreateningly as possible. "My name's Alex. What's yours?"

The man turned and fled.

Alex watched him go. He stumbled and fell a couple of times, but he was running as if his life depended on it and presently he was just a little speck in the distance.

Alex sighed. "Bollocks," he said, and *stepped back*.

The next time he tried it, he imagined clothes first, and found himself standing in someone's living room, surrounded by sparks. A very fat man was kneeling in front of him, eyes shut and hands clasped together. Alex knew who the man was, and where he was, and that made sense. That was how dreams worked. He *stepped back*.

He thought he knew what to expect the next time, but he found himself standing at the side of a road at night. There was a full moon, and from the fields behind him he could hear small creatures moving around. From the chill in the air, he judged it to be early autumn, and looking up he could see the blinking lights of an aircraft crossing the sky. This was all entirely unfamiliar to him, and he wondered where it had come from. He stood where he was for quite a while, then he went away.

He thought perhaps he was beginning to get a handle on it. The howling silence of that blinding white darkness was still a shock, but it was becoming more familiar the longer he spent there, and he no longer panicked when he tried to move between it and what presented as the real world.

When he was five years old, his father had decided it was time he learned to swim, so they went over to the pool at the local leisure centre in Leith. Alex remembered being really excited to be going on this outing. They took the bus, which in his memory suggested that this was one of his father's long periods of unemployment, when he couldn't afford to run a car, and that was exciting too.

At the leisure centre, everything was new and wonderful and confusing. In the changing rooms, his father helped him into his swimming trunks, then held his hand while they walked barefoot along the textured tiles, through the footbath, and out onto the edge of the pool.

He remembered it was hot and humid in there, and the air stank of chlorine and that made him feel a little queasy, but that didn't matter because before him was the pool, and it was huge, like the Atlantic, and full of people splashing about and enjoying themselves. He was virtually vibrating with happiness as his father blew up the little inflatable armbands and slipped them over his hands and up near his armpits. Then they walked right to the edge of the pool, and without warning his father picked him up and threw him in.

That was where his memory of the trip to the pool ended, with a baffled impression of weightlessness, hanging above the pale blue surface of the water.

His next clear memory was of sitting beside the fire in the living room, his nose running and the smell of chlorine still on his skin and hair. In the kitchen, his parents were arguing in loud voices. There were no more trips to the swimming pool with his father.

He learned to swim, eventually, in his own time. At the beginning he still felt a rising sense of panic when he got into the water, but it passed. This was like that. After the initial shock, he was learning that there was nothing to be afraid of. Each transition was smoother, more confident, as he tried to work his way bit by bit back to where he wanted to be.

So he stood in his backyard, and in his kitchen while Pam Shanahan screamed her head off behind him, and outside a hotel door, and in his spare bedroom looking at himself, using each of these things as waypoints to anchor himself before moving on, and finally he found himself standing outside the main building of the SCS.

Except everything was wrong. The building looked shabby and dirty, its paint peeling and a couple of windows broken. It seemed to be deserted. He turned in a slow circle. The lawns around the building were overgrown and the trees had grown wild and unpruned. He tipped his head back and looked at the upper floors of the building. And looked up. And up.

"Fucking *hell*," he said.

Hanging directly over the building was an immense slowly turning spiral of cloud, like a slow-motion tornado. It rose into the sky until it pierced the cloudbase. He watched it, mouth hanging open, as it turned silently above him.

And all of a sudden he was writhing on the ground in agony. He tried to *step* away, but he was in too much pain to be able to focus. He was dimly aware of someone walking up to him, bending down, and thumping his fist down on his thigh. When the figure took its hand away there was a thin plastic tube sticking out of his leg and then there was a wild roaring in his head and a wave of blackness broke over him and washed him away, and that was how they caught him the second time.

He regained consciousness sitting in a chair. No, not a chair. A wheelchair. A wheelchair parked in the middle of a small cement-walled room with a single door and no furniture. It was featureless apart from an armoured light fitting in the middle of the ceiling and the black bubble of a surveillance camera set high up on one wall. His wrists and forearms were bound to the armrests of the chair with about a dozen cable ties each, and it felt as if his ankles were similarly fastened to the footrests. He could feel restraints across his chest and forehead holding him upright, and there seemed to be something on his head, like a metal bowl. He was wearing an orange jumpsuit, and over that some kind of waistcoat with wires trailing from it and away out of sight. An IV line had been inserted into the back of his hand. He couldn't move his head to see where the line went.

Well.

A voice behind him said, "Good morning, Mr Dolan. Please remain calm." He couldn't sense anyone else in the room with him, so presumably the voice was coming from a speaker.

He said, "Who are you?"

The voice continued, "We have you under light sedation, for your own safety. You'll notice you're wearing a vest and a skullcap. We're monitoring your heartrate and brain activity, and should either or both of these deviate from certain narrow parameters, the equipment you're wearing will administer an electric shock powerful enough to stun you. If you continue to misbehave, it will kill you. Please indicate that you understand this."

"If you want me to remain calm, you're going about it all wrong," he said.

"Please indicate that you understand," the voice said again.

He thought about it for a while. Then he said, "I understand."

"Very well," said the voice, and a moment later the door opened and three men stepped into the room. One was in late middle age, wearing the uniform of an Air Force general, while the other two were younger and in civilian clothes. A distant part of him noted that it was actually rather brave of them to be in the same room with him.

"We apologise for this, Mr Dolan," the general said. "We couldn't risk you... *leaving* again."

Alex sat looking at them. He said, "I have questions."

"So do we," said one of the younger men. "How much do you remember?"

"There was some kind of accident," he said. "I remember a *flash*. Then I was... somewhere else."

"Do you know where you were?" the other civilian asked. "Can you describe it?"

He tried to shake his head, but it was too firmly restrained. "I can't put it into words."

"Can you remember what you've been doing since the incident?" the general asked.

I've been having a dream. Except I haven't, have I. He felt a shudder of panic go through him, waited for the electric shock, but nothing happened. "I've been trying to come back."

"Were you in Cairo?"

"*Cairo*? No. Why would I be in Cairo? What the fuck happened at the SCS?"

"We don't know," said the first civilian. "We don't dare go into the control room. We sent in bomb disposal robots with remote cameras and there's... *something* there, but there are no people, no bodies."

"*Something*?"

The civilian shook his head. "We don't know. The cameras won't image it. It's just a dead point in the middle of the room. Can you remember anything of what happened?"

I was busy attacking Larry Day. "They were doing a full-scale run," he said. "Everyone was counting down and then there was..." He looked at them. "Sorry."

"Did anything seem out of the ordinary? Anything at all?"

Yes, I'd just found out Larry Day burned my house down. "No, everything seemed normal. But I'm not a physicist, I'm a journalist."

"Where do you... *go*?"

"I don't know. Somewhere. Nowhere. *Anywhere*."

The general said, "We'll go now, but others will want to speak with you. Thus far, you're the only survivor to whom we have access, and we want to understand what happened at the SCS as much as you do. If you continue to cooperate, I don't see any reason for unpleasantness. But for now, I think we'll leave the vest and the sedation in place. Please don't try to go, um, *anywhere*."

After they'd gone, he sat quietly in the chair—after all, there was nothing much else to do—and tried to address the probability that this was not a dream. Something really *had* happened at the SCS, and it really *had* done something to him. Which meant that everything else was real too. And what was that *only survivor to whom we have access* about?

HE THOUGHT THE IV must be remote controlled, or at least on a timer, because he drifted away periodically into a dreamless sleep, and when he woke there were usually a couple of people in the room with him asking questions. They were mostly the same questions, and he mostly gave the same answer: *I don't know*. But they broke up the monotony, and he gradually, bit by bit, learned stuff himself.

The accident had happened over a year ago, which was a shock. He had... reappeared? *manifested*? eight months later at Fort Bragg, where he had caused some unspecified emergency before disappearing again. Quite why he had appeared at Fort Bragg was a mystery to him; he didn't even know where it was. The entire facility had been evacuated and was under quarantine; a patrol had spotted him and brought him down. Nobody would tell him where he was. They kept asking him about Cairo.

Time passed, he supposed, but there was no way of telling

how much. He woke at one point to find an IV in his other arm, presumably to feed and keep him hydrated, and occasionally he regained consciousness wearing fresh coveralls and a feeling that he had at least been sponged down. Apart from that, nothing changed.

One day, he woke up and he was being wheeled along a corridor. Someone in all-black combat gear was walking in front of him carrying an automatic rifle, and he could hear the footsteps of perhaps four more bringing up the rear.

The lead guard stopped at a door and opened it, and Alex was wheeled into a room with a desk and several chairs. There were two men in the room. One was tall and thin and in late middle age, with a face that was all hard angles. The other was younger, with dark curly hair, wearing chinos and a polo shirt and a windbreaker.

"Mr Dolan," said the older man. "My name is Flynn. This is my colleague, Mr Maserati."

"Dominic." The younger man raised a hand in greeting. "Everyone calls me Dom."

Flynn looked at the guards. "Get those things off him," he said.

"Sir, we're under orders—" began one of the guards.

"Yes," Flynn interrupted. "You're under *my* orders. Now get them off him."

There was a moment's pause, then the guard who had spoken came round and cut the cable ties attaching Alex to the chair. Alex sat where he was for a moment, then allowed himself a delicious *slouch*.

"And the rest," Flynn said.

The guards unbuttoned the execution vest and helped Alex out of it and all the other paraphernalia. They left the IVs in place.

"Okay," Flynn said. "Dismissed."

"Sir—" said the first guard, but the look on Flynn's face

changed his mind. The men left the room, then it was just Alex and Flynn and Dom Maserati looking at each other.

"It might be best if you sit where you are while we have this conversation," Flynn said. "You've been in that chair for over a week and you'll probably pass out if you try to stand up."

"I feel fine," Alex told him.

"You feel fine because you're under sedation. We'll get you off that, presently."

"Who are you?"

Flynn and Dom glanced at each other. "There has been something of a turf war going on over you, Mr Dolan," Flynn told him. "A turf war which I have won, for the moment."

"We're the good guys," said Dom. "The other guys are good guys too, I guess, but we're better."

"You've been treated badly," Flynn said, "and I apologise for that."

Alex looked at them. "Where am I?" he asked.

"You're in Quantico, Virginia," said Flynn. "At the FBI Academy."

"That's one of the reasons why we're better," Dom said. "We don't mind telling you where you are."

"Are you the FBI?"

"I was CIA," Flynn said. "Now I'm without portfolio, so to speak. Dom here comes to us from the DEA. His career's been *much* more interesting than mine."

Dom grinned and shook his head and said, "Nah."

"I don't get it," said Alex. "Are you comedians or something?"

Flynn sighed heavily, pulled a chair round, and sat down almost knee-to-knee with Alex. "Your little visit to Bragg caused two fatal heart attacks and put six people into comas, Mr Dolan," he said evenly. "Two of them still haven't recovered. So, no, we're not comedians."

"I didn't know that," said Alex. "I'm sorry." He tried to make it sound convincing.

"We've been tasked with working out what to do with you," Flynn went on. "Whatever happened at the SCS, it seems to have left you with certain... *abilities*. We don't know how it happened, and we don't know the extent of those abilities, and that has made certain authority figures somewhat excitable. I see my job, chiefly, as trying to get everyone to calm the fuck down." He looked Alex in the eye. "Are we on the same page here?"

Alex nodded. "Calm is good."

"All that fancy paraphernalia," said Flynn. "The portable electric chair. It wasn't a problem for you, was it."

Alex didn't know for sure, but he suspected not. He put a finger to his lips. "Don't tell anyone."

Flynn nodded. "So, we can't confine you. And bearing in mind your... unique situation, exploring the limits of your mortality might prove counterproductive."

Exploring the limits of your mortality. Alex liked that. He said, "I think you could probably kill me. If you took me by surprise. I'm still exploring limits myself."

"Duly noted," said Flynn. "So, we have something of a problem. Here you are, with certain abilities, the parameters of which we're all still uncertain."

"Yes."

"And here are we, frankly shit-scared of what you might turn out to be able to do. If you think about it enough, you might be able to see the advantage of coming to some kind of accommodation with us."

They had not, so far, threatened him or his family, Alex noted. Whether that was a good or a bad thing, he had no idea. He said, "What kind of accommodation?"

Flynn thought about it. "We can't, as we've noted, force you to cooperate with us, but I think you'd like to understand what's happened to you. We can try to help with that. We have the resources."

Alex doubted whether Flynn's resources were adequate, but he didn't say anything.

"In return, we need to know what happened at Sioux Crossing. What is *still* happening. You're the only survivor, and we believe you're our best chance of doing that."

"Actually," Dom put in, "we're more worried about that than we are about you right now. We can reason with you."

Flynn glanced at him, then back at Alex. "I've had some briefings over the past week or so where some very very smart people have used the phrase *extinction-level event*," he said. "I don't know whether it is or not, and neither do the very very smart people. And personally, I find that extremely worrying. We have to try to understand it, and to reverse it if it turns out to pose a threat. Myself, I'd like to reverse it anyway."

"You want me to go back in there," Alex said.

"Not right away," said Dom.

"I don't want to do that."

"Well," Flynn crossed his arms and sat back in his chair, "we have a problem, then."

"You have a problem," Alex said. "Not me." And he *stepped* out of the room for a moment.

When he came back, Flynn and Dom were where he had left them. Neither of them looked particularly freaked out, but nor did they seem particularly impressed.

"We've seen the footage of you doing that," Dom told him. "Old news."

"But thank you for reminding us," Flynn said heavily. "And you might want to put some clothes on."

Oops. Alex conjured up jeans and a hoodie. Flynn and Dom didn't seem impressed by this, either.

"Tell me," Flynn said. "Why did you come back?"

"I want you to find someone for me."

* * *

Flynn co-opted a military transport from the Marine base which surrounded the FBI Academy and flew with him to Duluth. Apparently, Alex's request had sparked a monumental discussion among Flynn's superiors.

"We'd rather you didn't do this at all," he said. "The official line is that there was an explosion; you're listed among the dead."

Much of the discussion, Alex gathered, had centred around the mechanics of how to do this. Flynn and the people he worked for had finally come down on a least-worst scenario which concealed Alex's involvement with them. But they were still not remotely happy with him.

At Duluth airport, Alex was hustled into a windowless van and driven into a hangar, where he and Flynn changed vehicles for an anonymous Nissan. Following the GPS, Flynn drove them around the edge of the city. Alex looked watched the buildings go by, not wanting to talk. He supposed he could have come here under his own steam, but he was still uncertain about his accuracy. He could just as easily have wound up in Doncaster as Duluth.

Eventually, Flynn pulled up on a pleasant, wooded street. "Just down there," he said, nodding through the windscreen. "Number 103. Apartment 12. You've got an hour; I'll be here waiting for you."

Alex put his hand on the doorhandle. "What will you do if I don't come back?"

"I'll spend what remains of my life simultaneously appearing in front of closed Congressional hearings and trying to find another job."

Alex nodded. "Okay."

Number 103 was a newish apartment building. Someone was just leaving as he arrived, and he caught the door before it closed and locked, and slipped inside. He took the stairs up to the first floor, found apartment 12, and stood in front of the door for a few moments trying to gather his thoughts before knocking.

The door opened and Wendy spent quite a long time looking at him. "So," she said finally, "not dead then."

"I DIDN'T EVEN know anything had happened until two days later," she said, opening her fridge and bringing out a couple of bottles of Budweiser. "Bud was so pissed he threw me in your old cell. Next thing I knew, he was opening the door and the town was under martial law." She popped the tops off the beers, brought them into the living room, handed one to Alex, and sat down.

"Martial law?" he asked.

"Soldiers, Marines, Army Rangers, helicopters. They sealed the place off. Haven't you seen the news?"

Alex shrugged. Wendy's apartment was small and neat. The home of someone who had thought it was just temporary and was now starting to face the possibility that it might be permanent.

"It was like a movie," she said. "You know? One where an alien spaceship crash-lands in some little town and the military move in and take over?"

He nodded and sipped his beer. "Is it still under martial law?"

"So far as I know. They questioned me for *weeks* and then they suddenly let me go. No thank you, no nothing. Just put me on a bus with about a dozen other people from the Facility, drove us to Mason City and left us to take care of ourselves. Alex, what *happened* in there?"

"I don't know," he said.

"Charles said you were in the control room."

For some reason, he felt rather happy to learn that Charles had survived. "I never made it," he said, which was the story he and Flynn had come up with. "I got to the top of the stairs and there was this *bang* and I turned and ran for it."

"Charles didn't remember you coming back downstairs," she told him.

"Charles was already gone by the time I got back into the lobby."

She frowned at him. "They say you're dead."

"I'd just busted out of a cell," he said, sticking to the story. "The police were after me. I stole a car and I got out of there, went out of state. I've been keeping my head down ever since."

"You're looking well, for a man on the run."

"I've still got some contacts from when I was at the *Globe,*" he said. "They helped me out." It sounded terribly thin, and he'd told Flynn that, but it was the best they'd been able to come up with. "It might be best if you don't mention you've seen me."

"I think Bud has more things to worry about than arresting you."

"I didn't see Larry at the Facility. He might still be out there somewhere."

"He was listed as dead."

"So am I."

She sighed. "You should go to the police."

He shook his head. "I don't know what to do," he said, and it was more or less the first true thing he'd told her since he arrived. "Did you get a chance to see Ralph?"

She shook her head. "I heard they evacuated the town but some people were refusing to leave. For all I know, he's still there. I tried to find out but nobody's talking. I managed to track Danny Hofstadter down and asked him, but he never got back to me."

Alex sighed and rubbed his eyes. "What about you?"

She looked around the apartment. "I'm kind of in freefall. The Facility's been sealed off but I'm still getting a salary. Nobody's seen Stan Clayton in months, so we don't know what the status of the project is." She shrugged. "Don't know. I'm waiting for someone to tell me what to do. We all are. A lot of the researchers got tired of waiting and went on to other projects. I got a call from Mickey Olive a couple of months ago and he's in the same boat. He was talking about going back to England."

What a mess. "Does anyone have any idea what happened?"

"They say it was a bomb. I can't see what else it could have been; there was nothing in the control room that could have caused an explosion."

"Doesn't that seem at all odd to you? Why would they evacuate Sioux Crossing if it was just a bomb?"

She spread her hands. "Defense," she said, as if that explained everything. "I guess they wanted to secure whatever it was they were working on, if they were working on something. National security." She drank some more beer and looked at him. "It's been over a year, Alex. I should punch you."

"I know," he said. "I'm sorry."

"You're sorry."

He opened his mouth to make an excuse—something about being on the run, her being hard to find—thought better of it, and closed his mouth again.

"What are you going to do now?" she asked. "You can't stay dead; your friends won't look after you for ever."

Oh, I think they might. "I'll be okay for a while. What's your phone number?"

She looked at him a few moments longer, then went to find a pen and something to write on. She came back with an old envelope, scribbled the number on it, and held it out. "Where are you staying?"

"Better you don't know," he said, taking the envelope. "I'll be in touch, though. I'll try to come back again."

She looked sadly at him. "I don't think you should make promises you can't keep, Alex."

* * *

Driving back to the airport, Flynn said, "How did it go?"

"Is it possible for you to forget all about this?" Alex asked.

Flynn thought about it. "If it was just me, maybe," he said. "But too many people are in the loop to just pretend it didn't happen."

"I don't want her messed around with," Alex said. "No surveillance, no phone taps, no hacking. Nothing. I want her left alone."

"I can make recommendations..."

"No, Arthur," Alex said. "You don't understand. If Wendy gets dragged into this, however tangentially, I'm off, and you'll never find me again."

There was a long silence in the car. Finally, Flynn said, "Okay."

They drove for a while longer in silence. Alex said, "Why do people keep asking me about Cairo?"

Flynn glanced at him. "You sure you want to hear this?"

"I won't know until you tell me."

"Okay. Well, a day or so after you lit out of Fort Bragg, there was an incident in Cairo. Half the city centre was destroyed. There's no footage of what happened, but some of the survivors say they saw a *djinn* walking through the city, a human figure that walked through buildings and wrecked them."

"And you think that might have been me?"

"You keep telling us you weren't there, although it's possible you didn't know *where* you were. But there's another reason for us to think it wasn't you. There was another incident, while you were unconscious at Quantico. A small town called Spicerville. Eight hundred people dead."

Alex looked out of the window, thinking about that.

"We're calling it an explosion in a railcar full of chemicals," Flynn went on. "The Egyptians are saying theirs was a meteorite strike."

You're the only survivor we currently have access to. "You think someone else made it out of the SCS. Someone like me."

"That's the theory we're working on. It might all be unconnected, but what are the chances?" Flynn turned the car off the freeway and onto the airport approach road. "Whoever it is, they don't seem to be coping as well as you."

"They're in real trouble then," Alex told him. "Because I'm not coping at all." He thought for a few moments. "There's something else I want you to do."

Flynn glanced at him. "I thought we had established who was running this operation, Alex."

"Without my cooperation you can't do anything," Alex reminded him. "And you can't make me cooperate."

Flynn sighed. "You and I are going to have to establish some *parameters*," he said. "What do you want?"

THEY BROKE IT to her gently. As gently as they could, considering it involved flying her to Quantico, sitting her down in a conference room, asking her to sign a six-inch-high stack of NDAs, and then showing her footage of Alex disappearing and reappearing, Alex making other things disappear and reappear, Alex taking a motorcycle to pieces just by looking at it. They didn't show her the footage of him putting it back together again, because he hadn't quite managed to do it right and what they'd wound up with looked more like a modern sculpture than a motorcycle.

When the videos ended, she turned to him and said, "You lied to me."

"I did," he admitted.

"You came to my home and you lied to me."

He glanced at the screen. *But look what I can do with my brain.* "I'm sorry."

"I helped you bust out of that cell and you lied to me."

"Wendy," he said.

"You let me think you were dead and then you just turned up out of the blue and you lied to me."

"Dr McCoy," Flynn said, stepping in smoothly. "We have a situation here which we think you could help us with."

She looked at him. "Who are you?" she said. "What's going on here?"

"As far as we understand it, Mr Dolan's proximity to the accident at the SCS resulted in him gaining certain... abilities," Flynn told her. "We're currently assessing those abilities. Our long-term objective is to study the ongoing situation at Sioux Crossing and, if possible, reverse it."

Wendy narrowed her eyes at him. "'Ongoing'?" she said.

"The accident blew a hole in space-time," Alex said. "That's the best guess, anyway. The hole's still open."

She looked at him, then at Flynn, then back. "Did anyone else survive?"

"There are... indications that there may be one or more others," Flynn said carefully. "We still don't have enough information."

She sat back in her chair. "Jesus."

"I need a friendly face, Wendy," Alex told her.

"You'd better go find someone else, then," she said. "Liar."

Alex sighed.

"I should mention that quite a few people were opposed to your being made aware of the situation, Doctor," Flynn said, without adding that he had been one of them. "Mr Dolan was very insistent."

"I'll bet."

"As of this moment, your security clearance is roughly equivalent to that of the Joint Chiefs. That's how serious this is."

She blinked at him. "Does that mean you can tell me who really killed Kennedy?"

Flynn said, "Dr McCoy."

"How about Roswell? Can I see the bodies?"

"Dr McCoy," Flynn said, infinite forebearance in his voice. "Do you recall me saying, just a few moments ago, 'That's how serious this is'?"

Wendy gave Alex a final glare. "As far as I know, I'm still employed by Clayton Dynamics. They're still sending me paychecks, anyway."

"And we'd prefer it if things remained that way," Flynn told her. "The longer they remain unaware of your involvement here, the better. The amount of work you could do for them is limited, anyway. At this point, it seems unlikely that the SCS will reopen in our lifetimes."

That gave her pause. "Have you *any* idea what happened?"

"We have a theory."

"And it... " She nodded at Alex.

"That, we still don't understand," Flynn told her. "Perhaps you could help us with that?"

"Can I vivisect him?"

"Hey," Alex said.

"All we can promise you is a government salary and research that no one else on earth is currently doing," Flynn said.

She looked at them again. "Well why didn't you say that in the first place?"

THERE WERE MORE weeks of tests, visits back *there*. The scientists were eager to try their theories out on him, calling the other place 'Calabi-Yau space', or, if they were trying to be particularly mysterious that day, 'the Manifold'. The theory was that Calabi-Yau space existed a tiny fraction of a nanometre away from what Alex had once thought of as 'normal space', if he had thought about it at all. Under normal circumstances, the scientists said, it would take more than the total energy output of the entire universe to force a single photon to cross between the dimensions, but travel from one space to another seemed to be more of a judo trick than a karate move, more a manipulation of force than a direct application of it. Somehow, the high energy run at the SCS had caught the universe at *just* the right angle, pitching everyone in the control room into a terrible emptiness and leaving behind Point Zero, a pulsing, open wound between the worlds, a point that *wouldn't be imaged*. One of the researchers told him that the odds of the accident happening at all were billions and billions to one against. Like going into every casino on The Strip in Vegas and playing every slot machine and winning the jackpot on all of them, all in one evening. But that was the thing about odds and probability. You could talk about them as much as you wanted, do all the fancy math, but in the end there was only Either/Or. That was all that mattered. Either you won all the jackpots on The Strip, or you didn't. Either it happened, or it didn't. It had, and here he was.

He suspected the scientists wouldn't have told him anything at all, but he was their only eyewitness—the only one they had access to, anyway—and he was the only person they could bounce their ideas off, even though the concrete information he gave them wouldn't have covered the back of a postage stamp. One of the scientists asked him, "What's it like there? How many dimensions does it have?" and all Alex could tell him was, "Not enough. Too many. I don't know."

Flynn's lead researcher was a woman named Sierpińska, an untidy, genial Pole in her early fifties. "Ah, Alex," she said, shaking her head sadly. "You mess with Nature, you see what you get?" Which he thought was an unusual point of view for a scientist.

The latest session was taking place in what had become their informal Situation Room at Quantico, a big roomy boardroom with a table large enough for twenty people. Usually it was just four of five of them, crowded down at one end and talking in low voices about what had happened at Sioux Crossing. Alex's contribution usually consisted of saying, "I don't know," at strategic points in the conversation.

Today's theory involved the structures Alex had reported

seeing while in the Manifold. "We think—we hypothesise—that some of them at least are the people who were in the control room with Alex when Point Zero was formed," Professor Sierpińska said.

Everybody—Dom, Professor Sierpińska, Wendy, a couple of the other scientists—looked at Alex, who said, "I don't know." He was thinking of having the phrase printed on a little flag that he could hold up when circumstances demanded.

One of the other scientists rubbed his eyes—they were all tired—and said, "Did we rule out gravitational shear? I can't remember." There had been a theory that Point Zero had produced a short-lived but steep gravitational gradient, a kind of subcritical black hole—the irony was not lost on Alex, remembering what he had told Ralph—which had torn everyone else present in the control room into microscopic pieces but somehow left Alex unharmed.

"There's no evidence of it," said Professor Sierpińska. "Not on the footage, anyway."

Everyone looked again at Alex, who was still putting off a visit to the SCS, and he just scowled and waved it away.

"So we can't rule it out yet," the scientist, whose name was Greene, went on. Greene was very big on gravitation, Alex remembered. He believed Point Zero was some kind of event horizon.

"No, Chris," Professor Sierpińska said patiently. "We cannot rule it out yet. There are many things we cannot rule out yet. Too many things."

"So if they're in there and they've been changed, the way Alex says, are they dead?" asked Dom.

"Maybe, maybe not," said Wendy.

Everyone looked at Alex again. He sighed. Maybe not a little flag. Maybe a tee shirt. "They're not moving," he said. "They're just *there*."

"You know, Alex," said Professor Sierpińska, "it's really time you went back to Sioux Crossing." She pronounced it 'Susie Crossing', which Alex found rather charming.

"I'm not ready yet," he said. Nobody mentioned that he had not been ready for several months now, and didn't seem inclined to give anyone an idea when he *would* be ready. Sometimes he thought they treated him like a very expensive and delicate piece of lab equipment. Other times, they behaved as if he was just a camera on legs. Taking an actual camera, or any other kind of recording equipment, into the Manifold was impossible. They simply disappeared. It was left to Alex to try and describe or draw what he saw, which was beyond him. And so they struggled on. He'd already done two trips today and it was hard not to see the gaps between the walls.

The Professor sighed. She was not, he thought, an unkind person, but he knew she was becoming frustrated by a lack of on-site work. Nobody else dared go anywhere near Point Zero. The Army had put a fence around the main building, at quite a distance.

"The time is coming," she said gently, "when you will have to *be* ready, Alex."

He nodded. "I know." He looked at Dom, who just shrugged. No help there. "Where's Arthur?" He hadn't seen Flynn for several days.

"Out in the field." Which was Dom-speak for stuff which someone had decided Alex didn't need to know about.

The meeting stalled. They drank coffee and ate stale pastries. Alex turned a croissant into an apple, and back again.

"Dude," said Greene.

Alex sat back. "Sorry. Mind wandering." It was surprising how quickly a miracle could become prosaic and then simply annoying.

"We're all tired," Dom said. "Let's pick it up again tomorrow, yeah?"

This was received with grunts of relief from almost everyone else at the table. The Professor sat looking at Alex, lips pursed.

"You know," she said when everyone else but Wendy and Dom had left, "I'm maybe not so good at man management, so I apologise if it seems that I'm hassling you, but we *need* you in there. Because of the other one."

'The other one' was Flynn's *djinn*, the presumed second survivor, who had so far not manifested again. Alex said, "How's an on-site survey going to help with that?"

"That's just my point," said Professor Sierpińska. "We *don't know*. It could be of vital importance, it could be utterly useless. Until we actually *do it* we don't know."

Alex closed his eyes and rubbed his face. "I'll think about it."

Professor Sierpińska looked mildly annoyed. Dom, who Alex had noticed *was* good at man management, said nothing.

"I DON'T KNOW whether to thank you for getting me mixed up in this or punch you," Wendy said.

"At least you had a choice," said Alex.

"Don't be snarky, there's a dear."

"You were just threatening to punch me; I think I'm allowed to be snarky."

They were sitting in a Chinese restaurant in a town about an hour's drive from the base, Alex didn't know exactly where. The food was indifferent but at least he was away from Quantico for a few hours.

"You think I have to go back," he said.

"I don't see any alternative," Wendy told him, poking at her beef in black bean sauce with her chopsticks. "We've sent in pretty much every recording device known to man and they all say there's nothing there, but we know *something*'s there. We need someone to have a physical look-see."

He scowled and looked around the restaurant. It was packed with diners; the waiter had found them a table tucked away in a corner away from the door. "It might be as dangerous for me as for anyone else."

She sat back and looked at him. "What we can say with some confidence is that there's no radiation in there," she said. "Air samples have come back clean." She nodded around the dining room. "This is probably a more hostile environment."

"Point Zero isn't here," he said.

"Scaredy-cat." She wrinkled her nose and went back to her food. "Kasia's right," she said, meaning Professor Sierpińska, with whom she had bonded within about a second of being introduced. "There's no other way."

They ate for a while in silence. He said, "Well."

She sighed. "Look," she said, "I'm still more pissed off with you than you can imagine. Okay, so maybe you couldn't let me know any earlier that you were alive, but did you have to come to my apartment and lie to me like that?"

"It was Flynn's idea."

She gave him a hard stare. "Don't you dare blame Art," she said. "You didn't have to go along with it."

"I did if I wanted to see you."

She snorted. "Like anyone can make you do anything."

"Not that it stops them trying," he pointed out.

She pointed a chopstick at him. "You're in a bad situation, Alex, and you need all the friends you can get. You can't afford to alienate people."

"Okay," he said. "Okay." This entire conversation was, of course, classified. Fortunately the people at the tables nearest them were cleared for anything they might overhear—scientists and techs from Quantico. Further out into the restaurant were more researchers, and a scattering of Security staff with high clearances. And beyond them, out of earshot, a semicircle of Marines, dressed in casual clothes but still recognisably military. Flynn had packed the place with his people, quietly booking up the entire restaurant for this one evening. The only civilians in the building were the restaurant staff. Alex looked around the room again, and saw his future, a place where he couldn't go anywhere without bodyguards—not to protect him, but to stop him letting the secret slip. It was not a future he liked very much.

Wendy was eating again. "What about Ralph?" she asked, lowering her voice so that no one, security-cleared or otherwise, could hear her.

"I'm still thinking about that," he said.

"Don't think for too long," she told him. "Last time I saw him, he looked sick."

FLYNN MAY HAVE been ex-CIA but he had fought long and hard to have Alex brought to Quantico. "Always handy to have the Corps on your doorstep," he told Alex. Quite apart from several thousand Marines, Quantico also had both Marine Corps and FBI R&D facilities, which other possible destinations for Alex—Langley, for instance—did not. It also had the DEA training school, Dom's alma mater.

They had set up an outdoor firing range for him, tucked away in a newly built compound in the woods surrounding the Academy. It was basically just a big windowless two-roomed cinderblock building, which had acquired windows shortly after Alex, during an early exercise, had burned out the lights.

Other early triumphs included the infamous and never-repeated Levitation Experiment, when he had done something very bad but thankfully temporary to gravity inside the range, and the time he had taken apart an office chair and reassembled it, from the atoms up, into what he had thought was a more pleasing shape. The shape had not been remotely pleasing to the two observers on duty that day, and both of them were now on indefinite medical leave. Flynn had given him a hard stare while he—only just—accepted Alex's apology that he hadn't realised what he was doing. "Try not to break any more scientists,

Alex," he said. "They're expensive to train."

The smaller of the range's two rooms housed the researchers and their recording equipment. The larger was a big echoing space with a cement floor and scorch marks on the walls. The new windows were high up near the roof and sometimes let in shafts of sunlight in the late afternoons.

Down at one end of the room was a row of targets. These had originally been shop-window mannequins, but Alex hadn't liked that so now they used big circular archery targets, which he blew to bits when he got bored.

The exploration of his abilities was something of an adventure for everyone, even if it sometimes seemed to Alex that the researchers were using a stack of superhero comics as a reference. *Does he have x-ray vision?* Yes, as it turned out. Kind of. *Can he leap tall buildings in a single bound?* Don't be so stupid. The thing that struck him most, as the weeks and months went by, was how matter-of-fact everyone was about the whole thing. It was as if generations of comic books and movies had made them view superpowers as something to be taken for granted. He waited for someone to suggest, casually, in a meeting that he should have some kind of uniform, but that never quite happened. Perhaps they realised he wouldn't suit spandex.

At one point, someone somewhere had become interested in whether he could raise the dead. This more or less confirmed to him that he was in the hands of mad people, because one morning he was presented with a dead frog in a Tupperware container and invited to return it to life. He failed, but failure was no reason, in and of itself, to abandon an experiment, so in the following days the corpses of two white mice, a cat, and a small monkey were delivered, and there he called a stop. "If you bring me one more dead thing," he told the researcher who had come in with the monkey, "I'll turn you into a fucking wardrobe."

"Stop frightening the researchers," Flynn told him in passing a couple of days later. "If they sue you, you're on your own."

He was conscious that, in parallel with the scientists trying to work out what had happened to him, there was another programme which was seeking to weaponise that knowledge, but there was nothing he could do about that. Well, there was; he could leave and never come back, but then he would never know if he hadn't walked away from a chance to be normal again. He thought the chances were slim, but they were there.

So what was he? A superhero? A wizard? A god? What he mostly was, he felt, was a long way from home. Flynn's people had made him as comfortable as they could, bearing in mind the circumstances. He had a nice apartment on the Academy campus—once the home, he thought, of some senior administrator or instructor. He had the very best medical care, good food, and in the unlikely event that Larry Day was still out there somewhere bearing his incomprehensible grudge, he was surrounded by an unusual concentration of some of the most capable and heavily armed people on the planet.

And yet, he was dead, and that hurt. His mother, and everyone he knew, had been told that he had died in an explosion at the SCS. Flynn had told him there had been a rather nice little memorial service for him back home in Leith. He'd considered, several times, popping home to tell his mother he was still alive, but he didn't quite know how he'd approach that. *Hi, Ma, there's been a bit of a mistake, and oh, by the way, I can kill people with my brain now.*

So he sat in his nice room at Quantico and ate his nice meals and submitted to scans and samplings and exercises to see if he could turn himself into a gigantic invulnerable green rage monster (yes, he could, and then they asked him not to do that again) and late at night he lay in bed staring at the ceiling wondering how the fuck he was being so calm about it all.

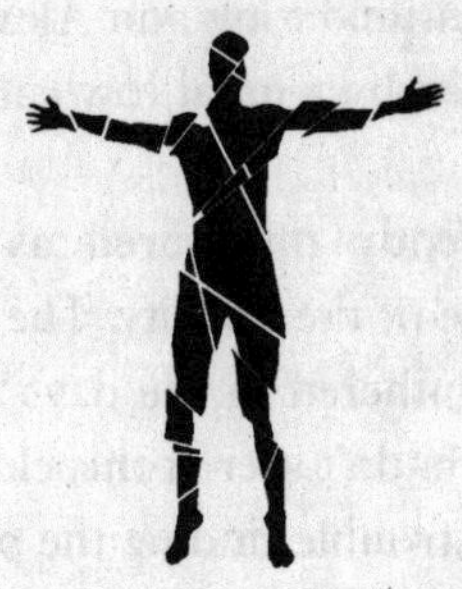

THE EXPLODING MAN

IN THE END, it was a little like a school outing. Alex, Flynn, Dom, Wendy, Professor Sierpińska and half a dozen researchers flew in to Sioux Crossing's airport one morning. Looking out of the window as they taxied to a halt, Alex couldn't see a single civilian aircraft.

From the airport, they were helicoptered to Rosewater High, where a forward base had been established on the sports field, a ring of modular housing and office units stacked five high and dubbed Camp Batavia, for reasons which were never explained to any of them.

They loaded themselves and their gear onto a convoy of Humvees and Marine drivers took them to the Facility. The countryside looked wilder and more overgrown than Alex remembered, but there was no sense that a disaster had happened here. Was still happening.

He'd seen the cloud from miles away, as they began their descent into Sioux Crossing airport, a great slowly rotating spiral of vapour that rose all the way into the stratosphere. Flynn had told him that a tornado had tracked across this part of Iowa earlier in the year, and it had disturbed the cloud not at all. It was huge and intimidating and Alex thought its rotation should be accompanied by a great low rumbling sound instead of eerie silence.

"Jesus Christ," Wendy murmured as the convoy passed through the front gate of the Facility. The cloud hadn't formed immediately; it had gathered in the days and weeks following the accident, and she hadn't seen it this close up before.

"At least there's no trouble finding the place," Dom said.

Of course, the cloud also made it impossible to pretend that something big and weird wasn't happening in Sioux Crossing. There was an official explanation—something about the edge effect of intense magnetic fields being created by the collider—but Alex gathered this was being regarded with a certain amount of cynicism by most of the population of the United States, and he couldn't blame them.

A new, inner fence had been constructed within the campus, with the main building at its centre. A patrol of special forces soldiers met them when they pulled up at the fence, and helped unload their gear and carry it to a little cluster of tents a few yards away. Alex stood where he was, hands in the pockets of his windbreaker, looking through the fence at the cloud and the main building in the distance.

"Quite a thing, isn't it," Dom said, standing beside him.

"Yes," Alex said. "Whatever it is."

Dom glanced at him. "Having second thoughts? We can scrub it, come back another day."

It seemed unlikely that this would please anyone, considering how long it had taken them to get him to agree. He shook his head. "Let's get it over with."

THEY DRESSED HIM in black coveralls like the special forces soldiers, although they looked better in them. Over this was a webbing harness weighed down with sensors and tools and bits of kit nobody thought worth explaining to him, and a heavy backpack with more recording gear. The whole outfit was topped off with a cycling helmet with cameras mounted on either side and an LED flashlight on top.

"Absolutely badass." Dom grinned, looking him up and down.

"Fuck off, Dom," he said.

"We'll be recording everything here, and there are separate recorders in your rucksack," Professor Sierpińska told him, "but I want you to give us a running commentary as well. Everything you see and do, please. If you believe you're in danger, I want you to leave immediately."

"Can I leave now, then?"

She smiled and patted him on the cheek. "You're a good man, Alex," she said.

The leader of the special forces patrol, a warrant officer named Stetson, walked him around to the gate. "You might see things in there," she told him.

"What sort of things?" Nobody had mentioned things to him.

"We don't know for sure, we've never been able to get a good look at them. Coyotes, probably. Raccoons."

"Okay." That didn't sound so bad.

"They mostly avoid us, but they move fast and they might startle you. You're not carrying a weapon."

"Do you think I need one?"

Stetson shrugged. "I know *I* wouldn't go in there unarmed," she said. "There's some spooky shit going on here."

You have no idea. "It's just edge effects from magnetic fields," he told her. "It's perfectly safe."

Stetson grunted. "Yeah. That's why we put a fence round the whole thing and stationed half the US military outside."

Stetson let him through the gate and he paused just inside the fence to run a final comms check, then he set out towards the building. The grass was almost knee-high, and surprisingly hard to walk through. He found himself having to lift his feet high and put them back down carefully. He kept the building in front of him and concentrated on walking in a straight line.

He was about halfway across the space between the fence and the building when he heard something moving in the grass to his left and a little ahead of him. He stopped and said, "There's something in the grass."

"Can you describe it?" asked Wendy's voice in his earpiece.

"No, I can't even see… wait." The grass had started to twitch, then vibrate, as if whatever was in there was shaking itself violently. "Oh." Abruptly, something small and possibly bipedal stood and looked at him, and just as suddenly dropped out of sight again sped off through the grass. "Did you get that?"

"Affirmative," she said. "That was… weird."

"That wasn't a raccoon, was it? It had too many eyes."

There was a moment's silence over the commlink, then Professor Sierpińska's voice said, "Do you feel under threat, Alex?"

"Sure," he said. "Every day since the accident."

Another brief silence, then the Professor said, "Proceed with caution, please. And don't forget to describe what you see."

He reached the front of the building and gave them a long tracking shot with the cameras. "It looks the same as it did when I came back here," he said. "Some windows are broken, it needs a lick of paint, but the structure looks sound. One of the doors is open. I'm going to go in."

Inside, the lobby was ankle-deep in blown-in leaves and bits of vegetation. He smelled mould and animals. He reached up onto the top of his head and switched on the lamp, turned in a slow circle. "No obvious damage," he said. "No sign of people, no sign that anyone's been in here since the accident." He looked at the floor, where two narrow lines had been scuffed in the leaf litter. "I can see the tracks of your remote; they haven't been disturbed. Is there anything here you want a closer look at?"

"No, thank you," said Professor Sierpińska. "Carry on, please."

"Okay. I'm going up the stairs now." He passed a panel of light switches, flipped them up and down one at a time. "Power's out," he said.

"The circuit breakers are in the basement," said Wendy. "We'll leave them for another time."

"You sound awfully sure there's going to *be* another time. Going up the stairs now."

He took the stairs carefully, pausing on each landing, until he reached the top floor and shone his light down the corridor. "Looks deserted," he said. "Animals have been in here; I can see pawprints on the carpet." He bent down to give the cameras a good look at a clutter of old bones and feathers at the base of the wall. "Someone's dinner," he said. He straightened up. "I'm going down the corridor."

He tried the doors on either side as he went. About half of them were locked. He stood in the doorways of the others and shot a minute or so of footage before carrying on.

The door at the end was open. He looked inside, remembering the control room as it had been when he'd last seen it, full of people. Now it was dark and empty and cold and it smelled very strongly of animal piss. He shone the light on the desks and workstations and screens. "Nobody home," he said. "No sign of bodies." He paused and looked at a mug on one of the desks. It was half full of mould. He moved slowly between the desks, filming everything, making sure he kept well away from the thing in the middle of the room until he was ready to turn and look at it.

"There's nothing there," he said.

"Could you be more precise, please?" asked the Professor.

So there it was, Point Zero itself, the thing which would not be imaged. Or rather, there it wasn't. "It's like a blind spot," he said. "You're conscious something's there, but you can't see it. It's hard to tell how big it is, precisely. Maybe a couple of metres across. I couldn't tell you what shape it is; I'm getting an impression it might be spherical, but it's only an impression. It doesn't seem to be doing anything, just sitting there."

"Sitting, or floating?"

"I can't tell. It seems closer to the floor than the ceiling, that's all I can make out."

"We're not reading any kind of activity in there at all," said the Professor. "No radiation. Nothing."

"That's because there's nothing here," Alex told her, moving around Point Zero. "I don't know how to describe it."

A sigh. "Very well. Give us another five minutes of footage, then move on to the next phase, please."

The next phase had been very hotly discussed back at Quantico. He said, "You're really sure you want me to do that?"

"I'm sorry, Alex," she told him. "We have to know."

"Okay. Well, it's been good working with you."

"We'll see you soon," she said.

"Right."

He took off his gear and put it on the floor by the door, where a bomb disposal robot could retrieve it if necessary. He balanced the helmet on a filing cabinet, where the cameras had a good view of the room. Then he walked over to Point Zero. "I'm standing right next to it," he told them. "I don't feel anything."

"Copy that," said the Professor. "Good luck, Alex."

"If I had any good luck at all I wouldn't be here in the first place," he said, and he stepped forward into Point Zero...

...AND OUT INTO familiar howling notlight. *Ah well. Home again home again.* The theory was right; Point Zero was the point where the dimensions touched, a hole between the real world and the Manifold. Looking behind him, he saw that it existed here as a faint *craquelure* hanging in the air. He made a mental note of its position and moved on.

He came upon the structures again, the ones the Professor was theorising represented everyone from the control room. She thought they were caught in some kind of intermediate state, neither dead nor alive. He counted them, as best he could. There had been thirty people in the control room when the accident happened. Minus himself and the still-theoretical second survivor, that left twenty-eight. But he counted twenty-nine. Did that mean they were wrong about the *djinn*? That it was just some natural phenomenon after all? He didn't think so. There were too many bodies here.

He drifted for a while. The team back at the SCS had no idea how long this would take him—there had been a real possibility that it would kill him outright—so he had some spare time. He took a very short *step*.

And found himself standing on East Walden Lane. All the houses looked dilapidated and deserted, their gardens gone wild. But there was a light on in one house, so he walked up the path onto the porch and knocked on the door, and after a minute or so Ralph opened it. "You're dead," he said.

"I get that a lot, these days."

Ralph grunted. "Come on in, then."

The house was a mess. It looked as if Ralph had abandoned the upper floor and was living and sleeping downstairs. He'd lost a lot of weight and moved very slowly, as if he ached all over.

"Why aren't you dead?" he asked as they sat down in the living room.

"I wasn't there," said Alex.

"They said you were."

"They were wrong. What are you still doing here? I heard they evacuated the town."

"Where am I going to go?"

"Danny would have helped you."

Ralph said, "Danny," and made a rude noise. "He beat feet the first chance he got."

Alex suspected this was untrue. He pictured Danny standing on Ralph's porch, and Ralph telling him in no uncertain terms to fuck off. "You can't stay here, you stupid old man," he said. "How the hell are you managing?"

"We got *militia* here now," Ralph said. "Montana militia. Survivalists looking for the End of Days. Moved into town a couple of weeks after the accident. They had a standoff with the Army, then the Army decided to leave them be, so now they just growl at each other every now and again. They bring me food and water, make sure I'm okay. They're batshit crazy, of course, but they look after me."

Homer wandered into the room. He'd lost weight too, but his digestion hadn't improved. He farted in greeting, then left again. Alex said, "Ralph, seriously, you have to leave. Look at the state of you."

Ralph shook his head. "This is my *home*, Alex. I don't understand why apparently smart people can't understand that."

Alex *looked* at the old man. In his right lung, shining a steady blue like the light over the front door of an old police station, was a tumour the size of a tangerine. It had thrown off a bunch of secondaries, and they twinkled in his other lung and his lymphatic system and his liver and spleen. Alex sighed and snuffed out the lights one by one. Then he repaired the worn-out mitral valve in Ralph's heart and cleaned out his arthritis, and finally he reset his telomeres. And then, because why not, he did the same thing to Homer.

This all took a fraction of a second, and Ralph never felt a thing. He put his hand in his pocket and brought out a fat envelope. "There's ten thousand dollars here," he said. He wasn't sure whether it was *exactly* ten thousand, but that was what he had imagined.

Ralph eyed the envelope as if Alex had decided to offer him a rattlesnake. "Where did you get that?"

"You wouldn't believe me if I told you. But there's more where it came from. Take it, get your act together, take Homer, and *get out of here.*" He didn't know how many more years he'd given the old man and his dog, but eventually someone would notice that Ralph hadn't died of old age, was in fact starting to look positively *chipper*, and that would attract the attention of Flynn and his friends. "The militia guys must know a way through the quarantine; get them to take you out, get on a bus, and just *go*. I'll call you and we'll sort things out from there."

There must have been something in his voice, this time, because Ralph gave him a long, steady look. Then he reached out and took the envelope. "That guy who came to see you," he said. "The big guy with the red car."

"Larry?"

Ralph nodded. "They say he killed some folks. Is that true?"

Alex stared at him. "I have no idea. What are you talking about?"

"He died in the explosion, right?"

"Yes."

"Well, when they finally got round to checking out his house they found some bodies there. That's what I hear."

Alex thought about it, then shook his head. "That's ridiculous. Who told you that?"

"Bud Rosewater. He was pissed because he was trying to deal with that while the emergency was going on. Said it was a big guy with white hair, drove a red car. Asked if I'd seen him around."

"What did you tell him?"

"Said he'd been round here one day but you weren't home. Said I thought the guy worked at the Facility, maybe he was here to do an interview with you or something."

"That's ridiculous," Alex said again.

"Well, that's what he told me." Ralph regarded him calmly. "You got time for a game?"

"No. I have to be somewhere else." He felt as if the world had suddenly taken a ninety-degree turn. Another ninety-degree turn. He stood up. "Two days," he said, nodding at the envelope in Ralph's hand. "I'll call you in two days, and if you're not somewhere else by then I'll get you out of here myself, and I promise you won't enjoy that."

Ralph tipped his head to one side. "You're different."

"You have no idea. I'll be in touch, okay?"

"Okay."

"And take Homer with you."

Ralph snorted. "Where the hell do you think I'm going to leave him?"

HE WENT BACK to the SCS via the Manifold, stepped out into the control room and picked up the bicycle helmet. "Hi, honey. I'm home," he said for the benefit of the cameras.

Back outside the fence, Professor Sierpińska said, "You were gone a while. We were worried."

"You were right," he told her, taking off his rucksack and handing it to one of the techs. "It's the front door into the Manifold."

She nodded happily. "That's good news. But what were you doing in there for so long?"

"Time doesn't work like that over there, I keep telling you that. But I did a count of the things you think are Professor Delahaye and his team and there's one too many." He saw Flynn and Dom, standing behind the Professor, exchange a glance. "So," he went on. "What are you not telling me?"

"WE DON'T KNOW this for an absolute fact," Flynn said. "There's no evidence, no eye-witness testimony."

"Okay," said Alex. They were sitting in a small room in one of the office modules that made up Camp Batavia, just himself and Flynn at a cheap table. There was an irritating whine in the background, almost too high-pitched for human hearing. Alex presumed it was electronic bafflers to prevent eavesdropping, but equally it could be a mosquito caught in ducting behind the wall.

Flynn said, "It's being kept very quiet, but nobody's seen Stanisław Clayton since the accident. We know he was in Sioux Crossing because he was having a meeting with someone at the New Rose Hotel. Where he went after that, we don't know. None of his people know."

Alex remembered Wendy saying something about Stan going missing.

"We think it's possible that he went to the Facility when he heard about the accident," Flynn went on. "Again, nobody we've spoken with remembers seeing him there, but by all accounts it was chaos in the first few hours and days after the incident. It's possible he could have gone into the control room and got too close to Point Zero, either accidentally or on purpose."

Alex sat back on his uncomfortable chair. "Well, shit," he said.

"Obviously, the board of Clayton Dynamics doesn't want this becoming common knowledge. Their share price is already in the toilet after the accident. It's equally not beyond the realms of possibility that when he heard about the accident he took himself off to a quiet corner of Rosewater County and killed himself."

Alex shook his head. "Stan wouldn't kill himself. He's not the type."

Flynn looked at him sadly. "There's no 'type' when it comes to suicide, Alex. But if you're right, it seems more likely he wound up in the Manifold, and I'll pass that on to the board in due course."

"You should have told me about this right away," Alex said.

"Why? What possible good could it have done you to know about it?"

"It would have demonstrated a certain amount of trust."

"It would, and I apologise," Flynn said. "But while we're on the subject of trust, you didn't spend all that time in the Manifold counting heads, did you. You were over the other side of town chatting with your old neighbour."

Alex gave him a hard stare. "Ralph's house is bugged."

"Ralph's house is bugged," Flynn agreed. "He's been dealing with the preppers who moved into Rosewater County; we thought we might pick up some useful gossip. And so we did."

They stared at each other for quite a while. Alex said, "Larry Day."

"I'm not going to apologise for that," Flynn said.

"Good."

"I wanted you clear-headed and cooperative, not obsessing about Professor Day." Flynn knew everything, of course. Kitson, the raccoon, the fire, Larry. Alex had told him all that in the earliest days of his debriefing.

"Is it true?"

"Professor Day had a house over on the west side of Rosewater County, near the county line. Quite a secluded place. It took the County Sheriff's department a couple of weeks to work around to visiting it; the authorities here were extremely busy in the early days of the emergency. Professor Day lived alone, so they broke in, and they found human remains. I'm not going to tell you the circumstances in which they found them, but it was more than one person."

Alex blinked at him.

"We still don't know who they were or how they met their deaths," Flynn went on. "As to why, well, we're still working on that. One of the profilers at Quantico assembled a view of him from sources in the public domain, which is probably the worst way of doing it, but it's not pretty. Equally, he could have suffered some form of breakdown."

"A breakdown that made him kill people?"

Flynn drummed his fingers on the tabletop for a moment. "One of the profilers at Quantico thinks he became fixated on you when you were arrested in Blackfish County. I understand you were released first?"

Alex nodded mutely.

"Well, they think that offended him somehow and he decided you were next. We still don't know what the Englishman was doing in Rosewater County, or how he wound up in your car, but it looks like Day mistook him for you and drove him off the road."

It took Alex a long time to even begin to process this. "Well," he said, "this has been a hell of a day."

"Everyone's tired," Flynn said, standing up. "Have a bite to eat, then get some sleep. We've got to do it all again tomorrow."

"What about Ralph?"

"Your friend?" Flynn paused at the door. "He can go; we've been trying to get the old fart to leave ever since the accident." He gave a tired smile. "But next time you decide to counterfeit US currency, don't tell people about it where you can be overheard, okay?"

Over the next five days, Alex made a dozen trips into the control room, bringing out laptops and hard drives and notebooks and anything else that looked as if it might have details about the experiment Delahaye and his team had been running on the day of the accident. When, at the end of that time, nothing awful had happened, Stetson and her people moved into the lobby of the building and cautiously started to search the offices on the lower floors.

Back at Quantico, Flynn disappeared into a fog bank of meetings, Professor Sierpińska and her people busied themselves analysing the data Alex had brought back from the control room, and Dom found himself embroiled in an old Enforcement operation he had once run which had suddenly become live again.

Which left Alex twiddling his thumbs, repeating exercises, and smiting targets on the range. The techs tried to keep him busy, but after two weeks of nothing much happening he was starting to get cabin fever. "I'm supposed to be a superhero," he told one of the techs. "I can't just sit about all day watching Netflix." The tech gave him an understanding smile and then went off to do something else.

Ralph had been exfiltrated from Sioux Crossing and was now on the way to Philadelphia, where he still had a few friends. Getting money to him proved complicated. Wendy asked a friend to set up an offshore bank account for him, then Alex created cash, a few thousand dollars at a time, and she took it out of Quantico and gave it to her friend, who banked it. It wasn't ideal, but Alex had discovered he couldn't directly manipulate data the way he could manipulate matter and it was the best solution he could come up with. He'd visit the old man when he was settled in, but for the moment there was nothing else to do but destroy stuff and binge-watch box-sets of old television shows on his laptop.

Finally, it got too much for him. One morning, without telling anyone, he *stepped* into the Manifold and then back out again.

He was standing in the middle of Main Street in Sioux Crossing and the place looked like the set for one of the post-apocalyptic shows he'd been watching lately. All the stores were shut, many of them boarded up, the buildings were dilapidated, rubbish was strewn across the street and along the pavements. Cars were parked haphazardly, left where they'd been when the Army first moved into the town and began its evacuation. At Stockmann, he saw signs of looting—windows broken, items of merchandise dropped on the pavement. It was all, he thought, heart-crushingly sad. He'd liked the town, liked its people, had actually, even after Larry started harassing him, felt at home here, and now it was all gone. Flynn said a lot of the population had been dispersed to family and friends across the state; the remainder were in a relocation camp near Mason City. The government was working hard to help, said Flynn, but he didn't take into account the farmers suddenly spirited off their land or the store owners or the people whose family had been in the county since before it had been named after Bud's great-grandfather. It was unlikely any of them would ever be allowed back; the people now in control of Sioux Crossing wanted as big a *cordon sanitaire* around the SCS as they could manage.

He turned and looked back up the street. The cloud rose above the buildings, turning unhurriedly up into the sky. There was now a big fat civilian no-fly zone over Rosewater County; commercial flights were diverted a long way to the south and north. That would probably be permanent too.

Of the supposed Montana militia, he saw no sign. Perhaps they were out on manouvres. He walked down the street and tried the doors of the Telegraph, but they were locked, and peering through the windows he could see it was deserted, abandoned in the middle of a working day, plates and cups still on the tables where people had left their meals behind. The *Banner* offices were similarly locked up. He wondered if he would be able to locate Dru Winslow without Flynn's help. He could turn a block of cement into a three-course meal just by thinking about it, but he couldn't navigate the labyrinthine backwaters of US bureaucracy without at least an initial clue where to look.

The New Rose was locked, all the lights turned off. He stood looking through the glass doors into the lobby, and to be honest apart from being in darkness it didn't look all that different from when he was living there; he'd always suspected the staff outnumbered the guests by about ten to one. How Danny had managed to keep it going was a mystery, although he'd probably received a fairly chunky stipend for the government's occasional use of the top floor.

The whole town was growing wild. In a few years you wouldn't be able to see the houses for overgrowth, the roads would be cracked by weeds and frost and snow. Sioux Crossing would eventually be like those old abandoned gold mining towns in California, except tourists would not be allowed to come here to poke around and take photographs. If they couldn't close Point Zero—and probably even if they could—the town was going to be out of bounds for ever.

He walked back to the road and stood there with his hands in his pockets. In the distance, he could hear helicopters landing and taking off at Camp Batavia, but apart from that it was eerily quiet. He'd always thought the county was quiet, but he hadn't noticed how much background noise there actually was. Traffic, farm machinery, human voices. All gone. It probably hadn't been this quiet in Rosewater County since before the first settlers arrived.

He wondered why Flynn and Professor Sierpińska hadn't asked him to close Point Zero. He didn't know if he could, but surely it was worth a try?

"You went walkabout," Flynn said casually while they waited for the meeting to begin.

"I got bored. I went and had a look at Sioux Crossing," Alex said, looking around the conference table. There were some unfamiliar faces here today, all of them not quite managing not to glance at him.

"Hm." Flynn reached out for one of the water jugs in the middle of the table, filled his glass. "Let us know the next time you want to do that, would you?"

"Cause a bit of a stir, did I?"

He replaced the jug on its coaster. "How was it? Sioux Crossing?"

"It's sad. I liked the town." He wondered briefly if this was the right time to broach the subject of Dru Winslow's whereabouts, then decided it wasn't.

"I never saw it, before." Flynn sat back in his comfy chair. "We got some new guys, I see."

"I was thinking that. Recognise anyone?"

He shook his head. "I'm getting too old to spend my days in committees. Everyone looks about twelve. I should be out fishing somewhere. Do you fish?"

"I never have, no."

"You should try it, sometime. Calms the spirit."

"Unless you're the fish."

"Can I ask a personal question?"

"You can *ask*..."

"If you could change what happened, would you? If you could go back to that day and stop yourself visiting the collider, knowing what you do now, would you?"

Alex looked at him. "What do you think?"

"Well, I don't know, that's why I asked. I was thinking about this the other evening. Sure, you want your old life back; this stuff sucks, you wouldn't be human if you didn't. But on the other hand, you're *not* human any more, are you. You teleported from here to Iowa and back, that's pretty cool. That would be hard to give up and go back to being normal."

Alex thought about it. "I wouldn't miss the meetings."

Flynn grunted. "You'll not hear me argue about *that*. Speaking of which, try not to lose your temper."

Alex said, "What?" but he didn't get a chance to answer because a young man in a business suit had walked to the front of the room and taken the audiovisual remote control from the podium.

"Ladies, gentlemen," he said by way of calling the room to order. "Before we begin, this meeting is classified FORAGE. Could anyone who is not FORAGE cleared please leave now. If you are not FORAGE cleared and you do not leave, you risk prosecution."

There was a moment's silence. Nobody made a move. Alex had never heard the codename before, so he started to get up, but Flynn put a hand on his arm. "You're cleared, Alex," he murmured. "Don't be a dick."

The young man in the suit gave the room a last once-over, then nodded and said, "Thank you." He thumbed the remote and the screen behind him came on with the words OPERATION FORAGE centred on it. "Ladies and gentlemen," he said. "First I'd like to detail the decision process which led to Operation Forage." He thumbed the remote again and an image of Point Zero came up. It had been taken from quite a distance, the spiral cloud hanging over the abandoned main building.

"Eighteen months ago," the young man went on, "an accident of unknown nature occurred at the Clayton Dynamics supercollider at Sioux Crossing, Iowa. As far as we can judge, everyone within a two-hundred-foot radius of the site of the accident was somehow translocated into a dimension which we are still struggling to understand.

"A year later, a naked human being was seen to appear out of thin air within the security perimeter of Fort Bragg. This individual was interviewed by base security, and partway through the interview they disappeared. The individual subsequently made a number of reappearances over a period of two months, and was eventually designated Resource Bravo."

Alex wondered if he should stand and take a bow.

"To date, Resource Bravo is the only individual to have visited the dimension to which the Sioux Crossing accident opened access. A working group was convened to address this fact, and reported that steps should be taken to broaden access."

Alex felt a dim stirring of concern.

The young man changed the image on the screen. This one was of a group of eight men and women in desert camouflage, carrying automatic weapons and equipment. Their faces had been pixellated out. "Oh, you *didn't*," Alex said, so quietly that only Flynn heard him. He put a hand on his arm again.

"To this end," the young man continued, "four days ago, on executive order, a SEAL team was transported to the site of the Sioux Crossing incident. Their orders were to access the adjacent dimension and carry out a full reconnaissance, with a view to establishing a foothold situation on the other side."

"Now just a fucking minute," Alex said out loud. Every head in the room turned to face him.

"Alex," Flynn murmured.

Alex shook the hand off his arm. "Did it not occur to anyone to ask *me* about this?" he demanded. "I mean, just for my *opinion*?"

"Alex," Flynn said again. "Calm down and hear the man out, would you?"

Alex looked at the young man, who was regarding him as if he was an unexploded bomb. "Did they come back?" he asked. When there was no reply, Alex said, "No. They didn't. Jesus Christ."

"It was a direct order from the president," said one of the other men sitting at the table, an older man with a deeply unconvincing combover.

"Your president's an asshole, and so is whoever talked him into signing off on this," Alex told him.

"Alex," Flynn snapped. "That's enough."

Alex suddenly realised he was halfway out of his chair. He sat down again. "Muppets," he muttered. Then louder again, "You've killed them all, you realise."

"*You're* not dead," someone, Alex couldn't see who, pointed out, and a heavy silence descended on the room.

He cornered Flynn in the secure breakout room and jabbed a finger at his chest repeatedly. "That stuff about wanting a *foothold* situation is bullshit," he said quietly. "You wanted a squad of superheroes and you thought you could get them by sticking a bunch of SEALs through Point Zero. And now they're all dead and you want me to clear up your mess."

"It was a decision taken above my head," Flynn said. "For what it's worth, I argued against it."

"Well you didn't fucking argue hard enough, did you. Jesus." Incandescent with rage, he turned away and approached the refreshment table. Everyone there moved away, which was fine by him. He poured himself a coffee and glared at the pastries and sandwiches and bowls of fruit.

"There are those," said a voice at his shoulder, "who say you're getting too big for your boots, son."

Alex turned, found himself looking at the unconvincing combover. "I beg your pardon?"

The combover looked Alex up and down, a smoothly plump operator in a suit worth more than a month's rent on Alex's old apartment in Boston. "You're pretty important right now," he said. "Got everyone running around and dancing to your tune."

"I hadn't noticed much dancing going on," Alex said in a low voice. Across the room, he sensed Flynn starting to move towards them.

"Maybe if you weren't the only one, you wouldn't be so important any more, Mr Dolan," he went on. "Maybe that's why you're so royally pissed."

Alex looked at him a moment longer. Flynn had almost reached them. He smiled at the combover. "Sure," he told him. "That's exactly it." And then he was gone.

"Alex!" Flynn shouted, but by then it was too late. He was gone too.

"So," said Flynn. "Have we got that out of our system now?"

"Don't patronise me, Arthur," Alex said. "I'm not in the mood." They were sitting in the Situation Room at Quantico, along with Dom Maserati and Professor Sierpińska and a couple of staffers.

"Where did you go?"

"None of your business."

"There's been another incident," Dom said from the end of the table. "A village in India. Looks like a bulldozer the size of a cruise ship went through there."

Alex thought about it. "I wasn't in India."

"Can we believe that, Alex?" asked Flynn. "Really?"

"I don't care what you believe," he said. "I wasn't there."

Dom opened a folder and tossed a sheaf of photos on the table. Alex saw aerial shots of a forest with a wide, neat slot cut out of it down to bare earth. "About twelve hundred people," he said. "Just gone. No bodies, no rubble, no nothing. Just gone."

"Not me," Alex told him.

"Right," Flynn said. "Okay. So, we still have an ongoing situation and we still don't know how to respond to it. Alex, we need you to go over there and locate the SEAL team, assess their condition, and do a headcount. Are you good with that?"

"Sure."

"Fine." He closed the folder in front of him, dropped it in his briefcase, and stood up. "Professor Sierpińska will brief you. We'll make the insertion at ten o'clock tomorrow morning." And with that he left.

"He's still pissed with you," Dom said.

"No shit."

"He tried to stop them. We all did."

"That's not good enough, Dom. Trying to give people superpowers like that. What were they thinking?"

"There's a faction in Washington," Dom said, "which is more pissed off than you could imagine that the world's only superhero isn't an American. I know you don't think that matters; you have your own problems. Myself, I think it's insane. But these people think their superhero should sound more like Steve Rogers than Billy Connolly."

"I don't sound remotely like Billy Connolly."

Dom looked levelly at him. "Alex," he said. "You can't just go round making US senators vanish. I mean, that probably qualifies as an act of war or something."

"He's an asshole."

"Well, it took him a day and a half to hike down off that

mountain and find someone with a phone, but he says thank you for his unexpected vacation in New Zealand." Dom grinned. "He might be an asshole, but he's a tough asshole. Adults are running this operation for the moment; Senator Pulver could change all that, if he got it into his mind to, and we've just seen what things are like when that happens."

He had a point. Pulver, and people like him, were completely irrelevant to Alex, but for the moment at least the damage they could do wasn't.

"I guess I should apologise to Arthur."

"Nah." Dom shook his head and stuffed the folder of photos under his arm. "He'll be fine. He's a tough asshole too." He reached out and touched Alex's elbow. "People like Pulver, they don't like things they can't control. It makes them angry, and they don't ever forget. Art spent twelve years with the CIA, running agents into China; he just rolls with this stuff, gets up, dusts himself down, gets the job done. The Pulvers of this world, they break things that don't go their way."

"Point taken, Dom. But keep me in the loop from now on. I could have prevented this, and now it's a disaster."

"It was handled badly, and Art would be telling you that himself, if he wasn't so pissed off right now." He gave Alex's elbow a little squeeze and let go. "Let's get the job done, Alex, eh?"

"We'd prefer it if you didn't interact with them at all," Professor Sierpińska said. "The simple act of observing them could collapse them into a rest-state."

"They're going to be hard to count if I can't look at them," Alex said.

She sighed. "This is so unnecessary."

"Yes." Alex looked down at the file in his lap. It was two inches thick and detailed the military career of Lieutenant

Sarah J Bowman, one of the SEALs who had been sent through Point Zero. The cover of the file was thickly decorated with classification stripes and warnings that any uncleared persons who read it would be prosecuted or shot or thrown into a cage full of tigers. Its pages were a mass of black redactions, but from what was left it was obvious that Lieutenant Bowman had had quite a time in the Navy; the names of half a dozen international flashpoints over the past eight years or so appeared between the crossings-out, and one or two places that hadn't been international flashpoints, at least officially. There was a photo near the front of the file of a blonde, capable-looking woman in a dress uniform, standing in front of a huge Stars and Stripes. Alex wondered whether Bowman and her colleagues had been ordered to go, or had been invited to volunteer. It would take quite an unusual person to volunteer for a mission like that. What did they tell them? 'When you come back, you'll be able to do magic'? He closed the file and sighed.

The Professor looked up, raised her eyebrows.

"I'm not up to this," Alex told her. "I'm a journalist."

She looked at him for a few moments, looking sad. "You're all we have, Alex." She thought about it and added, "That came out all wrong. I'm sorry."

He smiled. "It's okay. I feel that way too."

She sat back in her chair and looked at Alex across the desk. "It's sometimes easy to forget, as scientists, that real lives are involved," she said. "For me, this is..." she gestured at the ceiling, searching for the words, "... the opportunity of a lifetime. The research we're doing here would win every single one of us a Nobel Prize, always assuming it was ever declassified. But in our eagerness, in our *excitement*, we sometimes forget that... well." She nodded at the file on his lap, the stack of similar folders on his side of the desk. "Real human beings are getting hurt, and maybe worse."

He remembered Delahaye saying something similar, in a rare moment of candour back at the SCS, something about riding off across the wild frontier of physics and into a strange new world. Well, he'd certainly managed to do that.

He said, "You're doing okay, Prof. I wouldn't still be here if it wasn't for you and Art and Dom and the others. There wouldn't be any point in staying." He saw her glance at the door at the mention of Flynn's name. Maybe she was expecting Flynn to turn up to see him off, as he had on the previous occasions he had crossed into the Manifold. But the door stayed closed.

"Ah well," he said, and he *stepped* away.

THE HYPOTHESIS THAT the structures in the Manifold somehow represented the people who had been in the control room on the day of the accident had never been tested, but here they were, eight new structures, Lieutenant Bowman and her squad of would-be superheroes. Alex did it by the book, counting them twice, assessing them as closely as he dared, conscious of Professor Sierpińska's fears about waking them up. There was no way to identify them as individuals—they were just *objects*, insofar as anything here was an object—but they had been people, and it made Alex angry to see them here. There was still no coherent theory about how he had avoided the same fate, and until there was one it seemed criminally reckless to try to repeat the experiment. He should, he thought, have sent Senator Pulver here instead of New Zealand. See if *he* liked being an all-American superhero.

"Can we retrieve them?" Flynn asked when Alex had returned to the Situation Room.

The question raised a Mexican wave of sharply indrawn breath from the techs around the table. "It's dangerous to even *look* at them, Arthur," said Professor Sierpińska. "I was telling Alex this earlier. At the moment they're not dead or alive; they don't even *exist* as we understand it. If we drop them into a rest state it could be one in which they are not alive."

"The president wants them back," Flynn said.

"The president can go and get them," Alex said. This earned him a sharp glance from Flynn, but he was past caring.

There was a knock on the door and one of Flynn's staffers came in. He bent down and whispered in Flynn's ear, handed him a folded slip of paper, and left again. Flynn unfolded the piece of paper, read it, and looked around the table.

"He's in Sioux Crossing," he said. "The other one."

"When?" said Dom.

"He's still there. At the SCS. Stetson and her team have pulled out; they say the place is full of static electricity."

There was a silence, around the table. For a moment, nobody seemed to know what to do. Alex said, "I'll go."

"No, Alex," said Flynn.

"By the time you get there, he'll be gone again," Alex told him, standing up.

"*No*," Flynn said, but Alex was already gone.

It was late afternoon in Rosewater County, the great spiral cloud twirling up into a low dark overcast that promised rain. Alex looked at the building. Blue sparks were running down the walls like electrical raindrops. He felt the hairs all over his body stand up. In the distance, beyond the fence, he saw figures moving around, and a little further away what looked very much like a tank.

There was the sound of breaking from around the corner of the building, and he walked towards it. Rounding the corner, he saw the moke garage, and hanging in the air beside it... well...

He'd been expecting someone like himself, a person with weird new abilities, but the thing beside the garage was not remotely like that. It looked like part of a comic strip illustration of a man blowing up. Here he was in Frame One, a solid, whole human being. Here he was, at the end of the strip, nothing more than a widely distributed scattering of bone and meat and other tissue. And here he was, three or four frames in, the explosion just getting going, his body flying apart, impossibly caught in the middle of detonating. His body looked repugnant and absurd all at the same time, an animated human-shaped cloud of meat and blood, about three times normal size.

Alex took one step towards him. Then another. The air smelled of electricity and burnt sugar. Part of the garage had been demolished, lying on the ground in smouldering fragments. Alex took another step.

"Hello," he said.

The figure—the *djinn*—made no sign of having heard him. It changed position slightly, the whole exploding cloud moving as one, and another part of the garage puffed smoke and flame and collapsed.

Alex took another step, and it crossed his mind that this was possibly the bravest thing he had ever done. It might actually be the last thing he ever did. He said, "Hello," again, and this time the disgusting meat sculpture turned and *looked* at him.

"Alex," it said. "Dude."

Oh, fuck. Fuck fuck fuck fuck.

"What happened?" the voice asked. It issued from somewhere other than his exploding larynx. It sounded as if it was coming from an enormous distance.

Fuck fuck fuck fuck.

"Larry?"

"What happened? I feel weird."

Alex felt himself take a step back, prepare to drop back into the Manifold. He said, "There was an accident."

"I feel weird," Larry said again. "Like..." He seemed to raise a hand and look at it. "Wow, that's horrible," he said. "Why don't you look like this?"

"I don't know. Larry, you've got to stay calm and stop breaking stuff."

The cloud of flying meat seemed to tilt its head to one side.

"Why?"

Alex took another step back. "We don't know what happened, but you've been hurt and you need help."

The exploding body was silent a while. "It doesn't *feel* as if I need help," Larry said. "It feels pretty good, actually. Weird, but good." It was impossible to read the expression on what passed for his face, but he made a noise that might, if one were psychotic enough, be mistaken for a laugh. "It's like something from a Marvel comic. You think I've become a superhero?" When Alex didn't answer, he said, "You'd think I'd get x-ray vision or something, not... this."

Alex felt *something* moving around him, a sensation of billions of tiny teeth in an invisible swarm. "What are you doing?"

The cloud of body parts suddenly twitched and drew closer together into a more obviously human shape. "Yeah," Larry said. "That's better. How long has it been, Alex?"

"Quite a while," Alex said, standing very still. "Almost two years." It occurred to him to ask why Larry had tried to kill him, but it seemed the very last thing he wanted to remind him of.

"That *is* quite a while." He pulled himself a little closer together. "You look well."

Alex had an extremely unpleasant feeling of being *examined* at some very deep level. "I'm doing okay."

"Better than okay, I'd say." He looked around him. "Do you think this is what it feels like to be God?"

Alex felt the storm of teeth try to take him apart. He did the only thing he could think of. He stepped forward, plunged his hands into the centre of the exploding man, and *pulled*. Larry was too surprised to resist, and they both *stepped* into the Manifold.

He found himself standing in that screaming notlight beside a structure which had once been Larry Day. It seemed perfectly inert, to the extent that anything here was inert. That awful sensation of *disassembly* had stopped. He looked around him, trying to work out what to do next.

* * *

"JESUS," DOM SAID when he finished his debrief. Flynn sat looking stonily at him. Professor Sierpińska regarded him with an expression he hoped was not pity. "It can't be that easy, can it?"

"It could be the shock of being returned to the Manifold forced him to aestivate like the others," said Professor Sierpińska.

Flynn looked down at his notes and said, "You should have waited for backup."

"He'd have killed anyone else," Alex said. "He almost killed *me*." He remembered that sensation of *disassembly*, and shuddered.

Flynn grunted. "I guess the question we have to ask ourselves is, what do we do now? Can we kill him while he's in this inert state?"

"I don't think I can sanction that," the Professor said. "Anything Alex did to him would almost certainly collapse him into a rest state. It could conceivably make things worse."

"I think we're all in agreement that he's probably the worst possible person to get bitten by the radioactive spider," Dom put in.

"I don't know if I *could* kill him, over there," said Alex. Everyone looked at him. "The rules are different; it's hard to explain."

"He could be in that state indefinitely," the Professor said.

"But you can't guarantee that," said Flynn.

"I can't guarantee anything, Arthur," she said. "We're dealing with a physics we still don't understand. If it's a physics at all."

"Could you kill him over *here*?" Flynn asked Alex.

"I don't know. I took him by surprise." *I took* myself *by surprise.* "He felt strong, and he's very smart."

Flynn wrote something on the notepad in front of him, and he sat back and looked at them. "Well," he said, "I don't know about you, but the prospect of a murderer with the powers of a god scares the living shit out of *me*. We can't just sit here and wait for something to happen."

But that, of course, was what they wound up doing.

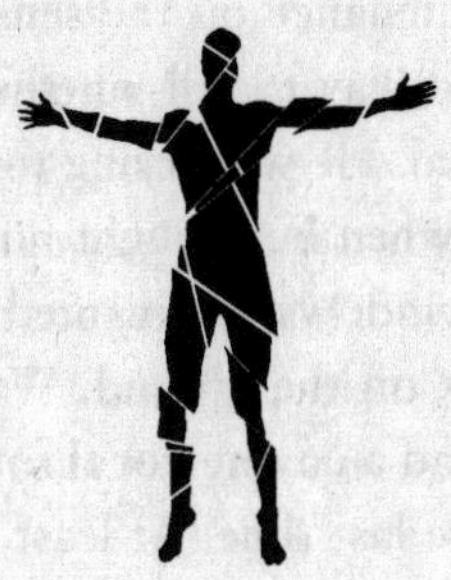

THE RETURN

THE CLOUD LOOKED eerie and frightening, hanging above the SCS, but it was just an edge effect, harmless water vapour in the atmosphere gathered by what was going on below. The really scary stuff at Point Zero was invisible.

The young lieutenant sitting across from Alex looked tired and ill. They burned out quickly here on the Perimeter—the constant stress of keeping things from getting through the fence, the constant terror of what they would have to do if something did. A typical tour out here lasted less than six months, then they were rotated back to their units and replacements were brought in. Alex sometimes wondered why they were bothering to keep it secret; if they waited long enough the entire US Marine Corps would have spent time here.

He leaned forward and raised his voice over the sound of the engines and said to the lieutenant, "How old are you, son?"

The lieutenant just looked blankly at him. Beside him, Alex saw Former Airman Fenwick roll his eyes.

"Just trying to make conversation," he said, sitting back. The lieutenant didn't respond. He didn't know who Alex was—or rather, he had been told he was a specialist, come to perform routine maintenance on the sensors installed all over the site. There was no way to tell whether he believed that or not, or if he even cared. He was trying to maintain a veneer of professionalism, but when he thought nobody was looking he kept glancing at the windows. He wanted to look out, to check on his responsibilities on the ground. Was the site still there? Was there a panic? Had a coyote got through?

It had been a coyote last time. At least, that was the general consensus of opinion—it was hard to be certain from the remains. The Board of Inquiry had found that the breach was due to gross negligence on the part of the officer in command. The officer in command, a colonel Alex had met a couple of times and rather liked, had saved Uncle Sam the cost of a court martial by dying, along with seventeen of his men, bringing down the thing the coyote had become. You could tell, just by looking at the lieutenant, that he had terrible nightmares.

The animals had been unexpected, although there were reports going all the way back to the very early days of the emergency. The control room had been sealed off, but some edge effect occasionally affected small mammals outside. Alex had been shown photographs of a bobcat that looked like something dreamed up by HP Lovecraft. Nobody knew why it happened, or why it didn't happen to plants and birds and insects. There was nothing they could do to stop it; the best they could do was carry out periodic culls of wildlife on the old SCS campus, and try to stop anything getting out.

The Black Hawk made another wide looping turn over Sioux Crossing, waiting for permission to land. Looking out, Alex thought he saw East Walden Lane pass by below, but it was hard to tell, everything was so overgrown. The town itself, a little further away, looked deserted. The government had finally lost patience with the Montana militia, and had handled the situation with a typically heavy foot. The militia were gone now, but there had been casualties.

The pilot eventually got permission to make final approach and they landed at Camp Batavia. The place had grown, over the years, from a temporary fortress of prefabricated modules to a full-scale military camp complete with a PX and a cinema, offices and barracks and mess halls and control rooms and armouries and garages. If you looked carefully, you could still spot, from the air, the original buildings of Rosewater High, repurposed into barracks and workshops. The lieutenant jumped down as soon as the door was opened, and the last Alex saw of him was his back as he strode away from them towards the control centre.

"Talkative fucker," Former Airman Fenwick commented, hopping down from the helicopter beside him.

Alex sighed. A figure in fatigues was coming towards them from the control centre. The figure passed the lieutenant, and they snapped salutes at each other without breaking step.

"Welcoming committee," said Fenwick. "Nice. I approve."

"Shut up, Fenwick," Alex muttered.

The figure was the base commander, Colonel Newton J Kettering. He marched up to them and saluted. Fenwick returned the salute sloppily, as usual. Alex didn't bother.

"Sir," Kettering said smartly. "Welcome to Camp Batavia."

"Well thank you kindly, Colonel," Fenwick said. "Looks like you're running a tight ship here."

"Sir. Thank you, sir." Unlike the lieutenant, Kettering didn't look tired and ill. He looked alert and bright-eyed. He looked alert and bright-eyed to the point of madness. He was a veteran of Iraq and Afghanistan and he'd done three tours here, and Alex didn't want to spend a minute longer in his company than he had to.

He said to Fenwick, "I'd better supervise the unloading."

Fenwick gave him his big shit-eating grin. "I think that

sounds like a fine idea, Mr Dolan." Alex wanted to punch him. "Perhaps Colonel Kettering could give me the guided tour while you're doing that thing."

"Sir, I was hoping you could join me in the Officers' Club," Kettering said. "We have a luncheon prepared."

Fenwick's grin widened. "Colonel, I would love to."

"We need to get onto the site as soon as possible," Alex said to them both, but mainly to Fenwick. Kettering regarded him with a keen look of hostility. Fenwick pouted; he hated to miss a free meal. Alex said, "Colonel, it shouldn't take more than half an hour to unload my gear—"

"Hell," Fenwick put in amiably. "That's *plenty* of time for luncheon. Right, Colonel?"

"Sir. Yes, sir." Kettering gave Alex that hostile look again. His carefully groomed routine had already been interrupted; he wasn't about to let Alex ruin lunch too. Neither was Fenwick.

Alex looked at them both. "Half an hour," he said. "No longer."

Fenwick and Kettering exchanged a knowing glance. *Civilians*. Then Fenwick clapped Kettering on the back and said, "Lead the way, Colonel," and they walked off. A few yards away, Fenwick looked over his shoulder and called, "Would you like us to send a plate out for you, Mr Dolan?"

Alex shook his head. "No thank you, General, I'll be fine," he called back. Fenwick flipped him the bird surreptitiously and turned back to Kettering. The two of them, deep in conversation, walked towards the nearest buildings.

Alex watched them go for a few moments, then went back to the helicopter, where, in the style of bored baggage handlers and cargo men the world over, half a dozen Marines were throwing his metal transport cases out onto the grass.

"Hey!" he shouted. "Careful with those things! They're delicate scientific instruments!"

Actually, the cases were full of old telephone directories, for weight, but he had to keep up the charade.

* * *

He had the Humvee loaded by the time Fenwick and the Colonel returned from their lunch. In the end he'd told the Marines to go away, and done it himself. Down the years he'd noticed that Marines tended towards a certain disdain for people who were not themselves Marines. Alex was a *civilian specialist*. To most of them that was a euphemism for *CIA*, which was a direct invitation to dick around and try to get a rise out of him, but he wasn't going to play that game.

"How was your lunch, General?" he asked when Fenwick and Kettering arrived.

Fenwick looked at Kettering. "I think I can report that this camp is not lacking in creature comforts, Mr Dolan," he said, and Kettering smiled in relief.

Alex looked at his watch. "We really should be making a start, General," he said. "I'd like to be out of here before nightfall."

Fenwick snorted. "You and me both." He turned to Kettering. "Newt," he said, "if you're ever down at Bragg, I'll throw a party for you at the BOQ that'll make your head spin."

Kettering grinned. "Sir. Yes, sir." They shook hands and Kettering stood to attention while Fenwick and Alex got into the Hummer.

Alex said, "I do hope you didn't breach any security protocols in there, Airman."

Fenwick grinned and tapped the stars on his fatigues. "*General.*"

Alex put the Hummer in gear. "Oh, fuck off, Fenwick," he said. "You're no more a general than I am." And he drove the Humvee out of the gates of the camp and onto the road to the site.

At ground level, fifteen years of abandonment were more obvious. There were Green Berets stationed at the main gate, and they spent a good half hour checking documents and establishing their bona fides before letting them through. As well as animals, the world's Press were always trying to sneak through the fence. Nobody had made it yet. Nobody they knew about, anyway.

The buildings were weathered and dirty, the grass waist-high, despite regular helicopter inundations of herbicides, and it was starting to encroach on the cracked asphalt of the roadways. A few years before, the inner perimeter around the main Facility building had been moved about a thousand yards further out, and reinforced with a second fence. Soldiers in black combat gear repeated the security checks performed by the Green Berets.

Alex drove until they were a few hundred feet from the building, directly under the slowly twisting spiral cloud. The government, even after all this time, was sticking to the story that it was caused by some electromagnetic effect, but the truth was that nobody knew, although if they'd told everyone that it was caused by aliens more people would have believed them.

Fenwick looked up at the white helix and curled his lips. He was a man of many attributes, very few of them admirable, but he was not a coward. He had been told that there was no danger in him coming this close to Point Zero, and he believed that. It had never occurred to him that a significant fraction of the Defence budget was devoted to stopping animals getting this close to the building.

There had been much discussion about what to do about him after Alex appeared out of thin air in front of him. A quick look at his file suggested that appealing to his patriotic instincts would be pointless, and that giving him large amounts of money would be counterproductive and fruitless. A working group of thirty very very bright men and women had been convened simply to study the problem of What To Do About Airman Robert E Lee Fenwick, who one night while out on patrol at Fort Bragg had seen a screaming Scotsman appear from a direction that no one in the universe had ever seen before.

Their solution was elegant and, Alex thought, unusually humane. Airman Fenwick was a simple organism, geared mainly to self-gratification, and his loyalty—and his silence—had been bought by the simple expedient of promoting him to the rank of four-star general. What fascinated Alex was that Fenwick never showed the slightest gratitude for this. It was as if the alternative never even occurred to him. He seemed totally oblivious to the concept that it would have been simpler, and far more cost-effective, to simply kill him.

"Here we are, then," Fenwick said.

"Yes," Alex said. "Here we are. I cannot argue with that." Alex looked at the cloud, looked at the building. Fenwick had surprised everyone by taking to his new rank like a duck to water. He was still *in* the Air Force, but he was no longer *of* the Air Force. He had no duties to speak of, apart from the duties that involved Alex. His general's pay had been backdated for a decade, and he had bought his parents a new house in West Virginia and his brother a new car, and he lived with his child bride Roselynne and their half-dozen squalling brats in a magnificent mansion in Alexandria, Virginia. The kids went to the best schools, and in moments of despair Alex hung onto that. The eldest girl, Bobbi-Sue, was starting at Princeton next year. Because of what had happened to Alex the Fenwick boys would not work all their lives in the local coal mines; the Fenwick girls would not marry the high school jock only to see him become a drunken wife-beater. They would be lawyers and doctors and Congressional Representatives and Senators, and maybe even Presidents. In his darkest moments Alex looked at Former Airman Fenwick, and he almost thought this was all worth it. Almost.

"How long do we have?" Fenwick asked. He always asked that.

Alex shrugged. "Minutes?" He always said that, too. "Days?" He opened the door and got out of the Hummer. Fenwick got out too, and together they unloaded the transport cases. They carried them around to the ruined moke garage, and emptied them of their telephone books. Then they put them back into the Humvee and dumped Alex's gear on the ground beside the vehicle.

Fenwick checked his watch. "Better be getting back," he said.

Alex nodded. In a couple of hours there would be an overflight. An unmarked black helicopter without an ID transponder would pass overhead, ignoring local traffic control until the last moment, when it would transmit a brief and curt series of digits that identified it as belonging to the NSA. It would dip down below the radar cover, hover for a few moments, and then lift up and fly off again. And that would be the *civilian specialist* leaving. "This is stupid. Someone's going to work it out one day," he said. He had no idea who had come up with this ridiculous charade. It would have been a lot simpler, and a great deal more covert, for him just to *step* directly into the building from wherever he happened to be at the time, but someone somewhere had overdosed on bad spy novels and liked the idea of having him *infiltrate* the site, with Former Airman Fenwick in his general's guise to lend authority.

Fenwick shrugged. "Nobody ever made any money trying to figure out why the government does what it does." He put out his hand and Alex shook it. When they had first met Fenwick had been rangy and fidgety. Now he was calm and plump and sleek, and in Alex's heart he couldn't grudge him that. "Happy trails, Alex," he said.

"You too, Bobby Lee. See you soon."

"Let's fucking hope, right?"

Alex smiled. "Yes. Let's."

Fenwick got back into the Hummer, gave a wave, and drove off back towards the gate, where he would tell the Special Forces and the Green Berets and eventually Colonel Kettering that the *civilian specialist* had arranged a separate means of departure. Which would, in its own way, be the only true thing about the whole operation.

Alex watched the Humvee disappear into the distance. When it was gone, he picked up his stuff and carried it into the lobby of the building. A pretty good job had been made of cleaning it up and making it habitable again. Alex dumped his gear on the floor, unrolled his sleeping bag, pulled an armchair over to the window, and sat down.

The longest he had waited, so far, was two weeks. There was no way to predict it, but that had been an unusually long time. Food and water were no problem—he could conjure those up out of thin air, he barely even thought about it now—but the waiting produced a sort of nervy tedium that he didn't like.

He wasn't entirely sure who was running things now. They had lost Flynn early, a massive heart attack a couple of years into the operation. Dom had been hit by a car while crossing the road in DC. Alex felt bad about that; he had liked both men and he could have prevented their deaths if he'd had some forewarning. Professor Sierpińska was still working hard, lost in a research team that was now almost as large as the one that had worked on the Manhattan Project but had produced little more hard science than it had back in the early days when they were all still floundering around. He saw less and less of Wendy; she was at CERN at the moment, having extremely classified discussions with some of the scientists at the LHC. At one point, the government had wanted to deploy him as a weapon, their very own caped crusader, but he had refused, and now, really, he only had the one purpose. Without it, he would have left years ago. They were never going to find a way to make him normal again.

He finished his dinner and sat by the window drinking coffee and smoking a small cigar. The cigar was from a tin he'd found in his rucksack—a little gift from Fenwick. He'd heard the helicopter fly over while he was eating; it had dipped down momentarily a few hundred metres from Point Zero—which was actually an act of insane bravery on the part of its pilot in order to maintain what Alex considered the fatuous and transparent fiction of his 'departure'—and then lifted away again to the West. Now everything was quiet and night was falling.

He remembered when this whole place had been busy and bustling. He thought about Delahaye and all the others who had been with him in the control room on the day of the accident. Rob Chen, who was out of the room at the time, looking for Security, had survived, which was a small blessing. At least he'd saved one of them, even if he hadn't known it at the time.

He looked down at his arm. As he watched, the hairs on his forearm began to stir slowly and stand up.

He went outside and stood in front of the building with his hands in his pockets. About seven hours ago, he had been sitting in a briefing room in a White House basement with the president and about a dozen NSA and CIA staffers, watching a video.

The video had been taken by a Predator drone flying over Afghanistan. It was the spearpoint of a long-running operation to kill a Taliban warlord codenamed WATERSHED, who had been tracked down to a compound in Helmand. It was the usual combat video, not black and white but that weird mixture of shades of grey. The landscape tipped and dipped as the Predator's operator, thousands of miles away in the continental United States, steered the drone in on its target. Then a scatter of buildings popped up over a hill and the drone launched its missile, and as it did a human figure came walking around the corner of one of the buildings. The crosshairs of the drone's camera danced around the centre of the screen for a few moments, then the building puffed smoke in all directions and disappeared.

And moments later, unaffected, seemingly not even having noticed the explosion, the figure calmly walked out of the smoke and carried on its way.

"Well," said the president when the video was over, "either the war in Afghanistan just took a *very* strange turn, or we're going to need your services, Mr Dolan."

Alex looked into the sky. The moon was low down on the horizon and everything was bathed in a strange directionless silvery light that cast strange shadows. There was an electrical *expectancy* in the air, a smell of ozone and burnt sugar, a breeze that blew from nowhere, and then he was there, standing a few yards away, looking about him and making strange noises. Alex sighed.

"Larry," he called.

Larry looked round, saw him, and said, "Jesus, Alex. What the hell happened?"

It was always the same. He always manifested as a suspended cloud of meat and body parts and if the techs had a theory about this, no one had bothered to tell Alex. For Larry, every time was the first time, everything was new. He didn't remember the accident, which was good, and he didn't remember what came later, which was even better, but he was ferociously smart and Alex couldn't afford to relax, even for a moment.

"There was an accident," Alex said. "Something happened during the last shot, we still don't know exactly what."

Larry's awful voice said, "What happened to your hair, Alex?"

Alex ran a hand over his head. "It's been a while, Larry. I got old."

"How long?"

"Nearly fifteen years."

Larry looked around him and made those strange noises again. "Delahaye..."

"All dead," Alex said. "Delahaye, Warren, Bright, Morley. The whole team. You and I are the only survivors."

Larry looked at his hands; it was impossible to read the expression on what passed for his face. "I don't seem to have survived very well, Alex. *You* seem to be doing all right, though."

Alex shrugged. "As I said, we still don't know exactly what happened. You need help."

Larry laughed. "Oh? You *think*? Jesus, Alex." He started to pace back and forth. Then he stopped. "Where was I? Before?"

"Afghanistan. We think you were just trying to find your way back here."

Larry shook his head, which was an awful thing to watch. "No. Before that. There was... everything was the wrong... *shape*..."

Alex took a step forward and said, "Larry..."

"And before that... I was *here*, and we were having this conversation..."

"It's just *déjà vu*," Alex told him. "It's hardly the worst of your worries."

Larry straightened up and his body seemed to gain coherence. "Alex," he said, "how many times have we done this before?"

Alex shook his head. "Too fucking many," he said, and he plunged his hands into the seething exploding mass of Larry Day's body and pulled them both back into Hell.

HE WALKED AN unimaginable distance. It took him an impossible length of time. Nothing here meant anything or made any sense, but he passed the structures representing Professor Delahaye and his scientists, and the SEAL team, all of them still in a dreamless half-death, colossal things that were almost too small to see.

And here, somewhere, was Larry Day, returned to his Schrödinger state until the next time.

Existing in the Manifold, being able to step between dimensions, being able to use that insight to manipulate the 'real' world, really *was* like being a god. Unfortunately, it was like being one of the gods HP Lovecraft used to write about, immense and unfathomable and entirely without human scruple. So far, the human race had been lucky that Larry seemed unable to quite get the knack of godhood. No one could work out why Alex had acclimatised to it so easily, or why it remained so difficult for Larry, why returning him *there* screwed him up all over again while Alex could cross back and forth at will, without harm.

The only thing Alex could be certain of was that every time they met—and they had played out this absurd little pantomime twelve times so far—Larry seemed to recover more quickly. One day he was going to come out of it bright-eyed and bushy-tailed and Alex wouldn't be able to drag him into the Manifold. He would have to fight him *here*, and it would be like nothing Stan Lee ever imagined. Either/Or. Either the world would survive, or it wouldn't.

And the wonderful, extravagant cosmic joke of it was that Larry was not even the Nightmare Scenario. The Nightmare Scenario was that Delahaye and the SCS scientists and the SEAL team somehow all dropped into a rest state at once and found their way into the real world. If that happened, it would make the Twilight of the Gods look like a quiet morning in a roadside diner. Alex planned to be somewhere else on that day. He was happy enough to present the appearance of humanity for the moment, but he didn't owe these people anything.

Eventually, he came across a room. Although this wasn't a room in the sense that anyone *here* would recognise. It was all distributed planes of stress and knots of mass, open on all sides, too huge to measure. He stepped into the room and sat down in a comfortable chair.

Nobody screamed. Nobody ran away. They were expecting him, of course, and he had learned long ago how to clothe himself before he came *here*. People hated it when naked men appeared out of nowhere in the Situation Room at the White

House. Someone brought him coffee. The coffee here was always excellent.

"Mr Dolan," said the president.

"Madam President," he said. He sipped his coffee. "He's recovering more quickly."

"We noticed," said Professor Sierpińska. "The others?"

"I saw some of them. They're still aestivating. I couldn't see any changes. We got away with it again."

"You look tired," said the president.

"I look how I want to look," Alex snapped, and regretted it. The president was not an unkind person, and unlike her predecessor, the one who sent the SEALs into the Manifold, she was not an asshole. And he *was* tired. And anyway, it was ridiculous. Why would a godlike transdimensional superhero want to look like a tubby balding middle-aged man? If he wanted, he could look like Lady Gaga or Robert Downey, Jr., or an enormous crystal eagle, but what he *really* wanted was to be ordinary again, and that, of all things, he could not do.

He looked up at the expectant faces, all of them waiting to hear how he had saved the world again.

"Do you think I could have a sandwich?" he asked.

ABOUT THE AUTHOR

Dave Hutchison is the multi-award winning author of the critically acclaimed Fractured Europe series for Solaris: *Europe at Autumn*, *Europe in Winter*, *Europe at Midnight* and *Europe at Dawn*.

FIND US ONLINE!

www.rebellionpublishing.com

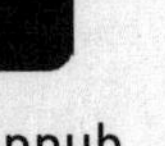

/rebellionpub

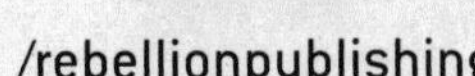

/rebellionpublishing

/rebellionpub

SIGN UP TO OUR NEWSLETTER!

rebellionpublishing.com/sign-up

YOUR REVIEWS MATTER!

Enjoy this book? Got something to say?

Leave a review on Amazon, GoodReads or with your favourite bookseller and let the world know!